Synergy Publications Presents...

A Dollar Outta Fifteen Cent IV:
Money Makes the World Go 'Round

Another Caroline McGill Exclusive

Published By:
Synergy Publications
P.O. Box 210-987
Brooklyn, NY 11221

www.SynergyPublications.com

© Copyright 2010 Caroline McGill All rights reserved. No part of this book may be reproduced in any form without permission from the author, except by reviewer, who may quote brief passages to be printed in a newspaper or magazine.

Publisher's Note:
Sale of this book without a front cover is unauthorized. If this book was purchased without a cover it was reported to the publisher as "unsold or destroyed." Neither the author nor the publisher has received payment for the sale of this stripped book.
This novel is a work of fiction. Names, characters, places, and incidents are either products of the author's imagination or are used fictitiously. Any resemblance to actual persons, living or dead, actual events, establishments, organizations, and/or locales is entirely coincidental.

Library of Congress Control Number: 2010922509

ISBN: 978-0-9752980-5-3

Cover Design: Matt Pramschufer for E-Moxie Data Solutions

Written by: Caroline McGill for Synergy Publications

Edited by: Caroline McGill for Synergy Publications

Printed in Canada

For Jerry "Jay Money" McGill

My cuz and my comrade

December 3, 1973 – March 30, 2009

Gone too soon

God bless, and Rest in Peace

ACKNOWLEDGEMENTS

All praises due to God first and foremost. You make all things possible, so thank you Heavenly Father. Next up is y'all, my readers. Some of you've been waiting on this book for a while. You've been calling, sending emails, storming into your local bookstores demanding a release date, rushing the book vendors, contacting me through the website, hitting me up on Facebook and MySpace, and some of you've even approached me on the street. I LOVE YOU ALL!!!!!!! And my sincerest apologies to those of you that pre-ordered this book, and then waited long weeks, and even months for it. Thank you for your patience. I worked really hard on this, so I pray it's worth your wait. Thank you all so much. I really appreciate your support. God bless.

I'd like to thank my mother and father, Carolyn and Carnell. Love to my sisters, brothers, nieces, nephews, cousins, and friends. Shout out to the homies, my homegirls, the bookstores, book vendors, book clubs, libraries, wholesalers, distributors, and all my people in the penitentiary. I see y'all. Thanks.

Shout-outs to Casino, Bless Bigz, Connie, Carleata (Keya) and Ty, Keiecha and Chris, Kishah, Musa, Sha, Fanerra, NaQuanda, Jemik, Jaylin, ShaMauri, Zapanga Milan, Kendell, CJ, the whole McGill family, the McKoy family, Lucky and the Norfort family, Fee-fee, Sparkle, Mo, Tammy, Paulette, Tara, Bennie, Angel, Angie, Ice, Maisha, Lisa, Nicole, Tasha, Makeeba, Kadeasha, Kiana, Tashonda, Avis (Dee Dee) and Rahsheedah, Carlene,

Boobie, Lisa, Sandra, Terry, and Otis. What up Man, Jamie, Mighty, Silk, Sherron, Zayquan, K-Lo, Quick, Dun, Caine, Hov, Diamond, Ty, and Micah.

Special shout to my dudes at Green Haven Correctional. Respect to the Brooklyn crew; my bro, my partner, and my heart Casino, Boom, Deezo, Sike, Twin Villain, the whole Dirtbomb crew, Stick, Diamond, E-Glama, Surfer, Wayne-head, Bigs, George, and Tripple O.G., and Prada. Assalamu alaikum to Nobel, Young Lah, Pooch and the whole Hustle Hard crew. Amir finish that book. Bibin, Jihad, Hakeem, Tabliq, Success, Yah-yah, Shabazz, all my 914 niggas, the Jamrorcks, Gee, Yusef, Life, Koolaid, Psych, Lincoln, Bad Boy, Butta, Big Show, and Brazy.

And I see ya'll out there at Collins Correctional. Bless Bigz, CEO of King City Records. What up, bro? Shouts to the whole crew. Thanks for the card, fellas. Six, Black, Big C, King, Doc, Dee Rugz, Lah, Jazz, Keo, Doggs, Blackness, Big Willz, Islam, Stone, Terry, Man, PI, Mar, Alim, V, Fifty, KK, Lex, Beanz, Trife, BG, Infamous, Jeezy, Spank Loc, Slim, Tone, Funny Styles, Charlie Miller, Mel, Cat, Nut, Q, Jamie, Shanette, Sherry, D-Block, Trife, Rugz, Debbie, Gunz, BG, Beanz, Big Trips, Shawn, Cash, Nut, Q, and Jeezy. Geronino in Bertie Correctional down in N.C. Hold your head, my dude. And keep ya' pen on the paper.

A sugar coated shout to Lucky. Love ya' babe! Shout to Anthony and Jason, Street Literature Review magazine, Hakim, Tyson, and the crew from Black and Nobel in Philly, K'wan, Erick Gray, all my author friends, and of course Urban Book Source. To my peoples in the north, the dirty south, the east, the mid-west, the west, the Caribbean, Canada, and even the UK. I see ya'll. Thanks for the love.

A special shout-out goes out to Justin "Amen" Floyd, the newest addition to the Synergy family. You next, son. "Anything 4 Profit", a'ight. Y'all be sure to cop that. Check out the excerpt in the back of this book.

Gone but not forgotten... Grandma and Granddaddy, (Rosa McKoy and Cary Lee McKoy), and Grandma and Granddaddy (Zante McGill and Bennett McGill). Uncle Dake, Uncle James, Uncle Fred, Lindsay, Blue, Knowledge, Polite, Kendell, Jay, Davell, Michael Norfort, Rab, EP, Jesse, Lloyd Hart, Thomas, Mary, Kimyatta, Ernestine, and all the rest of my deceased loved ones, and fallen soldiers. Rest in peace, and God bless.

If I forgot your name, please give me a pass. Ain't no love lost. I been in the lab working on this book so long my mind is mush. If your name ain't in here, it's written on my heart. I LOVE EVERYBODY OUT THERE WHO'S READING THIS! EVERY SINGLE ONE OF YOU! Thank you SO MUCH for supporting my movement! Live, laugh, love, and dare to dream! God bless!!

P.S. – Follow me on Twitter so I can keep you posted on my upcoming releases. And log onto www.SynergyPublications.com to join the mailing list for our upcoming newsletter.

CHAPTER ONE

Six months later...

It was a bleak and dreary night in Brooklyn. It was spring, but it was pretty cool outside. It had been raining hard all day. At just after two AM, Jay drove through the mean, wet streets of East New York. He was laid back in the driver's seat listening to an old school CD.

The song "It's a Thin Line Between Love and Hate" was blaring from the speakers of his newest toy, a luxurious '09 Bentley Mulsanne. The record had Jay feeling a little emotional. That particular night he was melancholy, so the music and the weather matched his mood perfectly. To say he had the blues would have been understating his pain. He was downright depressed.

Jay wasn't a complainer. He knew he was blessed, and overall life was good. He was just missing something at the time. It was Portia. He needed to get into something that night to take his mind off her. Jay was en route to an after-hours gambling spot, but he was thinking about her the whole time.

He thought about the last time he had seen his wife, which was in court about two weeks before. Portia looked good too. That was the day they'd finally dealt with those assault charges they got for fighting with the police at the hospital when Wise died. Their attorneys had held off that case for some time. That's why it was good to have money. That's what made the world go 'round.

Those hot guns Portia had hid in Laila's room were never recovered, so Jay and Cas hadn't been too worried about the outcome of their charges. They didn't know what happened to the guns, but they knew those bastards couldn't do much without them.

But Portia and Fatima were a little nervous. They didn't want to go to jail, but they were scared for nothing. When their court date finally came, they just paid a fine, made a donation, and the four of them were each given 20 hours of community service.

They had all completed their community service the week before. Those cock suckers ordered them to clean up the court house halls, of all things. As dirty and corrupt as the system was.

Jay pulled up down the block from a g-spot he'd frequented a time or two in the past. It had been a while since he'd been there, but an old buddy of his had called him and told him he was having a game there. It was his old crimie, BJ. BJ had been away in prison ever since their man, Nate, was killed. Nate was the older brother of Jay's deceased protégé, Humble.

Thinking of Humble made Jay feel guilty as usual. In his heart, he still felt like he failed to protect him. That was his little man. He really missed him. Humble and Nate were both good dudes, and both were gone too soon. So was his main man, Wise.

Jay took his mind off the dead. He was sad enough. He thought about BJ. He and Cas had last seen BJ at Nate's funeral. Right after that he got knocked in Maryland. He was just now coming home from doing a six year bid, so he was trying to get on his feet. Jay just came out to support. He knew his man got a cut of every play, so he came to gamble a little bit.

As soon as they found out BJ touched ground, Jay and Cas extended their financial assistance. They all went pretty far back, so they knew he was a real dude. Together they gave him fifty grand, and an employment opportunity. But BJ was a street dude. He took the money, but the job was another story. He said he appreciated the offer, but he wanted to try something else first.

Jay and Cas had no beef with that. They knew dudes had lots of pride. But they told him their offer was still on the table. BJ was one of the last real dudes left. That was pretty rare nowadays, so breaking bread with him was nothing.

Cas had sat that night out. He didn't come out because something he ate had given him the bubble gut. Jay didn't blame Cas for not coming out when he had the runs. He wouldn't have either. Jay had teased him, and said it was one of those super healthy seaweed smoothies his ass was always drinking.

BJ assured Jay that there would only be bosses at the game. He said he wouldn't have to worry about nobody standing around scheming. That was good to know, but Jay had been around long enough to know that shit could still happen. So he wasn't going in anyone's gambling joint off point. Shit, he was double strapped. He always toted two guns. That was his trademark.

Not on no sucker shit, but he thought about removing his jewelry and putting it in the glove compartment. Jay didn't fear anything walking on two legs, but he knew he wouldn't exactly be amongst his peers in that joint. He wasn't bragging, but he knew the average dude couldn't match half his bank. It was a recession, and niggas were thirsty. There was no need to rub his wealth in their faces.

Jay was no chump, but he didn't feel like he had to shine on dudes. He'd never been a fronting type of cat. There was no need to be shining in that environment anyway. He wasn't trying to impress a bunch of dicks. He drew enough attention as it was. He didn't want anybody to try him. He had zero tolerance for shit like that. He didn't want to have to kill a mothafucka.

Jay wasn't even in the mood that night, so he removed the impeccable black and white diamond ring from his pinky. That ring drew lots of attention, and he didn't come out for that. Jay was on some grown man shit now, so he was pass the excessive jewelry stage. Dudes didn't even rock their Street Life medallions anymore. Shit like that was for those young ass new money niggas.

The only other piece of jewelry Jay donned was his Cartier watch. Its bezel was icy, but he left it on so he could tell time. That watch was a gift from Portia the year before. Jay thought about her again for a second, and wondered what she was doing. Was she asleep, or was she up watching television, or writing a scene in her next novel? If she was in bed, he hoped she was sleeping alone. He thought about riding by her house. She was only about ten minutes away.

Pissed off at his own thoughts, Jay put Portia's ass on a back burner just like she did him. Fuck all that, he was going to gamble. He pulled his black fitted Yankees cap down so it shaded his face, and stepped out the car.

It was late, in the wee hours of the morning. The average person was probably just turning over in their sleep. Walking down the block, Jay noted some impressive vehicles parked along the street. When he got to the g-spot, there were a few dudes standing around outside. Jay nodded at a couple of them he recognized, and gave another dude he knew from back in the days a pound. After that, he headed on inside.

There were two dudes posted up right at the front, who were acting as security. They looked familiar to Jay. They must've recognized him too because they both nodded at him, and let him pass. Jay nodded back, appreciating the reverence. He noted that they hadn't searched him.

As soon as he stepped inside, he was hit in the face by thick cigarette smoke. He couldn't stand that smell. The thought of inhaling all that secondhand smoke was a real turn-off, but that was what came along with the territory in a "sin den".

At the stage he was at in his life, Jay really had no business down there. He just liked to gamble. He figured you could never have enough bread. He loved to win. It gave him a surge. Everybody loved money. It made the world go 'round. The only thing money couldn't seem to do was fix his marriage. So he had learned that it couldn't buy love.

Mother's Day was coming up that weekend. The year was almost half gone already, and for Jay, it wasn't going so well. He was glad to be alive, but unhappy that he and Portia were still split up. She was still on her bullshit.

2009 had come in sort of rough because that was the first holiday season they were on the outs ever since they'd been together. Portia had bought the girls home for a few days, and she and his mother had cooked for Christmas. They had all spent the day together like a family. But that night, Portia slept in one of the guest rooms. Imagine that. He felt mad stupid. That was his wife.

It was weird, but Jay had still liked having her in the house. Unbeknownst to her, he had tiptoed in the room and watched her while she was asleep. Not on no freak shit, but he just really missed her. She looked so pretty sleeping, and that was the only time she let her guards down around him.

Before he left the room, he had prayed to God for their reunification. But his prayers had been in vain that time. On New Year's Day Portia took the girls, and burned the road up. She said they had to be getting on "home." That shit really made Jay tight, but he didn't show it. It hurt him like hell, but women took advantage when they knew a dude was down on his knees.

Portia was acting real Hollywood, so he basically gave up trying to get her to come back. He was no lame. Wife or not, Jay didn't wear his heart on his sleeve. Women played on shit like that anyway. If Portia didn't come around that was her loss. And it was already May, so it didn't look like she was.

Jay acted like he didn't care anymore but he was miserable. He had resorted to piping a couple of other chicks, just to take his mind off Portia. He had protected himself, but the broads he screwed might as well have been mannequins. They were pretty, but he couldn't have been less connected to them if they were plastic. His mind had been on Portia every time.

Jay was sick of her flip-flopping on him. One minute he thought he had a chance, and they were going to work it out, and the next minute she led him to believe they were finished. Jay would never admit it, but she had him on an emotional roller coaster. Like some fucking puppet on a string. And he didn't like it. Not one bit. He oftentimes thought about the irony of his situation and found himself frowning in distaste.

Jay made it a point not to let his emotions govern him, especially in an unstable environment like the place he was in. He'd recently had a dream about being in a gambling spot when some knuckleheads ran up in there. Jay took his mind off Portia and his family for the time being, and got on point.

He headed to the designated "high roller" section, and commenced to place a bet. He glanced around the room for BJ. He saw him emerge from a side door seconds later. BJ noticed him at the same time, and his face lit up. Each grinning, they headed towards each other and exchanged daps.

The jolly men said their "what ups", and chatted for a while. BJ thanked him for coming out and supporting him. Jay told him the situation with Cas, and BJ said he hoped everything "came out all right". They looked at each other and laughed.

Jay knew a few heads there, and was quickly introduced to those he didn't know. The ones of relevance anyhow. He shook hands with his opponents, and they got down to business. Before long, Jay was engrossed in the game.

Time flew by. He was losing at first, so he was aggravated. He was nine large in the hole, but then he got up by about sixteen grand. After that, he was actually enjoying himself. Gambling was always more fun when you were winning.

Jay even accepted the drink BJ offered him. He poured him a shot of Chivas Regal Gold. Jay didn't really do whiskey but it was the good stuff so he tried it. He was usually a cognac drinker.

Jay was feeling good. He was in a zone. He had found his rhythm with the dice, and was on his A-game. He was just about to roll again, when he and the other gamblers got a rude awakening. Suddenly there was a thunderous thud, as the door was kicked in. *Boom!*

An ominous crew of gun toting, would-be stickup men stormed in the joint. They were three deep, and disguised in baseball caps, with stocking caps over their faces. They immediately commanded everybody to lay down, repeatedly shouting, *"Get on the floor! Everybody on the fuckin' floor!"*

Jay cursed under his breath. Wasn't that a bitch? Damn, he was caught in a robbery. It was so similar to the dream he'd had, he wondered if he was psychic. He couldn't believe it. He should've taken that to be a premonition. He thought about his kids, and prayed he would see them again.

Jay told himself that, if he made it out of there alive, there was nothing in the world that would stop him from getting his family back. He realized now how irresponsible of him it was to be hanging out in a place like that. He owed it to his kids to make responsible decisions so he would be around to see them grow up. He had no business in that spot. That was exactly why he needed his family back. Being a family man kept him grounded, and that kept him out of trouble.

Jay looked around at everybody getting down on the floor. He started to get down too, but he must've taken too long. One of the stickup dudes walked up to him and stuck his gun in his face.

The first thing Jay thought about was the last time he had killed someone. He had mercilessly pulled the trigger, and blew off Lite's face. That was months ago, but he couldn't help but wonder if this was his punishment for that work. In his eyes that little nigga Lite had it coming, but was that really up to him to determine? He knew how God worked.

Jay was human, so he was uneasy with that gun in his face.

What really made him nervous was the fact that the nigga didn't have a steady hand. He already got shot in the face once. Jay remained calm, and tried reasoning with the dude. "Be easy, man. I don't want no problems. Just take the money."

The dude acted like he was real tough. He snarled, "Get on the mothafuckin' floor, nigga, 'fore I shoot ya' fuckin' face off!"

Jay realized that his lights could get put out at any second. He wasn't really afraid to die, but he certainly wasn't ready. He had a lot to do, and his kids were still babies. He looked in the eyes of his could-be killer. He sensed that the dude didn't have a lot of heart, but he was no idiot. A coward or dude with something to prove could shoot you just as quick as a lionhearted killer. A bullet was a bullet, no matter what type of gun it came from.

Jay had too much to live for. He just wanted those clowns to take the bread, and go. But if that little street-fame thirsty asshole kept waving that gun at him, he would have to take his chances. If he was dying that night, he wasn't going peacefully.

Jay got down on one knee with his hands up. The gunmen must've been under the impression that everyone was unarmed. They were clearly amateurs because they didn't even pat anyone down and check. Jay had steel in the front and in the back of his waist. He wanted to make a move. He just had to strike at the right time, or he could get himself killed.

Jay knew he wasn't invincible. He was smarter than that. And then there was the question of the safety of the others in there. If he pulled out and started blasting, he knew those dudes were going to answer. Other people could get shot in the crossfire. On the low, he glimpsed around for a place he could run for cover. Jay thought about his kids once more, and silently prayed that he would see them again.

The amateur was getting impatient. He said, "Nigga, you heard what the fuck I said! Get all the way down! Is you *deaf*? Yo, matter of fact, let me get that watch! Send that right now!" Flossing that watch on bitches would get him mad pussy. The thought alone put stars in the amateur's eyes.

Jay thought about the way he'd debated leaving his watch in the car, and he had to laugh.

The dude didn't appreciate that one bit. He screwed his face up and moved closer with the gun. "Get on the floor, nigga! All the way down! And run that watch *now*!"

In the corner of his eye, Jay saw his man BJ making a move on another one of the stickup men. That dude was focused on a guy he caught reaching for a gun in his sock. He squeezed and let off on the guy who was reaching.

At precisely the same time, BJ gracefully pulled out and shot the amateur stickup man in the back of the head. BJ had a pretty quick draw. The shots were fired so close together it was almost simultaneous.

The loud gunfire caused the little dude with the gun on Jay to instinctively turn around to see who had fired. Jay took the opportunity to reach. He had to go all out. Fuck that, his life was in danger. With the speed and precision of a marksman, he produced his .45 and fired on that clown. *Blaow!* The slug hit him dead in the face.

Meanwhile, the owner of the establishment had seen the opportunity to take down the third accomplice. They got into a physical struggle, and he managed to wrestle the nigga's gun from him.

The owner's name was Zaggy. He was a big Bajan dude, who had come to America twenty years ago from Barbados. He had pulled himself up by the bootstraps, determined to become a successful entrepreneur. The work he had put in on the streets had qualified him to be well-respected enough to run a gambling spot in the heart of the slums of Brooklyn. As much as half a million dollars exchanged hands in his establishment on a regular, so he didn't take kindly to being violated and disrespected by some wannabe goons. He was a guerilla from the slums of Barbados, and had murdered more than a few men in his youth. Zaggy used that nigga's gun to blast three holes in his torso. His body danced a little jig, and then he dropped.

Now all three of those mothafuckas were on the floor dead. Jay and BJ snatched some of their bread off the table, and quickstepped up out of there. Just about everyone else in that joint followed suit. Dudes were tearing the door down trying to get out of there.

On the way out, they stepped over two more dead bodies. It was the two security dudes. Jay saw two busted potatoes on the ground. Now he knew why they hadn't heard any shots outside. Those shots could've warned them.

Jay hurried to his car so fast, he was out of breath when he got there. BJ was right behind him. Jay looked down at his shirt and noticed there was a little blood on it. That was okay. He would rather it be duke's blood splattered on him, than his blood splattered on duke. He shot the nigga before he got shot. That was the golden rule.

Jay was glad he had managed to come out of that situation alive. He gave God a quick shout-out, and hopped in his Bentley. BJ hopped in on the passenger side, and Jay peeled off. When they got a few blocks away, he slowed down a little. After what had just gone down, he didn't want any extra attention from the police.

Jay told BJ he wasn't stopping until he got to Jersey. BJ didn't even protest. He figured it might be a good idea to get low and camp out at Jay's crib for the night. They both had blood on their hands, so there was no point in sticking around.

Along the way, Jay talked to his man about leaving that street shit alone. He told him if he wanted to profit off the night life, he needed a legit setup like their man Wings had. A classy, legal establishment.

BJ had to agree with him that time. After what happened, he was glad to be alive. He felt disrespected by the way those niggas ran up in his game, but that was street life. Maybe Jay was right.

He had children to live for too. Maybe it was time to square it up.

BJ just wanted to have something in life. He had plans. He just had to get his bread right. Jay must've read his mind because that very second, he offered him a lifeline again. He told him he would set him out, and back him on whatever he wanted to do. He said he should just think of it as a gift, and if that was difficult, he should think of it as an interest-free loan.

BJ put that in his pipe and smoked it. That cowboy shit was sort of fun back in the days, but at that stage in his life he preferred not to be actively involved in gunplay. He saw how wealthy his mans Jay and Cas had become while he was away. And they were both good dudes. They had looked out for him and his family.

BJ was proud of his dudes, but he wanted to make some type of mark in the world too. He needed to establish himself, and acquire something he could leave his kids. He told Jay he wanted to take him up on that offer, but he had to think hard about what it was he really wanted to do. He said he didn't want any favors, so he would get back to him after he devised a serious business plan.

CHAPTER TWO

Portia woke up around eight that Saturday morning. She laid there in bed for a few minutes, prioritizing her "to do list" for the day. It was Mother's Day weekend, so she had to get her and the kids ready for church the next day. Portia briefly thought about Jay, like she did every time she woke up. She whispered her usual prayer for his wellbeing, and wondered what he was up to.

They were still split up. It had been over six months now. Two whole seasons had passed. It was spring again, and the weather was slowly starting to get warm. It hadn't been easy getting through those cold winter months without the warmth and comfort of her husband. A part of her wanted to get back with Jay more than anything, especially for the sake of her children. But Portia's pride just wouldn't let her.

During their time apart, she proved to herself that she could be independent again. But she didn't believe she proved her point to Jay yet. Or at least he wouldn't admit it. She missed him a lot, but he was still playing this nonchalant role. He acted like he couldn't care less if she returned.

Portia knew he wasn't the type to grovel, but she wanted him to look her in her eyes and apologize. She wanted him to say he was sorry, and she wanted him to admit he needed her the way she needed him. She wanted him to mean it.

Portia refused to return to some half ass marriage. If they couldn't start over, she wanted out. It was ridiculous to believe they could just pick up where they left off, and go on like nothing had ever happened. A lot had happened. Jay had completely shattered the trust she had in him. He put her through some pretty heavy stuff. Portia didn't appreciate the way he was acting like she was the one who'd broken up their home.

Jay had made a couple of attempts to reconcile. But his attempts were half assed, so she had shut him down. It didn't seem like he really got it yet. One time he just said, "P, stop playing games, and come home."

Jay didn't quite understand. She wasn't playing. If he couldn't love her like she loved him, she didn't want to be with him. To her, having half of him was worse than not having him at all. She wasn't about to settle. If he wanted that type of relationship, he should marry someone else.

It hadn't been easy, but God had given her the strength to get by. The only time Portia slipped up was when she had slept with young Vino. That happened when she and Fatima went to Los Angeles to catch Callie, their deceased friend Simone's trifling sister, in the act of stealing Fatima's identity. The sex with Vino was great, but the guilt trip afterwards was not worth it. Portia would never play herself like that again. She was too virtuous of a woman to have even stooped to Jay's level. She didn't feel too good about herself afterwards.

Then the fact that Vino was sort of Jay's friend made it worse. There would always be the possibility that mess could come back to bite her one day. She prayed otherwise, but she had slept with a man she knew Jay associated with. A man he had hired to look after her. That was pretty foul.

At the time, there had been something inside of her that had wanted revenge, but now she regretted it. Vino had treated her like a lady and all, but she was married to Jay. They were split up at the time, but she still played herself. Portia was old-fashioned in a sense, and believed marriage was sacred.

The more she thought about it, she wanted to get back with

her husband. She couldn't front, she missed him like crazy. But he had to understand that she wasn't the one to cheat on. Portia laid there and contemplated going back home to Jersey. Their wedding anniversary was coming up soon.

But that time apart had also done her some good. She had thrown herself into her work to keep herself occupied, so she had almost completed her fourth novel.

She and Jay acted civilized towards each other. For the sake of their children, they did the whole "weekend visitation" thing. Jayquan came to stay with her sometimes, and some weekends Jazmin and Trixie went and stayed with their father. Every time Jazz came back home, she told Portia she missed living with her daddy.

Portia took that into consideration, but it was so late in the school year now she wanted Jazmin to finish it out. There was no point in shifting her around in May. Her summer vacation would be starting soon. But after that, who knew.

Portia wanted Jay to be in the kids' lives. Trixie was fourteen months old now, and she loved him just as much as her big brother and sister did. Jay had missed a lot in her life, including seeing her take her first steps. Portia knew how much he loved his kids so she felt bad about that. He smiled when she told him the baby was walking, but he looked pretty sad.

Portia reminisced about the way Jay used to make love to her. She couldn't front, she missed being in his arms. And she missed him being inside of her. She'd been pretty horny lately. To be frank, she was in dire need of some dick. Portia knew she was attractive, and probably wouldn't have a problem getting laid. But she didn't want just any man. She wanted her husband. Jay had the best dick she'd ever had anyway. Damn, she missed Rocky. Thoughts of Jay's penis aroused her.

Portia ran her hands across her breasts, and then she stuck her hand down the front of her panties. She closed her eyes and thought about the way Jay used to kiss her down there. He wouldn't stop until he knew she was satisfied. He knew how to please her. Portia rubbed her pussy and began masturbating. It wasn't long before her juices were flowing, and her fingers were wet.

She was breathing heavier and heavier. She continued to rub her clit with her thumb and forefinger until she was about to erupt. Portia imagined that was Jay eating her out. She started moaning, and got so into it she cried out.

Just as she was cumming, she heard her daughter's voice. Mortified, Portia opened her eyes and saw Jazmin standing in her bedroom doorway. Wow, she could've just died.

Jazz looked concerned. She asked, "Mommy, why are you crying? Are you okay?"

Portia was so embarrassed she must've turned beet red. As dark-skinned as she was. How long had that child been standing there? She tried to play it off. She said, "Mommy's fine, baby. I'm not crying."

Jazz said, "So why were you squirming in the bed, and making all those noises? Are you in pain, or something? Mommy, what hurts?"

Portia didn't even know what to say, so she just brushed it off. "Oh, I guess I was just dreaming. I must've had a nightmare."

She changed the subject quick before Jazz could ask anymore questions. Portia urged her kids to be inquisitive, but that wasn't the time. She thought of a reason to make her run along. She asked, "Did you brush your teeth, sweetness?"

Jazmin shook her head. She blew her mommy a kiss, and headed for the bathroom. Portia was relieved she got out of that one. Having kids basically meant that your right to privacy went out the window. She couldn't even get one off without gettng busted.

Jazz had brought her back down to reality. It was time to get their day started. The following day was Mother's Day. Portia put her sexual thoughts of Jay on a back burner, and got up and ran Jazmin a bath. While she was bathing, Portia washed in the shower box across from the tub. When she was done, she woke her little sleepyhead Trixie up, and got her ready.

After her girls were dressed, Portia made them breakfast. When they were all done eating, she got the garbage ready to take outside. She hoped to run into her new neighbor soon. The house next door had just recently sold, and the new owner hadn't been around much to clean up.

The Department of Sanitation had issued Portia a $25 fine, all because their rubbish kept blowing in front of her gate. They'd put the violation on her property because the garbage was littered in front of her house. She had been hoping she would run into the new owner so she could ask them to come around and sweep up more often. But she'd had no luck thus far.

Portia didn't see anybody over there again, so she put her trash to the curb and went back inside. She washed her hands, and they got ready to go to the hair salon. She wanted to get an early start so they could beat the pre-Mother's Day rush. Jazmin was getting her hair done that day too. She'd been begging for Shirley Temple curls all week. Portia didn't want to be in the beauty parlor all day, so they left the house before ten.

Three hours later, they were done. Lucky for Portia, Trixie had been a good girl. She took a nap in her stroller while Portia got her hair washed, and roller set. By the time the baby woke up, her hair was almost dry. Jazmin's too. And you couldn't tell her nothing with her bouncy curls. Baby girl thought she was too cute.

Portia spent the rest of the day getting her little girls' outfits together. They were moving a bit behind schedule because Trixie's little grown butt wanted to walk everywhere like a big girl. Her tiny footsteps slowed them down a little bit.

When they were done shopping, they stopped by a beauty supply store to pick up some pretty barrettes the same color of Trixie's dress, and a satin cap to hold Jazmin's curls in place. After that, they hurried home. Jayquan was due to arrive at four.

Portia was thrilled that he had called and let her know he was coming over to spend Mother's Day with her. That meant a lot to her. Portia may have not birthed Lil' Jay into this world, but she loved him like she did. He was her son, and she was honored that he wanted to spend that day with her. That had almost moved her to tears. After church, she was taking him to put flowers on his mother's gravesite. She planned to do the same for Patty Cake, may her mother rest in peace.

She and the girls got back to the house around a quarter to four. Jazmins was excited about her brother coming over. Portia knew she missed him when he wasn't around. She planned on taking the kids somewhere nice that evening. When Jayquan arrived, she would give him the honor of deciding where they would go.

Portia looked out the window for the car Lil' Jay was coming in. He wasn't out there yet, so she called up Laila and Fatima to make sure they were still going to church with her the following day. Both of her friends said they were still on. They were bringing the kids too. Portia, Laila, and Fatima were all raised in church.

Portia thought about her two best friends briefly. She was proud of them both. Fatima had finally gotten it together, and was on her job with her daughter. She was clean, and actually seemed happy for a change.

Laila was happily in love with Cas. And she was out of that wheelchair, thank God. Every now and then she used a scooter to help her get around, but not often. Girlfriend had made amazing progress.

Portia smiled at the thought, and looked out the window for Jayquan again. For some reason, she thought about her cousin, Melanie. She hoped she was okay. The last time they spoke, which was about two months ago, Mel had informed her about her new "occupation". She said she was a proud porno star.

While they were on the telephone, she went on and on about being "the next big thing" in the business.

Portia couldn't believe how lost her poor cousin was. And in this day and time, when so many STDs existed. Portia asked her if she was doing it because she was broke and desperate, but Mel told her she was good. She said she even still had money left in her savings from her lawsuit against Wise, God bless the dead. She told Portia that doing porn just empowered her, and made her feel appreciated.

Portia had tried to talk to her. She told her to utilize her intelligence and try something different, but Mel wasn't trying to hear that. Portia gave up, but she prayed Mel was just going through some type of phase. And she hoped she was really protecting herself, like she claimed she was. She was in an extremely high-risk business.

Portia did what she did back in her day, so she didn't want to be a hypocrite and pass judgment on her crazy cousin. And it was no secret that Mel had always been promiscuous. Melanie used to carry on like a broke hoe, so Portia had told her she should get something in exchange for all the ass she gave away.

Mel had taken her advice, but she took it and ran with it. That chick was wilding. Portia didn't approve. Melanie was moving backwards. She was thirty now, and she just started doing porn. That was something she should've gotten out of her system years ago, if she wanted to try it. Portia just prayed that God would make her cousin see the light so she would quit risking her life, just for a little money and self-esteem.

$ $ $ $

Jay and Cas were riding along the way to meet with few of their clergy associates. There was money business to be discussed. Afterwards, they planned to play a little golf. Cas was anxious to try out this new set of top of the line golf clubs Laila got him.

Cas was driving at the time, and Jay was thinking about his son. He had just sent Jayquan to Brooklyn in a hired car a little while ago. He went to stay with Portia for the weekend. Jayquan told him he wanted to go to church with her on Mother's Day. Jay was so touched by that, he decided to go to church with his mother too. Out of all the money, jewelry, cars, and furs Jay had given his mama for Mother's Day over the years, the thing she always said she wanted most was for him to go to church with her.

Jay's mother preferred a simple life. She wore a lot of white linen, and she used Carol's Daughter beauty products, and wore her hair natural. Mama Mitchell had retired from the Department of Agriculture five years ago, and her favorite hobby was gardening. She had a garden in the backyard of her Clinton Hills brownstone. She had a green thumb, and grew all of her favorite organic vegetables back there.

Sometimes she declined the gifts Jay gave her, and referred to them as "meaningless". Especially flashy vehicles. Mama Mitchell drove a European car, but it was a wagon. She told him she needed something she could carry her soil and other gardening necessities in, so he got her a BMW 535i xDrive Sports Wagon. Jay loved his mom the way she was. She had raised him to be meek, and she still kept him grounded.

Now Cas' mom was the complete opposite. Ms. B loved flashy cars. She currently drove a pearl white Bentley. And that was just her everyday car. The average person couldn't even pronounce what she stepped out in on the weekends.

And Ms. B loved to travel. In fact, she had just flown off somewhere Friday morning. Cas had sent her on her annual all-expense-paid Mother's Day voyage. She got a fabulous vacation as a gift from him every year. Cas was her only child, and he treated his mama good. Over the years, Ms. B had gone just about everywhere in the seven continents. She was truly an international diva.

Jay looked over at Cas driving. He looked like he was deep in thought. Jay wondered what that dude was thinking about. He'd been pondering something himself. He figured he'd let Cas know what it was. He broke the silence, and asked him to go to church with him the following day.

Cas looked at him kind of strange. The first thing he thought about was the fact that they had been cleared of that federal investigation they were under. The pigs couldn't find anything solid that tied them to corruption. God was good. After a second, he said, "A'ight. What time?"

Jay said, "I'll find out, and let you know." He made a mental note to call and ask his mother what time service started.

Cas nodded. Jay and Casino didn't usually talk much about the dirt they did after it was done. Jay had already given his right hand man the rundown on that incident in the gambling spot at BJ's game, so he didn't bring it up again. But it was on his mind. He'd taken another life. It was self-defense, but it was bothering him.

Jay thought about the time they'd been forced to kill little Lite for trying to snake them. He wished they had never even run into that dude. Against his will, Jay thought about all the others whose lives they'd taken as well. He even thought about their former artist and crony, Hip Hop. Hop's two-faced ass had set them up that time when Jay got shot in the face, so he deserved to get it.

Jay was a good dude, and he really didn't like hurting people. He only did it when they tried to hurt him first. But at that point in his life, he just wanted to live right. He was tired of that life. He was getting older now. At almost thirty six, enough was enough. It was a brand new day. A black man not much older than him was the president of the United States. President Obama had raised the bar. Dudes had to straighten up, real talk.

Cas hadn't spoken about it, but he'd been experiencing some similar changes within. So it was funny that Jay had suggested going to church. He knew Jay, so he could tell he wasn't happy about the shit he had to do the other night. Cas was tired of living like that too. But some dudes were real dickheads, so you had to answer. He and Jay were getting older now, and so were their children. Their kids were watching them, so they had to be role models for them.

Cas talked to God a lot, and he constantly prayed he wouldn't have to kill again. He had a family now, and God was blessing him too much to create bad karma. He thought about all of the ruckus he and Jay had encountered throughout their lives. They were living examples that God heard sinners' prayers too. So why not go to church? God had been good to them, so surely they could give Him a little of their time. And if they wanted to live right, change came from within.

The song "Pretty Wings", by Maxwell came on the CD that Cas was playing. Jay noted that every song that had played so far was some old mellow, laid back shit. It wasn't hard to tell that dude was in love. Jay decided to fuck with him. He joked, "Damn, son. You on some Romeo shit today. Laila got yo' ass whipped."

Cas just laughed, and didn't say anything. He knew Jay was just busting his balls.

Jay was straight fronting. Maxwell's song lyrics were making him think about his Kit Kat.

"Your face will be the reason I smile, but I will not see what I can not have forever…I'll always love you, and I hope you feel the same…Ooh-h, you played me dirty. The game was so bad. Toyed with my affection, had to fill out my prescription, found the remedy. I had to set you free-e-e. Away for me- to see clearly- the way that love can be- when you are not with me. I had to live, I had to live, I had to leave, I had to learn…"

"If I can't have you let love set you free to flap your pretty wings around. Pretty wings, your pretty wings, your pretty wings, pretty wings around…"

Portia had flapped her pretty wings right out of his life. Damn, he had to get her back. She was his rib. A lump rose in Jay's throat. It was real tough without her. That damn song was getting to him.

Jay reached over and turned the volume down. He said, "I'm in here with this old R&B ass, in-love-ass-nigga. Take that slow shit out, man. Play somethin' hard."

Cas really liked that song, and he knew Jay did too. But he didn't protest because he understood. He knew his man was hurting. He ejected the CD, and turned the radio on and searched for some Hip-hop.

Cas left it on Hot 97, and said a quick prayer for his best man. Jay really needed to be back with his family. The dude was low.

CHAPTER THREE

The next morning Portia's alarm clock went off, and the radio came on. She was tuned in to WBLS, and they were jamming. They were playing "I'll Always Love My Mama" by The Intruders. She smiled and listened to the lyrics.

"I'll always love my mama. She's my favorite girl...I'll always love my mama. She brought me in this world. You only get one, you only get one, yeah... Talkin' 'bout mama...sweet ol' mama..."

It was Mother's Day Sunday. Portia started her day with a prayer. She missed her mother more than anything in the world so they were playing the right song. There was no other like a mother. She wished Patty Cake could've been there for her to confide in. Portia was glad her mother had taught her to believe.

Portia and her babies were going to church that day. She thought about when she was small. Her mother used to pin red flowers on their dresses every Mother's Day before they went to church. In the spirit of tradition, Portia had purchased flowers for her, Laila, Fatima, and all their kids to pin on their shirts and dresses. She had picked up red for those whose mothers were alive and well, and white flowers for those of them whose mothers were deceased. Out of their group, Laila, Portia, and Jayquan were the ones with white flowers.

When her mother was on her dying bed, she told Portia to raise her kids with God, the way she had raised her. Now Portia got it. They needed spiritual guidance in their lives. What other

31

way but teaching them about God could she instill morals and values in her children? There had to be some type of belief system present. They had to recognize that there was a higher power to answer to.

Three hours later, they were all sitting in church. They were side by side, in the third pew. The pastor, who was Portia's aunt, Gracie, was warming up to preach a heartfelt sermon.

Pastor Grace Mills greeted her parishioners warmly. "Glory be to God! Happy Mothers Day, ladies! Today is *your* day. *Mother's* Day. Church, I'm talkin' to all y'all, young and old. You got to be good to your mama. God only gives you one. And I sure miss my mama. Lord knows, I miss her. My *mama.* What y'all know 'bout a mama? A mother is the strongest, most beautiful creature God ever put on this earth. I *miss* my mama. God, she was *good* to me! She got down on her *knees,* and she *prayed* for me! Hallelujah! Lord, if I could just hear her pray for me one more time."

The choir rose, and began to sing a gospel hymn Portia had always loved, "If I Could Hear My Mother Pray Again."

When they got to the chorus, Portia tried to sing along. *"If I could hear- my mother pray again. If I could hear - her tender voice again. How glad I would be. It would mean so much to me – If I could hear my mother when she prayed again…"*

She was in tears before the song ended. Along with half of the other folks in the church. After the choir selection, Pastor Mills said a prayer for the sick and afflicted mothers who could not be there. And then she addressed the folks with deceased mothers. She told them their moms would always live on through their ways, and the examples they set out in the world.

Next, she prayed for the mothers with children that weren't with them, either because they were dead, in prison, or at war. That prayer broke Laila. She thought about the way her baby, Pebbles, was brutally raped and murdered. She started crying, so Portia reached over and squeezed her dear friend's hand.

Jayquan even had a little water in his eyes, but he played it cool. Macy held his hand. She knew he had lost his mother when he was little. That couldn't have been easy for him.

Fatima had tears of guilt in her eyes. She thought about all she had put her mother through when she was doing drugs. Her mom was a class act. She had loved her regardless. Even when she couldn't love herself. Fatima and her daughter were heading over to the afternoon service at her mother's church next. Their Mother's Day program started at three o'clock. They were going out for dinner afterwards.

Sitting next to her two best friends, whom had both lost their mothers, reminded Fatima how blessed she was. Her heart went out to her girls. Portia and Laila had lost their fathers as well. That was sad. She realized she should really cherish the time she had with her mom and dad because life just wasn't promised. Not to anyone.

$ $ $ $

Jay and Casino were sharp that Sunday. They were decked out in tailored suits, designed by Tom Ford. Jay was wearing gray, and Cas had on a tan number. To say they were pimping would've been understating their swag. The dapper brothers had gone to church with Mama Mitchell that morning. They got out of service just after twelve 'noon.

Jay's sister, Laurie, was also there. And so was Cas' son, Jahseim. Jahseim had been staying with Cas while Kira was locked up, but he spent a lot of weekends with his grandmother. That was one of them. Jah had been at Mama Mitchell's since Friday.

Jahseim was happy to see his father and uncle at church that morning. He had no idea they were coming. After the service, he had hugged them and excitedly told them he was going to visit his mother that day.

Cas grinned at his son affectionately. That little dude was his heart. Jah was his firstborn. He thought about his incarcerated baby mama and ex-wife, Kira. Mother's Day was probably hard for her that year. But she only had a few months to go, and she would be home.

Since Cas and Jay were just kids, they had been calling each other's mothers "Ma". Cas turned to Mama Mitchell, and said, "Ma, that's nice of you to take Jahseim to visit Kira today."

She just smiled, and waved her hand at him. Kira was her daughter, so that was nothing. Mama Mitchell said all her children better come see her on Mother's Day every year too, even when she was gone. She said they'd better be at her gravesite every year then.

Jay and Laurie both made a face. They hated when their mother talked that way. Jay told her to knock it off.

Mama Mitchell said, "Son, we all have to go one day, so just make sure you're right with God. None of us are promised tomorrow."

Jay said, "I know. But not you, lady. You gon' live forever."

Cas smiled, and said, "I second that, Ma. All saints live forever."

Mama Mitchell laughed. She said, "Okay, if you boys say so."

Jay leaned over and kissed her on the cheek. His mother was a queen. And he'd enjoyed attending service with her. So did Casino. They couldn't front, both of their hearts felt lighter.

Although Jay had flowers delivered to his mother and his sister that morning, he reached in his pocket and peeled off his usual cash Mother's Day blessings. After Laurie collected her money from Jay, she turned to Cas with her hand out. He laughed, but he peeled off and followed suit. Laurie hit Cas up every time she saw him. That was how it had always been. Ever since back in the days. But it was all good. They were all like family.

Mama Mitchell asked Jay about Portia. He looked sad when he told her the truth about them still being split up. She urged him to go on and be with his family. Jay was her only son, and he had made her very proud. She could honestly say that she had raised a man. He had done well for himself, and she wanted him to get back with his family. He had a good wife.

Mama Mitchell was a wise woman. She could see right through people. Portia was a good girl. She could tell she really loved her son, so she was worth him fighting for.

Jay did want to see his wife. He thought about going over to the program at her church. His kids were there too. He knew where the church was. That was where they got married. Jay made up his mind, and he voiced his decision out loud. He and Cas kissed his mother and sister goodbye, and they broke out.

Cas rode with Jay across town to Freewill Baptist Church. When they got there, Jay parked the Bentley, and they hopped out and headed for the church. The men entered as quietly as they could.

It was Mother's Day, so the women inside were dressed to the nines. There were matching hats and suits in just about every color, from aqua to zebra print. Unbeknownst to Portia and the gang, Jay and Cas had a seat at the back and listened to the end of the sermon.

When the pastor was done, she turned it over to the children to give them a chance to show their mothers how much they appreciated them. The little ones went up there one by one, and the church clapped.

Jay was so proud when his daughter, Jazmin, went up there. She said, "I wanna tell my mommy "Happy Mother's Day." She's the best mommy in the world."

Falynn went up next, and said "Happy Mother's Day" to Fatima. Even Macy and Mr. "Too cool for everything" Jayquan went up there.

At the end of the program, Jayquan and three other young men were selected to hand out long-stemmed, red roses to all the mothers in the church. The women on the receiving end of the solitaire roses were all smiles.

When they were done, everyone applauded. The pastor smiled and stood up. She asked the congregation if anyone had any closing remarks. Jay smiled to himself. He knew the pastor well. She was Portia's aunt, and she bore a striking resemblance to Portia's mom. She had also married him and Portia years ago.

When the last church member was done speaking, Pastor Mills asked if there were any visitors. Jay didn't know what came over him, but he stood up. He walked to the front of the church. It felt like all eyes were on him.

Portia's aunt recognized him. She smiled, and extended her arms to Jay. She said, "Welcome, son", and embraced him.

Jay appreciated the warm welcome. It meant a lot to him. He was pretty sure the pastor knew he and Portia were split up at the moment, so he was glad she didn't judge him.

Jay took a deep breath, and turned around to face the congregation. It was a pretty big church. He saw Portia, her friends, and all the kids in front. They were sitting in the third pew. Jay was nervous for some reason. He almost choked up.

He was already up there, so he spoke into the microphone and introduced himself as a visitor. He mentioned that he and his lovely wife had been married in that church eight years ago.

Jay cleared his throat, and began. "First, I'd like to say Happy Mother's Day to all the mothers present, in body or spirit. I came up here because I'd like to apologize to my wife. The mother of my three children. She's here, and I hope this doesn't embarrass her. She's been upset with me for a while, but I'm offering her my *sincerest* apology. And I pray she accepts."

Jay unbuttoned his suit jacket, and loosened his tie a little. He looked around at everybody, and then he continued. "I'm not proud of this, but I messed up. I had the *perfect* marriage. The *best* family in the world. Then I did something stupid. I messed up. So my wife left me."

Jay paused for a second, and nodded sincerely. "I guess I deserved it. Because she was the best wife I could've ever asked for. She was good to me, so yes, I deserved it. I've been miserable these past months. But I've been doin' a lot of praying lately. A *lot*. I'm actually praying right now. I hope my wife will forgive me, and just give me one more chance to show how much I love her. That would really be a privilege."

Jay paused thoughtfully. A few seconds later, he said, "I'm not gon' front, I've learned somethin'. I get it now, y'all. I *need* her. She's my better half, so I don't wanna spend another day without her. I don't think I could. Her and my kids, we're supposed to be a family. If she would give me the opportunity, I promise her, right here before God, that I will *never* hurt her again. As long as I live."

Jay had spoken from his heart, but he wondered if he'd said too much. He decided he had been up there too long, so he wrapped it up. He looked around, and said, "Thanks for listening. God bless, and enjoy the rest of y'all day." After that, he just walked off.

After he was done talking, it was just quiet for a minute. Jay felt awkward so he made a beeline straight for the door. All of a sudden somebody started to clap, and then the whole church erupted in applause. Just about every woman in there was stretching her neck, looking around to see who the lucky girl was. At least a third of them envied her. That man was fine, well dressed, and he was up there begging her for another chance.

Portia had to restrain Jazmin and Trixie while Jay was up there speaking. When they saw their daddy, they wanted him. When he was done speaking, Portia let them go. The girls ran straight to Jay.

Jay picked his daughters up and hugged them. He kissed them on their foreheads, and told them to go back over there to their mother. They looked unhappy that he was leaving, but he promised them he would see them real soon. Then Jay continued walking to the back of the church.

He looked over at Cas, and pointed at the door. Cas was on

point. He stood up and started making his way toward the exit too.

Jay meant every word he said up there, but now he felt like that was sort of lame. He didn't wear his heart on his sleeve. What had made him do that? Come on, people were applauding him. He hadn't gone up there for that purpose. It wasn't a performance.

Portia just sat there for a second. She was so touched by Jay's public apology she had tears in her eyes. She mentally replayed his words. Wow, he was really sorry. She could tell he had meant everything he said. That man loved her. She knew it and felt it. Now she was ready to take him back. It just felt right.

Just then, Jazmin and Patrice came running back over there. They were both in tears. Jazz stammered, "Mommy, D-daddy left! He l-l-left! Again!"

Portia wiped their faces and told them not to cry, and then she hurried to the back of the church. She didn't see Jay anywhere. Jazmin was right, he was gone!

Portia felt like an idiot. She had taken too long to respond. She knew how Jay was. He probably left because he was embarrassed. She should've stood up and acknowledged him. He was her husband, and he was speaking to *her*. She didn't mean to hurt his pride. She forgave him. And she missed him, and she loved him. Where was he?

Portia ran back and asked Laila and Fatima to keep an eye on her kids for a minute, and then she ran outside, and jumped in her car. She drove around the block three times looking for Jay, but to no avail. Distraught, she went back to the church to get her children.

Laila and Fatima were waiting outside the church. They all hugged, and said goodbye to each other. Portia and her kids went home to change, and Fatima and her daughter headed to her mother's church.

Laila and her daughters went to visit Khalil's mother, Mama

Atkins, because Macy had a gift for her. Laila always made sure her kids got their grandmother something for Mother's Day when they were little, so Macy did it every year now. Laila knew Khalil lived in his mother's basement apartment, but he was incarcerated for a little while. He was locked up for some dumb stuff. He still called and harassed her every chance he got, so she wouldn't have gone near there if he was home.

When Portia and the kids got home, she told Jayquan to change his clothes so they could head to their mothers' graves with the flowers she'd picked up. And then they were heading for the movie she'd promised them. Portia laid out Jazz's clothes for her, and then she got the baby ready. Both her girls were wearing their pink Pradas that day.

Portia was stepping into her Rock & Republic jeans when doorbell rang. She yelled for Jayquan to answer it, and continued getting dressed.

A few seconds later, Lil' Jay hollered, "Our new neighbor's at the door!"

Portia yelled, "Tell them to give me a minute." She was glad her neighbor had finally showed up. It was the perfect opportunity to tell them about that $25 sanitation ticket she got because of their negligence. Maybe they would offer to pay it. It was the principle of the matter. She quickly tied her Gucci sneakers, checked her hair in the mirror, and headed to the door.

When Portia got out front, she got the surprise of her life. Jay was out there! And he looked so good. She gave him a big Kool-Aid smile, and playfully balled up her fist at Jayquan. He just grinned, and walked off.

Portia turned back to Jay. She said, "Hey. Your son's lil' storytelling ass said my new neighbor was at the door."

Jay just smiled. After a second, he said, "That's not a story. He was telling the truth. I *am* your new neighbor. I bought the house next door. A few months ago, actually. I did it to prove a point, but then when I thought about it, the shit seemed a little weird. I didn't wanna make you feel awkward. I figured the last thing a woman who left a guy wants is him moving next door to her. I wanted to be closer to the kids, and you, but I didn't want you to think I was stalkin' you. I decided to give you your space. So I just left the house sitting there, until I figured out what to do."

Wow, Jay was crazy. Portia couldn't believe him. Neither of them said anything for a minute. He just took her hand and held it for a second, grateful for the opportunity.

Jay looked around, and nodded in approval. He smiled, and said, "It looks good in here. Real nice, P."

Portia thanked him, and smiled.

All of a sudden he looked at her real serious. Jay said, "Listen, P… I can't do this. I can't be wit' out you and my kids no more."

He looked so sincere, Portia almost cried. She held it in and allowed him to finish.

Jay said, "I remember when you told me that things are different now. You said you had to get *you* back, and I understand. I can live with that. Sometimes we need our own space. But I gotta be in your life, P. And I need you in mine. You really are my better half. Please, Ma. I'm so sorry about all this."

Portia couldn't hide it anymore. She let go, and let those tears fall. That was what she was talking about. The moment she had prayed for. It sounded like he loved her as much as she loved him. That was the reciprocity she needed from him.

Jay couldn't have said another word if he'd wanted to because Portia wrapped her arms around his neck, and kissed him. Jay hugged his wife tight and enjoyed the makeup kiss he had been praying for. He rested his hands on her ample bottom and squeezed it. He loved the shit out of Portia. He would never jeopardize what they had again. She was his backbone. As they stood there embracing, Jay stood up tall, and felt complete.

They heard the sound of laughter. He and Portia looked over and saw the kids standing there watching them. They were all cheesing. It looked like they were pretty happy. Jazmin was laughing and jumping up and down, and Jayquan was dancing around with the baby grinning. Even Trixie was laughing. She was smart so she knew what was going on.

Portia and Jay opened their arms to their rug rats for a group hug, and they all shared a long one. It was a happy family reunion. Jay kissed all his kids on their foreheads. He was so happy he had tears in his eyes. He had missed his family so much. He was nothing without them. Absolutely nothing.

CHAPTER FOUR

A week later, Portia and her little girls were back in Jersey. They had unofficially moved back into what Jazmin affectionately referred to as "the big house with Daddy". Portia still had a lot of stuff at her house in Brooklyn, but she enjoyed being home with Jay. The only thing complicated was that Jazmin had to commute to school everyday. It was the end of the year, so there was no point in transferring her. Jay just left the house a little earlier every morning, and dropped her off on his way to the City.

They had talked about everything that happened, and Jay was honest with her. Portia forgave him, and they agreed to put it all behind them. They both wanted to start over.

Portia hadn't been nasty about it, but she had demanded that he go to the doctor to get tested for sexually transmitted diseases. She loved him and forgave him, but the fact was that he'd been with someone else. They just had to play it safe.

Jay had respected her wishes. He got tested, and came back clean. Portia was relieved. He didn't know, but she had gone to the doctor to get checked out herself. She'd only had sex with Vino that one time, and they used a condom, but she wanted to be a hundred percent sure everything was good. Thank God, her tests came back clean too. Portia was so glad. She would never put herself in that position again.

After they got all that out the way, she and Jay started having make-up sex everywhere. They were screwing all over the house. Especially when the kids weren't home. The lovemaking was amazing, and worry-free. They were going at it so much, Portia decided to get on some form of birth control. She didn't want to get pregnant again. Trixie was still a baby, and she didn't want anymore kids.

Jay was romancing Portia hard. They were going out on dates like twice a week. They even went dancing. They were having the time of their lives, and behaving like newlyweds again.

Since they had agreed to start over, Portia wanted to recreate their very first encounter. One evening she was in a silly mood, so she decided to send Jay a sex text. On her BlackBerry, she typed, *"Hurry up and cum home, baby. I wanna give you a milk mustache tonight."*

Jay was just jiving around with a few dudes, and shooting dice when his phone vibrated in his pocket. When he got Portia's text, he laughed. She always wanted her pussy eaten. After reading that, he felt naughty too. He sex texted her back, *"I'm wit' that Ma. Do u want a milk mustache too?"*

After he sent it, Jay chuckled to himself. He knew how Portia felt about cum in her mouth. She didn't play that. He waited for the slick response he knew would follow.

To his surprise, the text she sent him read, *"Who knows? I'm n the mood for sum freaky shit 2nite. Get home within the hour, and double your pleasure. Now bet on that."*

Jay got rock hard at the thought. P was crazy. Now he was ready to say goodnight to his mans. He and Portia's sex life had been on fire lately. That pussy was smoldering, and it matched his fit like a glove. He felt at home in it. It was his.

Portia's body was calling him, so Jay started giving out pounds and daps. After he said goodbye, he got started on the journey home to his sexy chocolate Kit Kat. He had a sweet tooth. He called and let her know he was on the way.

When he got there, he was in for a treat. Portia was waiting for him at the front door with the music playing. It was party time. She was dressed in a little hot pink spandex dress, with hot pink thigh-high fishnets, and stilettos. She had put black lights in the room, so it looked like her outfit was glowing.

Portia's tities looked like they were about to bust out of that dress. Needless to say, Jay had wood in his pants already.

She eyed him sexily, and said, "Hey handsome. My name is Mystique. You wanna slide to VIP for a private dance?"

Jay smiled. He got it. She was reenacting the first time they met, which was in the strip club she worked in as an exotic dancer. He started to ask Portia where the kids were, but he skipped that and played along.

He said, "I'm not really into that. But you sexy, and I respect your hustle. So I'll tip you anyway." He dug in his pocket and pulled out a roll of money. He peeled off five bills, and handed them to her.

Portia took the money and tucked it in the front of her dress. Those dead presidents were probably thrilled to be nestled between those twin chocolate mounds. She smiled at Jay, and ran her finger across his chest slowly. She murmured, "Come on, let me rub this hot chocolate all over you."

Jay gave her a sexy once-over, and smiled at the thought. He said, "A'ight, let me see what all the *Mystique* is about."

Portia took his hand, and led him to a chair across the room. He sat down, and she danced for him seductively. She winded her body like a snake, and caressed herself. Befittingly, the record she danced to was "Wetter", by the rapper Twista. She sang along with the hook.

"You done been good, but you can do it better. I done been wet, but I can get wetter…Come and make it rain down on me-e-e. You done been good, but you can do it better. I done been wet, but I can get wetter…Come and make it rain down on me … "

"I'm calling you daddy, daddy. Can you be my daddy, daddy? I need a daddy, daddy. Won't you be my daddy, daddy? Come and

make it rain down on me…"

Portia sang to her man, and gave him a lap dance he would remember for the rest of his life. His dick was rock hard. He ran his hands along her body and squeezed her the whole time. Damn, she was soft.

She bent over and placed her hands on the floor, exposing all that ass and pussy. Jay slid her g-string to the side and ran his finger along her slit. She was wet.

Portia sat up and licked her juices off his fingers, and then she kissed him. She was so nasty. Jay liked that shit. She tasted good. He was ready to go headfirst. He stood up, and bent Portia over. Then he knelt down on one knee and spread her ass cheeks open, and stuck his tongue in from behind.

Portia murmured, "Yeah, baby… Aah yeah, tongue fuck me."

Jay was happy to oblige. He knew she loved that. He stuck his tongue in her love canal as far as it would go. She backed her ass up and started humping his face, grinding her juices allover him. That only excited him more. He loved eating her pussy. Only his wife could get that type of treatment. Anything went with P.

Jay turned her around so that she faced him. It was easier to lick her clit like that. In a minute Portia was moaning and trembling. She held onto the back of his head. Before he knew it, she was crying out and begging him to stop.

Jay was enjoying himself too much to quit. He wrapped his arms around her thighs, and wouldn't let up until she came again. After that, he just laid beside her and held her for a minute. She was putty in his arms.

When Portia caught her breath, she joked, "So you was really try'na get that milk mustache, huh?"

Jay laughed. "Hell yeah. You already know. Now you ready for yours?"

Portia grinned. "You did get home within the hour. I told you I would double your pleasure, right? A promise is a promise." She started to go down on him, eager to show him a good time.

Jay laughed, and stopped her. He said, "Nah, Kit Kat. We can do that later. Your pussy is so wet, I just wanna slide up in you right now."

Portia was turned on by the way he said that. She gave him the "I wanna fuck you" eyes. She said "Take this pussy, baby. I'm yours! Just take off those clothes first."

Jay got undressed like she asked, and Portia stared at him with lust hooded eyes. Damn, he was a sexy chocolate mothafucka. She wanted to give Rocky a kiss. Jay's penis was so beautiful, she couldn't help it. It looked like it was made of chocolate.

Jay didn't protest the French kiss Portia gave his erection. She made his toes curl. When she stopped, he laid her down and positioned himself atop her. Before he penetrated her, he laid there for a minute caressing her. He loved squeezing Portia's soft ass. And she smelled so good. Her hair did too. His dick was throbbing, so he knew he wouldn't last long the first round.

Portia massaged Jay's back and shoulders, and coaxed him. "Make love to me, baby. *Please.*"

Jay took a deep breath, and slid inside of her. Her pussy was sweet and sticky like hot fudge. He could tell it hadn't been tampered with while they were apart because it was always nice and tight. All the time. Damn, he loved that girl.

Jay was breathing real heavy. It didn't make any sense how good that pussy was. He said, "Damn, Ma. Oh man!"

Portia told him she wanted to get on top, so they rolled over. She rode Jay slow and sensual at first. While she slid up and down his pole, she talked to him like she knew he loved. Between moans, she said, "Ooh, Jay! Baby... I love you so much... You got the best dick in the world! Rocky, I love you!"

Jay palmed her ass and squeezed it like dough. He had a sexy ass wife. He said, "Work that pussy, girl. Show me how much you love this dick."

Portia surprised him after that. Without any warning, she hopped off his dick and took him in her mouth. When she did that, Jay was done. He couldn't stand it. He came as soon as she slid her lips down his dick. He groaned, and then shuddered for a few seconds.

Portia realized Jay was cumming, so she pulled her head back. Most of it squirted on her lips and chin.

Jay looked at her with this real lazy grin on his face. That ejaculation had him feeling a little weak. He laughed, and pointed at Portia's face. "Look, Ma. Now *you* got a milk mustache."

Portia said, "Oh, you got jokes, huh? Real funny." She wiped her face with the back of her hand, and she laughed with him.

The days that followed were busy for Portia. She was happy and in love, but she had a lot on her plate. She and Fatima had been busy with the publishing company, and they were all still actively involved in AIDS Walk NY. Portia, Laila, and Fatima had been busy raising money for the cause. The march was coming up the following weekend.

Since Laila was still getting around a little slow, they didn't plan to finish the walk that year. But they raised a lot of money. And they still got tee-shirts made with their deceased friend, Simone's photo on them. That was a tradition they planned to carry out forever.

$ $ $ $

Thursday evening, Cas was driving through the Lincoln Tunnel on his way home. He'd had a long day. He had attended a meeting a little earlier, where he'd butted heads with an associate for almost two hours. He was sort of uptight because the deal winded up falling through. Cas had pretty much told the guy to go fuck himself. He didn't kiss anyone's ass for anything.

He quit thinking about that asshole associate, and thought about Jay. The prick had pissed Jay off too, so he had stood with Cas on his decision to tell that nigga to fuck off. Cas and Jay almost always saw eye to eye. They had been friends a long time, and over the years they rarely disagreed with each other. And if they did, they never expressed it in public.

Cas was grumpy and aggravated. He just wanted to get home, take a shower, and get some rest. His week had been long, so he was pretty tired. He turned up his car stereo, and listened to an old song he used to really like. The record was "Don't Wanna Be a Player No More", by Joe. Cas hummed along, and thought about Laila.

"...Girl, I feel like you could be the one - to make a difference in my life - 'cause I'm tired of living trife. Don't wanna be a player no more. I think I found someone I can live my life for. Don't wanna be a player no more. I think I found someone I can live my life for ..."

The music helped the ride go pretty smooth. He got home in thirty two minutes. When Cas walked in the house, he saw Laila sitting by the bay window holding their baby. Skye had recently turned a year old. Laila was singing "Hush Little Baby", and staring at Skye with love filled eyes. You could see the sunset through the window behind her.

It was picture perfect. Laila really looked beautiful. Cas stood there silently for a moment, and admired her. That was what life was all about. Family. At that point in his life, he needed a strong, intelligent woman in his corner. He was in his mid-thirties now, and on some grown man shit.

Laila was the first woman he'd ever really fallen in love with. He was sweet on her before he even got with Kira. The only reason he winded up dealing with Kira was because Laila chose to stay with her husband, and work her marriage out. But that was before. This was their second time around.

Cas had what he had with Kira, and he didn't have any regrets. She had given him a great son. But he and Kira hadn't mixed well, mainly because she was a drama queen. He could never be at peace around her.

Laila was the complete opposite. They had basically resolved all their issues, so it was pleasant being around her. Cas overlooked Laila's behavior when she first had the baby. She had been going through something, so she wasn't herself around that time. But they got pass all that. Now they got along great.

Staring at Laila holding their daughter made all the residue from Cas' bad day just vanish. That was what he wanted to come home to. Love and peace. He needed that in his life. Having a family was important to Cas. It was a cold world.

Cas was touched. He was moved to let that woman know how he felt. She was the one. Every time he looked at her, he felt something. He couldn't explain it. Cas realized then that Laila was his muse.

He made up his mind. He wanted her to be his wife. He was ready to "put a ring on it". He didn't say anything at the moment because he wasn't prepared.

The following afternoon, Casino spent an hour with a well known, elite jeweler. The exquisite five carat Harry Winston diamond he walked out of there with was well worth his time. It cost a handsome ransom, but Laila was worthy. He couldn't wait to see the look on her face when he proposed.

Cas was short for "Casino", not "Casanova". He wasn't the Romeo type, but he definitely wanted to make that night special for Laila. Not on no sucker shit, but he had some pretty romantic things in mind.

Before Cas left the City, he called Portia and asked her if Macy, Jahseim, and Skye could come over to spend the night. She told him they were welcome anytime. The whole bus load.

Cas laughed, and kept it real with Portia. He let her know he was planning something special for Laila. He thanked her for the solid, and promised to do something nice for her. He jokingly apologized for cutting into her and Jay's make-up sex-athon.

Portia laughed, but she dared not deny it. She and Jay had been making love as much as two or three times a day.

Cas already knew. Outside of the meeting they'd attended the day before, he had barely seen his man Jay the last two weeks. Cas was genuinely happy they were back together. He knew those two would make it. They had something special.

That was something Cas had sort of envied when he was with Kira. He and her just couldn't connect all the way, but Portia and Jay completed each other. Shit was just natural between them.

That was how it was with him and Laila. Just pure love. It was time to take it to the next level now. Cas was no lame, but he felt like that was their destiny. He believed Laila was his soul mate. She completed him. And he knew she felt the same way about him. He could tell when she looked at him. Her eyes lit up when he was around. It was real.

After Portia and Cas hung up the phone, she smiled. She had a good feeling about what he had just told her. She loved the fact that Laila was so special to him. He went out of his way to do something nice for her, so Portia took it upon herself to go pick up their kids.

When Portia got to Cas and Laila's house, Laila was surprised, but she didn't object to her sudden urge to come kidnap the brat pack. The kids wanted to go too. They were all traitors. Even Skye was whining to go with Portia.

Skye had just started walking, so she was a handful. Laila warned Portia about this, but Portia reminded her that she had a child the same age. Their little girls were only two months apart.

Before Portia left with the kids, she suggested that Laila wash her vajayjay good, and put on something nice. She said just in case Cas wanted to go out, or something. Laila just laughed, but she should've known something was up then. But nothing would have prepared her for what happened later that night.

Cas started out their evening by giving Laila one hundred red roses. There were so many flowers, all she could do was admire them. After that, Cas had a chef he'd hired serve them a romantic dinner of French Cuisine. They sipped on chardonnay while they dined.

When they were done eating, Cas thanked the chef and cleared out the house. Laila didn't know, but he was ready to pop the question.

In the backyard of their new house, they had a luxurious but cozy outdoor living space. The ground was covered with the finest stone tile, and it was complete with trendy outdoor furniture, and an outdoor fireplace. Cas took Laila's hand, and led her out back. He had a fire burning out there, and it was nice out.

When they got outside, he thought about getting down on one knee. He wanted Laila's second time around to be special but that wasn't really him. So instead, he just pulled out the ring box.

Laila smiled so big, her cheeks hurt. Was Cas about to do what she thought he was? He opened the box, and showed her this huge Harry Winston diamond. She gasped, and almost choked. That rock was sparkling in the dark. It was awesome.

Cas looked at Laila sincerely. He said, "Laila, there's something about you that brings out the best in me. You make me better. So, what up? Let's get married."

Laila just nodded because she was choked up with tears. She couldn't believe Cas was proposing. And in such a romantic setting. How thoughtful. She was so overwhelmed she couldn't find her voice for a minute.

Finally, Laila said, "Yes, Cas! Yes, baby! I *love* you with all my heart!"

Cas grinned, and placed the ring on her finger. She admired it for a second, and then she wrapped her arms around his neck, and kissed him on the lips.

That was the reaction he was hoping for. Cas kissed his fiancé back. Laila was going to be his wife. Everything felt right this time. They stood there by the fireplace under the stars embracing for what seemed like an eternity.

Cas' touch sent shivers down Laila's spine. She was no slow leak. She knew what her man wanted. She wanted it too, bad as hell. She caressed his back and shoulders while his hands roamed all over her body.

Cas was wearing a nice Issey Miyake shirt. Laila took it upon herself to help him remove it. She wanted him out of those clothes, and then she wanted him inside of her ASAP. Her desire was almost animalistic. She felt like she needed him right then and there.

While Laila was undressing Casino, Casino was undressing Laila. She took off his shirt, but he was working from the ground up. He slid his hands under her dress, and took off her panties first.

Laila was so excited, she was practically panting like she was in heat. Cas helped her out of her dress, and then her bra. After she was nude, he knelt down in front of her and kissed her belly button.

Laila traced Cas' broad bare shoulders with her fingernails. He was so fucking sexy. She played in the waves in his hair, while he licked and sucked on her left nipple. It felt so good, she just leaned back and enjoyed the moment.

Cas worked on the other breast for a little while, and then he licked and nibbled his way on downtown. Laila breathed heavier and heavier. He stuck his tongue in her belly button and twirled it around. It tickled, but it felt great. She was on fire. Her pussy was throbbing.

Cas stood up and palmed her ass. Laila pressed up against him, and saw that he was hard. She wanted him to stick it in so bad. She unbuckled his belt and loosened his jeans, and then she bent down and ran her tongue along his waistline.

Cas saw where that was going, so he stopped her for a minute. They may as well get comfortable. He took the fur throw from the sofa and spread it out in front of the outdoor fireplace. Afterwards, he laid Laila down there.

Laila caressed herself while she watched him undress. Cas held back a smile, and stripped down to his boxers. He could tell the way she was looking at him, she was feeling real naughty.

Cas knew what she wanted, but he wanted to tease her first. The sight of her laying there naked was so tempting. The light the fire cast on her body gave her this sexy glow. That, along with the thrill of outdoor sex turned Cas on so much, he got down there and buried his face between her thighs. He kissed all around her honey pot at first, teasing her until she practically threw him in a leg lock.

Cas laughed to himself, and spread her lips and twirled his tongue in her essence. Laila squirmed. He gently sucked on her clit, which stiffened more each time he ran his tongue across it. She was holding his head, and moaning like it felt real good.

While Cas pleasured Laila, he squeezed her fat, juicy ass. It was soft and round like a ripe peach. He ran his index finger lightly along the crack a few times, and then he slipped it in her soaking wet pussy. He fingered her for a minute, and then Cas decided to do something they had never tried. He removed his finger from her pussy and slid it in her ass.

At first, Laila tensed up a little, but she relaxed after a few seconds. Cas fingered her ass while he licked her pussy. They had never gone there before. It felt strange at first, but it felt good before Laila knew it. Real good. She got in the groove, and started humping Cas' face. He asked her if she liked it, and she admitted she did. She didn't want him to stop.

He kept on licking her pussy, and fingering her ass until she came. Laila started shaking when she reached her peak, and he just kept on. The next thing she knew, she was having an out of body experience. She had never experienced an orgasm like that.

Laila and her homegirls jokingly referred to anal sex as "HBL", or Hot Butt Love, but she had yet to experiment with it. She didn't know if she was quite ready for that, but there was definitely something to that finger up the ass thing. Cas had turned her out. He made her feel wonderful, and she wanted to repay him by making him feel good too.

Laila was feeling a little naughtier than usual. She got bold and told him what she wanted to do to him. "You made me feel so good, baby. Come here, Cas. I wanna suck your dick."

When she said that, something went through Cas. He took off his boxers fast. He said, "Come here, girl. Wit' your nasty, pretty self."

Laila could tell he meant that in a good way. And he was right. That night she planned on being nastier than ever. They were getting married, so there would be no holds barred. She got on her knees, and stroked his long, thick pole with admiration. It was lovely. She brushed her lips against it, and gently sucked on the tip.

Cas fought back a series of moans. Damn, that felt good. All of a sudden, Laila just opened up her throat and swallowed him. He couldn't hold it in that time. He let out a moan, and a little groan. She was really going in. He didn't know how much of that he could take.

Cas didn't want to cum yet, so he shied away from her for a second to recuperate. Laila didn't want Cas to cum yet either, so she quit pleasuring him for a while. She knew he wanted to fuck her, and she was ready. Her pussy was dripping wet.

Casino got on top of Laila, and lowered himself in her valley. She gasped when he entered her. Cas was built large, so he filled her up to capacity. Laila hugged him, and caressed his back. She loved it when he got on top.

Cas deep-stroked to the left, and to the right. That pussy was amazing. The warmth of her canal was so overwhelming the pace of his heartbeat quickened. She was so wet. That stuff was good and gushy. He slowed down his pace so he could last a while.

The second he slowed down, Laila cried out in bliss. She was cumming again. She yelled "don't stop", so Cas kept stroking her. It wasn't long before he exploded too. Damn, that sex was so official he called out her name.

Cas laid there panting for a minute, and then he rolled off her. Laila snuggled up under him on the fur throw and just laid there in his arms for a while. Together, they looked up at the sky and admired the stars. It was a calm June night, and the sky was clear. If that night was any indication of how their new life together would be, it would be peaceful. Perhaps even perfect.

CHAPTER FIVE

Laila was up on her feet again, but she was still doing her therapy three times a week. She wanted to make sure her spine was working one hundred percent. And it really paid off. She could walk on heels now. And pretty good too. She wasn't quite ready to wear five inch stilettos, but she would get there.

Laila wasn't a quitter. And perseverance combined with strong faith was the main reason she was back. Her girlfriends didn't quite know she could walk on high heels yet. Laila was waiting until the time was right.

She had fantasized about walking down the aisle to marry Cas in some bad ass Jimmy Choo shoes, and now it looked like that would actually happen. He had asked her to be his wife. That meant he really did love her. For better, or for worse. Laila would never give that type of love up, as long as she lived.

That Saturday afternoon, she hooked up with Portia and Fatima so they could go turn their money in for the AIDS Walk NY fundraiser. They all wore their new Simone tee-shirts, designer jeans, and sneakers.

When they got there, they hung around at Central Park and socialized with some of the familiar faces from previous years. That day they were all united for one cause, and love was in the air.

Before dusk settled, the three friends decided to head to a restaurant to eat and drink, and reminisce about Simone. While they were dining, Laila told Portia and Fatima that she and Cas were engaged, and she pulled the ring out of her jeans pocket.

When Portia and Fatima saw that big ass Harry Winston rock, they both squealed in delight. Then those crazy bitches got up and started screaming, and jumping up and down. They told Laila they were planning an engagement party immediately.

Laila begged them not to make a big deal out of it. She said that was too much. Cas had made the proposal beautiful for her, so she was happy with that.

After Laila gave them complete details about everything he did, both of her best friends were teary-eyed. Portia told her that sounded like a fairytale. Fatima said that was the proposal of every woman's dreams.

Portia and Tima were hardheaded. They still wanted to have the engagement party, but they assured Laila that it would be a small, private affair. They said it was her second chance at lifelong happiness, so a celebration was definitely in order.

Portia and Fatima hustled and bustled all week long making preparations. The following Saturday evening they hosted a Black Tie Affair at Portia and Jay's house. It was truly elegant. Portia hired a cook, a butler, and a full staff of uniformed servers to cater to their guests.

Portia and Fatima had promised Laila they would keep it very private, and they kept their word. The only guests there were them, and all their children. To everyone's surprise, Laila showed up that night in heels. When they saw the amazing progress she had made, that made the occasion even more joyous. They were all thrilled. And she looked stunning. She was still rocking her new trademark short, layered haircut, and it was tight as usual. She was donned in a black satin St. John pantsuit that flattered her figure, and red Chanel kitten heels, with the matching handbag.

Everyone at the dinner party was dressed to kill. Even the babies. Laila, Cas, Portia, Jay, Fatima, and the two oldest kids, Macy and Jayquan, sat together at the dinner table. The smaller ones, Jahseim, Jazmin, and Falynn ate at a smaller table that was set fancy, just like the big table. They also had their own menu. They didn't like certain foods the adults ate.

After dinnertime, the little ones were going upstairs with the babies. Trixie and Skye were in the rec section with a sitter, being entertained by a clown Portia had hired. Jazz and Fay were so excited about that they didn't even want to eat.

At the dinner table, Portia suggested they all join hands in prayer to commemorate the occasion. It was nice to gather for a happy reason. There was no tragedy this time. Everyone at that table knew the adversities they had faced over the past couple of years. But they had gone through it all together because they were a family.

Portia led the family in prayer. She started out by thanking God for each and every one of them. Then she prayed for the souls of those no longer with them. There were so many loved ones gone from their lives. Wise, Patty Cake, Pebbles, Humble, and Simone, to name a few.

Next, Portia asked God to watch over all of them, and their extended families. She prayed for peace and prosperity within their circle, and all across the world. And then she prayed that God would bless the union soon to happen between Cas and Laila. When she was done, everyone said "amen". Then they were all silent for a minute, each perhaps taking a moment to reflect on their many blessings. There were ups and downs, but God had been good to them.

After they were done praying, Jay popped a six hundred dollar bottle of vintage merlot, and he proposed a toast to Laila and his bro's future. Jayquan and Macy were feeling themselves because Jay and Cas let them join in on their toast, and drink a glass of wine. They both tried to act all sophisticated like it was something they did everyday. The adults at the table found them hilarious.

Portia and Laila told them not to get open because they

wouldn't get another opportunity until their asses were grown, and could purchase their own wine. Everybody laughed again. Then it was time to grub.

Portia signaled the butler. He immediately snapped his fingers and summoned the servers, and they brought out the food. It was a full course feast, starting out with hot, freshly baked breadsticks, and a choice of Caesar or garden salad, with an array of dressings.

The main course came next, which was a choice of rosemary braised baked salmon, or grilled primavera stuffed chicken breast, either served with a side of rice pilaf or garlic roasted mashed potatoes, with steamed broccoli. There was good music playing while the family dined, and conversed.

For desert, there was a sinfully delicious six layered mocha chocolate cake, and raspberry mint sorbet. When they were all done eating, everybody said they were stuffed. The servers kept the drinks flowing, so they were all tipsy too. Portia smiled around at everyone. They all appeared to be having a good time.

Fatima sipped on another glass of wine, and tried to keep a smile plastered across her face. But truthfully, it was hard. It wasn't that she wasn't happy for Laila and Cas. She really was. They were like her sister and brother. But she couldn't help but question God. Why did she have to be the one left alone?

Things were going great for her friends. Jay and Portia had reunited, and Laila and Cas were engaged to be married. And she was sitting there all alone. Fatima couldn't help but be a little bit envious. Wise was her soul mate, and he was just snatched away from her. It wasn't fair. She would never understand why life had been so cruel to her. She missed her husband more than anything in the world, and she would've given a limb and a vital organ to have him back.

Fatima's lesbian friend, Charlene, had called her the day before. She had been tempted to go hang out with her, but she had to avoid that lifestyle before she got caught up again. Fatima finished her wine, and tried to force herself out of the dumps. When she was done, she held her glass up for the uniformed server standing to her left to refill.

Fatima didn't want to spoil the evening for her friends. She loved them all like family, and wanted their unions to always be blessed. Fatima whispered a little prayer. That was the only way she'd made it through. God had given her strength, and she had the best friends in the world.

They were playing all Michael Jackson's songs to commemorate his recent unfortunate passing. Portia and the kids were getting down to all the hits, from "Beat It" and "Billie Jean", all way back to "ABC". Fatima was glad to see everyone having a good time but she was so downhearted, she couldn't get into it.

The next record that played was "I'll Be There". Fatima couldn't hold back her tears anymore. She sat there and put her head down, and had herself a good cry. Nobody had to ask why she was so sad. They all just wished there was something they could do.

Jay looked at Fatima for a minute. He didn't stare openly, just from the corner of his eye. His heart went out to her. He knew she was still hurting. Jay felt his cell phone vibrating in his pocket, so he checked the number to see who it was.

Jay sighed to himself. It was Ysatis calling. Again. She had suddenly started calling him again that day. Out of the blue. He hadn't spoke to her in about eight months. Jay pressed ignore, and sent her to his voicemail. He didn't know how he was going to deal with that situation, but he wasn't ready to address it just yet. She was really annoying the shit out of him, calling like that. Right now just wasn't the time.

He knew her lease would be up soon. That was probably why she was trying so hard to contact him. Jay wasn't a creep, so he would call her before then. But that night, he didn't want to be bothered. He was with his family and closest friends. Ysatis had caused enough trouble in his life. After all he'd gone through with his wife, he really didn't want to have anything to do with her. Portia was home now, and he wasn't trying to fuck that up.

When Portia and Laila saw that the song was getting to Fatima, they went over to comfort her. Fatima squeezed both of her best friends' hands appreciatively. Their presence automatically strengthened her. She loved those girls with all her heart. It was good to have friends. Every time one of them suffered, they felt each other's pain.

"Just call my name, and I'll be there…"

They were all touched by that song. God had brought them through plenty trials and tribulations. Neither of their lives had gone unscathed, but they made it. God was so good.

Jayquan saw how the mood had changed, so he got up and switched the music to some upbeat party stuff. He put on Wise's latest CD, and they all started dancing. Now the party was live again. After a minute, even Fatima was moving and grooving.

Jayquan put on Jamie Fox's hit, "Blame It", and that was it. Everybody was getting down, and singing along. *"Blame it on the Goose – got ya' feelin' loose. Blame it on the 'Tron – got ya' in a zone. Blame it on the a-a-a-a-a-alcohol. Blame it on the a-a-a-a-a-alcohol. Blame it on the vodka, blame it on the Henny, blame it on the blue top got ya' feelin' dizzy. Blame it on the a-a-a-a-a-alcohol. Blame it on the a-a-a-a-a-alcohol…"*

After Lil' Jay played the hip-hop, Portia put on some oldies for them to dance to. Jayquan and Macy hung around for a while, and then they went on upstairs. The adults partied that night until almost four A.M.

After the party was over, Fatima tried to drive herself home. She was pretty hammered so Portia took her car keys. Jay insisted that she crash until the morning. Cas wasn't as drunk, so he and Laila headed on home. They only had about a fifteen minute drive.

The kids were all asleep, so Portia told them to take advantage of the overnight babysitter she'd hired for the occasion. They agreed, and Cas said he would pick up their rug rats that afternoon.

They all hugged, and Jay gave Cas a pound. Everyone bid the newly engaged couple a good night, and told them to get home safe. It was good to see Laila getting around so good.

$ $ $ $

Meanwhile, Ysatis was in New York Presbyterian Hospital. She had been in painful labor all day, and was just about to have the baby she was secretly carrying. That was the reason she'd been calling Jay's phone so much earlier. She wanted to tell him she had gone in labor. He still didn't know she was pregnant. When her water broke, she figured it was time to confess.

But Jay hadn't answered any of her thirty-plus calls, so Ysatis went in the delivery room alone. And she was afraid. It was nothing like she had imagined it would be. She had hoped that when Jay found out, he would've dropped everything and ran to the hospital to be by her side. She was bringing their child into the world.

Ysatis prayed she hadn't made a bad decision. Jay not answering his phone indicated that he was done with her. What if her plan had backfired on her? She was hit by another contraction so she breathed deep, and tried not to scream.

Ysatis didn't know what she had gotten herself into. She didn't want a baby. She just wanted Jay. She hoped it would all be worth it. That baby was supposed to be her security. But Jay wouldn't even take her calls.

She had another contraction, and gasped in pain. They were getting real close now, coming every few seconds. The doctor told her it would be any minute now. He said she was crowning, so he could see the baby's head. Ysatis took a deep breath, and commenced to push. She yelled out in pain, and brought forth the child who was merely a product of her trickery and scheming.

CHAPTER SIX

Smoke arrived in New York City at the Port Authority on a Tuesday morning. He was just coming from South Carolina. It had been a minute since he'd been up top. He would've preferred to roll back in town with class, on some high roller shit. But due to a string of unfortunate events, that Greyhound bus ticket was all he could afford. Smoke had been having a stream of bad luck, and he was in a serious financial slump.

After Callie got arrested, he had migrated from L.A. down to Myrtle Beach, South Carolina. He had been petty hustling there ever since. Nothing he had tried worked out. He had found this White girl, and he was making a little change off her sucking and fucking down there. But the bitch was hooked on crystal methamphetamine. She did so much her brain was just fucked up.

She was a dingy, dumb blonde, but she had a bad ass body. When he first met her, Smoke thought he had stumbled across a gold mine. He had bagged her in less then thirty seconds, and she agreed to work for him that same day. He had imagined he would clean her up, and make her his new sidekick. He just knew she would be the blue eyed, Malibu version of his down-ass-bitch Callie.

But he should've known that was too good to be true. At first he thought she was just slow, so he kicked her ass and tried to make her sharp. He figured he could beat some sense into her.

But she kept doing the same dumb shit over and over, so he realized the bitch's brain was chopped liver. And then that dumb bitch almost got him locked up. That was the straw that broke the camel's back.

The trouble started the day before, when he had lined up a trick for her with this old cracker from out of town. The dude was vacationing down there to play golf, and the shit was sweet. Smoke got the money up front. All she had to do was go in the hotel room and take care of him. Smoke had taught her how to jostle, so she was supposed to try and rob the dude too. But only if the opportunity came up.

That dizzy bitch got caught slipping. The man caught her searching through his pants pockets, so he pulled a gun out on her. She started crying, and confessed to being only fifteen years old. She also told him she was a runaway from Kansas, who'd been missing since she was thirteen.

The dude came outside where Smoke was waiting, and wanted to be righteous all of a sudden. He told Smoke he was going to call the cops and have him arrested for pandering, and kidnapping a fifteen year old child. He said it was wrong to take advantage of a kid that way, and then he had the nerve to demand his money back. Smoke refused to give him back his bread, so that cracker dialed the police on his cell phone.

Smoke got angry and punched that lame in the jaw. He knocked that nigga out, and then he broke out before the pigs got there. He got low that night, and caught the bus to New York in the next town over. He wasn't going down over no bitch. That druggie broad looked way older than fifteen, so he really didn't know.

Smoke missed Callie. He had trained her so well she would've never done anything that stupid. But she was locked up now, so that was a wrap. He was glad he got out of Myrtle Beach before he got picked up, but he had arrived in New York worse off than he was before he left.

Smoke was broke as shit. He had used the last bread he had to purchase that bus ticket to get back up top, so he was on the prowl. He was hungry, so somebody's ass was in trouble.

Smoke had a plan. It was far fetched, but he had nothing else to go on. He was literally going for broke. If all went well, he would have a nice lump sum soon. Then he could get low, and try his hand at the drug trade again. He just needed some transportation. He didn't give a fuck how raggedy it was, as long as it was dependable enough to get him to New Jersey.

He ran through his mental rolodex trying to think of someone he could borrow a car from, but he came up blank. He realized he would probably have to steal a vehicle. He hadn't stolen a car since '92, but he had to do what he had to do. New Jersey was like the rainbow right about then. He had to get over there somehow, to get to that pot of gold.

$ $ $ $

That Tuesday, Fatima and Falynn spent the day in New York with her parents. They stayed for dinner too, so they returned home kind of late that evening. On the way home, Fay fell asleep in her car seat. Fatima saw her nodding in the rearview mirror.

After she parked in the garage, Fatima decided not to wake Falynn up. She knew she would be cranky if she did. She picked her baby up as carefully as she could, and carried her inside the house. When Fatima got inside, she took Falynn upstairs and laid her down in her bedroom. She undressed her, and wiped off her face and hands, and then she slipped her Dora the Explorer nightgown on. She tucked Falynn in, and kissed her little angel on the cheek. Fay was scared of the dark, so Fatima turned on the nightlight. She left the door cracked on her way out, and turned off her bedroom light.

Fatima turned around and looked at Falynn one more time. She was so adorable. Fatima smiled, and then she went across the hall to her bedroom to wrap her hair. She also wanted to change into some comfy sweats. She was in for the night so she just felt like relaxing, and watching a couple of movies. She had Tyler Perry's film, "Daddy's Little Girls", and Denzell Washington's "American Gangster" on DVD. Those were two of her favorites.

Fatima stood in front of her mirror and wrapped her hair, and tied a silk scarf around it. After that, she took off her clothes, underwear and all. When she took off her bra, she breathed a sigh of relief. It felt so good to set the twins free. Her breasts itched from the lacy bra she'd had on, so she massaged them a little. Then she pulled one of Wise's old tee-shirts and a pair of gray sweatpants out of her bottom dresser drawer.

Fatima sat on the foot of her bed, and put the shirt down beside her. She stepped in her sweatpants one leg at a time. Still topless, she stood up and pulled up her pants. When she got ready to pick up her shirt, she almost had a fucking heart attack.

Oh shit! There was a man in her bedroom! Fatima gasped, too terrified to scream. She was frozen in fear for a second.

Her first reaction was to cover her breasts and run. She tried to flee but that nigga stopped her dead in her tracks. She found herself staring down the barrel of a very large gun. Damn, he must've come to rob her. There were a lot of reports about home invasions on the news recently, but she would've never guessed it would happen to her.

Fatima was frightened beyond her imagination. She looked in the stranger's eyes, hoping she could figure out where his mind was. The windows to his soul were like black ice, so she knew he meant business. There was something extremely cold and unsympathetic about him. He looked like he was a real killer.

Something like this had happened to her homegirl Portia years ago, when she and Jay first got together. Portia was at Jay's house when some niggas ran up in there to rob him. She was pregnant at the time, and those bastards raped her and shot her.

Fatima prayed she would get out of her situation alive. She

was no fool. That dude could kill her, so she kept on praying. She kept a gun in the house but it was put away for safekeeping from her daughter, so faith was all she had.

Fatima finally found her voice. Careful to keep her breasts covered, she demanded some answers. "Who *are* you?! And why are you in my house? What the hell do you *want*?!"

Smoke leered at Fatima's voluptuous knockers for a second. Temptation was a bitch. But since he lived by the code "Money Over Bitches", he kept it icy and told her the reason he was there. He got right to the point. He said he wanted currency. A lot of it, or she would die. He told her he was a friend of Callie's, and that he knew all about the money she had confiscated.

Smoke wasn't playing. He would really kill that bitch if she didn't come up off that bread. He didn't come up there to leave empty-handed. So far, everything had gone smoothly. His entrance in the house had been a piece of cake. It wasn't even forced. He had the key Fatima gave Callie when she was staying there, and he had used it to walk right in. He'd had some doubts that the key would still work, so he came prepared to muscle himself inside. But getting in had been easier than he could've dreamed. Smoke took that easy access as a good sign. Now nothing would stop him.

Fatima told Smoke she didn't have any money in the house. He looked at her like that was the wrong answer. She felt like an idiot because she didn't change the locks after Callie left. She told herself she would get around to it, but she was lax about it because she knew Callie was in jail for stealing her shit. The district attorney told her Callie wouldn't see daylight for a while, so she had slept.

Fatima had changed the security code on her home alarm system, but she forgot to activate the system when she and Falynn left the house earlier. Now as a result of her negligence, there was an intruder in her house. And the mothafucka had a gun. She prayed he would just take what he wanted, and leave.

But it was personal for Smoke. After he had found out about Fatima destroying Callie's car with that bat, and getting her arrested, he was ready to execute that bitch. She should've just left that money in the hotel room. He checked the room before the police got there, and the money was gone. All that fucking money. It hurt just thinking about it.

In minutes, he had gone from buying a mansion in Mexico, to being fucked up and dead broke like a nigga just coming home. He even had to sell his new Benz. And he had let it go for dirt cheap because he knew it was hot. He was really tight about that shit too. He let it go for a third of what it was worth. Every time he thought about that, he was ready to murder something.

Smoke took that situation personal. He and Callie were almost in Mexico   home-free, but that bitch had intervened. He wasn't just upset because Callie got locked up. It wasn't just about that. That bitch Fatima had snatched away his dreams. He had finally touched it, and she took it all away. Smoke knew she went in that hotel room and got his suitcase full of money, so he wanted it back.

Homegirl was under the notion that she and her money would just return to safekeeping, but she must've been crazy. He was going to get right again, if it had to be over her dead body. He planned to take that bitch for everything he possibly could.

Smoke's mentality was such that of a criminal's, he actually believed he was the one who'd been crossed and done dirty. He really felt like Fatima had taken his bread. He never took the time to think that it was never rightfully his money from the gate. He was ready to kill Fatima for something that belonged to her.

He had left Callie in jail out in L.A. She was a good girl, but he couldn't mess with her at the time. She had played her part, but now she was too hot. There was nothing he could do for her right now anyway. He was fucked up too, so they were at their crossroads. She got locked up, and there was no way he was going back to jail. He was just glad he got a chance to see where that bitch Fatima lived.

Smoke warned Fatima that if she tried anything stupid, he would blow her brains out. He allowed her to put a shirt on, only because seeing her big tities exposed made his dick hard. That was a distraction. He wasn't there for that. Fuck getting some ass, he wanted that money.

He forced Fatima downstairs, where he made her sit in one of her dining room chairs. He made her put her arms behind her back like she was under arrest, and he stuck his gun in his waist and tied her to the chair. He tightened the rope around her wrists and legs so she couldn't move.

After Fatima was tied to the chair, Smoke held her hostage at gunpoint. He told her he would let her go when she stopped playing games. He promised her she would die if she didn't tell him where that money was.

$ $ $ $

Portia and Jay were up late that night making love. When they were done, they stayed up talking. Portia brought up the European vacation they had forfeited the past two years, due to all that was going on. To her surprise, Jay told her they should go that summer. He said sometime around August would be a good time.

Portia was so excited, she gave him another blowjob. After she was done, he fell right asleep. She cleaned up, and then she called Laila and Fatima to tell them about the trip.

Portia wanted to invite her friends to go along. She wanted them to all go together. She imagined her and her girls on a European shopping spree, and squealed with delight. Paris, London, and Milan, oh my! It would be so much fun.

When Portia called Laila, she answered her phone on the fourth ring. She said she would love to go, but she had to ask

Cas first. They were both pretty sure he would agree.

Laila asked Portia if they were taking the kids with them. Portia said yes. She felt like that would be a great cultural experience for them. Laila agreed, and reminded her that they had to get passports for their babies. The rest of the kids already had theirs.

When Portia hung up with Laila, she called Fatima. Fatima didn't answer the phone, so Portia wondered why. She hoped homegirl was still on the right track. She knew Fatima had her daughter that night, so where was she?

Portia redialed Fatima's house and cell phone numbers three more times, and still got no answer. She decided to try her friend again the following morning. She was probably already asleep.

$ $ $ $

Four hours later, Fatima was afraid and absolutely miserable. She'd been forced to sit completely still because every time she moved, those ropes cut into her flesh. She was glad her daughter was still asleep up in her bedroom, but she knew Fay would be waking up soon.

Smoke told Fatima she had a decision to make before the sun came up. He said if she didn't give him back that money, he would shoot her and her little girl dead in the head. His last words were arctic and extremely mean, but he certainly meant what he said.

Fatima was honest with him. She had put that money back in the bank a long time ago. Smoke had searched the house thoroughly before she got there, so he believed she was telling the truth.

He ran down his plan to her. They were going to the bank the first thing in the morning, and she was going to withdraw as much money as she could for him.

Fatima said she didn't have a problem with that. She told him she agreed to his terms, as long as he wouldn't hurt her child. She said she would go to the bank and get him the money if he gave her his word that he would leave, and go on about his business afterwards. She swore to him that she wouldn't even tell a soul he had been there.

Smoke nodded, and agreed to the terms. He gave her his word that after he got paid, he would leave them unharmed. But he was lying through his teeth. He had no plans whatsoever to leave Fatima breathing. She would be able to identify him, so why would he? He'd already seen how she had gotten Callie arrested. He wasn't going to let her put the pigs on his trail.

That night was a long one. Smoke untied Fatima two times so she could use the bathroom, and he stood there and watched her each time. He was glad she only had to pee, but he would've stood there while she took a shit too. Just to make sure she didn't try anything while she was in the bathroom.

She was lucky he was no rapist because she definitely had a fat ass. And some pretty knockers too. And the fact that Callie told him Fatima messed with girls also aroused him. He knew all about her little Chinese girlfriend, Cheyenne. That really made him want to fuck her. But again, Smoke lived by the words "Money Over Bitches." M.O.B. Pussy made a nigga slip, and love for it was a weakness. Therefore, his main focus was that bread.

Neither Smoke nor Fatima slept a wink that night. He occupied his time by flipping through the cable channels on the huge flat screen mounted on the parlor wall. He ignored Fatima's request for food, but he let her sip water and cranberry juice through a straw.

When morning finally came, he went upstairs to check on the little girl. When she saw him she started crying and shit, probably because he was a stranger. He told her to go use the bathroom. After she peed, he took her downstairs where his rope was.

When they got downstairs where her mother was, he gagged

her so he couldn't hear her screaming, and then he tied her little ass up too. She was still wearing her pink Dora the Explorer nightgown.

Fatima was helpless while he tied up her child, but she protested the whole time. She didn't want him to hurt her baby. He could do what he wanted to her, but he couldn't hurt Falynn. He couldn't. She yelled for him to leave her daughter alone, over and over.

Smoke got annoyed with her hollering, and rewarded her with a hard punch in the face. After he hit her, he growled at her menacingly. "Shut the fuck up wit' all that noise, *bitch*. Or you gon' make me *really* hurt y'all."

Fatima yelped out in pain, wondering if that nigga broke her nose. It was throbbing like crazy. The pain spread throughout her whole face. Tears came to her eyes, but she shut up like she was told. Fatima continued to pray silently.

She felt completely powerless. Her baby was looking at her, crying and afraid, and there was absolutely nothing she could do. Fatima remained as calm as she could, only because she didn't want that mothafucka to hurt Falynn.

All of a sudden, that bastard picked Falynn up, and took her outside. Fatima watched him take her away through panic filled eyes. She just prayed, and prayed. *"God, please take care of my child. Please don't let him hurt her."*

A minute later, Smoke came back inside the house alone. Fatima was petrified. She demanded to know what he had done with her daughter. She prayed he hadn't harmed her.

Smoke told her she was outside in the trunk of her car. He said if she just got the money from the bank like she was supposed to, her daughter would remain unharmed.

Fatima was anxious to get to the bank after that. And she hoped they wouldn't give her any problems when she got there. She just wanted to get that money so that mothafucka would just leave.

Smoke untied her, and they left the house together. He kept his pistol pressed in the small of her back. Fatima was afraid, but she demanded to see Falynn before she got in the car. Smoke looked at her real mean at first because he didn't appreciate her tone of voice, but he opened the trunk and let her have a look.

Thank God, Falynn was alive. But Fatima didn't know how well she was. She would never forget the look in her little eyes when she looked at her. Her baby had never been that afraid before in her whole life. She promised Falynn that she would be okay, right before that bastard slammed the trunk closed.

The sad and scary part was that she wasn't even sure if she meant that. How could she be sure if either of them would be okay? She just told her baby that to make her feel better. She couldn't guarantee her anything. But Fatima knew one thing. She would lay down her life before she let him hurt Falynn. Only over her dead body would he be able to.

When they got in the car, Smoke kept his pistol pushed in Fatima's ribs. She didn't want anymore trouble, so she didn't give him any problems whatsoever. All she could think about was her daughter alone and afraid in the trunk, tied up and gagged. Falynn had to be scared to death. Fatima knew she was.

The thought made her push the pedal to the metal harder. Smoke warned her to slow down before the police pulled them over. She did as she was told, and drove a safe speed until they pulled up in the bank's parking lot.

They walked inside the bank, and Fatima behaved as normally as she possibly could. Smoke walked right beside her, with his fitted cap pulled down over his face as far as it would go.

Fatima marched up to an open teller window, and asked what the maximum amount of money she could withdraw was. The teller asked for her account number, and looked up her account. She told her there was a one hundred thousand dollar daily withdrawal limit at the window.

Fatima filled out a withdrawal slip, and showed her two pieces of I.D. She withdrew a hundred grand, and she acted as normally as possible. That was less money than that bastard was expecting, so she prayed he understood that was all she could get on such short notice. Fatima tried to alarm the bank teller with her eyes, to let her know she was in trouble. But the girl didn't seem to get it.

Smoke was disappointed at the amount of money she took out, but he was standing right there when the teller told Fatima there was a hundred grand limit at the window. Anything greater would require consent from the bank manager, and Smoke didn't want to go through all that. He was no dummy. He decided to cut his losses, and take that money and run.

After the teller counted out the money in the big bills Fatima had requested, Smoke hugged her around the waist like they were a couple, and escorted her out of the bank. When they got back in the car, he removed his gun from his waist, and stuck it in her ribs again. And then he took the hundred dollar bill filled bank envelope away from her.

Fatima figured they could go ahead and part now. He had the money. She asked him if he wanted her to drop him off anywhere in particular. She told him he could even take the car, and she and Falynn would find their own way home.

Smoke told her to shut up, and made her drive back to her house. He told her not to ask him any questions. Fatima was nervous, but she did as she was told. She was just anxious to get rid of him. She had to get Falynn out of that trunk. As she drove home, she prayed he would keep his word and leave them alone.

CHAPTER SEVEN

Back in New York, Ysatis and her newborn were in the back of a yellow cab, on their way home from the hospital. The baby was a boy, and he was handsome like his father. She named him after Jay too. Jaylin Mekhi Mitchell.

Ysatis looked at her baby. She still couldn't believe she had him. He was so tiny and cute. He had Jay's eyes.

At the time, she couldn't help but feel a little hatred towards Jay. It was three days later, and he hadn't even called her back. After all those messages she had left him, saying she urgently needed to speak to him. She was starting to hate him for the way he was doing her.

It took willpower and determination, but she had finished out the semester at NYU. She graduated just weeks before she had the baby. And now she was on the last months of her apartment lease. If Jay didn't come around soon, she didn't know what she and the baby were going to do. She had her degree, but she couldn't do anything with a baby that small.

Things weren't exactly going the way Ysatis had planned. She had imagined her and the baby going home from the hospital in a luxury hired car, or in Jay's Bentley. She decided to give her baby daddy a little bit of time, but she really did need his help. She needed to go shopping for the baby. She had purchased a few things with the little money she had, but it wasn't nearly enough. She had to get in touch with Jay soon. Even if that meant she had to go over his house.

Ysatis thought about it. That would be her last alternative, but she would find out where he lived and do what she had to do. She had a child by Jay. He was obligated to look after them.

But she had to give him the benefit of a doubt. She couldn't label him a deadbeat dad because he didn't even know about the baby yet. Now after he found out, that would be a different story. If he shunned them then, she would make sure he suffered for it.

Right now, Ysatis just wanted to rest. Her body was tired. In the hospital, they had poked and prodded on her all night. She was new to the baby thing, so she preferred to tackle it when she was fully rested. She would get at Jay again soon. After she and Jaylin got settled at home.

$ $ $ $

After Fatima and Smoke pulled up in front of her house, she asked him to please go ahead and leave like he said he would. She told him she just wanted to get her baby out of the trunk. She told him Falynn was claustrophobic, and promised him she wouldn't say a word about anything.

Smoke made Fatima get out of the car, and he forced her back inside the house. Fatima's heart was pounding in her chest. She felt like she was wearing lead filled combat boots. Every step she took got heavier and harder. Why was he coming back inside her house?

Fatima feared for her life. She had a feeling he was going to kill her. She just knew it. Dear Heavenly Father, it was getting harder to breathe.

Smoke shut the door, and cocked his gun. He smirked at Fatima, and aimed the pistol at her head. He got what he came for, so she was no longer of any use to him. He didn't get as much bread as he'd intended to, but he wasn't leaving empty-handed.

When he pointed that gun at Fatima, she was absolutely horrified. She opened her mouth to protest, but Smoke coldly pulled the trigger without a second thought. Fatima flinched, and saw her life flash before her eyes. With her and Wise both dead and gone, who would take care of Falynn? She just prayed God would look after her.

Fatima had seen Smoke squeeze, but she didn't hear the gun go off. She was so scared she was shaking like a leaf. But she never once stopped praying. If that coldhearted bastard was going to kill her, she wanted to go to heaven.

Fatima watched him pull the trigger again. She covered her face with her hands, and squeezed her eyes shut. She silently prayed that God would take her soul. *"God, please forgive me for all my sins. And please don't let this maniac kill my daughter."*

Falynn was her main concern. She knew her daughter was afraid in that dark trunk. She hated small places. Fatima wondered if she getting enough oxygen in there. Her poor baby.

She heard the gun click again. Fatima flinched, and realized she was still alive. That had to be God. She cried out for more help to come from heaven. "God, help me! *Please*, Lord Jesus!"

Since God gave her a chance, Fatima decided to fight back. She opened her eyes just in time to see him squeeze the trigger again. But there was nothing! Something had to be wrong with his gun! She charged at Smoke, digging her nails in his face. She clawed at his fucking eyes, and kneed him in the nuts as hard as she could.

Smoke hollered out, and crouched down for a second. He tried to fire the gun at her again. Then a sixth time. His firearm was obviously jammed. Fatima had her fingernails dug in his eyes, and it was pretty painful. To get that bitch off him, he backhanded her hard across the jaw. She stumbled backwards, and fell to the floor.

That stupid bitch was lucky as hell. Smoke had heard her praying, so God must've really been with her. He got frustrated and bent down and grabbed Fatima by the hair, and then he conked her in the temple with the butt of his gun. He hit her hard as hell three good times, and managed to knock her out cold. Fatima dropped, and hit the floor with a thud. She was silent, and her body was still.

Smoke tucked his faulty gun in his waist, and made a mental note to get rid of the bullshit as soon as he had the opportunity to discard it properly. It had failed him once, so he wouldn't give it a second chance. If that bitch had been spitting back at him, he would've been done off.

He thought about finishing Fatima off simply by clubbing her in the face, but he wasn't in the mood for bludgeoning. And all that blood would be messy. He couldn't afford to stain his clothing at that point. That could hinder the smooth getaway he had planned. That bitch was lucky. Smoke opened the door, and just broke out.

He had made sure Fatima left the key in the ignition when she got out of the car. His plan was to drive her car down the road to the stolen hoopty he had waiting there. He had parked down there and walked down, so she wouldn't notice any strange cars by her house.

He started to run down the front steps and jump in the car, but he remembered the little girl was still in the trunk. He had originally planned to shoot her too, but now his gun was jammed. He contemplated whether he should choke her to death, or break her neck. She only looked about five years old, but she was old enough to identify him.

While Smoke was busy trying to decide how to kill Falynn, a figure in all black appeared out of nowhere. The man's face was partially covered by the long dreadlocks he adorned. Dressed in a black hat, and black clothing, he quietly crept up on Smoke's left. He was holding a black 9 millimeter in his right hand.

In his haste, Smoke didn't even realize he had company. After debating with himself for a few seconds, he decided to choke the little girl to death. Anxious to get it over with, he started towards the car.

Smoke took one step. Before he could take another one, the stranger stealthily placed his gun right behind his ear. The cold gun metal startled Smoke. He jumped, and turned around.

Before Smoke could get a good look at his assailant, the man fired and dropped him right on the steps. The bullet pierced his skull, and exited his forehead. Blood splattered all over his shirt, ultimately messing up his clothes anyway. Smoke's body twitched and jerked on the ground. It was apparent that he was dying.

He had done an enormous amount of dirt, so he knew his day was coming. It was inevitable. You got it just how you gave it up in life. After thirty three years, most of which he'd spent criming, Smoke's number was finally up. He'd always told himself that when he faced death, he would do so with honor. He swore he would go out blazing, and not be afraid to look death right in the eye.

But now that the time had come, Smoke didn't feel so courageous. He was afraid. He didn't want to die. After the life he had lived, he knew where he was going. Straight to hell. He felt his stomach turning, like he was about to shit on himself.

The assassin stood over him and bit his lip in rage. Without a word, he emptied the clip in his chest. Smoke had gone through all that trouble to get Fatima's money, but now he would never get a chance to spend it. After that brutal barrage of bullets hit him, he died instantly.

$ $ $ $

Later that day, Fatima woke up in the hospital. She didn't know what had happened, but she had a hell of a headache. At first, she couldn't remember anything. She laid there for a few minutes, and then it all started coming back to her.

She remembered Smoke trying to fire that gun in her face. She had counted every time he pulled the trigger. It was six times. The gun jammed, so she had narrowly escaped death. After his gun jammed, he used it to hit her in the face. Fatima thanked God out loud because she could've really been dead. Her face was swollen, but she was alive.

Suddenly, it came back to her that Falynn was in the trunk of her car! Fatima sat straight up in her hospital bed. Just then, her room door opened. In walked a middle-aged, Caucasian man, who was obviously a detective. She could tell because he had that cop walk. Fatima wondered if she was under arrest for something. She thought about her and Portia's last encounter with the police, at the hospital when Wise died.

The detective introduced himself. It turned out he just wanted to question her. Fatima decided to question him too. She wanted to know where her daughter was first. And then she wanted to know how she got to the hospital.

The detective answered her last question first. He told Fatima that there had been an anonymous 911 call for help at her address. He said that when the paramedics arrived, they found her unconscious on the floor in her home. She was bleeding from the head.

Fatima noticed he hadn't responded to her question about Falynn, so she knew something was wrong. She prayed to God that mothafucka hadn't killed her baby. She didn't know what happened after he hit her in the head with that gun. She decided to ask the detective one more time, even though she was terrified to learn the outcome.

"*Sir*, do you know where my *daughter* is? Can you *please* tell me the truth?" Fatima's voice was shaking, and so were her hands. She was literally worried sick.

To her horror, the detective informed her that Falynn was missing. When Fatima heard that, she almost had a heart attack. She broke down, and just started crying.

Her mind was in a whirl. Everything was a blur now. Did that bastard kidnap her baby, and take her off somewhere and kill her? That was exactly what had happened to Laila's baby, Pebbles. Poor Pebbles was raped and murdered, God bless her soul.

And not long ago, the actress from the movie "Dream Girls", Jennifer Hudson's nephew was abducted. That poor baby was later found dead too. The unlikelihood of Falynn being returned to her unharmed was so great, Fatima almost threw up when she thought about it. She tried to block the unthinkable from her mind. Dear God in heaven, where was her child?

The detective looked at her sincerely. He assured her that every possible measure was being taken to find her daughter, and then he handed her a tissue. After she stopped crying so hard, he told her there was something else he wanted to talk to her about. He said there was sort of a twist to the incident. He asked Fatima if she knew anything about the dead man on her front steps.

When Fatima heard that, she was completely shocked. She made a face, and shook her head. And then she asked, "What *dead man?*"

The detective told her he believed it was the person who'd assaulted her. He said a First Federal Bank envelope filled with brand new hundred dollar bills totaling one hundred thousand dollars was found in the dead man's pocket. He said that had prompted him to go to the bank to investigate.

The detective told Fatima he had viewed the security tape from the bank's cameras, and they had captured the perpetrator on video. He said he'd seen her and the man at the bank teller window, and he figured she'd been forced to make a withdrawal. He said the ropes around the chair in her home also indicated that she had been tied up, and held hostage for some period of time. He pointed to the rope burns on her forearms, and told her that was evidence as well.

The detective pulled a photo from his back pocket, and asked

Fatima if that was the guy who had invaded her home. When she looked at the mug shot, she recognized him immediately. She told the detective that was him. She would never forget that mothafucka's face as long as she lived.

The detective told her the man's name was Ivan "Smoke" Williams, and armed robbery was the most reoccurring charge on his long rap sheet. He told her Smoke would've probably winded up dead sooner or later because of the way he was living, but his job was to find out who killed him. He said he had reason to believe whoever had killed Smoke was the person who had taken her daughter. He told Fatima he needed to know if she had any information that would be helpful to the case.

Fatima just shook her head. She really had no clue who could've killed Smoke. And why would they have taken her baby?

Fatima's mind started racing. Did Smoke have an accomplice, or something? Did his partner flip on him, kill him, and then kidnap Falynn for some ransom money? But if that was the case, why didn't they take the hundred thousand dollars from him before they fled?

Fatima was honest, and told the cop she didn't know anything about Smoke's death. All she knew was she didn't kill him. She told the detective that she remembered he tried to shoot her in the face, but lucky for her his gun had jammed. She said after that, he hit her in the head with the gun and knocked her out. That was all she remembered.

She asked the detective if they had checked the trunk of her car. She knew Smoke had put her baby in there. He told her they had already searched every inch of her house, and every vehicle in the garage and driveway diligently. He let her know that her parents and her friends had been notified about what happened to her. He said they were all worried sick, and adamant about finding her daughter. He said everyone was in the hallway waiting to see her. They had kindly respected his request to speak to her first.

As he was telling Fatima all of this, all she could think about was her daughter. By the grace of God, where could Falynn be? There was no way she could have just disappeared like that. Where the fuck was her child?

Fatima just kept shaking her head in disbelief. This shit couldn't be real. Someone had to have some answers. There was no way in the world her daughter could just be missing. Falynn was all she had. She needed her baby. Fatima knew she had neglected her once upon a time, but she wasn't living like that anymore. She had to get her child back. She couldn't rest until she knew Falynn was safe.

The detective gave her a business card, and told her he would be in touch. He wished her a speedy recovery, and a good day.

As soon as he left, Fatima tried to get up out that hospital bed. She had to get out of there! She realized she had all these wires and stuff hooked up to her, so she cursed out loud. "Shit!"

Fatima snatched the oxygen out of her nose, and tried to figure out what those wires were attached to. She had to get dressed fast, so she could get the hell out of there. She had to find her baby.

Fatima couldn't figure it out, so she called for a nurse to come take that mess off her. If someone didn't remove that I.V. from her arm, she was about to yank that damn thing out. There was absolutely no time to waste. She had to find her daughter. She prayed to God her baby was okay. If someone hurt Falynn, there was going to be a whole lot of fucking bloodshed.

Just then, Portia ran in the room with a huge grin on her face. She informed Fatima that Falynn had just turned up okay. She said someone had dropped her off at the hospital. Fatima didn't know how or who, but she was grateful to God for answering her prayers. Her eyes filled up with happy tears. God was so good.

CHAPTER EIGHT

Kira was locked up in an all women's prison in the hills of New Jersey. She was on the end of her bid, and due to return back to the streets in just months. As far as she knew, everything was good so far. Her prison stay had been virtually drama-free.

She was cool with most of the chicks in there, but Kira also had some pretty big haters. Especially this one in particular. There was this broad named Big Red, who called herself a rapper too.

Big Red had initially tried to befriend Kira. It was no secret that Kira was signed to her brother's label, so Red thought she could get close enough to snag a record deal, or something. But Kira was basically a loner. She was alright with a few chicks, but she wasn't there to make friends. She spent most of her time in her cell writing. And judging from the stories she'd heard about Big Red, Kira knew she was dirty. So she stayed away from her.

Big Red didn't like that shit. Not one bit. She put the word out that she was going to get at Kira. It was purely sour grapes, but she felt her motivation was justified because she felt disrespected and overlooked. She ran that mothafuckin' house, and bitches in there better act like they knew. Including Kira. She didn't give a fuck how famous and paid she was.

Needless to say, they had a confrontation. Red waited until one of the rare times Kira came out in the yard. Anxious to prove she was the head bitch in charge, she approached Kira and told her she owed her some money. She said if she didn't pay her, she was going to do major damage to her face.

Kira looked at that bitch like she was crazy. She told her ass quick, "You got it fucked up, bitch. Ain't nothin' sweet! I'll pay yo' ugly ass no mind! Bitch, fuck you! 'Fuck outta my face!"

Red crossed her arms, and had second thoughts. That wasn't the response she had expected. Kira didn't seem afraid. Red had an image to uphold, so she ignored the little voice in the back of her head that told her to fall back.

She moved closer, and put her hand in Kira's face. She scowled, and replied, "Bitch, I tried to be nice, but I see I'ma have to show you. I *run* this shit, and *bitch*, I said you *owe* me!"

Kira tried to be easy because she was supposed to go home in a few months. She didn't want any trouble, but that bitch was testing her. She was straight invading her space. Kira had a cup in her hand that was filled with hot tea. She threw the scalding liquid in Red's face, and spat, "There you go, *bitch*. Hold that!"

Red grabbed her face and screamed. Kira didn't give her time to recover. She moved in to finish her fast. She pulled the weapon she carried in there from her pocket, a combination lock in a sock, and clocked that bitch in the head.

Big Red's forehead split open and blood gushed out of the wound. She charged at Kira blindly, but Kira sidestepped and hit her two more times. She lumped that bitch up for disrespecting her.

A crowd had gathered, and they cheered them on. The officers in the yard saw the commotion, and quickly ran down on them. They saw Kira swinging that sock, so they rushed her first. She surrendered and didn't resist, but they still handled her like she was a violent criminal. They got her down on the ground, and one of those pig bitches had the audacity to put their foot on her neck.

Kira wanted to kill that bitch for violating her like that, but she knew she couldn't win. Not that day anyway. She made sure she got a good look at her face. When she looked at her good, she recognized her. The bitch's name was Officer Burton, and Kira had a little run-in with her jealous ass a few weeks before. Now she would definitely remember her face. And her name. She knew she would see that bitch again. It was a small world.

For fighting in the yard, and using her lock in a sock as a weapon, Kira was sent to the box for ninety days. She was on 23-hour lockdown, and she lost her right to receive packages, her telephone calls, and everything else those pigs considered a privilege.

Kira was tight about that, but she would have done it again if she had to. She wouldn't subject herself to be punked by anything walking on two feet. Especially another bitch. She had to maintain her respect in there.

$ $ $ $

Ysatis was struggling with single motherhood. It just didn't come naturally to her. She learned everything by trial and error. She didn't have anybody to show her what to do so she winged it, and hoped for the best.

She didn't know what to do. Her lease was up in a month. She had reached out to Jay, but to no avail. She wondered if he expected her to just move out, and move on. What the hell was going to happen to her? Was the landlord going to evict her, and put her out in the street?

Ysatis held onto hopes that the baby was her saving grace. But Jay didn't even know about the baby yet. Jaylin was a month old already, and she couldn't reach his father to tell him. He wouldn't answer the phone when she called, so she still hadn't talked to Jay in months.

Ysatis was desperate, so she started doing her homework. She dug and dug, but she couldn't find Jay's home address for anything. But she was able to obtain his office address.

When she finally got up the nerve, she got the baby ready

early in the morning and went over there. Jay wasn't at the office when Ysatis showed up, but she told the girl at the front desk she would wait.

Ysatis was told to have a seat, so she camped out in the waiting room with her son. She had bought along three bottles of formula, just in case the wait would be long. She was really desperate so she couldn't leave there without seeing Jay.

Ysatis was there waiting for over three hours. She did her best to keep the baby quiet, but he kept on crying. And the little fellow had some strong lungs. He really made his presence known. You could tell he was going to be a man of power like his father.

Jay's new assistant, Robin, had a bad feeling about the girl with the infant who was waiting to see her boss. When she realized she had no intentions on leaving, she made an urgent call to Jay.

Jay was on the other line when she called. He recognized his office number on his cell, so he switched over. He figured his assistant, Robin, was calling to tell him he was running late for some meeting, or something. He had a lot on his plate, so he forgot about appointments sometimes.

Jay didn't even give Robin a chance to talk because he was close to the office. He told her he was parking, so she could update him in person. He said he was on another call on the other line, and hung up.

Robin frowned at the phone after he hung up. She hoped her boss wouldn't chew her out for the Jerry Springer episode she had a feeling he was about to walk into. She had tried to warn him. Now she was staying out of it.

When Jay walked in the office, he was still talking business on his cell phone. He was engrossed in his conversation, but he wasn't off point. The life he'd lived caused him to always make it a point to be aware of his surroundings, so he saw Ysatis peripherally.

At first, Jay got angry. What the fuck was she doing showing up at his office? He cursed the day he got involved with her. Was she some type of psycho bitch, or something?

Jay was a master of disguising body language, so he was cucumber cool as usual. He nodded at Ysatis, and headed in his office.

Jay closed his office door, and wrapped up his telephone conversation. When he hung up, he paged Robin, and told her he needed to speak to her.

Robin had a feeling what that was about. When she walked in Jay's office, she was already prepared. She said, "Yes, sir?"

Jay liked Robin. She was a twenty four year old punk rocker type of chick. Robin was a cute brown skinned girl with a lot of tattoos, and she wore crazy half shaved hairstyles all the time. But at work, she was always business. They had a good rapport because she did her job, and she thought on her toes.

Jay knew Robin didn't know he didn't want to be bothered with Ysatis, so he didn't chew her out. Instead, he asked her what Ysatis wanted. He hoped she hadn't said too much.

Robin shrugged, and said, "I don't know, but she's been out there for hours. She said she needs to speak to you. I tried to convince her to leave because you'd be a while, but she said she would wait."

Jay was tight about that, but he didn't show it. He told Robin to give him a few minutes, and then send Ysatis in. Jay was a little nervous for some reason. It wasn't like Ysatis had him under pressure, so he didn't know what that was about.

Deep down inside, he knew what it was. He had handled that situation like a coward. He hadn't officially told Ysatis that he didn't want to have anything else to do with her. But he figured she would've got the picture. Damn, he'd thrown her nothing but shade lately. He didn't even take her calls. Couldn't she read between the lines?

Ysatis had got two semesters at NYU, and a fancy duplex apartment for a year out of him. That was it. Jay wasn't playing either. He and Portia just got back together, so he definitely wasn't fucking that up again. Not for anybody.

He knew Portia. She told him she forgave him, but he knew she would never forget about that shit. If she even suspected something was up again, she would be right on top of it.

Once again, Jay cursed the day his do-good ass had stuck his neck out, and tried to be nice. He had complicated everything. But he was done with Ysatis now. If she had come there for money, or the guarantee of a lease renewal, he wouldn't be able to assist her. That bitch better go get a job with the college degree he'd helped finance.

Jay wondered if he was being too harsh. Damn, she was so pitiful he kind of felt sorry for her. But shit, Ysatis wasn't his responsibility. He had promised Portia that he would sever all ties with her, and he wanted to keep his word.

Just then, Robin paged him. That snapped him out of his thoughts. She asked if he wanted her to send the girl in yet. Jay told her he was ready.

In his haste to avoid Ysatis, he hadn't really looked at her when he walked in. So he was surprised when she entered his office carrying a little baby. He really hadn't noticed that before.

Jay could see that she had put on a little weight, so he guessed the kid was hers. That was actually good. That meant she had found herself a little boyfriend, or something. If she had somebody she was into, she should be willing to move on.

Now Jay felt better. Getting rid of her wouldn't be as difficult as he had imagined. But he wondered why Ysatis was at his office, instead of running to the arms of the guy who'd knocked her up. The dude was probably some deadbeat, or something.

Jay didn't even wanna know, so he was curt. He said, "What up, Ysatis? What are you doing here?"

She just stared at him like she was bewildered about something. Finally, she opened up her mouth and spoke. Ysatis said, "I want you to meet somebody, Jay." After that, she nervously but proudly presented him with the heir to his throne.

Jay just nodded. "I see that you had a baby. Congratulations. Is it a boy, or a girl?"

Ysatis looked right at him, and said, "A boy. You have a son, Jay. His name is Jaylin. Jaylin Mekhi Mitchell."

Jay sat up in his chair, and looked at her like she was crazy. That bitch had lost her mind. There was no fucking way. He wasn't trying to hear that. Annoyed, he said, "Look, don't come around here starting no crazy shit. What is *wrong* with you? You know that ain't my baby."

Ysatis knew better, so she stood firm. She said, "Trust me. I know it's hard to believe, but this *is* your son."

Jay took a deep breath. He wasn't in the mood for no crazy ass, delusional broad lying in his face. He was seconds from dismissing her from his office. He was trying to be nice, but now he thought about having security throw that crazy bitch out on her head. She was wilding.

Jay didn't really show his emotions, so he appeared a lot calmer than he was. He didn't even raise his voice. He said, "If things aren't working out between you and your baby's father, that's terrible. But do not play like that. That's a real baby you're holding, and fatherhood is not like playing a game of Pin the Tail on the Donkey."

Ysatis sighed, and said, "Jay, I'm not playing any games. I would *never* do that. This is your son!"

When she said that again, Jay got fed up with her. He was done. He had initially felt sorry for her, but she was really pissing him off. What the fuck type of shit was she trying to start? He had a condom on when he hit that, and she knew that. In an extremely aggravated tone, he told her, "Girl, you must be fuckin' crazy! Stop sayin' that shit! That baby is not mines!"

Ysatis was young, but she could be a fireball when she wanted too. She was upset that Jay was denying his child, so she gave him attitude. She said, "*Like I said*, this is your son. And you can take whatever test you want. You the only person I was with! I swear!"

Jay took a deep breath. He was running out of patience. "Look, Ysatis. You know I used protection. You *know* I did! So what the fuck is wrong wit' you?"

Ysatis was so hurt she had tears in her eyes. But Jay could be a cold mothafucka. He didn't give a fuck about no damn crocodile tears. He was disappointed that she was even willing to stoop to that level. He was disgusted with Ysatis. He would've never expected that from her.

Jay had her all figured out. He knew that was a ploy to get some money out of him. He offhandedly told her, "Damn, if you need money, then just say that. I know you gotta renew your lease next month. And I was gon' call you about that. But don't be gettin' down greasy, lying and talkin' about that's my baby. Don't *ever* fuckin' come at me like that. You should know better."

Ysatis said, "Look, Jay. I didn't stay here all day waiting for you for nothin'. Word on my *baby's life*, this is your son. Why don't you at least look at him before you make an assumption? I know we used a condom, but it must've broke, or something. You're the only person I was with. I swear to you, Jay!"

She shoved the kid in his face, and Jay felt like hitting her. He started to not even look. He said fuck it, and glimpsed at the tiny little dude. He was cute, but he wasn't about to own up to some other dude's kid.

Hold up, what the fuck? Jay noticed the baby sort of had eyes like his. He kind of looked like Jayquan when he was a baby. But was he bugging? That was impossible. Now that retarded bitch had him tripping.

Jay didn't say anything, so Ysatis started yapping, "Jay, I tried to call you to tell you, but you wouldn't *answer the phone.*"

Jay was really pissed off, so he just kept it real with her. He said, "My wife thinks it best that we not associate any more. I think that's best too. I'll give you money to move, and after that, go have a nice life." He gave her a look that showed he wasn't playing with her ass. Crazy ass bitch.

Ysatis pretended those words didn't hurt the way they did. She had figured that was what was going on. She wasn't stupid. She knew he'd been avoiding her. But now she didn't give a fuck about what he and his wife thought was best. She had a kid by him so she let him know. She and Jaylin weren't going to just fade away.

She said, "Jay, this is your son. If you think you can just wash your hands with us, then you better get ready to go to court. I'm trying to give you a chance, but you're not making this easy. I need your help to raise this baby. I can't do it alone."

Ysatis didn't like the way Jay was looking at her. He looked like he wanted to spit on her, so she tried to soften it up a little. "Jay, I'm not trying to threaten you, but I don't have money for the things the baby needs. I'm getting W.I.C. to buy formula, but that's it."

Jay reached in his pocket. Not because he believed that kid was his, and certainly not because Ysatis had him under pressure. He just wanted her to be on her way.

And Jay just had a good heart. That baby didn't ask to come there. He peeled off twenty five hundred dollar bills, and handed her a folded stack. That was about half the cash he had on him. He only did that because he felt sorry for the baby. A child should never be made to suffer, even if his mother was insane.

Jay told Ysatis to take her baby, and go home. He told her he would call her at a later date, and warned her not to pop up at his office again.

Ysatis put the wad of money in her pocket, and she took her baby and left. It wasn't a happy reunion, but it was a reunion nonetheless. She had showed Jay she would go to any extent to locate him, so she was pretty sure she'd be hearing from him soon.

She knew it would take time, but she was holding on to the notion that Jay would come around. She knew she had shocked him by bringing his son to his office, but she was optimistic that he would eventually grow to love them both.

After she left, Jay sat there for a minute regretting ever messing with that broad. He wished he'd never met her. She just wouldn't go away, and that really irked him. All Jay could think about was Portia. He didn't believe that kid was his, but he still didn't want Portia to know anything about that mess. But he had this nagging feeling that situation was going to blow up in his face.

CHAPTER NINE

Fatima sat in her living room going through old photos of her baby. She was choked up, but thank God her tears were happy ones. Falynn was okay. Fatima was just thinking about the way she felt when she thought she had lost her baby. That made her get all emotional.

She still didn't know who had Fay, but her daughter was returned safely. That was all that mattered to Fatima. But it was still weird. Fatima had asked Falynn over and over again to describe the person who dropped her off. Fay only told her it was a nice man. She said he bought her ice cream.

The police were still trying to figure out who killed Smoke on her front steps, so they wanted to question Falynn too. Fatima had allowed them one opportunity to speak with her daughter, and she made sure she was present. Fay had told them the same thing. All she remembered was that the man had a beard and dreadlocks.

It was now a month later, but Fatima was so happy she was still thanking God. That day Falynn was safe at her parents' house. Fatima looked around her newly securitized home, and breathed a sigh of relief. She was glad to be alive. She could still see Smoke pulling that trigger all those times. She'd had a few nightmares about that incident.

But Fatima vowed she would keep living, and not let that hinder her. She was getting ready for their summer European trip. She, Portia, Jay, Laila, Cas, and all their kids were going to spend two weeks in Europe. They were going to London, Milan, and Paris. And then they were ending their vacation with five days in the South of France.

Fatima loved the thought of being on the French Riviera. She looked forward to luxuriating on the beautiful beaches of Saint Tropez. She was excited about vacation more than anything. She needed to get away. That brush she had with death had given her a new appreciation for life. Now she wanted to see the world. She could've died that day without getting a chance to do all the stuff she wanted to do.

She'd suggested to Portia and Laila that they take the kids to Africa the following summer. Both of her girls thought that was a great idea. They agreed to start planning the trip that winter. That way, they could line up a full itinerary of cultural importance.

Another thing they had started planning was Laila's wedding. She and Cas had set a date for Valentine's Day weekend of 2010. It was only August, but time was going by so fast. Laila said she didn't want anything ridiculously extravagant, so they had decided on a small guest list of no more than a hundred people.

Fatima and Portia had already hired a wedding planner. They were going to make sure that day was special for their girl.

$ $ $ $

Portia was busy making preparations for their upcoming trip. She was pretty much in a good mood all the time since she got back home. Her family was together, and life was great.

She took the kids to the doctor to make sure they had all their necessary shots for traveling abroad. She also braided Jazmin and Trixie's hair in small cornrows. That way she wouldn't have to mess with their heads for a while. All that was really left for her to do was pack. They were leaving town in a few days.

$ $ $ $

The news about that kid was eating at Jay. He had to get it off his chest, so he told Cas about Ysatis' crazy ass coming to the office with a baby she claimed was his. Cas couldn't believe it. He said Ysatis was just another skeezer trying to come up. He told Jay not to worry too much about it, but to make sure he didn't put himself in that position again.

Jay asked Cas if he thought he should tell Portia about the incident, just in case Ysatis somehow leaked it first.

Cas knew Jay and Portia just got back together, so he knew how he felt. He didn't want to risk losing his wife again. Cas couldn't fault him for that. He told Jay to think smart. He didn't think he should mention it to Portia yet. He said he should get a paternity test first.

Cas told Jay if he found out that baby was his, he had to tell Portia. He couldn't let her find out about that kid any other way.

Jay appreciated the advice. He told Cas he had strapped up, so there was no way that was his kid. Cas said he should still get a blood test done, to get that money hungry bitch out his face. Jay agreed with him. After that, he didn't say anything for a while.

Jay was deep in thought. He really hoped that baby wasn't his. But the type of dude he was, he had to make sure. He made a mental note to arrange some type of confidential paternity testing. He was anxious to prove to Ysatis that he was not her kid's father, so she could get on with her life.

The timing was real fucked up because the family was going to Europe in a few days. Jay knew how excited Portia and the kids were about that trip, so he decided to just keep quiet and poker-faced about the matter. For the time being, he would pretend it didn't exist.

$ $ $ $

Laila looked at her ringing cell phone, and checked the caller ID. She had a feeling that "Unavailable" number was Khalil. She sent the call to voicemail, just in case. She didn't want to hear that jailhouse shit. She wasn't in the mood.

Laila had run out of patience with her loser ex-husband. He had signed those papers, so he was Black history. She didn't have time for his small-mindedness. She had two kids to take care of. Macy, her fifteen year old, was in high school. And her baby, Skye, was already one.

Khalil had called her from Riker's Island a few times. Each time, he was talking some stupid "I still love you, you're the best thing that ever happened to me" shit. Laila didn't want to hear that mess. That fool was out of his mind. They were divorced, and she wasn't thinking about his ass.

Laila was done with Khalil, and she would never look back. She was in love with Cas. Her fiancé treated her like a queen. Cas was her king, and he had moved her into a castle. Their property was storybook beautiful. And the landscaping was breathtaking.

Portia had suggested they have the wedding at the house. She said Laila could walk down their palatial spiral staircase to "Here Comes the Bride", or they could have the wedding on their picturesque foliage filled lawn. Laila was only against the outside thing because it would be cold that time of year.

Laila thought about Khalil again. She and his mother had talked when she took Macy to visit her on Mother's Day. Mama Atkins had greeted her with open arms. She gave Laila her blessing to move forward.

Laila was grown and could do as she pleased, but the fact was that she and her mother-in-law always got along. She had a lot of respect for Mama Atkins. She was a sensible woman, so Laila didn't want any bad blood between the two of them.

And she was Macy's grandmother, so they had to communicate. In spite of her distaste towards Khalil, Laila wanted Macy to be close to her father's side of the family. And she wanted Khalil to partake in his daughter's life. But he was busy worrying about Laila. And Macy was his only living child.

Now Mama Atkins cared. She had taken it upon herself to reach out to Laila. She expressed her unhappiness about not being in her granddaughter's life. Macy mattered to her, so she had extended the invitation for them to come by. Laila had handled the situation like a woman. She went over there to sit and talk with her.

Laila thought she was going to act kind of funny towards her, but Mama Atkins had embraced her. She even held her baby. She told her she understood that she had moved on with her life. She said her son was weak, and offered no apologies for him. She said she didn't blame her.

At the time, Laila wasn't engaged yet but Mama Atkins had hinted about it. She had asked her when she planned to marry her baby's father. She told Laila that shacking up was tacky. Mama Atkins was religiously old-fashioned, and she firmly believed in the marriage ethic. She had married twice in life herself, so she didn't view it as taboo. She was from a time when a woman was supposed to be married to the man she bedded. That was the way God said it should be.

Laila had told her at the time that there were no wedding plans in their near future. At the time, she really didn't know. But now things had changed. She made up her mind to invite Mama Atkins to the wedding. They were still family.

Laila's mother died when she was young, so when she first had her kids, it was Khalil's mother who had given her helpful advice. And she oftentimes babysat Macy and Pebbles for her, while she went to school and earned her nursing degree. Laila would never forget those things. And when Pebbles had passed away, Khalil's mother had offered her support, and tried to stand in for her sorry ass son. And she took Pebbles' death hard too.

Laila didn't have a problem with Macy going to Brooklyn to stay with her grandmother sometimes. She encouraged it. Especially now. Macy was a good girl, but she was getting older. Laila knew her grandmother would be a positive motivating force in her life. After Laila's parents died when she was small, her grandmother had raised her. The jewels of wisdom she left her with were priceless. That was what grandmothers offered.

Macy was going to be sixteen soon. She would be in her junior year that fall. She had been hinting about a Sweet Sixteen party at the new house. Laila hadn't ruled it out, but she hadn't said yes yet.

Macy was a good kid, and thank God, she was still a virgin. She got good grades, helped out around the house, and helped take care of her little sister. So she deserved a party. Laila wanted to throw her an extravagant Sweet Sixteen gala, but she wanted it to be a surprise.

They were all going to Europe in a few days, so she made a mental note to start planning the party when they returned.

CHAPTER TEN

The following morning, Jay couldn't sleep past seven. He had tossed and turned all night long, so he got up early. When Portia asked if he was okay, he made up an excuse about having an early meeting.

Jay decided that would be the day he'd end all the bullshit. Ysatis had been blowing up his cell phone so much, he was on the verge of changing his number. He had an idea, and he prayed it would work. He was going to call Ysatis' bluff that day. He was demanding a paternity test. He hoped that would cause her to shy away, and quit accusing him of fathering her child.

Jay showered and got dressed, and then he called for a car to take him to the City. Along the way, he called Ysatis and told her to get herself and the baby ready. When she asked where they were going, he was honest with her. He told her he wanted to test the baby for paternity.

To Jay's surprise, Ysatis agreed without hesitation. She didn't sound nervous at all. He told her he'd be there within the hour, and hung up. The whole way there, he prayed she'd call him back with some lame duck excuse. That would be a clear indication that she was unsure about who got her pregnant.

When Jay pulled up in front of her building, he still hadn't heard from her. He was pretty uptight about that, and his jaw line reflected it. He called that damn girl and told her to come downstairs. Jay figured she might've needed help getting the baby down there, but at the time he resented Ysatis too much to be the gentleman he normally was.

When she came downstairs, Jay barely glimpsed at her. But he did tell the driver to get out and give her a hand. After they were loaded up, the driver got back under the wheel and pulled off.

Ysatis tried to make small talk but Jay wasn't in the mood. He acted so distant towards her, she eventually just shut her mouth. Sitting there beside him, she wished he would at least peek at their son and acknowledge him. Jay's demeanor showed her that her dreams of them being a happy family were farfetched.

Jay gave the driver directions, and those were the only words he uttered the entire ride. He had his assistant, Robin, find him a place for discreet and fast paternity testing. Some places said it took 1-2 days to find out, but he needed to know sooner than that. He was willing to pay the extra cost associated with expediting the results. He just wanted that shit to be behind him.

When they got to the Upper East Side office, Jay kept his distance from Ysatis and her baby when they went inside. After they signed in, there was a short wait.

Before Jay knew it, it was time to do what they had to do. They were ushered into a private room and asked to sign some papers. Afterwards, this lady used these long swabs to take samples of everyone's DNA from inside their cheeks.

When they were done, the people told Jay they would notify him by telephone with the results. They told him they automatically tested the DNA twice to make sure the results were conclusive, no matter what they were.

That was good to know. After that, Jay put Ysatis and her baby in a yellow cab and sent them right back home. There was no need for them to spend any more time together. They weren't some couple with high hopes on The Maury Show.

Jay went on home too. That day he and Cas had promised Jayquan and Jahseim they would take them shopping to get ready for their trip. Portia, Laila, and Fatima were shopping for the girls. The little ladies on their team were all different sizes, from teenaged Macy, all the way down to the tots, Skye and Trixie.

Around five hours later, Jay, Cas, and their sons were out shopping when Jay got the call. When he answered the phone he was full of hope. But by the time he hung up, he was flabbergasted. To his extreme disappointment, they said the baby was 99.99% his.

The first thing he said was he wanted another test. They said they weren't against it, but in their professional opinion it would be a waste of time and money. They reminded him that they tested the DNA two times, and told him the paperwork documented it.

Jay was done. He couldn't believe it. He really could not believe that shit. That was some of the worse news he ever heard in his whole life. The fucked up part was that he couldn't express any type emotion because he was with his son and nephew at the time. Jay was no bitch, but he felt like crying. Why him? Damn!

Cas was standing to Jay's left when he got the call. He was checking out his son trying to mimic his big cousin's fashion taste. Lil' Jay was a funny dude. He was pretty cocky lately. Cas was amused because he recognized that cockiness. Jay was the same way when they were younger.

The boys had expensive taste like their old men. Especially Jayquan. Every outfit he picked out cost at least three or four hundred dollars. Cas looked over at Jay, ready to crack a joke about his strong genes, but his bro's face looked like he'd just seen a ghost. Out of concern, he asked Jay if he was okay.

Jay just kept his game face on, and nodded. It wasn't the time to spill the beans. Both of their sons were within earshot.

Cas just let it go. He'd ask Jay about that phone call later on, when the kids weren't listening.

Jay threw on a fake smile like everything was okay, and they finished their shopping. Meanwhile, he mentally replayed the events leading up to his intercourse with Ysatis. He had only messed with her one time, and he knew he hadn't slipped up. He had no choice but to suspect foul play. He believed Ysatis had tampered with that rubber. That condom didn't break. He would have remembered.

He should've never used one that she provided him with. That was real stupid of him. That wasn't the way he usually got down. He was way smarter than that. That bitch had to tamper with the rubber.

Knowing how foul Ysatis was caused Jay to develop a severe case of contempt for her. His marriage was probably destined for disaster now. All because of her. Jay felt like he was starring in a tragedy in the making. Damn, he felt like killing that bitch.

$ $ $ $

Ysatis' reaction to the call about the paternity results was the complete opposite of Jay's. She knew he was the father already, but she gleefully shouted for joy. She picked up her son and danced him around. Her little Jaylin was a crowned prince now. The son of a king!

Ysatis chuckled in delight, and repeated the sound of a cash register opening. "Cha-ching, cha-ching!"

She kept dancing, and started singing next. *"Cha-ching, cha-ching, cha-ching!"* Ysatis laughed happily, and then she sang that old hit by The O'Jays. *"Money, money, money, money...Money!"*

Jay had been handling her real fucked up lately. But having the child of a wealthy businessman entitled her to certain benefits. She was no fool.

But Ysatis didn't just want money. She wanted a family. She had feelings for Jay. On impulse, she called him to congratulate him about his new son. She was sure he would learn to love him sooner or later. Jaylin was a handsome little fellow.

Ysatis tried Jay three times, and didn't get him. She realized he had no plans to answer the phone. She guessed he wasn't happy about the news. All she could do was keep hope alive. But with those results, she had the courts on her side. That being said, she wasn't that worried.

$ $ $ $

Later on that evening, Jay and Cas hit up a sports bar to check out the game. Jay told Cas about his situation over a stiff drink. He admitted that he felt like he was doomed.

Cas was so cool about it, he made Jay feel like there could actually be a silver lining to that cloud. That was virtually impossible, but that was just how sincere he came across. But when Jay asked for his advice, Cas kept it real with him. He told him he had to tell Portia, but not yet.

Jay was low. That baby came at a bad time. It was a horrible mistake. He felt bad for thinking that way about a human life, but it was fucked up. He and Portia had just reunited months ago. What could be worse?

Jay felt terrible. He wondered how he'd gotten himself tangled up in that mess. It was because he was always fucking trying to help somebody. He had really learned his lesson this time. He wasn't dealing with anyone else outside of his circle. No new mothafuckas. When you started messing with new people, they disrupted your fucking life.

Portia had already showed Jay that she would leave his ass. And he knew damn well she might skate again after this. He didn't want to tell her. But he also didn't want any secrets between them. Damn, he had to tell her. If she left him again, that would probably serve him right. He was a fucking idiot.

Jay knew how much she was looking forward to their family vacation, so he decided to wait until they got back. He used the excuse that the news would rain on her parade. He would tell her when they returned to the States.

That night Jay went home feeling guilty as hell, but he couldn't show it. And to make matters worse, Portia was horny. She was in "nasty girl" mode for real. She told him she wanted him to fuck her.

Jay loved his wife, and relished making love to her. He prided himself in being able to give it to her when she wanted it. He knew there were lots of men who couldn't even perform. That was evident by all the new "male enhancement" drugs on the pharmaceutical market.

And Portia gave it to him whenever he wanted it too. That was part of the reason their marriage was successful. They had a few bumps in the road, but overall they had always been happy.

In the spirit of Black love, Jay gave it to his woman that night. And then he gave it to her again. That night Portia told him she was more in love with him than ever. She said they belonged together. She fell asleep in his arms murmuring how much she adored him.

Jay held her, and gazed at her sleeping. He was torn. Damn, he was in a fucked up dilemma. He and P were caught up in each other. What they had felt so new. You could even tell by the way they looked at each other.

Then on the other hand, he had this fucking bird completely annoying him with this baby shit. And it couldn't have come at a worse time.

Jay figured it out. He decided he would pay Ysatis to go away. No matter what the price was, it would be worth it. He had to get her out of the picture fast. He would offer her some bread to split, and never look back.

That was it. He would have his attorney draw up an agreement stating that he would forfeit his parental rights and everything. He wanted nothing to do with that broad. He hoped she would just take the money and run. Jay would ask Cas what he thought about his idea first.

CHAPTER ELEVEN

Since they were going abroad for a while, Jay decided to go visit his little sister, Kira. He chose to go on a Sunday visit, and he took his kids with him.

They got up to the prison at around eleven that morning. Kira was happy to see them. When she came out, she had a big Kool-Aid smile plastered across her face. She said, "Wow, look at my babies! Oh my God, all y'all gettin' so *big*!"

Jayquan and his little sisters grinned back at her. They all loved their zany aunt. And they missed her. Kira just kept on cheesing. She hugged them all tight, one by one. When they all sat down, she held Trixie on her lap while the rest of the kids filled her in on their latest activities.

After a while, Jayquan went to the vending machine to get some refreshments. Jazz and Trixie ran behind him. That gave Jay and Kira time to talk. They talked on the phone every week, but he hadn't seen her in person in a minute. He updated her on some current company business, and then they talked about their plans when she came home.

Kira shared a few of her experiences in there with them, and they spent the rest of the visit laughing and joking. Everybody was enjoying themselves so much, time flew by. Before they knew it, it was 2:30. The visit was over.

Before they left, they told Kira about the European vacation they had planned. She said she wished she could go with them.

She told them to be safe over there, and bring her something back.

Jay told Kira she could go get it herself when she came home. Kira laughed, and hugged him tight. She hugged the kids too, and said goodbye. Then she got on line to go back inside.

$ \qquad $ \qquad $ \qquad $

The time had finally come to go on their vacation. The gang all met up at Jay and Portia's, and they headed to the airport two cars deep.

An hour later, they boarded their plane. The kids were ecstatic. Jazmin and Falynn were afraid to fly, but they got over it when they realized they could watch Nickelodeon the whole time.

About seven hours later, they landed at Heathrow Airport in London. After they were settled in the grandest suites the five star Westbury Mayfair Hotel had, Portia and her girls gathered their little ones, and got started on their agenda.

They were there for three days, and they visited Big Ben, Buckingham Palace, and the National Art Gallery in Trafalgar Square. Jay and Cas were the art lovers. And then to satisfy Jayquan, they also went to this world-famous horror attraction called The London Dungeon. Last but not least, Portia, Laila, and Fatima shopped at Burberry, Alexander McQueen, Saville Row, Jimmy Choo, and Stella McCartney until their feet hurt.

Next, they headed for Milan, Italy for three days. While they were there, they visited a few tourist attractions as well. They included the La Scala Opera House, the Sforza Castle, and the Civico Museum. On the last day of their stay, the ladies got up super early and shopped until they dropped. None of them could imagine leaving Milan without hitting up Gucci, Prada, Tod's, Armani, Zanotti, Versace, and Moschino.

Next on the agenda was Paris. There, the gang shopped first. In fact, they shopped until their feet were almost blistered. Especially

Portia, Laila, and Fatima. Macy was gradually becoming a little fashionista too, so she stuck with them. They all spent a grip on Christian LaCroix, Louis Vuitton, Chanel, Dior, and Chloe. The ladies ended their shopping spree at Christian Louboutin, where they each copped several pairs of notoriously famous, to kill for, shiny red bottom shoes.

During the last two days of their four day stay in Paris, they checked out some historical tourist attractions. They went to visit the Eiffel Tower, the Louvre Museum, and then they walked up over 280 steps to the top of the Arc de Triomphe. Most of the adults broke sweat midways up, so the kids decided to run up and show them up. Jayquan's silly behind ran up halfway backwards. Portia just laughed, and took her time. She was videoing the gang along the way.

Their last night there, the adults went out to dine and see a cabaret show at the Moulin Rouge. There was a lot more to it then they anticipated. The Moulin Rouge was classy, entertaining, sexy, and worth every penny. They all especially liked the part of the show when this beautiful woman gracefully dived into a giant aquarium filled with these huge snakes. The woman's performance was precisely choreographed, and it was spectacular. It was like she was an aquatic snake charmer.

They all drank fine champagne while they watched the show. Needless to say, they left the theatre quite tipsy. Portia and Jay couldn't keep their hands off each other. You could tell their night was going to literally end with a bang.

Fatima could see that Cas and Laila were eyeing each other too. Love was in the air. And she understood. She felt it too. Paris had that effect on you. It was really a magical, aphrodisiacal city. Fatima wanted to make love too. She was just short of a partner.

She knew she was the fifth wheel before they had gone out, but she wanted to see the show at the Moulin Rouge too. And they really had a great time. But it was the end of the night, and she was the only one returning to the hotel solo. She was feeling pretty lonely. Fatima knew her night would end with another drink, and a hot and steamy masturbation session. She'd been touching herself a lot lately.

$ $ $ $

The last stop of their vacation was Saint-Tropez, which was located on the French Riviera in the South of France. They all had adjoining suites at the luxurious beachside Hotel Byblos. It was breathtaking there. On the first day, they all chose to lay around and relax. They had done so much the last twelve days, everyone was tired. They were having a great time, but even the kids were beat.

After they had brunch, Jayquan and Macy announced that they were going out on the beach. They ran off and changed their clothes in what seemed like seconds. Macy put on a colorful two-piece and tied a wrap around her waist. Lil' Jay had on knee-length swim trunks. Portia reminded them to put on some sunscreen. After that, they got their towels, and were out the door.

Portia, Fatima, and Laila agreed that hitting the beach wasn't a bad idea. They changed into swimsuits, and got the little ones ready too. Jahseim had on striped trunks just like Jayquan's. The girls, Jazmin, Falynn, Trixie, and Skye, all had on different Disney Princess swimsuits. They all looked so cute, Portia lined them up for a picture.

They all put ample sunscreen on, and headed out to the beach to soak up some sun. Jay and Cas opted to take a little nap first. They said they would join them later.

Portia and her homegirls watched their children build a sandcastle, while they sipped on exotic French cocktails from the beach bar. Then they let the little ones bury their legs in the sand. It was so beautiful and relaxing out there.

There were lots of activities available on the beach, and they did it all. The ladies tried sailing and canoeing, and Jayquan and Macy went windsurfing. After that, they tried their hands at some of the motorized water sports the beach offered. They had a ton of fun riding on jet bikes, and water skiing.

Jay and Cas came out around five o'clock. They rented a power boat big enough for the whole team. After they found lifejackets in everyone's sizes, they took the whole gang out to sea. Everybody went except for Fatima. She wasn't feeling well, so she sat that one out. She decided to go back to her suite and lay down.

Fatima had a light headache. She knew her daughter would be safe under her friends' supervision, so she took a nap with her terrace doors open.

Fatima fell into a deep sleep, and she slept for a while. When she finally woke up, everybody else was asleep. And they were out for the night. It was after three A.M. When Fatima called Portia and Laila, they were both knocked out. Portia told her Falynn was okay. She said she was asleep in the room with Jazz. Fatima thanked her for watching her.

Her stomach growled, indicating that she was hungry. She realized she hadn't eaten anything since brunch. And the cocktails she drank on the beach had long since burned that food up. The five star hotel they were staying at had amenities and entertainment available twenty four hours a day. She decided to go downstairs to the hotel grill and bar for a late supper. And she was bored, so maybe there was someone else up that time of night she could chat with.

Downstairs, Fatima sat at the bar and ordered a cocktail while she thumbed through the menu. She realized it was in French, so she requested the English version. She wasn't famished, so she just ordered an appetizer. There was a lot of French stuff on the menu, including frog legs and escargot. The thought of eating frog and snail turned her off, so she just stayed true to her

American roots and ordered a cheeseburger.

Fatima looked around and saw that there were quite a few folks still out. Everybody was chilling. There was good music playing too. She estimated that there were about twenty people down there. A few of them were dancing. The DJ, who was this internationally famous dude named Blade, was spinning some good stuff. Fatima chatted lightheartedly with her neighbors at the bar, and sipped on a Nouveau.

Her neighbors at the bar were some White guys who said they were from Germany. They were loud and jovial, and they were getting bent. They insisted that she drink with them, and ordered her another cocktail. Fatima accepted the drink, but she finished her food before she drank it. She didn't want to get sick on the stomach.

The guy sitting closest to her, whose name was Wolfgang, confessed that he was developing a crush on her. He told Fatima she was stunning. He said the fact that she could drink with him was the icing on the cake. After that, he ordered them another round. Fatima laughed, and gave him a toast.

After that drink, Wolfgang asked her to dance with him. There was no harm in dancing, so in the spirit of having fun, she got up to shake a leg with him. They danced to "Single Ladies" by Beyonce, and a few more upbeat songs.

After that, the DJ played a slow jam. Fatima didn't want to slow dance, so she took a step back. Wolfgang laughed, and told her he didn't bite. He stepped in and placed his hand on the small of her back, and began to sway to the rhythm. They were so close he was breathing on her neck.

Their pelvises touched, and Fatima could see that he was hard. He wasn't a bad looking dude but his red hair, freckles, and green eyes did little to arouse her. So as far as she was concerned, they were too close for comfort.

Fatima wasn't attracted to him, so she didn't want to lead him on. She politely excused herself, and left the dance floor.

Wolfgang looked like he didn't appreciate her ditching him. But she was so tipsy from those drinks, she needed some air.

Fatima made her way outside on the boardwalk. She just stood there looking at the water for a while. She noticed there were two couples strolling down the moonlit seashore. They both looked so happy. One couple was laughing and holding hands, and the other couple was strolling intimately close together. The guy had his arm protectively draped around the woman's shoulder.

Fatima missed that safe feeling the comfort of a man offered. She felt a pang of loneliness, and wondered if she'd ever find true love again. Portia and Laila had great relationships. They were both so in love. She wasn't jealous of her friends, but she prayed that God would bless her with someone she could grow old with as well.

Fatima held back the tears threatening to spill down her cheeks. She was so preoccupied with self-pity she didn't see the gentleman walking up behind her. Only when she heard footsteps did she finally notice someone was approaching her. It was dark and she was teary-eyed, so all she could make out was a male figure. She just assumed it was her German admirer, Wolfgang, trying to strike up another conversation.

Didn't he get it? She wasn't interested. Now she regretted accepting those drinks from him. She had to tell him she wanted to be alone. Fatima wiped the tears from her eyes, and turned around to greet him with a fake smile.

The first thing Fatima noticed was that the man was Black. She couldn't see his face that well because he had a beard, and his hat was pulled down low. The second thing she noticed was how good the brother smelled. Who in the world was this good smelling stranger? There was something familiar about his physique. Damn, he was sexy.

He didn't say anything to her at first, so curiosity got the best of Fatima. She asked, "Have we met?"

The guy didn't say a word. He just walked up to her and

wrapped his arms around her. He was big and strong, and it felt so good Fatima almost melted. How did he know how bad she needed a hug?

The man held her close. That was inappropriate for a stranger, so she should've protested. A warning bell went off in her head but she just couldn't voice her alarm. There was something so familiar about his touch.

Fatima ran her hands along the familiar stranger's shoulders, and inhaled his masculinity. She closed her eyes and rested her head on his shoulder. Damn, that liquor had her tripping. He reminded her of Wise.

The guy said, "Damn, ma. I missed you so much."

Now Fatima really thought she had lost her mind. He even sounded like Wise! She just froze. She was so in shock she couldn't move. Her brain shut down, but her heart rate quadrupled. Dear God, could it be? Was it possible?

Fatima backed up two steps. She needed to look in his eyes. He took off his hat, and her mouth dropped. It was Wise! She rubbed her eyes and looked at him again.

It was him! But how could that be? Happy tears welled up in her eyes. Fatima just covered her mouth, and said, "*Oh my God!*"

Wise smiled at his wife, and hugged her again. He tilted Fatima's chin up to him and looked in her eyes. He wiped away her tears, and said, "Don't cry, ma. Shut those waterworks off. You ain't gotta cry no more."

He gave her a smile so warm she got lost in it. She couldn't speak. Was she dreaming? She wished she had a pin to stick herself with. Fatima was literally overjoyed. Her mind was racing, and her heart was pounding too fast. The euphoria was too much. She was so taken aback, she fainted.

$ $ $ $

A short time later, Fatima awakened in her suite. At first she thought she was crazy, or had too much to drink. That must've been a fucking dream. She sat up and rubbed her temples.

She heard a man's voice say, "Damn, I'm glad you a'ight. You scared me for a minute."

Fatima focused in on Wise, and she was speechless for a second. She pinched herself to make sure she was awake.

He smiled at her, and then came over and sat next to her on the bed. He pushed her hair back out of her eyes, and gingerly touched her face. Fatima's heart melted. She threw herself in Wise's arms and broke down in tears.

She wrapped herself around him, and placed kisses allover his face. After that, she buried her face in his shoulder and cried. She couldn't believe her husband was alive. Her prayers had been answered.

Wise wiped Fatima's eyes again and told her not to cry. She said she was so glad he was back, she couldn't help it. He kissed her on the forehead, and told her he never left her. He said he just had to get low when that shit happened at the hospital. There were reasons he had faked his death.

Fatima studied her husband's face. He had cut his braids off, and had grown out his beard. Other than that, he still looked the same. Wise was one good looking man. She told him she loved the beard. Fatima noticed there was a scar on his neck. She knew that came from when he got shot. She traced it with her index finger, and placed feather kisses along its length.

She hugged Wise again, and told him she loved him. She said, "Baby, I'm so glad you came back to me. I missed you so much."

A thousand questions ran through her mind, but she didn't even ask one. It didn't matter now what had happened. Her man was back. They were a family again. She would go to the end of the earth to be with that man. She loved Wise with all her heart.

God had answered her prayers, and did her one better. She had her husband back. Her daughter had her father. They were a family. Fatima kept thanking God over and over. She said, "Thank you so much, God. I just can't believe it."

Her nose was running from crying so much, but Fatima was unconcerned about her appearance. She knew she probably looked a mess but she didn't care. Wise didn't either. He planted kisses all over his wife's face, and slowly undressed her. He wanted to savor Fatima with fervor. It had been a long time.

Fatima helped him undress too. When he came out of his shirt she let out a whistle. He'd obviously been working out wherever he was because he was cut up. Damn, she had missed his sexy tattooed chest. Wise had "Only the Strong Survive" tattooed across his chest when she met him, and now it was so relevant. She kissed along his chest, and traced each letter with her tongue.

Wise looked down at his sexy ass wife licking his chest, and was super turned on. He wanted to use his tongue on her now. It had been a while since he'd tasted that. He helped her out of her bra and panties. When Fatima was completely nude, he planted a trail of kisses on her body that led south. When he got down to her honey pot, he eagerly stuck his face in it and took immediate delight in its sweetness.

Wise's mission was to please. He spread her lips and darted his tongue inside of her. Fatima gasped, and grabbed the back of his head. She murmured, "Don't stop, daddy. Don't stop."

Wise was a good listener. He didn't stop. Not until she begged him too. Fatima was shivering and trembling when he was done.

She got up on shaky knees to reciprocate the pleasure. She was thirsty with lust, and wanted to drink from his fountain. She took his immense pole in her mouth and eagerly milked him. She hand stroked him while she licked and sucked it.

Fatima reached down and traced her dripping pussy with two fingers. Then she rubbed her juices on Wise's lips. Her baby was a freak like her. He licked his lips and didn't even protest. Her pussy was soaking wet. Performing oral sex had never made her feel so good before.

Wise couldn't take it. Before long, he let Fatima know he was about to shoot off. Fatima didn't give a fuck that night. She loved the shit outta that nigga. She took every drop of his sweet milk in her mouth. Afterwards, she licked her lips and let it run down her chin. Again, Fatima was real freaky.

That did it for Wise. He liked it nasty. Hot damn, his dick was rock hard again. Fatima watched it grow, and saw that look in his eyes. She wiped her mouth with her panties, and spread her legs. She gazed down at his thick long dick with lust filled eyes. She wanted him more than ever. Wise mounted her, and slowly lowered himself inside.

Fatima hadn't been an angel the whole time Wise was gone. She'd messed with girls a few times, but she had only been with one dude. And that was a while ago, when her and Portia went to L.A. and met Five and Vino. Needless to say, her pussy was pretty tight.

Wise slowly worked his way in. When he finally hit the bottom, he paused and let out a long sigh. She was creaming so much, that pussy felt like warm butter. He was so overcome he couldn't move yet. He didn't want to cum that fast, so he just laid there still for a minute.

Fatima caressed his back and told him she loved him. She had really missed him being inside of her. And it felt like he belonged there. That was his pussy. His name was still on it.

All of a sudden, Wise started to stroke. She gasped, and lightly clawed his shoulders. He was stretching her walls and getting all up in it. Nobody could do it like he could. Fatima relaxed her vaginal muscles and took that dick. It was the most pleasurable beating her pussy had ever taken.

Before Fatima knew it, she felt like she was having an out-of-body experience. Her orgasm was like a volcano. It started in her toes, and then erupted between her hips. She cried out Wise's name over and over. It was so explosive she had tears running down her face.

Wise grabbed her ass while she was cumming, and thrust himself deep inside of her. He was smashing that pussy. It was so good! And so wet. He couldn't take it. Fatima had some good shit. About four seconds later, he climaxed too. After he came, he slumped over Fatima and groaned for about five seconds. "Aaaaaarrrrrrggggghhhhh!"

When they were done lovemaking, they took a shower together. Afterwards, the couple cuddled and played catch up. They talked about a little of everything, including their future, and their daughter. But even while they conversed, Wise couldn't keep his hands to himself. He was all over Fatima.

A little while later, she went down on him again. Wise spun her around so he could lick her pussy at the same time. He sat Fatima right on his face and stuck in his tongue. Meanwhile, she was French kissing his cock. After a hot, wet, and nasty 69, they went for round two.

It was a little after four A.M. when they had initially got started, but Wise and Fatima made love until the sun came up. Then they fell asleep in each other's arms.

CHAPTER TWELVE

Around eleven that morning, Wise and Fatima woke up to the sound of their daughter banging on the door. They knew it was her because she was screaming, "Mommy, open the door!"

Wise got up to open the door. He'd missed his little munchkin. When Falynn saw him, she yelled, "Daddy!" She broke into a huge grin and hopped in his arms.

Portia was standing in the hall by Fatima's suite door. She had walked Falynn over there to make sure her mommy was okay. Tima wasn't feeling well the last time they saw her, so Portia was concerned. And Falynn needed clean underwear and clothes so she could get dressed.

When Portia heard Falynn scream "Daddy", she couldn't help but be nosy. She had to see who the hell Fatima had laying up in there with her. And how did Fay know the nigga well enough to call him daddy? Portia thought Fatima was moving a little too fast, whoever he was.

When Portia peeked in, she saw some man pick Falynn up and swing her around. Who the hell was that? When she got a good look at his face, Portia's eyes almost popped out of her head. She screamed, "Oh my God! Wise!"

Wise grinned at Portia. She ran over there and hugged him tight. She could not believe it. She was so shocked she had to say it again. "Wise! Oh my God!"

Jay overheard Portia yelling. He heard her scream *"Oh my*

God" like something was wrong. He hoped everything was okay. Jay rushed out to the hall to see what was going on.

When he got out there, Fatima's door was open. He looked inside, and saw Portia hugging some dude with no shirt on. When Jay got a better look, he couldn't believe his eyes. It had to be a mirage. He was bugging.

Jay shook his head a few times. He had to be seeing things. Was that his mothafuckin' man standing there? His nigga? Wise? Jay said, "Get the fuck outta here! *Word, son?* No fuckin' way!"

Portia cried tears of joy as she stood aside and watched the two friends hurry towards each other grinning. Jay gave Wise a hearty pound, and they embraced like long lost brothers. Not on no sucker shit, but water came out of Jay's eyes. He really fucking cried. Wise was his man. That was his brother from another mother. And he was alive!

The big kids, Macy and Jayquan, had their own suite. They heard the loud talking in the hallway too, so they came out to be nosey. When they saw Wise, they both started jumping up and down, and screaming, "Uncle Wise! Uncle Wise!"

Wise laughed happily, and hugged them both. Falynn ran and got the other kids. Wise hugged all them too. The only two missing from the happy reunion were Cas and Laila. But not for long.

Jahseim ran down the hall to get his father. He banged on the door excitedly, screaming, "Daddy, Daddy!"

Cas jumped up and opened the door fast, afraid that something was wrong. He was relieved to see Jah smiling. Before he could ask him what was up, his little man blurted out, "Come and look, Pop! It's Uncle Wise!"

Cas looked at his son like he was crazy. The boy was clearly confused, and didn't know what he was talking about. Nonetheless, Cas took his outstretched little hand, and followed him down the hall.

When Casino got down there he saw that his son was right.

His man Wise was standing there just as plain as day. In the flesh. Cas' heart damn near stopped. Emotionally, he exclaimed, "*What the fuck?* Wise! *Oh shit!*"

Wise looked over and saw Cas, and grinned. He said, "Oh! My nigga! What up, boy?" He started towards him and gave him a pound.

Cas was kind of choked up for a minute. He gave his little homie a big bear hug. After that, he playfully jabbed Wise in the ribs. Wise just laughed.

Cas said, "Man, what the fuck are you doin' alive? Nigga, I should kill you for puttin' us through that!"

They all laughed, and the Three Musketeers shared a group hug. All of them were like children again, excited to be reunited. It was genuine crew love. The team was together again, and it felt damn good.

Jay, Cas, and Wise were all pretty tough guys, but there wasn't a dry eye in the circle. They weren't boohooing like sissies or anything, but there were definitely some happy tears shed.

Laila had heard Jahseim banging on the door, but at the time she was getting dressed. After she put on her shoes, she went out there to see what everybody was up to. Laila was amazed when she saw Wise. It was unbelievable. And the exuberance in the air was so wonderful. Everybody's eyes were a little red, so she could tell they had all been crying.

She hurried over there and hugged Wise, and it wasn't long before she was in tears too. His being alive was truly a miracle. Laila was especially thankful because she had oftentimes wondered if she was partly responsible for his death. She had got into that near fatal car crash, and he had come to the hospital to see about her. Even though she was in a coma at the time, she felt like it was sort of her fault he got shot. Like maybe if he hadn't come there, he wouldn't have died. But none of that mattered now. God was so good.

Fatima was still in the bedroom, but she overheard the reunion.

Her lovemaking session with Wise prompted her to take a quick shower. Afterwards, she threw on some clothes, and joined the gang about ten minutes later.

The whole family was in her suite. They were all laughing and reminiscing. Everyone looked so happy. It was great to see that. They were complete again. Fatima's heart was full of love.

Portia and Laila were so happy for Fatima. Their girl had her husband back. When they saw her, they ran and hugged her. Fatima grinned and embraced them, and they all cried happy tears. God was so good.

Jay, Cas, and the kids were all firing a million questions at Wise. And all at the same time. Wise laughed, and said he needed a minute to use the bathroom first. He joked about the morning breath he still had. Falynn had awakened him and Tima from a deep sleep, so he never got a chance to clean himself up.

Reluctantly, they all agreed to give him a little bit of space. It was like they just got him back, so nobody wanted to let go. Everybody said they'd wait right there for him.

Wise said he only wanted to tell the story one time, so he was glad everyone was together. Thrilled at the love he was being shown, he headed to the bathroom. It was clear that he'd been missed. He was really sorry for putting them through that, but he had his reasons. And it was all for their own good.

Around fifteen minutes later, Wise rejoined the family out front. The adults were all seated on the sofa and chairs. The kids were running around playing, with the exception of the teens, Macy and Jayquan. Those two were sprawled out on the floor, eager to hear Wise's story too.

While he was in the bathroom, Fatima told the fam how Wise had romantically crept up on her outside the night before. Still the same good natured dude, Wise just laughed at the teasing and ball breaking Cas and Jay gave him for being "all Romeo and shit" with his comeback.

There were two people there Wise didn't know yet, so he was

formally introduced to his latest nieces. Portia was pregnant when he "died", so he never got a chance to see the baby. Her and Jay's latest princess was named was Patrice, also known as Trixie. And come to find out, Cas and Laila had a baby too. Their darling little cherub's name was Skye.

Wise admired the little girls, somewhat amazed by the new additions to the family. They were both cutie pies. He congratulated his bros and sis-in-laws on their new heiresses, and then he made a comment that made Fatima show all thirty two teeth. He said him and her had to make some babies fast so they could catch up with them.

Fatima beamed when she heard that. She was ready to give him another baby right that second. As many times as they made love the night before, they may have already made one.

Macy couldn't take it anymore. She was outspoken, so she blurted out the question she was dying to ask. "So, Uncle Wise, how the hell did you find us out *here*? All way in the *South of France*?"

Wise just grinned. Macy was something else. He told her his mother had tracked them down. He said he figured them being out of the country was the perfect opportunity to show his face. He had a new identity, but he still wanted to be sure the time was right. He said he didn't want to incriminate any of them, so he just leaned back until some time passed.

Fatima smiled. Two days ago, she spoke to her mother-in-law. Rose had asked for the address of the hotel they were staying in, and Fatima's suite number as well. She said she needed it so she could "send Falynn something." That Rose was pretty slick.

Jayquan asked the million dollar question. "Uncle Wise, how did you do it? Tell us how you faked your own death. Pardon me y'all, but this seems like some television shit."

Portia popped Jayquan for cursing, but she couldn't help but laugh. Everybody did. Wise laughed too. Lil' Jay was mad candid, so all eyes were on him. It was time to tell his story.

Wise said, "I didn't plan it, but it happened like this. After I got shot…"

Portia interrupted Wise. After she gave it some thought, she thought it was best to send the kids across the hall. The details of Wise's ordeal were too explicit for them. She was there at that hospital when it all started. There was some serious gunplay involved in that incident. The children didn't need to hear a firsthand account about murder.

All the other grownups saw where Portia was coming from, so none of them disagreed. Jayquan looked at his father. You could tell he was about to ask if he could stay.

Jay shook his head before he could say a word. Jay said, "We'll fill you in later, lil' man."

Jayquan sucked his teeth, and mumbled something under his breath. He looked like he wanted to tell them something.

Macy had a funky little attitude too. She put her hand on her hip, and said, "Well, how 'bout the *babies*? Can they stay? They're not old enough to understand the stuff that y'all believe *we* shouldn't hear."

She had a point, so Trixie and Skye were allowed to stay. But Laila wasn't moved by Macy's attitude. She said, "You were right about that, honey. But I'll see *you* later."

Macy rolled her eyes, but she knew how far to go. You should've seen the pouts on her and Jayquan's faces. They irritably shooed Jazmin, Falynn, and Jahseim out the door. You could tell they didn't appreciate being treated like kids. But they would just have to get over it.

There was a lot to talk about, and they couldn't speak freely about guns and violence in front of impressionable children. It would look like they were glorifying negativity.

After the brats were gone, Wise went on to tell them how he and his accomplice had pulled everything off. He informed them that his sidekick was none other than his mother. He started at the beginning, right after he got shot. Like they all knew, the doctor had declared him dead. He said he was only sitting there now due to an act of God. God had given him another chance.

All of a sudden, there was a knock at the door. Wise grinned, and said, "Matter of fact, let her tell y'all."

Portia was the closest to the door, so she answered it. To their surprise, it was Wise's mother, Rose. She greeted everyone with a smile, and gave out hugs and kisses. She looked well, as usual. Rose was fit, and took care of herself. In fact, she had spent the entire morning getting pampered at the hotel spa. She was there right up until Wise called her while he was in the bathroom freshening up.

Wise had asked his mother to fly with him to Europe so he could reveal himself to the fam. Rose said she looked at it as an opportunity to vacation. But truthfully, she was afraid to let Wise out of her sight. Things had gone pretty smooth so far, but being a mother, she couldn't help but worry about her son. She prayed everyday that his cover wouldn't be blown.

Jay and Cas were happy to see Rose, but they wanted to know how she could have misled them to believe Wise was mistakenly cremated at the funeral home. They wanted to know why she didn't tell them so they could've helped.

Wise said it was for their own good that they didn't know anything. The stakes were too high, and they didn't know who was watching them. He reminded them about the shootout they had in the hospital parking lot, and the hot guns that could've put them away forever.

At the mention of the guns, everybody looked at Wise. Those things had just mysteriously disappeared after Portia hid them under Laila's hospital bed. Wise and Rose just smiled.

Rose said, "Why don't we just start from the beginning. And I'm sorry I lied to you guys, especially at the funeral parlor. Believe me, that wasn't easy. But as you'll hear in a moment, I had my reasons. Now somebody get me a glass of wine."

Rose got ready to tell it like only she could. Fatima sent for a bottle of chardonnay. Room service arrived with a chilled bottle on ice in two minutes. Fatima poured Rose a glass, and one for herself as well. She asked the others if they'd care for some. Portia and Laila accepted, but the men said they'd pass.

Rose sipped her wine, and began. "Now this is how it started. When Laila got into that terrible car accident, I just happened to be in the area meeting Wise for lunch that day. Me, him, and Falynn ate, and then we went shopping. We were shopping when Jay called and told Wise about Laila's car accident. When he got that call, he hurried to the hospital. I kept Falynn for him, and told him to call and keep me updated on Laila's condition."

Rose drank some more wine, and continued. "Not long after that, I got a call from you, Jay, saying Wise got shot while he was at the hospital. So I hurried down there to see about him as fast as I could. When I got to the hospital, there was a lot of turmoil in the lobby. There were police everywhere. There were news cameras, and everything. I slipped right by the chaos, and rushed upstairs to see about my son. I later found out that part of that commotion was you all getting arrested."

She sipped her wine again, and continued. "When I got upstairs, the doctor told me that my son had passed away. After hearing that news I was hysterical, but I asked if I could say goodbye. When I walked in the room, there was a nurse in there. She was a pretty young lady, and she was smiling. She told me not to cry anymore because I was the mother of a miracle. She said something told her to check Wise's vitals again before she pulled the sheet over him. She discovered that he had somehow regained a pulse."

You could tell that telling that story was emotional for Rose because her voice had cracked a little bit when she said that last part. She smiled, and looked up and said, "Thank you, Lord." After that, she was quiet for a few seconds.

Then Rose looked over at Jay and Cas. She and told them she wanted to tell them, but she found out they had trouble with the law before she could. She never got a chance to see them because they went straight to jail from the hospital lobby.

Rose said she sat by Wise's side and prayed. Then she and that nurse got to talking. That's when she learned all about the big shootout that left Wise wounded, and two other men dead. One of them was an innocent security officer. The nurse also disclosed to Rose the fact that the police were searching around the hospital for the murder weapons.

The nurse told her she witnessed how those detectives had detained Jay and Cas in the hallway, and called downstairs to have Portia and Fatima searched as soon as they stepped off the elevator. She said they seemed so sure the girls had those weapons, but she heard no guns had been recovered. A co-worker of hers who was down there had given her a firsthand account of what happened, so she gave Rose the rundown about the scuffle in the lobby, and told her all of Wise's friends had been arrested for fighting with the police.

Rose said she put two and two together, so she knew Wise would be arrested if the police knew he was alive. She couldn't stand the thought of him going to prison for murder, so she went for broke and propositioned the nurse. She told her she desperately needed her help, and would compensate her well for her services. Rose said she told her she wanted everyone to still think Wise was dead, and asked her to help her pull it off. After she laid it on her, she gave her the opportunity to name her price.

The nurse's name was Lillian Rodriguez, but everyone called her Lily for short. She was a 27 year old Puerto Rican sister who embraced the hip-hop culture. She loved the music, and often clubbed on the weekends. So she knew damn well who Wise was. Lily was multicultural, and she was tri-lingual. She spoke three languages; English, Spanish, and Money. She said she was in, but said Rose had to let her handle it her way.

Long story short, Lily never told the doctor or anyone else about Wise's pulse. She followed the normal procedures for death of a patient. She tagged his toe, and logged the time of his demise. She got the doctor who pronounced him dead to sign off on his death certificate, and had Wise taken down to the morgue.

She told Rose to trust her, and go find a funeral parlor she could have his body transported to. Rose did as she was told, and quickly made alliances with a mortician she could pay to help her pull it off. Before the day was over, the funeral home went to pick up Wise's body. Wise was heavily sedated the whole time, but he was alive.

Rose and Lily had exchanged telephone numbers so she could pay her when she got off work. Rose said she called Lily and asked if she knew whether or not the police had found those weapons yet. Lily told her she didn't think they had recovered them yet. Rose said she figured someone might've stopped off at Laila's room, and stashed them there. She asked Lily to please take a look in there for her if she got a chance. Lily said she would see what she could do.

Lily worked from 2 to 10 PM. Before her shift ended that night, she managed to nonchalantly get the guns from underneath Laila's bed. She put them in a bag, along with some antibiotics and medications for Wise. When she got off work, she met Rose and gave them to her.

Rose thanked her, but said she didn't know what to do with the medicine, since she wasn't a nurse. She begged Lily to accompany her to a place where she could look after Wise for her. Rose said she didn't want to take any chances with his health. The open gunshot wound he had left him susceptible to infection.

Lily was a sweetheart. She knew the odds, and she knew Wise's pulse was weak, so she went for it. That night, she and Rose personally drove Wise to Rose's summer home in the Hamptons. Lily took some time off work to stay there and nurse Wise back to health.

Rose had paid Lily about a million dollars for her services, and she took the liberty of destroying those guns so they would never resurface again. She said she left Wise in Long Island with Lily, and returned home to prepare his "funeral".

Rose asked Fatima to refill her wine glass. Afterwards, she said the next time she saw them all was at the funeral home. She said she was afraid to tell anyone Wise was alive, so she got the director to go along with her fabricated story about Wise being cremated. She admitted that the settlement money the mortician paid them had really come from Wise's bank account.

When Rose finished telling the story, everybody was just quiet for a minute. It sounded like a movie, or something. The setup she had masterminded was totally impeccable. And they finally found out what happened to those hot ass guns.

The gang couldn't thank Rose enough. Especially Portia. When those guns came up missing, she thought she was crazy. Wise thanked his mother again too. He said he couldn't really take credit for anything because by the time he woke up, he had already been "buried".

Rose was a genius. There was a death certificate that said Wise was dead, so he had a chance at a clean start. And he already had a new identity, so he was good. His new name was Marcus Jacob, and it was squeaky clean.

Wise reminded them that he was the one who had delivered the fatal shot to Mike Machete's dome. If he was alive, and the police had found those guns with their fingerprints on them, he would've been finished. He would've had to either own up to that body, or stand trial for it.

Fatima stood behind her man and massaged his shoulders. She couldn't believe it. All those times Fay said she saw her daddy, she was telling the truth. Fatima had figured Falynn was talking about photos Rose had of Wise, but her baby knew what she was talking about.

Fatima didn't want to seem narrow-minded because she was really thankful for the nurse who had saved Wise. But she couldn't help but wonder just how well she took care of him. She didn't bring it up yet, but she knew she wouldn't be able to rest until she asked him if he had sexed Miss Lily.

Rose looked over at the time on the clock, and announced that she had to go. She said she had a lunch date with a distinguished Frenchman she met. She stood up and smiled, and told the gang she would see them later. Rose waved at everybody, and made a graceful exit.

CHAPTER THIRTEEN

When they got back to the States, Portia and Jay were still getting along great. They were as close as they were the day they got married. Their love felt new and exciting. To make things even better, Wise was back in their lives. A missing void in the family had been filled, and the love in the air was genuine.

Cas and Laila were doing good, and Wise and Fatima were crazy about each other all over again. Portia was so glad that all her friends were happy. She felt superb. Jay appeared to be feeling the same way.

Portia had no idea that Jay was facing what was literally his biggest conflict ever. He hated having to string her along, but he felt like what she didn't know wouldn't hurt her. Jay had propositioned Ysatis about taking a lump sum of money from him, and breaking out. He gave her a copy of the agreement his lawyer had drafted. But he was pretty disappointed because she read it, and flat out refused. That bitch really pissed him off.

He doubled his already generous offer, and she still refused to sign it. Reluctantly, Jay tripled the offer. The bitch objected to that too. Now he was just waiting for her to make a move. He figured she was going to hire an attorney, or something. But she did nothing, except call him and leave messages about how much the baby looked like him, and how bad she wanted to see him.

That was the last month of her lease, and Jay wanted her to move on as soon as possible. Portia didn't even know he was still communicating with Ysatis.

At the end of the week, Jay got fed up and went to talk to her in person. When he got there, he didn't go inside. He just knocked on her apartment door and asked her what she wanted.

Ysatis rolled her eyes and made a face. She said, "I don't wanna talk about all that. Come in for a little while, Jay. Come sit down and hold your son."

Jay got impatient, so he came out on her hard. He said, "Yo, what the fuck is wrong with you? Don't you get it? It ain't gon' be none of that. I'm offering you a financial settlement, and that's it. You act like I wanted this. And I still don't know how you pulled this shit off. But that's it. I'm done with you. You better take this fuckin' money, and move on. I'ma give you enough so y'all be good. Go somewhere and start over. I don't wanna have *any* type of dealings with you. *None*. Do I make myself clear? Do you understand that?"

Ysatis looked hurt. She said, "So… So what you try'na say?"

Jay just looked at her like she was stupid. He didn't like repeating himself. He just said, "Look, I'm done talking."

Ysatis was on the brink of tears. He was being so cold towards her. She said, "Okay then, I guess I'll have to get back to you."

Jay said there was no need to call him. He told her to contact his attorney at the number on the agreement he sent her. She told him she threw those papers away. Jay shook his head like he was annoyed, and gave her the number again. He warned her that she'd better make up her mind quick, while the offer was still on the table. He let her know he wasn't about to be extorted, or anything.

She didn't respond, but it didn't seem like she was digesting what he was telling her. She just kept trying to get him to hold the baby. That broad was acting real dizzy, so Jay decided to break out.

On his way home that evening, he received a text message from Ysatis. It read, *"All I want is for us to be a family. You have to leave your wife ASAP. Tell her about us, before I do."*

Jay couldn't believe that bitch. She had to be crazy. All he wanted was her to get the fuck out of his life. She was really being impossible. He realized there was something really wrong with that girl. Against his will, Jay toyed around with the possibility of telling Portia. He would rather she hear it from him. If Ysatis started leaking, the word would be in the streets.

When he and Portia got back together, they promised each other there would be no secrets. The more he thought about it, he knew he had to tell P. But if Ysatis just took the money and broke out, he wouldn't have to hurt Portia like that. Jay kept his fingers crossed, and kept hope alive.

He mulled it over all week long. But still nothing. Another whole week had passed, and his attorney hadn't heard from Ysatis yet. But she kept on texting him these crazy lovesick messages that had little indirect threats in them. She must've been under the impression that she had him under pressure, or something. She kept saying she would expose him and tell his wife if he didn't come around. Jay wasn't going to give that bitch the satisfaction.

Jay prayed over it, and then he got some advice from his main mans, Casino and Wise. He decided it was time to come clean. The type of bitch he was dealing with, he knew it was only a matter of time before Portia found out. Everything in the dark always came to the light.

That Friday, Jay took the kids to his mother's house for the weekend. Saturday night, he finally got up the nerve to tell Portia he had to talk to her about something. Befittingly, the weather outside was rainy. It was dreary just like his mood.

Jay gave Portia flowers, and served her favorite wine to soften up the mood. Afterwards, he gave her a hot oil massage.

Portia enjoyed the royal treatment, but she had a feeling that whatever Jay had to talk to her about was pretty major. She wondered what it was this time. She was actually sort of scared. She prayed it didn't have anything to do with jail time again.

Was Street Life still under that federal investigation? Jay had told her they were cleared.

Jay massaged her lower back, and thought of the right way to start off. He said, "Listen, Kit Kat... What I'm about to say is not easy for me, but it's probably gon' be even harder for you. Believe me when I say that I *never* intended for this to happen. I *swear*, Ma. I don't wanna lose you. Not again. Seriously. I'm so *sorry*, P. I would *never* hurt you like this."

Portia was scared now for real. She didn't even know if she wanted to hear what he was about to tell her. It was big. She didn't know if she could take it. Lord, why her?

Portia took a deep breath, and sat up. Her stomach was turning. She felt like she was going to be sick, but she had to see his face.

Jay felt like shit. His stomach was turning too. He couldn't even look at her. But it was time for him to man up. He took a deep breath, and looked at his wife. Jay told Portia about the illegitimate child he had fathered.

After he broke the news to Portia, he stressed the fact that he hadn't cheated on her again. He explained to her that all that shit was a repercussion from that same incident she left him for. The same time with the same bitch.

Jay came clean about everything, including the fact that he had tried to pay Ysatis off. He even told Portia she threatened to expose him if he wouldn't be with her.

Portia's initial reaction was shock. She couldn't talk, or move. The pain in her chest had engulfed her. That mothafucka.

Jay kept yapping about how sorry he was. Meanwhile, Portia's emotions had shifted gears. The pain was replaced by rage, which triggered violence. She jumped up and slapped the taste out of Jay's mouth. She gave it everything she had, so she hit that nigga hard as hell.

Jay didn't even flinch. That shit hurt, but he knew she was hurting more. And he deserved it, so he would stand there and take as many slaps as he had too. Portia could vent by cursing him out, hitting him, or whatever else she needed to do to make herself feel better. He just needed to know she would stay.

Portia was mad as hell, so she should've kept fucking Jay up. But the truth was she didn't even have the strength. Not at the time. As angry as she was, that news had taken the breath out of her. She felt dizzy so she just sat down.

Despite her efforts not to cry, a lone tear ran down Portia's face. Just one. She wouldn't give that bastard the satisfaction, although she was crushed. Wow, Jay had a kid on her. Her husband had another baby. Damn, it hurt to breathe. How could she go on knowing Jay had fathered another woman's child?

Portia just stared ahead sort of blankly, but her mind was in a whirl. She wondered if Jay had known about that baby all along. Did that bastard fool her to come back to him under false pretense? Did he go through all that trouble just so he could shit on her again? Was their marriage some type of fucking charade?

Portia didn't say a word of what she was thinking to Jay. She just got up, and went upstairs to her bedroom. She needed some time to herself. She would've left the house, but she couldn't even see straight. And it was dark and raining out too. She didn't want to mess around and kill herself out there. That was how Laila got in the accident she had, driving while she was upset.

Upstairs, Portia began to sob like there was no tomorrow. She cried her heart out. The pain was unbearable. The poor thing was literally sick. She actually threw up twice.

Jay just sat downstairs where Portia left him with his head in his hands. He knew he had to give her some time alone. He just prayed she wouldn't start bringing suitcases downstairs.

About an hour later, he went upstairs to their bedroom. He turned the knob, relieved that the door wasn't locked. Jay paused, and pictured Portia sitting on the other side of the door with a fully loaded weapon, ready to discharge on him. That would probably serve him right. He walked inside the room.

To his surprise, she was just sitting up on the bed. Her eyes were puffy and red, so you could tell she'd been crying a lot. He knew he wasn't on his wife's favorites list, but he was compelled to tell her again how sorry he was.

Jay expected Portia to shout and tell him to go away, but she didn't. He quietly sat on the bed beside her, and placed his arm around her. At first, Portia was resistant. But after a minute, she began to quietly sob again.

Jay just held her in his arms and caressed her, as if he could massage away some of the pain. But her heart and soul were aching, so he knew that was impossible. Jay felt horrible. He knew how much Portia loved him. He was low for putting her through this. The fact that he'd hurt her so bad really hurt him too. Real talk.

Jay's eyes watered up. He too knew that their family would never be the same, so it was heartbreaking for him as well. He didn't know how he would look his children in their faces and tell them he had fathered another child. That definitely wouldn't be easy.

Jay just sat there holding Portia for a while. Sadly, he knew it could very well be the last time. That night he and his woman cried together, just like that song by the O'Jays. She wept openly in his arms, and he cried silent tears. Jay was no bitch, but the situation was fucked up. All Portia ever did was love him, and look how he'd repaid her.

Portia's emotions got the best of her for a while. But the more she thought about it, she wasn't pleased with the distressed damsel role she was displaying. And Jay was rubbing on her like he could sooth her pain.

Portia got fed up. She pushed Jay, and told him she didn't want him touching her anymore. The pain she felt was turning into anger again. She was on a real emotional rollercoaster.

Jay looked surprised, and a little hurt by her reaction. His eyes were red, so she could tell he'd shed a few tears. But what the fuck was he crying for? He didn't know her fucking pain. He was the one who had crushed her. The adulterous bastard.

Portia got up off the bed. She shook her head, and gave Jay the evil eye. She said, "Jay, I have to get away from you. *Right now*. I feel like *killing* you. Lemme go, before I hurt you."

Portia didn't yell, but her words cut through Jay like a knife. He knew he deserved that, but she really made him feel like shit. He didn't even protest because he had no wins. All he could do was give her some space, and pray to God.

Portia didn't say another word to Jay that night. She holed up in her office alone. She locked the door and rolled herself a nice blunt. She had some serious thinking to do.

She finally came out about three AM. She didn't see Jay, so she guessed he was asleep upstairs. She didn't want to see him yet, so she camped out on the sofa and half-watched a couple of movies. She was too wrapped up in her situation to really pay attention.

Portia stayed up all night long pondering. After some thought, she made up her mind. As hard as it was, she wasn't leaving Jay. She believed him when he said he loved her. She knew he hadn't intended to make a kid on her. She had seen those tears in his eyes. For him to cry, he must've really been sorry. She didn't know how she could forgive him, but she prayed over time she would be able to.

Over the next few days, Portia took care of her house and kids as usual. But she threw Jay a lot of shade because she was really hurt. She had once prided herself in having a respectable marriage, but Jay had singlehandedly managed to make a circus of their nuptials. She still couldn't believe he had an outside child. She just kept wondering how.

Every day she wondered if he lied to her about using a condom. Did he not protect himself when he ran up in another bitch? Portia had to ask him about that again. She couldn't help it.

She went up to Jay and begged him to tell her the truth. He swore on every bible they had in the house. He told her he didn't know how that bitch got pregnant. He said he remembered flushing the condom down the toilet, and he was a hundred percent sure that it hadn't broken.

Even though it was killing her, Portia wanted more details. Before she could accept it and make peace, she had to know how it had come to be. Jay was honest, and told her he got the rubber from Ysatis.

That's when Portia figured it out. She knew it wasn't like Jay to run up in no bitch raw. When she first met him, he was adamant about using protection. They had used condoms for years. Jay had even asked her to go get tested for AIDS. And only after they proved to each other that they were safe did he feel comfortable enough to engage in unprotected sex with her.

Portia believed her husband. Jay was a condom user. If he said he had strapped up, then he had strapped up. But she came to the conclusion that the fool had been set up. Portia was no dummy. She knew bitches were foul. If Ysatis had seduced Jay like he claimed she did, then she was smart enough to plan that pregnancy. Portia was just upset that Jay was stupid enough to fall for the okie doke. Or had she given him too much credit? Nah, he was smarter than that.

Portia told him her theory. She believed Ysatis stuck a pinhole in that condom before she gave it to him. She told Jay he was an idiot for letting some dumb, young bitch get the drop on him like that.

After she berated him, he just hung his head in shame. She could tell he felt like an asshole, and that was good for him. Portia wasn't being mean. Look what the fuck he had done to her. He was lucky she was still there. She told that mothafucka it would be a long time before she forgave him for hurting her the way he had. After that conversation, she went back into her shell.

$ $ $ $

Portia was really going through it about that baby, but somehow she managed. She spent her days putting up a front in front of her children, and her nights giving Jay the cold shoulder every way she could think of.

That Tuesday, she got a call from her cousin Melanie. Mel told her she was still starring in porn. And she wanted Portia to get into the business with her. She was referring to the behind the scenes aspect, of course.

Mel told her she had been given an ultimatum by this disrespectful, sleaze ball director. He told her if she didn't let her co-star cum in her mouth, she was fired. She said she had told him to kiss her ass, and stormed off the set. She told Portia that had prompted her decision to form her own porn production company. She said she left California to come and get her, so she could be her partner.

Mel said, "P, I'm tellin' you. We gonna blow this shit up. I don't see anything wrong with a couple of females capitalizing off of sex. Men been doin' it for centuries. Just think of it as another business venture, and keep an open mind. I got a whole team of beautiful, professional bitches who wanna be down. Everybody tired of these niggas' bullshit. These ladies are trained actresses, and they ready to do the damn thing. Come on, P. You the one who taught me to think big."

Portia laughed. Her crazy cousin wouldn't take no for an answer, so she just told her she would think about it. But that was the furthest thing from her mind. Pornography wasn't really where she was right now. And furthermore, her life was in shambles.

But Portia couldn't tell Mel what she was going through. That wasn't her business. She wished Melanie luck, and told her to be careful out there. As much as Portia disapproved, she couldn't judge her cousin. Not with the wild past she had.

$ $ $ $

Three more days had passed, and Portia barely said a word to Jay. She didn't leave him behind that shit, but she had him on ice. He couldn't even sleep in the bed with her. Jay slept in one of the guest rooms.

That was better than sleeping in separate houses, but that shit was getting to Jay. They were living like they were strangers under the same roof. He would hear her on the phone laughing and talking with her friends, and then when he'd come in, she'd walk out the room. Either that, or she just gave him the silent treatment and ignored him completely.

Jay was trying everything to get out the doghouse. He had upgraded Portia's Benz to a 2010, and he just splurged on an exquisite jewelry collection for her. There were diamonds of every color in the pieces, from canary to chocolate. He'd been leaving expensive gifts conspicuously placed throughout the house, but Portia wouldn't even acknowledge them. She acted like she couldn't have been more unimpressed.

Jay knew she needed time to cool off. He figured that was natural. But at the rate she was slipping away from him, he just didn't know. That shit really had him by the balls. But he wasn't about to let her walk out of his life again. No way.

$ $ $ $

Portia was acting like she didn't care, but she was driving herself crazy. She was just sitting around obsessing over Jay's little baby mama. Out of the blue, she got a text from her cousin Mel. It was one of those "Forward to ten people and make a wish" kind. The first line read, *"The woman reading this is strong and beautiful..."*

Portia smiled, and sent it back to Mel. She also forwarded it to

Laila, Fatima, and a few other contacts in her BlackBerry. After that, she called her crazy cousin to see what she was up to. Last time they spoke, Mel tried to get her in the business.

Mel saw the caller-ID when Portia called, so she knew it was her. She grinned, and answered on the third ring. "P-Ski in 'da place to be! My American idol! What up, big cuz?"

Portia laughed at the hearty way her crazy cousin greeted her. "Melly Mel. What's good, baby girl?"

Portia and Mel played catch-up. In minutes, Mel briefed her on the progress she had made with her porn production company. She excitedly told Portia she had already produced a film, and invited her to check it out. Portia said sure, so Mel agreed to come by the house later.

About eleven that night, Portia sat in her office with Mel and watched the first film. After the first three minutes, she shut it off. It was simply horrible. The film was poorly edited, and the director obviously didn't have a clue. There had been better sex tapes created in people's bedrooms.

Melanie looked sad when Portia told her the truth. She said, "Damn, P. If you think you can do better, then help me out."

Portia grinned, and said, "I can't get too involved in this, Mel, but I'll do what I can to help you."

Melanie looked at her like she didn't believe her. When she saw that Portia looked sincere, she screamed for joy. "That's what's up, partner! Lovers Lane Productions on the rise! Holla!"

Portia laughed. "I didn't say all that. Lovers Lane Productions?"

Mel said, "Yes. Lovers *Lane*, like our last name. Get it?"

Portia nodded, and laughed. She did need something to keep her occupied.

$ $ $ $

Jay couldn't take it anymore. That night he approached Portia and demanded that she talk to him. At first, that was like trying to make a stone statue speak. She wouldn't even look at him. And when she did, her stare was so blank it was like she was looking through him. He didn't know which was worse. Boy, Portia could make a dude feel low. But he knew he deserved it.

She tried to walk pass him, but Jay wasn't giving up. He had to make her talk to him. He grabbed her arm, and then he grabbed the back of her neck and looked her in the eyes.

He spoke from his heart. "I'm *sorry*, Ma. But we can't let this shit ruin us. You *know* what we got. I'd rather cut off my fuckin' arm than hurt you like this, P! Don't you know that? Come on! This shit is killin' me!"

Portia softened up a little. She did know what they had, and it terrified her that they were on the brink of obliteration. She loved Jay. He was her man, and she wanted him to fix it. They were broken, and she wanted them to be whole again. There was nothing more important to her than their family. They were a team. She needed him.

Jay felt what Portia was feeling. He needed her too. He hugged his wife tight. She didn't hug him back, but she didn't push him away either. Jay cupped her chin in his hand, and forced her to look in his eyes.

He said, "I love you, P. Ain't *nothin'* comin' between us. You hear me? *Nothin'*. That's my word! And *nobody* either. I *love* you. You hear me?"

Portia could tell he meant what he said. She was on the brink of tears, so she just nodded.

Jay said, "We gon' be a'ight, Kit Kat. I promise you."

Portia wrapped her arms around him. For the first time since she heard the news, she believed that too. They were going to be alright. She forgave Jay. She loved him, so she had to.

Portia wanted to step to that bitch Ysatis for coming between them but she wondered what relief that would bring. What was done was done already. And no matter how much it hurt her, she wanted to be involved with everything hands on.

Portia was a decent woman. She didn't believe they should penalize a child that didn't ask to come there, just because his mother was a conniving bitch. But she made Jay promise her he would avoid one on one time with Ysatis at all costs.

Jay didn't have a problem with that. They also agreed that they shouldn't tell their children yet. There was no point in disrupting their lives. School was about to start in a couple of weeks, so that's where their minds needed to be. Especially Lil' Jay. He was a sophomore in high school now.

CHAPTER FOURTEEN

Labor Day came and went, and the kids went back to school. Lil' Jay was on the basketball team that year, and he was amazed by the amount of attention he was getting from the girls. Macy's friends in particular. Some of them were pretty flirtatious with him.

Jayquan was no fool. He knew that meant they were jocking him. He had a feeling he would be getting a lot of action that year. And he got his learner's permit over the summer so he was driving. He couldn't wait until he turned sixteen. That's when he was getting a car. Then he would be getting more pussy that he could handle.

Jayquan was fronting somewhat. He was actually still a virgin. This girl gave him a blowjob one time, and he made it to third base with two other girls. But that was it. He probably could've scored if he'd wanted to, but he was sort of nervous. He didn't want to appear all inexperienced his first time. He decided he would speak to his uncles, Cas and Wise. He knew they would give him some pointers.

Jayquan was a sophomore in high school that fall, and Macy was in the eleventh grade. They were so close, everyone sort of thought they were related.

Macy couldn't believe the way her friends were sweating Jayquan. Those were the same girls who had pretty much ignored him when he was a freshman. But she had to admit, Jayquan

143

grew up over the summer. He was quite handsome. He'd always been a cute boy, but now he was maturing. Lil' Jay was even growing a mustache.

Macy got a little tight when all those other girls were checking for him. But she didn't say anything. She just told herself she had home court advantage. She realized she wasn't supposed to feel like that about Jayquan, but she couldn't help it. It was his swagger that she was attracted to.

One day, Macy and her friend, Nicole, were walking down the hallway at school. They were en route to their fourth period algebra class. For the umpteenth time that day, Nicole was begging her to hook her up with Jayquan. Macy told her she would, but Nicole's words went in one of her ears, and came out of the other. There was no way she was about to do that.

At the end of the school day, Nicole ran into Jayquan herself. She could tell that Macy wasn't going to help her, so she made her move. She cornered him, and pressed her phone number in his hand. After that, she licked her glossy lips to cement her intentions.

Lil' Jay didn't have that much experience as far as girls were concerned, but he knew to be cool. He had learned that from his father and his uncles, Cas and Wise. So he would never sweat a girl, no matter how pretty she was. Jayquan was a naturally laid back type of dude anyway, so he acted totally indifferent towards Nicole.

He just looked at the number and shrugged. His nonchalant response to her advance was, "I don't know, shorty... I *might* call you."

Nicole was turned on by his reluctance. It was a challenge. She said, "You really should. Trust me, Jayquan. Let me show you what you been missin', baby." She eyed him seductively.

Jayquan didn't like the way she was pressing him. Nicole came on too strong. Bagging her was so easy he didn't even want her. He just took the number, and brushed her off.

In Nicole's eyes, Jayquan's acceptance of her phone number solidified their relationship. Now she had bragging rights. She hurried to tell her friends she was his new girlfriend. She especially couldn't wait to tell Macy.

When Macy got that news from Nicole, she didn't appreciate it one bit. She didn't say anything to Jayquan, but she developed a serious attitude towards him.

$ $ $ $

Portia prayed about her situation for days. She talked to her girls about it and got some feedback. Fatima and Laila were sympathetic with her but they both told her to get over it, and get involved. They said it wasn't the time to be passive. Another woman had a baby by her husband. They said shutting Jay out could push him right into that bitch's arms.

After that, Portia thought about it hard. She changed her mind about six times, but she finally made her decision. She told Jay she wanted to go with him to see Ysatis. There were some ground rules that needed to be set. There were boundaries she didn't want crossed. Portia was honest with Jay, and voiced all her concerns.

Number one, she feared an ongoing affair between him and his little baby mama, so she didn't want him alone with her. Under no circumstances. He said she never had to worry about anything happening between them again, but Portia didn't care. If he was weak enough to hit that once, he might slip again. She knew how conniving hoes could be, and temptation was a bitch.

She told Jay she wasn't against him supporting his child. She believed he should keep a roof over the baby's head. She would hate for the girl to wind up in a shelter, or something. She wasn't that dirty. But she told Jay he had to downsize the bitch immediately. He could put her somewhere decent, but that Central Park apartment shit was unacceptable. It was okay to provide for the kid, but the goal should be to gear that bitch towards independence.

Jay couldn't agree more, so he didn't beef with a word Portia said. He knew he was asking a lot of her. And Portia was right. He knew that scallywag was going to make a move to sue him for support sooner or later, so they did need to come to some type of financial agreement. He had to address the matter. Portia being so understanding about the situation definitely made it easier. He was married to a class act.

Jay already knew what a woman he had, but Portia managed to supersede the already high regards he had for her. After what he did, he wasn't even worthy of her. And she was standing by his side. He would never fuck that up again. He put that on his life.

The next day, Portia accompanied him to Ysatis' apartment. Jay felt better having her there with him. He didn't want any secrets between them. And he damn sure didn't want her suspecting anything when it came to Ysatis. He didn't have any feelings for that girl whatsoever.

When Jay called that morning and told her he was stopping by to talk, Ysatis got excited. She had purposely dressed in a miniskirt, and rehearsed what she would say to him. She planned to somehow convince him that he should be with her. She opened the door with this big smile on her face, but she frowned when she saw Portia standing there. Words couldn't express her disappointment when Jay introduced her to his wife.

Portia saw the disappointed look on that bitch's face. She knew Ysatis would be surprised to see her. Portia gave her attire a disapproving once-over. The bitch had on a micro mini jean skirt with no stockings on underneath, a pair of tan Uggs, and a low-cut sweater. The sweater plunged so low in the front you could see the color of her lace push-up bra.

From all the legs and cleavage Ysatis was showing, it was obvious she was trying to tempt her husband. Portia already knew what type of bitch she was dealing with, but she still had a lot of fucking nerve. Portia wanted to punch that trashy skeezer right in the face, but she handled it like a woman. She marched inside the apartment before Jay did, ready to lay down the law.

Jay gave Portia total control. He barely said anything. The first thing she did was demand to see the baby. Ysatis reluctantly got the baby from his bassinette where he was sleeping. Portia took him from her arms and got a good look at him. The baby stretched, and opened his eyes.

Portia had thought about demanding another DNA test. There was a small part of her that was still in denial. But when she saw that baby, she knew there was no point. Jay was the father. The baby looked like him. He was a handsome little fellow. Portia felt like someone had just deflated the air from her lungs.

But she couldn't let that bitch feel like she got the best of her. She handed her baby back to her, and stuck to her original plans. Portia ran down a list of rules, and told her how things would be from then on. She told Ysatis she and the baby would be moving somewhere else, and said "they" would decide how much financial support "they" would give her. Portia told her that having a child by Jay wasn't going to be her retirement plan, so she should aspire to do something with her life. She reminded her about the college degree her husband helped her get, and told her to find something in her field.

When Portia was done laying down the rules, she told Ysatis she knew she got pregnant by sabotaging the rubber Jay used. Ysatis was so surprised when she said that, she didn't even deny it. She just wondered how Portia knew.

Ysatis watched and listened in disbelief. Jay let his wife do all the talking. She felt like a child when Portia was done with her. She especially didn't like the way she had examined her baby. Who the fuck did she think she was?

And Jay didn't even stand up for her. He barely said a word the whole time they were there. And he wouldn't even really look at her. Damn, he was really acting like he didn't love her. Or was he just trying to be funny?

Ysatis came to the conclusion that he was just putting up a front because his wife was there. She wasn't giving up on them. They were going to be together. Whether he wanted to, or not.

$ $ $ $

A few days later, Ysatis sat thinking about how unhappy she was. She hated the way things were going between her and Jay. She was still salty about the way Portia had shown up with him and started giving her orders. It was hard to believe Jay had given his wife that much authority. They seemed to be a pretty close couple. Jay having a new baby didn't appear to be tearing them apart, as she would have hoped and imagined.

Ysatis had planned on her and Jay being a couple, but shit wasn't going her way. She wanted him to move in with her, but his wife told her to start looking for an apartment. Her lease ran out in a few days so she had to move fast. She didn't have any money, so she had to do what Jay said.

That didn't sit well with Ysatis. She was seething about the way Jay was doing her. She believed he needed a wakeup call. Instead of sulking around and passively letting his wife control things, she decided to take a proactive stand.

That night, Ysatis called Jay and faked an emergency. She lied and said the baby was sick, and needed to go to the hospital.

Jay went for it. He showed up at her apartment pretty fast, but he brought Cas along with him. They were in the City when she called. By car, they were only about fifteen minutes away. Jay asked Cas to accompany him because he was determined to never be alone with Ysatis. He gave Portia his word that he wouldn't, and he didn't even want to.

When he got there and saw that the baby was fine, he got real mad. They weren't about to start playing those type of games. He told that crazy bitch that would be the last time he believed her lying ass about anything. Jay hated a fucking liar.

Cas saw how upset Jay was getting, so he told him they should break out. Jay decided to take his advice. He came to the conclusion that Ysatis was stupid, and unreasonable. He was done.

When she saw Jay about to leave, she begged him to stay so they could talk. Jay told her there was nothing to talk about. He said he would take care of the kid, and that was that. He told her he was done with her. He headed towards the door.

Ysatis made a face. She didn't want to let it go. She grabbed his arm, and venomously spat, "Jay, remember what happened to my brother? Don't forget, I got some *dirt* on yo' ass. Now I *said* I wanna *talk* to you."

Jay looked at her hand on his arm like it was covered in cockroach shit. He shoved her off him, and then he looked at her like she had lost her mind. Her violating his space almost caused him to blow his top, so he warned her. "Yo, don't ever touch me again. You's a dumb ass fuckin' broad."

Jay thought about what she said, and glanced at Cas. Cas gave him a look. Neither of them could believe she took it there. She brought up them killing her brother. The nigga who killed Humble. She had the nerve to throw that shit in Jay's face. They had done her a favor by killing that scumbag, Nasty Neal. She said he had molested and raped her for years.

Ysatis was young and dumb, but she should've known better than to threaten Jay. She already knew how he got down. And she said that slick shit in front of Cas too. Come on, they killed her brother.

Neither of them really responded to her little indirect threat, so she was foolish enough to believe that meant she had the upper hand. Assuming the ball was in her court now, Ysatis gave Jay a little smirk. Had she been smart, she would've feared for her life.

Jay had never been a talker, but anybody that knew him knew he would never tolerate that type of talk from anyone. Let alone some dizzy, conniving bitch. Who the fuck was she threatening? That girl was out of her mind. Jay could've choked the life out of that trick right then and there. She was asking for it, but he kept his cool. It was time for them to go. Ysatis didn't know what she had just done.

As they were walking out the door, she crossed her arms. Upset that Jay was still leaving, she said, "You better think about what I said. I'm telling you."

Jay just nodded. She could bet on that. He would never forget. Jay took threats very seriously, so she was digging a hole. He glanced over at Cas. He looked like he was thinking the same thing.

$ $ $ $

Laila hadn't told Macy yet, but she had been secretly planning her Sweet Sixteenth birthday party. When Laila told Cas, he wanted to go all out. He hired an event planner, and offered to pay for everything.

When Cas ran everything he had in mind down to Laila, she was really impressed. The only thing she objected to was the new car he wanted to buy Macy. She thought her daughter needed a little more driving experience. Maybe she would be ready in another year, when she was a senior.

Macy was turning sixteen, and Cas knew what a milestone that was. The more he thought about it, he wanted everything to be done her way. That was her day. That notion prompted him to let Macy know about their plans to surprise her. She could plan the party the way she wanted, and he would just finance it.

When Macy found out, she was absolutely thrilled. Especially when Cas told her the sky was the limit. She grinned, and gave him a big hug.

Cas just smiled. That hug made his day. He called Brianne, the party planner he'd hired, and instructed her to sit down with

Macy. He told her to concoct a bash fit for a teen queen. Brianne told him she would make sure it was the party of the year.

A few weeks later, they had the party at their house, which Macy referred to as "the castle". All her friends from school were there, and a few friends from her old neighborhood in Brooklyn as well. Some of the children of their wealthy neighbors, a few of which were celebrities and major players in the entertainment industry, also came out.

The party planner, Brianne, booked two of Macy's favorite artists to perform, Fabolous and Trey Songz. She even got MTV to come out and film footage for a feature on their "My Super Sweet 16" reality show.

Macy was delighted. The funniest part of the night was when Jayquan showed up fronting in his father's Ferrari. All her friends were sweating him. He looked good too.

Jay let Lil' Jay rock that night. He didn't mind because he knew his son was a pretty good driver. He had taught Jayquan himself, so he gave him a one-time pass. It paid off too. The girls were on him hard.

Needless to say, Macy and Jayquan both had a great time. Everybody had a ball, including the adults. The catered food was good too. At the end of the night, the servers brought out a huge cake made by Duff Goldman, the dude from the show "Ace of Cakes" on The Food Network. The cake was shaped like a candy apple red Mercedes Benz. What really made the cake hot was the chrome on it, and the wheels were actually spinning. Trey Songz sang a soulful, flirtatious rendition of "Happy Birthday" to Macy, and she blew out the candles.

Right before they cut the cake, Cas surprised Macy with the real live version of the same exact car. He copped her a candy apple red 2009 C-Class Mercedes Benz, with the wood grain dash and peanut butter leather interior.

Macy was ecstatic about her baby Benz. She was jumping up

and down, and screaming at the top of her lungs. Even though her mother said she couldn't drive it to school yet.

Cas kicked out a lot of money for that party. The cake alone cost two stacks. Laila told him he was crazy for spending two thousand dollars on a cake, but he didn't mind. He loved Macy. She was his stepdaughter, and she was a princess. Macy was a good girl. She got good grades all the time, and did what she was told. She always helped out around the house, and she also helped out with her little sister, Skye, a lot. She helped out with his son, Jahseim, too. Macy deserved to be spoiled. Her father wasn't able to do it, so Cas was glad he was in a position to make that happen.

At the end of the night, Macy was totally over. She had the party of her dreams. The only thing sad about the night was the fact that her sister, Pebbles, wasn't there to share the moment with her. They were born a year and a day apart. When they were small, their mother used to give them a double birthday party every year. Macy imagined what a smash it would've been if that was their party together. But she knew her sister was there in spirit.

Macy looked up at the sky. She whispered, "Dang, I miss you, Pebbles. You really should've been here, sis."

CHAPTER FIFTEEN

Fatima was on her cell phone, in the middle of a conversation with Portia. They were talking about Jay's new outside child, amongst other things. After they were on the phone for about an hour, the friends said goodnight.

After Fatima hung up, she went to check on her daughter. Falynn was asleep, and just fine. Fatima decided to lie down in her bedroom and watch a movie. As she flipped through cable channels, she said another quick prayer that Wise wouldn't be noticed while he was out.

She was glad her husband was alive and well, and she didn't want to risk him being spotted. Wise just couldn't stay his jackrabbit ass in the house. He had gone to play golf with Jay and Cas earlier, and hadn't returned yet. He had put on a hat and dark glasses before he left, and assured her that he wouldn't go anywhere he might be seen.

Fatima knew part of the reason he had left out was because they'd unofficially had their first argument. She was upset about the fact that he told her he'd secretly had cameras installed throughout the house. He told her he had been watching her just about the whole time he was gone. He said he had seen some pretty out of control footage of Fatima partying, doing drugs, and engaged in lesbian sex with her former live-in lover, Cheyenne. Wise referred to Cheyenne as her "little nasty Chinese bitch".

Fatima was ashamed of the fact that he'd seen her doing all that stuff. He was dead wrong for that. She felt like he had violated her privacy. Wise said that was his house, and she was his wife, so he had every right.

Fatima said if he managed to do all that, he could have found the time to let her know he was alive and well. She still couldn't believe he had put her through all that grief. A part of her had died with him. She almost went down behind that shit.

Wise reminded her that he had his reasons for not telling anyone he was alive. Then he smacked her on the ass and said he was glad she didn't have any men in his house. But he told Fatima he didn't appreciate seeing Cheyenne eating her pussy. He said he used to get real mad looking at that bitch's face in his pie.

Wise hated to admit it, but he jerked off to the footage a few times. He liked watching how much Fatima enjoyed it. He said he was glad he hadn't seen her eating any pussy. He laughed, and said she was a real "pillow princess".

Wise thought he was such a comedian. Fatima had to laugh when he said that, but she really felt violated. If she had known he was watching, she would have never done any of that stuff. She asked I-Spy how he'd pulled it off. He told her he had the cameras installed when she wasn't at home. He said there were even a couple of times he was in the house when she was asleep.

Fatima asked him about one particular night. Not long after he "died", she'd had this extremely vivid erotic dream that they were intimate. She wanted to know if that was real. Wise admitted that one night he put a "harmless little pill" in a bottle of water he knew she would drink. He said after she fell out, he made love to her. He said he had missed her so bad he couldn't help it. That was the only reason he took a chance.

Fatima shook her head. Back then she had thought she was crazy. When she woke up from her "dream", she ran over Portia's house and told her Wise visited her from the grave.

Wise had the nerve to laugh when she told him that. Fatima

wanted to kill him. She asked why he had stopped coming over and drugging her, and fucking the shit out of her. He said she started having too many people at the house. And then there were people actually staying with her.

Wise said he knew about Callie too. He said he saw Callie on camera searching through her shit. He wasn't even surprised that she stole Fatima's jewelry and identity. Fatima asked why he hadn't at least given her some type of sign about Callie.

Wise told her she needed to learn a lesson about no-good people on her own. He said Fatima was too naïve sometimes. People like her got taken advantage of. He said she set herself up for what happened to her, but the stuff Callie stole could easily be replaced. It wasn't important enough to blow his cover over.

Wise said he had seen Callie and her man sexing all over the house, but they left before she came back in town. After that, things seemed pretty quiet so he didn't feel the need to monitor the house as much. He said he just checked on her and Fay a couple of times a day.

Wise admitted that from time to time he was occupied with some female company he had imported for entertainment. So there were a few days that he didn't even look at any footage. He said one day something just told him to tune in, and see what was going on. He couldn't believe when he saw that nigga Smoke holding her hostage. He recognized that snake as Callie's boyfriend the minute he saw him on the video. He said he hurried to the house as fast as he could.

He said when he finally got there he saw that nigga Smoke trying to get away. He demonstrated how he crept up on him and dropped him. He said after that, he ran in the house and saw her passed out so he called the paramedics immediately. He said he checked to make sure she had a pulse, and then he ran around looking for his daughter. Wise said he found Falynn in the trunk of her car. She was so shook up, he took her with him so he could calm her down. He said they broke out just before the ambulance showed up. The paramedics must've called the police.

Fatima was speechless after she heard that story. Wow. Now it all made sense. It was Wise who had saved them. She asked him why Falynn said the man who took her had dreadlocks. He laughed, and said he was wearing a disguise.

Wise told her she should've been happy he had invaded her privacy. He said having those cameras put in turned out to be a good thing. Without them, he would have never showed up to save her and Fay's lives. Fatima couldn't argue with that. She was definitely grateful to him.

But while they were being so honest with each other, she told Wise she didn't appreciate him being "entertained" by other women during his hiatus. She said he better not have fucked around and brought something back to her. She scowled, and asked him if he'd used rubbers with those bitches.

Wise said, "Hell yeah, I used rubbers! I survived getting shot, so you think I'ma let some *ass* fuck around and take me out? Come on, ma."

That was the correct answer, but Fatima wasn't satisfied yet. She wanted to know if he'd messed with his nurse, Lily. She said, "So… Did you fuck the nurse too?"

Wise got tired of her questioning him. He sucked his teeth, and "No! That's what you wanna hear, right? You happy now?" He shook his head like he was annoyed with her. After that, he announced that he was going to play golf with his mans.

That was hours ago. Fatima prayed for the umpteenth time that he would be okay, and not be spotted out there. She was scared because she felt like he was only safe at home. Their property was now gated, and you needed a code to get inside the iron fence. And it was surrounded with an invisible electric fence as well. There were also cameras everywhere, so no one could get close to their house without being seen. They had really beefed up security, and it was all Wise's idea. After what happened with that bastard Smoke, they weren't taking any chances.

$ \qquad $ \qquad $ \qquad $

A couple of weeks later, Macy told Laila she wanted to go stay over Portia's for the weekend. She said she was supposed to help Jayquan with a school project. It was the end of the semester, and the project would count for thirty percent of his grade.

Laila didn't object. She knew how close those two were. They had grown up together, so they were like family. Laila reminded Macy to take some church clothes with her. Portia had been attending Sunday service lately, and she usually took the kids with her too.

Macy asked if she could drive her new car over there. Surprisingly, Laila didn't object. She rode in the car with her daughter quite a few times. She let Macy chauffer her around so she could check out her driving skills. She had to admit the girl drove pretty well. She was cautious, and she listened.

Laila had sent her to the local supermarket alone a couple of times, and Macy had done okay. Jay and Portia's home was only about fifteen minutes away, so Laila said a prayer and let her daughter go.

Macy got ready to go quick, as if she might change her mind. Laila laughed at her little thirsty ass, but she understood. She could only imagine having a pretty red Benz that she couldn't drive. It was probably killing her.

Jayquan was waiting for Macy when she pulled up at his house. She had called to let him know she'd be driving over. He opened her door, and told her to move over. He said he wanted to take the Benz for a spin.

Macy laughed, and hopped over to the passenger side. She warned Lil' Jay not to act stupid and drive too fast. He hopped in, buckled up, and took off. Macy giggled, and buckled her seatbelt too. They headed for the mall so they could floss a little bit.

Jayquan couldn't wait until he turned sixteen. He was dying to get his first whip. He wanted a new car now. He was working on his father just about everyday. He needed that joint fast. So what if he wasn't old enough to get his driver's license yet. He had a learner's permit, and he could drive his ass off.

After they came out of the mall, he and Macy rode around fronting for a while. Jayquan had his favorite record on repeat, "Empire State", by Jay-Z and Alicia Keys. Macy loved that song too, so she kept singing the hook while he rapped.

"Welcome to New York, concrete jungle where dreams are made of - there's nothing you can't do. Now you're in New York, these streets will make you feel brand new - these lights will inspire you. Let's hear it for New York, New York, New York…"

About an hour later, Macy suggested they get something to eat. They talked about Jayquan's school project over a burger and a milkshake. She told him they should stay up late, and start working on it that night. That way they could have some of their Saturday afternoon free to do something fun.

The next day was Saturday, and Portia had planned a family day for all of them. But she and Jay just winded up taking their little ones, Jazmin and Trixie, out with them. Lil' Jay and Macy were exempt because of the schoolwork they had to do.

Late that afternoon, Jayquan and Macy were putting the finishing touches on his project when Macy struck up a casual conversation about making out. She beat around the bush for a little while, and then she got bold. She asked, "Jayquan, have you done it yet?"

Jayquan paused for a second. He didn't want to seem uncool, but technically he was still a virgin. He had sampled the lips of this white girl named Becky when he was in the ninth grade. She gave him and his homeboy Reggie blowjobs in the football locker room.

He figured there was no point in lying to Macy. They talked

about all kinds of stuff, so Jayquan told the truth. "Nah, not really."

Macy's face brightened up. That was good news.

Jayquan continued. "But I got me some face before, though. From this White girl."

Macy looked at him like she didn't understand. "What's face?"

"Face is neck, silly."

Macy said, "And what the hell is neck?"

Lil' Jay humped the air and pretended he was holding a girl's head in front of his crotch. "You fuck 'em in the face and neck. Get it?"

Macy sucked her teeth and rolled her eyes. That boy was crazy. She crossed her arms, and asked him, "Oh, so you like White girls now?"

"Nah", Jayquan said quickly. "She just wanted to do it. Ain't no *Black* girl ask me."

Macy shook her head at him. "Just be quiet. Stop while you're ahead."

She moved on to the question she really wanted to ask. "So what's up with you and Nicole? You know she wants to have sex with you, right? She's been telling everyone it's goin' down next weekend."

Jayquan laughed. "I just told her that to make her back off."

Macy was relieved. She said, "Good, 'cause she get around."

Jayquan smiled. "Look at you hatin'."

Macy said, "I ain't hatin'. I'm just lookin' out for you."

He said, "Nah, I know. But Nicole was pressin' me too hard. Your homegirl is too pushy for me. It's like she wanna be the dude. *I'm* supposed to try to hit that, not the other way around. *I'm* the one with the dick. *I'm* the man. I don't like easy, *or* pushy bitches. So she ain't gettin' none of this." Jayquan popped his collar, like he was the shit.

Normally Macy would have said something to insult his conceited behind. That was the way they usually kidded around.

But there was something about the way Jayquan wasn't impressed with Nicole's sexual promises. Macy liked that. It was kind of sexy. Her mother and her aunts, Portia and Fatima, had drilled in her head that boys only wanted one thing. She hated a thirsty guy. That was a turnoff.

She had thought all boys were the same, but Jayquan was different. Macy didn't say anything, but she found herself very much attracted to him that moment. She briefly considered being intimate with him. Maybe he would be her first.

Macy had been toying with the idea of giving up her virginity for a while now. All of her friends were already sexing. She was what they jokingly referred to as a late bloomer.

Macy was a pretty girl, with hair down her back, and a killer smile that melted hearts. And she had a big booty. She got it from her mama. She could've easily got just about any boy at school to be her first, but she was real picky. She didn't have high enough regards for any of the silly boys at school to have the privilege of deflowering her. Macy didn't have any self-esteem issues. She knew what she was worth.

Her being smart and careful had a lot to do with what had happened to her baby sister. Pebbles was raped and killed by a sick old pedophile. When she was abducted, she was trying to hitch a ride to Brooklyn to be with some stupid ass fake pimp named Ice. All of that "boy crazy" shit had got Pebbles into a world of trouble, and led to her demise. So Macy was real careful with hers. She was determined not to let some asshole be her downfall.

But Macy was a mature young lady, and she was becoming quite curious. In a sense, she believed she was ready to make that move. She was interested in the whole myth of sex, and wanted to see firsthand what it was all about. Her hormones were all over the place, so she had sexual urges. She had even touched herself a time or two. Macy was comfortable with her sexuality, so she knew she wanted to do it. She just didn't want to be taken by some knucklehead.

Now that Jayquan had matured, he was looking more and more like the perfect candidate. He was smart, tall, and really good-looking. The fact that all of her friends were throwing themselves at him gave him even more appeal.

Macy wanted him, but she was no skeezer. She had to play it cool. Especially now that she knew he didn't like easy girls. She dismissed that thought immediately. Jayquan knew she wasn't easy. He knew her better than any boy in the world. And she knew him too. That's why he was perfect.

She thought about the fact that she was a little bit older than him. A year and three months, to be exact. But her auntie Fatima was a little older than her husband, and they were happy. And Jayquan's age didn't stop her friends from lusting after him. He acted older than fourteen lately. And his birthday was coming up real soon. Macy dismissed her qualms about their age gap. She made up her mind.

From then on, something changed between the two of them. At least on her part. She started throwing signals, like wearing perfume around Jayquan, flirtatiously touching his face when she spoke to him, and laughing at his stupid jokes like they were the funniest thing in the world.

CHAPTER SIXTEEN

Khalil sat in his cell, deeply engrossed in one of his favorite pastimes. He was brainstorming, and thinking of a hundred ways to kill his ex-wife. Instead of rehabilitating in jail, he spent all his time angry because he was full of resentment towards Laila. And even more so, that nigga she was fucking with, Cas.

There were lots of dick riding ass dudes locked up in there with Khalil. They talked about that nigga Cas like he was some type of guerilla. That further fueled the hatred he felt for that mothafucka. That nigga thought he could just take his wife, and get away with it.

Khalil often laid awake at night and imagined killing that dude. He had even thought about dropping some info about him to the police, but he didn't want to be labeled a snitch. Word traveled fast in the pen. He was going home soon.

But Khalil was salty because he had nothing to go home to. He listened to other dudes talk about how excited they were to be going home to their wives. Damn, he really regretted signing those divorce papers. The thing he couldn't really digest was the way Cas had forced him to sign them, like he was some bitch. He got a hundred gees, but that shit was just about gone. He had blown the bulk of it "partying", so he only had about two stacks left in the bank. If he hadn't have got locked up, he would've been broke.

Khalil usually stayed to himself, but he was human. Just like everyone else, sometimes he liked to vent. But he made the mistake of running his mouth around the wrong people. He forgot how small the world was.

One day he was fronting in the yard, talking tough about all the things he was going to do to that nigga Casino from Street Life when he got out. Khalil was just trying to let dudes know how he got down. There were only a few dudes out there that heard him, but one of them happened to know a dude named Eighty who really fucked with them Street Life niggas. The dude, whose moniker was Murk, had bidded with Eighty two times, at Clinton, and at Upstate.

Murk called home later that evening. He had his wife call Eighty on a three-way. After he and Eighty said "what up", he told him about the contempt the dude Khalil had for his peoples. He let him know duke said he was going to get at Casino. Murk asked Eighty if he wanted him to spit at that nigga. He said it was nothing to send some young gunners to shoot him up.

Eighty asked him to describe the dude to him. When he realized who the nigga was, he laughed. He told Murk that clown was no threat. He told him about the way he and Handy Andy had assisted Cas in getting him to sign those divorce papers.

Eighty said he would call Cas and find out if he wanted the nigga washed up for disrespecting his name. He told Murk to get back at him the following day, and asked him if he needed anything. Murk told him he would keep that favor in a bag, and pull it out later.

Eighty said, "You got it, man. Hold me to that." When they hung up, he thought about Cas. That nigga threw him a lifeline a few times when he was fucked up, so he was loyal for that. He had to call his homie, and run it down.

It wasn't long ago that Eighty had pulled Cas' coat about that little bitch ass nigga, Lite. That lame had called him, and tried to get him to line Cas and Jay up. The stickup game was Eighty's usual line of work, but those were his mans. He had called them to let them know what it was.

The very next day, he heard the word on the streets that Lite was killed. He knew that was Killa' Cas and Jay's work, but he never said a word. Eighty was a real ass cat. He called Cas and gave him the rundown again.

When Cas got the call from Eighty, he thought about it. He contemplated getting Khalil touched up for running his mouth, but he told Eighty to let it ride. He knew that lame was all talk.

Eighty told Cas that was the wrong answer. He said, "Son, that faggot ass nigga in there talkin' out the side of his neck like somethin' sweet. He needs to be taught a lesson."

Cas laughed, and said, "I'm not threatened by that dude. That nigga ain't nothin' but a bitch. Don't worry about it, son."

The old Cas would've got Khalil washed up on GP. He sort of wanted to, but that lame was Macy's father. Cas loved that little girl to death. That nigga was lucky. That was the only reason he got a pass.

Eight reluctantly said, "A'ight, son. I got you." They chatted for a few more minutes, and hung up.

The next day, Murk called again. Even though Cas gave that nigga Khalil a pass, Eighty told Murk to get somebody to go up in that nigga mouth. He told him to send a shooter at him, to see if he was really as tough as he claimed to be. Fuck that, Cas was his man. That nigga had violated by disrespecting his name.

Two days later, Khalil was walking down the hall on the way from his day program. It was one of the rare days he was in a pretty decent mood. He had thought about it, and he realized his time was too short to be spending his days stressing about that bitch Laila. He was scheduled to be released soon, so he needed to be thinking about what he was going to do. Khalil knew he needed to get his shit together. He used to be "that nigga". He wanted to bury Laila's ass, and move on.

Khalil was so engrossed in preparing the mental checklist of changes he needed to make in his life, he wasn't paying attention to the angry looking young dude coming toward him. He wasn't on point the least bit.

The dude marched up to him, and said, "I got a message for you, my man." He threw something in Khalil's face, and sucker punched him.

Khalil threw up his hands in defense, but not quick enough. He felt warm blood oozing from his face, and realized he was cut. Oh shit, the nigga had a blade!

Khalil's counterattack was pretty useless. His delayed reaction was no match for the dude's agility. The mothafucka was swift. He swung and sliced him again, just underneath the first cut. Khalil grabbed his face and hollered out in pain.

After that, homeboy appeared satisfied. He got Khalil good that time. He leaned in and menacingly growled, "Nigga, that was for Casino. Keep his name out ya' mouth, sucka' ass bitch!" The dude walked off fast to avoid being spotted by a C.O.

Holding his face, Khalil went running toward the bubble where the C.O. was. He needed some medical attention immediately. That nigga ripped his shit wide open. He knew he needed mad stitches. An officer saw him, and quickly had him ushered to the infirmary. An ambulance was called, and he was rushed to the hospital.

Khalil got his face stitched up, and the doctor gave him some antibiotics so it wouldn't get infected. After he returned to the prison, they questioned him about who the culprit was. He acted like he had no idea who attacked him. He didn't say one word. He was no rat.

But he was no fool either. He gladly accepted the spot in protective custody the pigs offered him. He remembered what that nigga said right after he cut him. Casino was behind that shit. Khalil didn't know how many foot soldiers that nigga Cas had in there. He didn't want to take any more chances, so he would finish out his time in P.C.

Khalil realized that if he wanted to do something to Cas, he should've kept it to himself. He had learned that the hard way. You weren't supposed to talk about the shit you planned to do to mothafuckas. You were just supposed to step to your business and handle it.

For running his mouth that one time, he got two buck fifties across his face. When he did the math it didn't make sense. And strangely, the two scars looked like they formed an "L". "L" for Laila.

Khalil had no choice but to eat what happened to him, but he vowed to see that nigga Cas when he got out of jail. He had to wear those scars on his face for the rest of his life, so that meant war. He meant it this time, and Cas wouldn't win again.

$ $ $ $

Portia was a good wife to Jay. She was sticking by his side, but she was getting impatient. She kept asking Jay if his little baby mama had found an apartment yet. The notion of Jay paying for that luxury Central Park apartment did not sit well with her. She understood that Jay had to financially assist that girl because she had a child by him, but he didn't have to spoil the bitch.

Jay had explained to Portia that it wasn't like that. He told her Cas' mother owned the building, and he had leased that apartment without even seeing it first. He told her how Ysatis' first apartment had been burglarized, so he'd moved her to a safer place.

Portia asked Jay why the fuck he cared so much. He reminded her that Ysatis was Humble's former shorty. He assured her that was the only reason he had looked out for her. Just on the strength of his little man Humble. Portia knew how Jay was. He had a good heart, so she believed him.

While they were on the subject, Jay decided to tell Portia everything. He had told her the truth already, but he withheld one thing. He didn't tell her the part about him and his mans killing Ysatis' brother. Now that Ysatis was talking out the side of her face about it, it was pretty relevant.

Jay started from the time Humble died. He said Ysatis came to them to collect the reward he and Cas had put out for his murderer. Jay went into detail about the way she'd told them her brother, Nasty Neal, had raped and molested her since she was twelve. She said he killed Humble just because she was dating him. Jay told Portia how Ysatis gave them the key to the apartment she and her family lived in, and set Neal up. She called them over, and then feigned sexual desire for her brother. Jay said they walked in and literally caught him with his pants down. He said duke was off point, and that was that.

Jay didn't say anything else about that. The story got pretty graphic, so he didn't go into details. Portia could read between the lines. She didn't need to hear about Neal and his accomplice, Chewy, getting their melons blown off at "The Meat House" that belonged to his good friend, Colombian Manuel.

Portia knew back then that Jay had taken care of Humble's killer, but she didn't know who it was, or how he did it. She never asked him any questions about stuff like that.

The way Jay looked at Portia, she could tell there was more. He sighed, and told her he was telling her all this for a reason. He said Ysatis had called him recently, and lied about there being an emergency with the baby's health. Portia made a face, and got ready to spazz. Jay told her to wait a minute, and just listen to him.

He said when she called him, he asked Cas to accompany him over there to see if the baby needed to go to the hospital. He said he only went because Ysatis was young and dumb, and didn't know shit about a baby. He told Portia that when he got there he discovered that the whole thing was a farce. He said he got mad, and started to leave as soon as he realized she had lied.

Jay paused like he was deep in thought for a minute, and scratched his chin. Then he told Portia that bitch had the nerve to "remind" him about what he did to her brother. She had insinuated that he'd better give her what she wanted, or else. Jay told Portia it was him she wanted. He showed her a few of psycho Ysatis' texts in his iPhone.

Portia was pretty upset about the latest 411 Jay gave her. She was ready to step to that crazy bitch. Jay was tight too. He said Ysatis had crossed the line by threatening him. He wanted to stay away from that girl because he didn't know what he would do to her if she said some slick shit like that again. People had died at his hands for less, so he just didn't want to deal with her.

Portia couldn't believe the way that bitch had been pressing her husband. She actually believed she had a shot at them being a family. To Portia's surprise, Jay asked her if she would handle things for him when it came to Ysatis.

Portia agreed. She didn't know how she would be able to deal with that conniving bitch without killing her, but she had her husband's back no matter what. She thought she had set that delusional heifer straight, but apparently they needed to have another conversation. If that bitch thought she was going to wind up with Jay, she was really crazy.

Portia knew what type of game she was playing, trying to use that baby to get to Jay. No wonder she was dragging her ass on her apartment search. Portia knew Ysatis didn't want to move out of that high-rise building, but there was no fucking way she would allow Jay to continue spoiling no bird ass bitch like that. She thought she would be living the highlife just because she had tricked Jay into getting her pregnant, but Portia didn't think so. She would show her otherwise.

Jay still owned the house he had bought next door to Portia's brownstone in Brooklyn, so she briefly thought about moving Ysatis in there. She immediately dismissed the notion, knowing she wouldn't even be able to sleep with that bitch living that close to her house. She hated that she had to have anything to do with Ysatis, but she had to move.

Portia took it upon herself to call Cas' mom, Ms. B. They greeted each other warmly, and then Portia voiced her desire to relocate Ysatis to a much more modest location. She told Ms. B she realized the lease was over, but they would pay her prorated rent.

Ms. B told Portia she was okay with that. She said she hadn't even called Jay yet because she knew he would take care of that. Then she told her about two apartments she had for rent in Brooklyn. One was in Park Slope, and the other was located in East New York. The rent was about an eighth of the price on the Central Park apartment Ysatis was staying in.

Portia told her they'd take the one in Park Slope because it was a two-bedroom. Ms. B admitted that one was the nicer of the two. When she said that, Portia started to choose the other one.

$ $ $ $

Halloween was on a Saturday that year. The week before, Portia was in a good mood because she had successfully downsized and relocated that whore Ysatis. So she really got into Halloween that year, "for the sake of the kids". She was having more fun then them.

With Lil' Jay and Macy's assistance, Portia created a spook-tacular horror house at their place. They had a Halloween party for the kids that evening, after everyone was done trick or treating. Most people showed up in costumes, including the adults. Portia wore a sexy she-devil costume. Laila and Fatima wore sexy costumes too. They helped Portia host, and they all had a great time.

Portia had invited some of her neighbors, and there were lots of Jayquan and Macy's friends from high school there. They partied until about three AM. Portia went all out, so there was plenty to eat and drink. They had so much stuff everybody went home with plates of food, cake, and lots of candy.

After Halloween passed, the holiday season was right on their heels. Fatima notified everyone about her and Wise's plans to host Thanksgiving at their house that year. The gang usually took turns. The year before, they all had dinner at Jay and Portia's house. The following year would be Cas and Laila's turn.

Fatima spent her days watching the Food Network, and looking for new twists on traditional dishes. She wanted to try something a little different that year. She was looking forward to showing off her cooking skills a little bit.

Fatima was excited about Thanksgiving because she had a lot to be thankful for. She was happy, and in love. And she and Wise had been getting along really well too, mostly because she had stopped nagging him so much. She had learned to back off and let him be a man. He seemed to appreciate that.

He and Fatima had started their love over. They were compatible in so many ways, they were good for each other. And they both had wild streaks, so they kept each other grounded.

Wise was a pretty smart dude. He had calmed down a lot. He was a family man now. When he did hang out, he made sure it was at places where he wouldn't likely be noticed. And he always made efforts to disguise himself in specs and a hat. He had a full beard now, which Fatima found sexy, and he'd even developed a new walk.

He was still just as attractive, and even more. Fatima couldn't keep her hands off him. They were still making up for lost time. In fact, she had a surprise for everyone. Fatima and Wise had been fooling around so much, she was pregnant. She hadn't told anyone yet. Not even him. That was the thing Fatima was most excited about. She planned to announce it over Thanksgiving dinner.

When the day came, the family gathered at their house for a grand holiday fête. Fatima's mother, Doris, had arrived early that morning to assist her in the meal preparation. Portia and Laila showed up with their kids at about noon. They were on dessert detail. Portia was in charge of the sweet potato pies, and Laila was making the homemade apple pies. Laila gave Macy the task of peeling the apples for her. Laila said she used to do it for her grandmother when she made pies.

Jayquan loved banana pudding, so he decided to tackle making one that year. He wanted to do it himself. He said he was getting the recipe from his grandmother when she arrived. Mama Mitchell also made the best macaroni and cheese in the world. As per Fatima's request, she showed up with a huge pan of it at around two o'clock. She supervised Jayquan while he made his banana pudding from scratch, and then she and Macy set the table for Fatima.

Jay and Cas got to the house right after Mama Mitchell did. Wise's mother, Rose came over next, and Fatima's father arrived a little later. The house was lively, and filled with laughter. The kids were running around playing happily, and the men were drinking top-shelf cognac, loudly discussing the Yankees' recent World Series win, and watching football.

Together the ladies hustled and bustled around the kitchen until a mighty feast was laid out. It was smelling good up in there, and there was enough food to feed a small African nation. Dinner was served at around seven.

The whole family bowed their heads in prayer while Fatima's father blessed the food, and then they got their eat on. It wasn't long before everyone was stuffed. Even so, they got started on dessert.

Fatima got ready to announce her news about the baby she was expecting. The first person she told was her husband, and she did it on the low. She presented him with a greeting card that said "Congratulations! We're having a baby!"

When Wise opened the card and read it, his eyes lit up. He jumped up with this huge grin on his face and pumped his fist in the air. He was mad excited so he shouted it out to his peoples.

"Hey, guess what! I'm about to be a father again!"

Every face in the room looked surprised. Fatima beamed, and nodded her head in confirmation. "Yup, he's right. We're having a baby!"

Wise was smiling so hard he was showing all thirty two. He was going to be a daddy. And he had a feeling that was his boy. His namesake. Wise was real proud.

Ever since he had survived that bullet he took to the neck, he had these little moments throughout the day when he just had to thank God sometimes. Having the blessed opportunity to be there to father another child triggered one of those moments. Wise looked up and said it out loud. "Thank you, God! Yes!"

Fatima smiled at him, and cosigned. "That's right, baby. God is so good!"

CHAPTER SEVENTEEN

Ysatis was just settling into her new apartment. She was back in Brooklyn, but in a different neighborhood than she'd grown up in. The new apartment had two bedrooms, but it was nothing like the duplex princess pad she just left.

Ysatis took the downgrade as a slap in the face. To make matters worse, she hadn't seen Jay the whole time she was moving. Ironically, it was his wife that handled everything. She found the apartment, hired the movers, and even had the baby furniture delivered.

Ysatis could read between the lines. Jay and his wife were both trying to be funny. They were obviously out to prove their little thing was unbreakable. She could see that. Ysatis didn't lack common sense. She was a pretty smart girl. She knew she needed to move on and leave Jay alone. She was starting to see how much he really didn't love her. It seemed like he didn't even want to see her anymore.

Jay's rejection was quite a self-esteem blow, but Ysatis wouldn't give up. She called him lots of times, but he never answered. She figured he was screening her calls, so she had called him from a different phone number. He answered his phone then, but he got mad when he realized it was her. He had the nerve to tell her to go through his wife, or his assistant when she wanted to get in touch with him. He treated her like she was nothing.

She was mad and bitter, to say the least. Not even her

threatening him had worked. In fact, Jay didn't even respond to that. Ysatis was unhappy so she became more and more vindictive each day. Now she even regretted having her son. Jay just wouldn't embrace him. He had given her a little money to help out, but that was it. He treated her better before she had the baby.

Nothing turned out the way Ysatis had planned. Jay's fucking wife was making decisions he should've been making. Ysatis should've just backed off, but she was determined to win Jay over. And if she couldn't, she would make his life a living hell. She wasn't going to allow him to just dismiss her like she didn't count. Enough was enough. It was time to show that mothafucka she wasn't some dumb little girl.

$ $ $ $

Laila was happy for the first time in a while. She and Cas were in love, and things were great. Thanksgiving had just passed, and she had a lot to be thankful for. She had her health and strength, and she was planning her wedding. She also had great kids. Her oldest daughter, Macy, was on the honor roll. She and Skye were the joy of Laila's life.

Just when she thought she couldn't be happier, Laila got a call about some pretty bad news. It always seemed to find her. Her luck was usually shitty, so she should've known it wouldn't be long. For her, life would probably never be simple.

The District Attorney who had prosecuted Harvey York, the maniac responsible for raping and killing her daughter, called her personally. Pebbles' murderer was being released on a technicality. In about two weeks, that sick bastard would be out on the streets.

When Laila heard that she was absolutely distraught. When she lost Pebbles, a part of her had died. And when she found out about that creep being released, she almost died again. She wondered how God would allow that to happen.

The more she thought about it, she decided that only over her dead body would that mothafucka walk the streets again. She wouldn't give him a chance to harm someone else's child. Laila was sick with the judicial system. She couldn't believe they were releasing that scumbag back into society. Now she wanted to punish that bastard the way he deserved.

She wanted to look him in the face, and let him know what he took from her. And then she wanted to take his life the way he took Pebbles'. That pedophile bastard had raped and killed her baby. The thought of it caused Laila to weep. That pain would never go away.

Laila made up her mind. She didn't know how, but she was going to kill Harvey York. That mothafucka was the scum of the earth. He didn't deserve to live.

When Cas came in later that night, Laila was sitting up in bed trying to think of a way to pull it off. She was usually asleep by that time of night, so he asked her what was wrong. Laila told him she couldn't sleep, and tears came to her eyes as she told him why. She said she was mad as hell, and wanted Harvey York to die with his dick in his mouth.

Cas loved Laila so he felt her pain. She had every right to feel that way about her daughter's killer. The poor thing was devastated, and he understood. She wanted that bastard dead.

Like every other time Laila was faced with adversity, Cas wanted to fix it. There was no way he could bring her daughter back, but he could certainly get rid of the creep responsible for her death. Cas believed in street justice anyway, so the pleasure would be his.

The following day, Cas spent a little bread to retrieve some information. Money talked, so he managed to get his hands on the address where that sick ass cracker, Harvey York, would be residing. He would be staying out in Bayside, a suburban community in Queens. He'd be staying there with his sister.

Cas thought about the way he and Jay had done away with

Ice, that young pimp Pebbles had got tangled up with. They had taken him to Manuel's "Meat House", and that was the last time he was seen or heard from. That cocksucker Harvey needed to be disposed of just as diligently.

While Cas was putting his plan together he thought about calling his good friend, Manuel, and asking to use his facility again. He decided against that since they had been recently cleared of that federal investigation. He didn't want to take any chances because you never knew who was still watching.

Cas knew how personal it was for Laila. He could really tell she wanted to kill that mothafucka Harvey. Cas wanted to fix it so that she could do it with no repercussions, but he didn't really want to involve Laila in any street shit. It was either her satisfaction or her safety, so he had to decide.

Cas waited for a few days after Harvey got out, and let him get comfortable. Pebbles wasn't the only child he had done harm to, so there was much ado about his release. People had petitioned and protested against him being let out on the streets, but the law was the law. So many feathers were ruffled, the judge ordered him police protection. There was a patrol car parked outside his house for the first five days.

Cas had personally drove by there a couple times to see for himself. The officers in the car looked bored, like they couldn't care less. You could see "I'm just here to get a friggin' paycheck" all over their faces. That was a good sign.

The first thing Cas needed was some men for hire. He didn't like talking over the phone, so he drove to the old neighborhood to holler at some dudes that were infamous for their work. In Brooklyn, he commissioned BJ, Eighty, and Handy Andy to aide him in a little "disappearing act". Cas knew he could trust those three.

It was no secret that most respectable criminal minded dudes detested the likes of child molesters and rape-os. That applied to those in the penitentiary, and in the streets. That being said, when Cas told the henchmen about that sick cracker raping and killing his stepdaughter, they were anxious to tackle their assignment. Especially when they found out he walked due to a legal technicality. The three of them were all fathers, so dudes would do that type of work for charity. But of course, none of them was foolish enough to refuse the compensation Cas offered.

Cas' original plan was to have the goons run up in the house and snatch Harvey up out of there. He wanted to tie that nigga up somewhere, and let Laila chop his dick off and shove it down his throat. Then after she watched him suffer, he planned to put a bullet in his head. But the more Cas thought about it, he couldn't bring his wife-to-be around such insidiousness. Laila wasn't even built like that. She was a lady, and he didn't want to tarnish that. He decided to just have that slime ball put out of his misery. Cas informed his henchmen of the slight change in plans, and upped the ante to their specifications.

The seventh night that pervert was home, they began their stakeout. Lucky for them, the patrol car wasn't there anymore. For seven hours, Cas' henchmen sat outside the Queens address where the scum lie. They were waiting for the perfect opportunity to run up in there. They wanted to avoid hurting the creep's sister, so they waited until the wee hours of the morning.

Lucky for them, Harvey's sister, Roxanne, had a little addiction. She was hooked on prescription drugs. She would've had enough Percocet to get her through the week if it wasn't for her bum-of-a-brother. He had been staying with her since he got out of the can, and kept insisting he needed something for his "bad nerves". Roxanne's supply of Percocet ran out that night, and she couldn't even go to sleep. So around three AM, she left the house to go across town to buy a few pills from her girlfriend, Judy.

When Roxanne pulled off in her old beat-up minivan, BJ, Handy Andy, and Eighty sprang into action. They quietly hopped out of their car and crept around to the back door. There was a big ass Rottweiler on a chain back there. He started barking, and charged at them, so Eighty quickly shot him in the face with his .380. Casino had supplied them all with silencers, so no one heard the shot.

With the guard dog dead, entering the house was relatively easy. Cas had requested notification when they gained access, so BJ called to let him know. They quietly tiptoed inside, and found Harvey in one of the bedrooms sleeping alone. Lucky for them, he was the only person in the house.

$ $ $ $

Cas hadn't gone home just yet. He was still in the area waiting on that job to be done. When he found out his peoples were in, he used a throwaway prepaid phone he'd purchased to call 911. He feigned a Jamaican accent, and excitedly told the 911 operator that two on-duty police officers had been shot. He named the location to be about fifteen blocks north of Harvey's address. The dispatcher quickly put the call out on the radio.

Cas didn't want any police riding by Harvey's house while his boys were inside, so the purpose of his 911 call was to create a distraction. Knowing how cops stuck together, every police officer in the area would rush to see about their comrades wounded in the line of duty.

Cas knew what he was doing. His plan worked. When they heard that two of their own kind got shot, every cop in the surrounding area rushed to the intersection Cas gave the operator. Cas laughed to himself. There were so many sirens, he could hear them where he was. The police dragged their asses when it came to a lot of stuff, but they responded quickly when it pertained to one of their own.

$ $ $ $

Harvey was high off his sister's prescribed medication, so he was in a particularly deep sleep. His bed was surrounded by his would-be murderers, and he wasn't even aware that he had company. He could've been the poster child for "Say NO to drugs".

Eighty, BJ, and Handy all grimaced at his snoring figure in disgust. They had to hurry up and get out of there, so Eighty snatched the covers off him. To their horror, the pervert nigga was wearing a diaper and a baby bonnet. He was asleep in the fetal position, with his thumb in his mouth, and there was a baby bottle on the bed next to him.

And you could see the crack of his flabby, milk white ass. The sight of that was a stomach turner for the whole gang. BJ hock spit on that freak mothafucka.

Handy Andy was the smallest of the three. He went under the bed with a rope, and they tied Harvey down to the bed. The men worked quietly, and didn't bother to wake him up until he was hogtied down. When they were done, BJ hit him in the head with the butt of his gun.

That blow to the head woke Harvey up fast. And much to his chagrin, he focused in on three angry Black men with big guns. His first reaction was to get up and run, but he couldn't move. Harvey realized he was tied to the bed. He was scared to death because he was laying there helpless in a diaper. He knew he was doomed. All he could do was plead for his life, so he begged them to let him go.

The henchmen knew what type of fecal matter they were dealing with, so his pleas hardly moved them to show mercy.

Eighty had a little girl, so the notion of Harvey being a pedophile infuriated him. He said, "Do you remember that pretty little Black girl you raped and killed? She was only twelve, you piece of shit!"

From the look on Harvey's face, what Eighty said rang a bell. They were all so repulsed by that mothafucka they started beating the shit out of him. While they hit him, they spit on him and hurled insults at him. Harvey cried out in pain the whole time. They wanted to kill that sick cracker on the spot, but they had to follow Casino's orders. He was paying them to do it his way.

They lumped Harvey up pretty good, and then Handy Andy reminded them of Cas' request. They were all wearing thick rubber gloves, but nobody wanted to volunteer to do the honor. Finally, BJ stepped up to the plate. He thought about the way Cas said that pervert brutally raped his stepdaughter before he killed her. Hatred and disgust gave him the stomach to snatch off that fucking diaper and grab Harvey's nasty little vienna sausage cock. When he got a good grip on it, he nodded at Eighty.

Eighty had these sharp, heavy-duty gardening shears. He clamped them on the base of Harvey's gross little pecker, and completely severed it in one motion. The next thing BJ knew, he had the nigga's shit in his hand.

Harvey hollered at the top of his lungs. The scream he let out sounded like it came from the depths of his soul. Handy Andy shoved a pillow over his mouth to shut him the fuck up. Harvey stared on in wide-eyed fear while BJ dangled his severed penis in his face. You could see the life draining from him already.

BJ grinned wickedly, and shoved the pervert's dirty little dick in his mouth. After that, Handy Andy doused him with gasoline. They each spit on him again, and Eighty struck a match and set him on fire.

They got up out of there, and left that cracker burning alive. His death would be slow and painful. Harvey's cries for help were muffled by his dick in his mouth. And you could actually smell his flesh burning. It was stomach-turning. That was some television shit.

The goons quietly exited the house through the same door they came in. They had ridded the earth of one less parasite of the worse kind, so each of them was filled with a sense of pride. Harvey York had preyed on innocent children and got away with it. But when you make your bed hard in life, you lay in it. So now he laid on his bed, burning in a makeshift hell. Needless to say, he died miserably and tortured.

The next morning, Cas and Laila were watching the news when the story broke.

There had been a grisly discovery of a Queens man who was burned to death in his bed. The man was identified as convicted child pedophile, Harvey York. Apparently, someone had broken into the home he was staying at, and tied him to the bed. The perpetrator then cut off his penis and stuck it in his mouth, and set him afire. The police had no suspects as of yet.

Laila couldn't believe it. That filthy bastard actually died with his dick in his mouth. That was the exact way she had wished him dead. Could that be just a coincidence? She looked over at Cas.

He just sort of smiled, and winked at her. That was the only indication he gave her that he was behind it, so Laila didn't ask him any questions. And he didn't volunteer any explanations. Cas didn't do that. He never talked about the stuff he did.

Laila smiled. Cas had done it again. Every time someone wronged her, he stepped in to take care of it. He took care of Ice, the young pimp she blamed for Pebbles going astray. And then when her ex-husband wouldn't release her from their marriage-gone-to-hell, Cas made Khalil sign the divorce papers. And now the scumbag responsible for her baby's murder got out of jail scot-free, and Cas stepped in and took care of that too.

Casino was such a man. Laila felt safe with him. He always had her best interest at heart, and she knew he really loved her. And she loved him just as much, and more. Christmas was coming soon, and she couldn't have asked for a better gift than the justice he had given her. Now Laila could sleep at night because Pebbles could rest in peace.

CHAPTER EIGHTEEN

Christmas Day came, and it was pretty good. The gang was very blessed, and so were their families. All the kids got everything they wanted. Except Jayquan. He really wanted a new car. He had convinced his spoiled self that his father would buy him one for Christmas, so he was disappointed.

What Jayquan had, he wasn't even aware of. Macy's crush on him was growing by the day, and it was fueled by his swagger. She liked his style. The way he walked, the way he talked, the way he wore his pants sagging just enough… The list was endless. He just had a way about him. It was sexy, and she was totally into him.

The day after Christmas was a Saturday. Macy let her mother know she was going over to Portia's house so she and Jayquan could play pool. As far as Laila was concerned, Macy and Jayquan were like cousins so she didn't think anything of it. She told Macy to take some church clothes just in case Portia was taking them on Sunday.

Portia and Jay had already left the house when she got there. They took Jazz out for her birthday, which was the following day. Macy knew they were gone because Jayquan had informed her that he had the crib to himself. He said his parents wouldn't be back until later that night, and his little sisters were staying at his grandmother's house for the weekend.

After Macy arrived, she and Lil' Jay chilled outside for a little while. She played Keri Hilson, Ne-Yo, and Kanye West's hit song "Love Knocks You Down" on her car stereo a few times. After that, she put on Beyonce's "Sweet Dreams", and watched Jayquan practicing tricks on his skateboard. About an hour later, she suggested they go inside because she was cold. It was almost January.

Jayquan agreed, and they headed on inside. They went up to the second floor to the rec section, and he flicked on the flat screen TV hooked up to his Xbox 360. Macy turned on his laptop, and logged onto her MySpace page. She called Jayquan over to check out her new photos.

He paused his game, and walked over and took a look. He laughed at the pictures of her trying to be sexy, but he said they were cute. He told Macy to go to his page to see the new stuff on his.

Macy checked out Lil' Jay's page for a minute. In the process, she pretended to suddenly have a pain spasm. Jayquan asked her if she was okay. She told him she hurt her back playing volleyball in gym at school, and asked him if he would mind massaging it for her a little.

Lil' Jay didn't think anything of it. He stood over Macy and massaged her shoulders. Macy told him he wasn't quite reaching the spot, so she probably needed to lay down and let him do it. He told her to stretch out on the floor, or the sofa. Macy said she wanted to lay on the bed, so they should go upstairs.

Jayquan shrugged. It didn't matter to him. Girls were so picky over stuff. Macy led the way, and they walked upstairs together. She swung her ample booty in his face. She stopped at the top of the stairs for a second, trying to decide if they should go in his bedroom, or the guest room she always stayed in. There were eight bedrooms in the house, and that one was basically hers. She even left clothes over there, and cosmetics in the bathroom.

Macy decided on Jayquan's bedroom, and nonchalantly headed down the hall. Jayquan followed her, wondering why she was acting so weird. He asked her what was up. "Yo, Mace. You a'ight?"

Macy said, "Yeah, my doggone back just hurts. I need you to massage the pain away for me."

Jayquan just shook his head. He said, "A'ight, man. Whatever. You lucky."

In the bedroom, Macy took off her shoes, and laid down on her belly. Lil' Jay stood up and leaned over her, and began to massage her back.

She said, "No, silly. Get on the bed and do it."

Jayquan didn't say anything, but he was trying to keep his distance because he had a hard-on. He didn't realize that was Macy's intention. Not yet. He took a deep breath, and then he climbed on the bed. He started massaging her back in circular motions. The deeper he pressed, the more he could feel her relaxing.

All of a sudden, Macy said, "Wait a minute, let me take this stuff off. It's in the way. Let me get up for a second."

Jayquan moved over. To his amazement, she took off her shirt. Macy had on a pink satin bra. Jayquan was almost drooling. He caught himself and closed his mouth. Macy peeped his reaction, but she casually laid back down.

Jayquan took another deep breath, and crouched down over her back. He hoped she couldn't feel his erection because now it was pressed on her behind. He went back to massaging again, and noted how soft her skin was.

Macy relaxed, and hummed softly. She suggested he turn some music on. Jayquan reached over and picked up the stereo remote from his nightstand. When he hit the power button, the sounds of one of Macy's favorite artist, Trey Songz, filled the room. *"When I pull back them sheets, and you climb on top of me-e. Girl you gon' think, girl you gon' think, girl you gon' think, you gon' think I invented sex…"*

That song had him thinking real naughty. Jayquan grinned

to himself, and massaged Macy's back. He asked her, "Yo, how that feel?"

She said, "It feels good. Is my bra strap in the way?"

It wasn't, but Jayquan said, "Yeah, sort of. I'ma just unhook it."

Macy said, "Okay, go 'head."

Jayquan struggled with the bra hooks for a few seconds but he finally got them open. He stared down at Macy's bare back, amazed by the fact that she was now basically topless. Her jeans were low-cut, so her Victoria's Secret panties peeked out at him just below the small of her back. They were pink satin just like her bra.

Jayquan took a slow deep breath. Macy's backside was sure looking sexy. Now he wanted to see the frontal view.

She must've read his mind because she said, "Watch out for a second. Let me turn over. My knee hurts, so can you massage that too?"

Jayquan understood the game she was playing now. He got off her back so she could switch positions. When Macy got up, he was very pleased. She had some nice ass titties. They were so full and perfect, Jayquan couldn't help himself. He reached over and palmed them. To his delight they were soft. He started rubbing them, and her nipples hardened under his touch.

Jayquan laid Macy down and started sucking one. It felt so good Macy caressed the back of his head and moaned. He got on top of her, and kissed her on the ear and neck. Damn, she smelled good. They found each other's lips, and had their first kiss.

Macy was the better kisser, so Jayquan followed her lead. He caught on quick, and their tongues danced in each others mouths. Jayquan played with her nipples while they were smooching. His hands felt experienced so Macy was panting. She caressed his back and shoulders, enjoying the way he felt against her. She guessed that was what women meant by "the comfort of a man."

Macy had kissed a boy before, but never had she been involved in a situation that heavy.

It seemed like Lil' Jay was enjoying himself too. She knew he was hard because she could feel his thing against her thigh. Macy got bold, and reached down and felt it. She was impressed, but almost frightened by its size. She hadn't seen many to compare it to, but she could tell it was big.

Macy rubbing on him that way almost drove Jayquan crazy. He stopped kissing her, and looked at her sincerely. "Yo, you sure you wanna do this, Macy?"

She breathily replied, "Yeah, I'm sure. Take off your clothes too."

Lil' Jay got up and took off everything except his boxers. Then he helped her out of her Guess jeans. Macy laid back on the bed in just her pink panties. Her hair cascaded over the pillow, and she looked real pretty. He had never seen her like that.

It was their first time, so Jayquan didn't want to mess anything up. He asked Macy what she wanted to do next.

"Come lay down, and let's kiss", she responded softly.

Jayquan got back on the bed with her, and they started smooching again. After a while, he slid her panties aside and slipped his fingers in her valley. She was real wet, and that aroused him even more. Damn, he wanted to put it in. He rubbed her clit for a minute, and then he asked her if she was ready.

Macy nodded, and told him she had a condom in her pants pocket. She wanted to play it safe so she wouldn't get pregnant like her sister did. Lil' Jay took the condom from her and tore it open, and he attempted to roll it on. He was a little nervous so he fumbled at first. He had practiced doing it a few times before, so he finally got it right. He laid on top of Macy and got ready to penetrate her.

He put it in slow but it really hurt at first. Macy cried out in pain and clawed his back. Jayquan took a deep breath to maintain control, and told her to relax. It felt good inside of her. She was real tight. He didn't have much experience but he knew what he was doing. He learned from watching his father's porno movies.

Jayquan slowly slid in and out of Macy's warm cocoon. She relaxed and stopped digging her nails in his back, so he moved from side to side too. He figured that was "deep stroking". He must've been doing something right because Macy started bucking and moaning like it felt real good. Jayquan met her rhythm, and their first lovemaking experience was consummated with mutual pleasure.

Afterwards, they laid in each other's arms. Macy snuggled up under him, and he planted a kiss on her forehead. At that moment, she realized she loved him. He had made her first time beautiful, and that was something she would never forget.

$ $ $ $

It was the day after Christmas, and Ysatis was way disappointed. The holiday hadn't been happy for her. She had waited up late the night before, holding on to the notion that Jay would pop up like Santa with a bag of goodies. But he didn't come through with shit. No gifts for the baby, or anything.

Ysatis was really hurt about that. All day she had been sipping on Alize, and planning her retaliation. The baby was crying so much she couldn't stand it, so she turned her stereo up to tune him out. She knew that was selfish but she couldn't comfort him at the time. She needed somebody to comfort her.

Ysatis was drunk, and she was tired of Jay hurting her. He needed a taste of his own medicine. He had shunned her, and now she was a woman scorned. She made up her mind. He had to feel her pain.

Jay's financial support wasn't enough. She was going to fix his ass. Since he wouldn't be with her, she would wreck his whole shit. She was going to tell the police she believed he was responsible for her brother's disappearance. She would tell them how Jay had given her a lump sum of cash to relocate, and maintained her living expenses and paid her tuition while she attended school.

She would lie and say she suspected foul play because the last time she had seen her brother, he was with Jay. She would say she believed Jay's generosity was some type of bribe technique to keep her mouth closed. When the pigs asked why she'd taken so long to come forward, she would say she had feared for her life.

Ysatis knew she was foul for planning to leak Jay's name like that, but she loved him. He should've fucking loved her back. He started it when he just discarded her. He broke her heart and ruined her life, so now she wanted to ruin his life as well.

Ysatis was down on men. She had thought Jay was the exception to the rule, but she hated them all. Her father never cared about her, her brother had stolen her innocence, and now Jay stole her heart. How dare he come into her life and rescue her, and then abandon her? What type of games was he playing? She was bitter, and unwilling to take any more shit off men.

Ysatis was drunk, the music was blasting, and the baby was screaming and hollering. She hit her breaking point and started crying too. With eyes full of tears, she picked up the phone and called Jay. She was giving that bastard one last chance. He didn't answer the phone, but she left him a message that let him know exactly what was on her mind.

When Jay's voicemail picked up, she slurred, "What up, Jay? This is Ysatis. This is the last time I'ma call you and tell you to come through. Christmas just passed, and you ain't do *nothin'* for us. Since you wanna play these type of games, and act like I ain't shit to you, I'ma do you dirty right back. You hear me, nigga? If you don't get at me within 48 hours, I'm goin' to the cops and telling them all about how you killed my brother. This is your final warning. I'm dead serious this time!"

She hung up the phone, and smugly patted herself on the back. She had finally put her foot down. Jay would get the message now. He would see that she wasn't playing with his ass.

$ $ $ $

It was the day after Christmas, and Jay was in a pretty good mood. He spent the day with his family. Well, everyone except Lil' Jay. He and Portia rolled out with just their daughters because Jayquan's big head didn't want to go with them.

It was Jazmin's birthday weekend, so they took her out on the town. Portia was also giving her a birthday party at the house in two weeks. She had learned in the past that it was best to wait until the holidays passed. The turnout would undoubtedly be better if folks had time to recover from the busy season.

After they took Jazz and Trixie out for a day of fun, they headed to Brooklyn to Mama Mitchell's house. She had birthday plans for Jazz as well, and then she was keeping the kids for the rest of weekend.

Jay and Portia hung out with his mom for a little while and played catch-up. Jazz was anxious to go out with her granny, so before long she shooed them off.

After they left, they went by Portia's house to check on things. Everything was okay over there, so they decided to go do something. They actually went to see a movie. That was something they hadn't done in a long time. And it was just like a first date. They held hands, shared popcorn and candy, and Jay even felt Portia up in the dark. After that, they went out for seafood and drinks.

While they were riding home in the car, Portia was pretty tipsy. She kept on eyeing Jay. She was lighthearted because they'd had such a great time, and she was also feeling naughty. She wanted to do something freaky. She decided to surprise Jay with some head on the way home.

She made her move subtly, and Jay smiled down at her. Portia told him to keep his eyes on the road. He laughed, and told her he had it. She pulled his joint out, and put her warm lips on it.

Portia talked dirty to Jay while she teased and pleased him. It felt so good he had to stop her before long. He had to maintain control. They were only minutes away from home, so they could finish when they got there.

When they got home, they went straight up to their bedroom. They would've done it downstairs, but they knew Jayquan and Macy were somewhere in the vicinity. Jay shut their room door, and he and Portia tore each other's clothes off. They went at it for about an hour. The sex they had was that hot, wet, and nasty kind. That was always the best.

Afterwards, they showered together. Jay finished and got out first. After he towel dried, he walked out the bathroom to get some clean boxers from his underwear drawer. He was pretty tired. Especially after all the sex he and Portia just had. His cell phone was on the dresser, so he noticed the message light was blinking. He picked up the phone and checked his voicemail.

When Jay heard that threatening voicemail from Ysatis, he got tight as hell. Steam almost shot out of his ears. That bitch was crazy, talking reckless on the phone like that. What the fuck was wrong with her? When Portia got out of the shower, he played the message again so she could hear. They both agreed that bitch was completely out of control. Something had to be done.

CHAPTER NINETEEN

It was New Year's Eve, and the countdown to the year 2010 was starting in about thirty minutes. Jay and Cas were amongst the well dressed individuals attending the grand opening at BJ's new night spot. The club was called "The Honeycomb", and all the hostesses were dressed in sexy black and yellow bumble bee inspired uniforms.

BJ had that plan in the works for some time, but he had finally managed to pull it off. He put up the bulk of the money himself, but Jay and Cas had also made substantial investments in his project. The two of them were silent partners, but they were each willing to let him buy them out when his thing took off.

BJ had also managed to get Eighty and Handy Andy to take the road to square-dom by offering them employment at his establishment. They were both placed in fields that were compatible with their personalities. Eighty was aggressive and never missed anything, so his job was supervising security. All he mostly had to do was sit in the back and monitor the door and floor security men on camera. He could come to work dressed up everyday if he wanted to.

Handy Andy was the more diplomatic of the two, so he opted to be the VIP Liaison. He said he was trying to do some things in the sports entertainment area in the future, so that gave him the opportunity to possibly cement some contacts.

Most people just wanted to be a part of something. Jay and

Cas were both glad to aid in something that could turnaround their cohorts lives. All of them would always be crimies at heart, but it was time for a change. Dudes were trying to be on a positive note, and that was great. Jay and Cas were both strong advocates for the "stay home campaign". They had all given enough of their time to the prison system. They could do better than that. It was about to be a new year.

The party had kicked off around ten, and the night was going well. They had advertised on the radio, so they had a pretty nice crowd. The music was good, drinks were half price until midnight, and there was a surprise guest scheduled to perform. Wise had wanted to come out, but Cas told him he didn't think that was a good idea because there were too many people there who knew him. Jay agreed with him.

Jay and Cas made occasional rounds to greet acquaintances who had showed up on the strength of them. But for the most part the two friends played the background. That night they were just there to show support for their peoples. It was BJ's night. They were proud that the dude had taken their advice and tried to do something legit.

These days Jay and Casino both preferred to stay more behind the scenes. It was all about business. They had their share of flossing, so they left that part up to their artists, and the homies from around the way. And dudes came out in droves that night to show love. They were dressed to kill too, on some real pimp shit.

About ten minutes to midnight, Jay's phone vibrated, indicating that he had a text message. He figured it was Portia, so he took out his phone and had a look. Jay frowned immediately. To his dismay, the text was from Ysatis. All week long he'd been trying to figure out what to do with her. That message she'd left on his phone the other day had pissed him off pretty bad. She was becoming a major problem.

Jay sighed. He wasn't in the mood, but he read the text

anyway. It said, *"Happy New Year, baby! Let's win in 2010! Don't fuck around and bring the year in behind bars! Stop pushing me!"*

Jay was angered and annoyed, so he put the phone away. He wanted to bring the New Year in on a positive note, but she was really trying to fuck that up. He didn't know who that dizzy bitch thought she was, but he wasn't going to tolerate any more of her threats. He had to really straighten that bitch out. He didn't want to have to hurt her, but Ysatis was too loose. He had to deal with her, and that was that.

All of a sudden, Jay got an idea. It might be at least a temporary fix. They were about to bring the New Year in, so he put it on a backburner for the time being. Just then, he saw Casino coming towards him with a bottle of rose champagne. Cas nodded at him, and they headed in the back.

Jay knocked on the door of the office, which doubled as a dressing room that night. A female's voice yelled, "Come in!"

Jay and Cas walked in on Kira sitting there getting the finishing touches on her makeup. She grinned at them, and said what up. They both greeted her, and Cas passed the rose bottle he was holding. Jay asked his baby sister if she was okay, and ready to go on.

Kira grinned, and nodded enthusiastically. The surprise guest was none other than her. She was performing that night at a quarter past twelve. She hadn't done a show in well over a year. She just came home four days after Christmas, so she was anxious to get back on the scene.

Cas asked Kira how her ride there was. She said it was okay, but something funny happened when she got to the club. She told them all about the incident.

When she pulled up outside in her limo, there was a long line of people waiting to get in. She just glanced at the faces on line, but one in particular stood out. This girl looked so familiar she did a double take.

Kira searched her mental database, and matched the face with a name. She couldn't believe it. It was that same C.O. bitch who put her foot on her when she was locked up, Officer Burton. Kira just smirked. She knew she would see that bitch again.

She rubbed her hands together in anticipation because she was about to get some get-back. Boy, it was a small world. Kira laughed to herself, and tried to conjure up the perfect plan to rain on that hoe's parade. She had violated her and treated her like a dog, so Kira wanted to ruin her night. The first thing she thought about was getting that bitch barred from the club. But she wanted to make her revenge a little more subtle.

The sound of people yelling snapped Kira back to the present. The club was packed, and the partygoers out there were shouting out the countdown to 2010. Kira jumped up and joined in. *"… five, four, three, two, one… Happy New Year!"* She grinned, and hugged her brother, Cas, and Allie, her makeup artist. She was so glad to be home.

They all laughed, and wished Kira a Happy New Year as well. Casino popped the bottle of Cristal Rose and filled everyone's glass, and they shared a New Year's toast. Kira threw hers back fast, and demanded a refill. She said she needed to get loose before she hit the stage.

Jay and Casino's cell phones went off one behind the other. They both received "Happy New Year" texts from the women in their lives, Portia and Laila. Kira noticed how Cas sort of smiled when he looked at his phone. Her woman's intuition told her that was some type of female correspondence.

A year ago she would've probably tried to fight him over that, but not anymore. She wasn't even tripping. Especially after that bid she did. She was glad she and Cas got pass all that. They had a son together, and that was it. All that mattered to Kira now was that they raise Jahseim the right way. She had really matured.

Cas poured them another round of champagne. They all joked around and laughed for a few minutes, and then Kira started spitting. She was feeling alright, so she said a quick sixteen bar rap. She sounded pretty good. Afterwards, she told them she had spent her whole bid writing, so she had some fire shit now.

Kira had on a red leather cat suit and these bad ass, thigh high, black leather Gucci boots. They were five inch platform stilettos. When she stood up, Jay asked her if she was sure she could still walk in high heels after doing that bid. He had jokes. He said jail had made her even more butch than she was before.

Kira laughed at her silly brother. She had always been a tomboy, but she set him straight real quick. She said, "Nigga, don't play. 'Cause I'm *still* a fuckin' lady." She took the champagne bottle from Cas and drank straight from it, and strutted out on stage.

Jay and Cas laughed at her bootleg impersonation of one of the queens of comedy, Adele Givens. Kira was back. And her ass was still crazy.

When they announced her on stage, the crowd went wild. When she got out there the first thing she said was, "Damn, it's good to be home! What up, New York? Happy New Year y'all!"

The crowd roared. Kira returned their love and energy, and then she went into her first set. She did four of her hit records. All the ladies in there seemed to know the words, and some dudes rapped along with her as well. Kira just loved it. She tore the roof off that mothafucka. The whole audience was rocking.

Kira was in her element. She was a natural so she knew how to work the stage. Jay and Cas watched her perform from the sidelines, and they were bobbing their heads too. She still had it. She didn't need anymore time off. She was ready. It was time to get her back in the studio.

She gave that performance her all, and she wasn't even getting paid for it. That was just a little test they gave her to see if she was still hot. And she had passed with flying colors.

Kira was a true emcee. She had love for hip-hop so she didn't mind the charity work that night. She jumped at any opportunity to rock the mic. She knew Jay and Cas were testing her but she loved shit like that. Being on stage gave her an adrenaline rush.

When Kira was done performing, she blew kisses at her audience, and then she picked up her half filled bottle of champagne and left the stage. She wasn't holding on to that bottle because she planned on finishing it either. She had something else in mind. She went back to her dressing room to carry out her plan.

Kira had to use the bathroom, so she headed to the private one in the back. She took the bottle and a plastic cup with her. When she stood over the toilet to pee, she caught most of it in the cup. After that, she carefully poured it in the champagne bottle.

The bottle wasn't quite filled to the top, so she mixed a little water with it too. Kira dried the bottle off good, and went back to her dressing room. The cork was in there. After she stuck the cork back in, she sat the bottle on ice.

After his sister was done performing, Jay went to tell her it was time to go. He knew Kira was feeling good off that champagne, but she knew the rule. There was no sticking around after a performance. She wasn't there to socialize. She was only there for business purposes.

Kira didn't complain about having to leave, but she told Jay she wanted to give somebody something first. She quickly ran down her plan to him, and then asked him to please have someone locate her "friend" Officer Burton. Jay shook his head at his crazy sister, but he went and got one of the hostesses.

He returned with a pretty hostess named Darlene. She had no problem taking the chilled bottle of bubbly out there to find the girl in question. Especially after Jay tipped her five hundred dollars as an incentive.

With the description Kira gave her, it only took Darlene about fifteen minutes to locate Officer Burton in the crowded club. She spotted her with two friends standing by the VIP section. They couldn't get in, but they were over there just trying to see who they saw.

Officer Janet Burton didn't live in the city. She was from the suburbs of New Jersey, so she was way excited about her annual New York City outing. She and her homegirls only came down once a year to party, so they tried to make it worth their while.

While she was on duty at the prison, she was what she called "professional". But she usually overdid it, and abused her powers on the job. Now Janet had a flipside too. Sometimes she took off that uniform and let her hair down. And when that happened, she was quite a party girl.

When the hostess approached her with "bottle service" and told her it was sent by a friend of hers, Janet Burton and her girls were absolutely thrilled. They felt like big shots. Especially Burton. Getting that type of love was reason enough to gloat a little bit. She told her homegirls they better recognize who they were with because she was a well-known bitch. Mothafuckas was sending her bottles of top of the line rose.

The ladies popped the bottle, and poured the expensive champagne in the glasses Darlene had provided them with. They made a toast, and happily drank up. They all took turns waving the bottle in the air and flossing while they got their dance on.

As if on cue, "Say Aah" by Trey Songz came on. They really started showing out after that. The ladies passed the bottle around and sang along, each of them fronting hard as hell.

"Go girl, it's your birthday. Open wide, I know you're thirsty. Say aah, say aah. We don't buy no drinks at the bar. We pop champagne 'cause we got that dough. Lemme hear you say aah. If you want it, say aah…"

The three friends kept pouring until that bottle was bone dry. They never once suspected that their Cris was full of piss. The funny thing was that none of them had ever tasted champagne that expensive before, so they were convinced that the bitter taste was just its natural flavor. That night they had the best time they'd ever had in their lives. They would talk about the way they did it up that night for many years to come.

After Darlene hand delivered the bottle to Burton, she kept her word and went back to notify Kira that it was done. She said she saw them open the bottle before she walked away. Kira thanked her, and then she laughed so hard she almost threw up.

Jay laughed hard too. That girl was a damn fool. After that, he had his crazy sister escorted home in the limo she came in. It wasn't long before he and Cas said goodnight too.

When they got ready to leave, BJ walked them outside. They congratulated him on a successful opening night. He smiled, and agreed with them. He thanked them again for helping him out, and assured them he would repay them as soon as possible. Cas and Jay told him they weren't even sweating it.

When they got in their limo to head home, Jay told Cas about Ysatis' threatening voicemail the other day, and then he showed him the text she sent him that night.

Cas just shook his head. He said, "Damn, son. These fuckin' bitches!" He asked Jay what he wanted to do.

Jay just sighed. He had no choice. After the driver pulled off, he ran his idea down to Cas. It wasn't a permanent solution, but at least it would buy him a little time. to come up with a concrete plan.

When he was done talking, Cas just said three words. "Call her now."

$ $ $ $

When Ysatis got the phone call from Jay, she smiled from ear to ear. That call had to mean she was finally getting through to him. To her delight, Jay said he'd called to wish her a Happy New Year. When she heard that she pinched herself to see if she was awake. Unbelievably, she was.

Ysatis played it cool. She thanked him, and said it back. Then Jay said he would talk to her soon, and they hung up. The conversation was brief, but Ysatis was happy like Jay had just serenaded her with a romantic Brian McKnight song.

She told herself he couldn't go into the New Year without making things right with her. She was the queen of making nothing into something, so she interpreted that call to be a declaration of his love. Now she couldn't wait to see him in person.

$ $ $ $

Meanwhile, Wise was at home with Fatima. He had brought the New Year in with his family, and that was a blessing. He wasn't complaining or anything, but he had to admit he missed hanging out and being on the scene. But he knew Jay and Cas were right. He had to lay low. Fatima was always telling him that too.

Wise thought his disguise was pretty sufficient. And he had I.D. in case the police stopped him. But there was still the risk of someone familiar with him noticing him. He had really wanted to be at BJ's grand opening that night, and he'd wanted to be there to support Kira too. That was her first performance since she came home. But Wise knew there was no point in taking a chance.

He glanced at the clock on his nightstand. It was a little after two AM. Fatima was knocked out already. She drank a little too much champagne, so she fell asleep right after they finished fucking. That was about a half an hour ago. He wore her ass out. Wise picked up the phone and called his main mans to see if they were still out.

Cas answered his jack jovially, and the friends wished each other a Happy New Year. Cas elbowed Jay and told him that was Wise on the phone. Jay grinned, and yelled, "Happy New Year, son!"

Wise was silly. He yelled it back through the phone. Cas laughed, and told Wise that he and Jay were on their way in.

Wise told him he put Fatima to sleep already, so now he was bored out of his ass. Cas laughed again, and asked him if he was hungry for something other than pussy.

Wise laughed then. He said, "I ain't gon' front, I ate a lot of that, but I'm starving."

He and Fatima did sort of O.D. on the champagne, so he needed to put something on his stomach. Cas told him they would swing through to get him in a few, so they could go get something to eat.

About an hour later, the three friends sat in a 24-hour diner, waiting on their food. They joked around and bugged out for a little while, and then they discussed some financial business. They talked about some overseas accounts and investments they had, and then some record label affairs.

Wise announced that he wanted to do another album. Jay and Cas didn't think that was a bad idea. The last EP they dropped after he "passed away" had done well. They could do it again. Wise said he and Jayquan had been in his studio laying down some new stuff he produced. He told them Lil' Jay had come by his crib to show off his skills a few times. He asked Jay if he knew his son could rap.

Jay looked surprised when Wise said that. Cas did too. At the notion of his boy being a rapper, Jay made a face. The business was so shady, he prayed hard none of his kids wanted to be stars. It was a dirty game. He wanted his son to go to college more than anything. After that, Lil' Jay could do what he wanted to do.

Next, they filled Wise in about the drama Jay had with that crazy bitch, Ysatis. When Wise heard the details, he couldn't believe she had threatened Jay with that old shit. That was pretty serious. Even though it happened a few years ago, Jay could still be prosecuted for it. And so could Cas, if she really started yapping.

Wise was honest with Jay, and told him he was really surprised that he got caught up in a situation like that. That wasn't even like him. Jay had always been the level headed one, ever since back in the days. He was the voice of reason in their crew.

Jay didn't comment, but he knew he was telling the truth. So did Cas, but he didn't say anything either. Wise was ball busting enough.

Wise told Jay he wasn't judging him. He said that was none of his business, but he agreed that something had to be done because Ysatis was out of control. He offered his assistance in eliminating the problem.

CHAPTER TWENTY

Portia tried to carry on as normal as she could and pretend that Ysatis bullshit wasn't affecting her, but it was no use. It was a new year, and she had accepted a lot of things. Ysatis had a baby by her husband, but she had to get it straight with that bitch that there was nothing popping between her and Jay.

Portia couldn't stop thinking about the fact that that bitch was actually trying to take her man. And she had the nerve to try and use the threat tactic. Nobody threatened her husband. Portia made up her mind to go over there and check that out-of-line bitch.

Portia didn't know about Jay's little plan to hold Ysatis off with lies. He didn't tell her that part. If she knew that, maybe she would've thought twice. But when Portia made up her mind, she made up her mind. She decided it had to be the very next day.

The next morning, she was anxious to confront Ysatis. She drove to Brooklyn right after the kids went to school. She popped up on that bitch early, knowing she wouldn't be expecting her.

Ysatis and the baby were asleep when Portia rang the bell. When Ysatis went to the door she was surprised, but she tried to act unfazed. Her words were drenched with attitude when she asked Portia, "May I help you?"

Portia said, "No, I came to give you an opportunity to help yourself." She pushed right pass Ysatis, and walked inside.

Ysatis couldn't believe Portia just walked up in her house

uninvited like that. And it was early in the damn morning. She had some fucking nerve. Ysatis just stood there with her arms crossed.

Portia said, "Obviously, this is not a social visit. I'll get to the point. I see you're the type of bitch that'll do anything to get what she wants. That was the only way you lucked up and got pregnant by my husband. But I don't think you understand how much my marriage means to me. And what *extremes* I'll go to just to protect it."

Portia looked in her eyes to make sure she got the message. "I assure you that I will annihilate, kill, and destroy any and everything that tries to come in between me and my husband. This is something you should know. Leave my mothafuckin' husband alone, bitch. Jay doesn't want you."

Ysatis wanted to curse Portia out, but she didn't want Jay to get mad at her. She was a little confused. She had just got a call from Jay days ago wishing her a happy new year, and now his wife was in her house telling her to stay away from him. What was really good?

Ysatis had doubts, but she was more was naïve than pessimistic. She figured Portia just didn't get the memo yet. Jay wanted her now, so she didn't know what to tell her. Ysatis just smirked, and said, "Yeah, whatever. I hear you." She just wanted Portia to leave so she could call Jay.

Portia scowled at her, tempted to snatch a knot in her little skinny ass. "I *hope* you hear me. Don't *make* me kill you, *bitch*. Stop calling my husband, and stop texting him too. If I have to come back, I won't be talking next time. I'll be gunning for yo' ass, tramp!"

Before Portia left, she wrinkled up her nose. "And take those shitty baby pampers outside. It stink up in here! When you have a child, you gotta have common sense! You can just stay ignorant, and act like you slow. You're a mother! Damn!"

$ $ $ $

Kira was enjoying being home. She was hungry, so she had a lot of work to do. Despite what the nay-sayers thought, she had just begun. She had come back to reclaim her rightful spot as the hottest female emcee. Second or third best just wouldn't do.

She was also focused on being the best mom she could be. She was trying to make up for lost time. She needed to bond with her son. She had been away from him for more than a year. Jahseim was growing up so fast. He was almost ten years old now, and he had a lot of sense.

He seemed a little distant since Kira had been home. She had the feeling he was sort of mad at her about something. He pretty much knew why she had gone to jail, so she suspected he had some issues with her. She knew he had been staying with Cas, and Cas was with Laila now. What Kira had done had probably put Jahseim in a pretty awkward position. He was staying with a woman whose house his mother had torched.

At first, Kira didn't like the idea of her son being around Laila. She believed she would mistreat him, so of course she had been concerned. When her family brought her son to visit her, she asked him how he felt about Laila. To her surprise, Jahseim said he liked her because she was nice to him all the time.

He knew what happened already, so Kira was forced to have that conversation with him. She gave him permission to speak freely, and get whatever he was mad at her about off his chest.

Jahseim told her he didn't understand why she had set Laila's house on fire. Especially when she and his little sister were inside asleep. He wanted to know how she could've done something so mean.

Kira felt small as hell, but she had to look him in his face and try to redeem herself. Jahseim was a young man now. She needed him to respect her. Kira had grown up a lot the last year, and her son's opinion of her meant everything. There was nothing more important. She told him she was sorry, and would never do anything to risk being taken away from him again. He made her promise.

After she reestablished her connection with her boy, Kira's main objective was to be hot again. It was all for her son anyway. Whatever she accomplished was going to be his one day.

Since she left the game, she sat back and watched all these new rap chicks coming out of the woodwork. She loved competition, so she was determined to get back out there and shut them down. Her objective was to make her career pop.

She hit the studio and laid down enough songs to create a mix CD. She was rapping over all the latest hot tracks. After that, she started booking lots of shows. Kira had sharpened her sword and honed her rap skills while she was away, so she was on fire.

She got at the so-called hottest female rappers in the game, and tried to spark beef. She publicly challenged all of them to step up and battle her. Doing this, Kira stirred up a lot of controversy. And that was just what she wanted. That would spark up anticipation for her upcoming album. She was all over the radio, and the internet.

She was focused this time around. She was doing some modeling, and also pitching a new reality show she had in mind. Her manager was just searching for the right network. She had talked Jay and Cas into putting up the bread for the pilot, so her big brother and ex-husband would be the executive producers of the show.

In literally no time, Kira landed a spot on primetime cable television. Her reality show was going to be airing on VH1 that coming spring. She had agreed to reveal the truth about her arson charges, the bid she'd just come off, and the whole nine. They were even going to film footage of her going to the group meetings and therapy sessions she was ordered to attend, as a condition of her release.

Jay and Cas were in because they saw dollar signs, and the

exposure was good for Kira's upcoming CD. Hell, everybody else in the world seemed to have a reality show. So why not?

Kira was so busy her days were a blur. That gave her less time to think about Cas being engaged to Laila. She had recently found out, and that news didn't sit well with her at all. She had moved on, but still. Kira secretly prayed that God would send her someone special. Sometimes she was kind of lonely.

Kira was preparing to record her album. She wanted to work with the best producers in the game. Amongst others, Vino and Five were two hot, up and coming producers out on the west coast. She really liked their sound, so she told Jay and Cas she wanted to meet with them. They told her they could make that happen.

Jay and Cas had their plates full of things Street Life had in the makings. They had the airwaves on fire, with four hit songs in heavy rotation. And they were releasing an EP of Kira's new music, strictly to be sold on I-tunes. That would heat things up until her album was ready. They had also signed a new artist, and were releasing another "posthumous" album from Wise. The New Year was going to be a prosperous one. They were going hard, so it had to.

$ $ $ $

Jay stayed in the house all day the following Monday. He needed to catch up on some rest. The last few days had been very long ones for him. He had been pretty busy. Jay had been taking care of company business, and he was even more exhausted from the web of deceit he had been spinning. He had been lying to Ysatis, and stringing her along. Just so she wouldn't think about going to the cops about her lousy brother, Neal.

Jay didn't know how long he could keep that up because she was annoying the shit out of him. She had called him and asked him if he really cared about her. He just lied and told her he did.

She sounded glad to hear that. After that, she told him Portia showed up at her house and threatened her life.

Jay could tell she wanted some type of reaction from him when she said that, but he wasn't into all the drama and shit. He started to tell her the damn truth, which was that he wished Portia or somebody would just kill her. That's how bad he wanted her out of his hair. She was calling him everyday and begging to go out, and shit. He wasn't thinking about her ass. If she only knew. That bitch really had no idea.

Jay laid there thinking for a while. He had quite a quandary on his hands. He was in a hell of a jam. Ysatis was lucky she had that baby. That was the main reason he wouldn't just kill her himself. Jay had a good heart.

He got up and stretched, and then he headed downstairs to the kitchen to get something to drink. As he walked down the hall, he heard loud music coming from his son's bedroom. The door was open when he walked by, so he glanced inside. He was just in time to see his son rapping in his dresser mirror.

Jayquan was fronting hard. He was popping his collar, dusting dirt off his shoulders, and the whole nine. The dude was really feeling himself. He said, *"Hop up out my bed, turn my swag on. Take a look in the mirror, say what's up. Yeaaahh. I'm gettin' money. Ohhh-ohhh…"*

Jay chuckled to himself. His boy was pretty confident lately. Some girl must've had his head swollen. Jay knew a lot of them were jocking him. He saw how they were on him at Macy's party.

Lil' Jay had birthright swag. He inherited it from his father. Jay was quite dapper, and the apple didn't fall far from the tree.

When Jayquan noticed his pops standing there watching him, he quit rapping and laughed. Then his face looked like a light bulb came on in his head. He quickly turned his music down, and jumped on the opportunity to hound Jay about a new car for himself.

Again, Jay told him it wasn't the time. Number one, he didn't even have a driver's license yet. And he couldn't get one yet because he wasn't even sixteen. Jay said, "You'll get a car when the time is right, son. But I don't understand what the rush is. Between me and Portia, there are five vehicles in our garage. So what's your hurry? All the cars we got out there, come on."

Jayquan made a face, and had the nerve to say, "Man, I want my *own* car. It's not like we don't got the money. *Come on*, Pop. Stop frontin'."

Jay laughed, but then he put that little dude in check quick. He told Lil' Jay that was his damn money, so he didn't have shit. He wanted his kids to have the world, but he also wanted them to understand that you had to work hard for what you wanted in life. He didn't want his son to go the route he had taken, so he told him he needed to make the right choices in life. And that way he could make his own bread. As much as he desired.

Jayquan made a face, and said, "I don't need to make no money. What for? I can just spend yours."

Jay just shook his head. Wow, that guy was hilarious. He said, "God bless the child that's got his own, son. Money makes the world go 'round."

Jayquan was looking at him like he was speaking Japanese. Jay gave up. That boy was spoiled as hell, so they would have that talk a little later. He said, "For right now, son, just get your education. Focus on finishing high school. And it's time to start thinking about what you wanna go to college for. With education, the sky is the limit."

Jayquan made another face. He and his father had a pretty cool relationship. Jay had always encouraged him to say what was on his mind, so Lil' Jay was usually outspoken with him. He said, "But Pop, you or my uncles Cas and Wise didn't go to college, and y'all are mad successful. So I'ma be just like you."

Jay just looked at him for a minute. That little dude was really something else. He checked Jayquan again. "First of all, you have *no idea* what it took to get here. You think what we did was easy? I did what I had to do so *you* wouldn't have to. So don't be like *me*. *Be better*. I didn't go to college, but *you are*. Right, man?"

Jay saw the way Jayquan looked at him. He detected a little defiance in his eyes. Damn, the boy was just like him. He didn't like to be pushed.

Jayquan was a young man now, so Jay decided to show him some respect. He softened his tone a little. "Man, just go to school and do the right thing. And I'll get you that car soon. Stay on the right track and make me proud, and I'll buy you anything you want. You already know."

Jayquan piped right down. He sighed, and shook his head. "A'ight, Pop. You got it." He gave his father a pound, and a hug.

After Jay hugged his son, he playfully threw him in a headlock and gave him a noogie. Lil' Jay made a face and protested immediately. He thought he was too old for shit like that now. Jay just laughed. He thought about giving him a wedgie too, but he decided against it.

Jay lived for his kids. He loved them more than anything, and they meant the world to him. It was his job to protect them at all costs. That was the main reason why he hadn't said a word to them about that baby yet. He didn't want to upset them with the news. He knew they would be hurt by it.

$ \qquad $ \qquad $ \qquad $

Ysatis was stuck in the house with her baby all the time, so she didn't have much of a social life for a girl her age. She got by on the notion that her life was about to change for the better. She was elated that she actually had a chance at love and happiness.

She had fought pretty hard for Jay, and she finally won. It wasn't easy, but he came around just when the New Year came in. He had called her first. And when she asked him if he wanted to be with her, he said "yes". He said that when the time was right, they were going to run away together. He just needed a little bit more time to tie up some loose ends.

His wife had come over her house talking shit, but Ysatis chalked that up to be Portia's last desperate attempt to hold on to her marriage. It was over between them. Ysatis asked Jay if he was going to get a divorce. He told her to just worry about her and him, so she decided to just focus on what they had together.

Ysatis was mad gullible, so she believed all the bullshit. One might say that she was blinded by love. The only thing she hated was the fact that Jay didn't want to go out, or anything. She told him she understood, and would give him some time to do what he had to do.

He told her it wouldn't be long, and she believed him. There was no reason for him to lie to her. Or so she thought.

$ $ $ $

Macy and Jayquan had been intimate, but they were cool about it. No one had any idea. The two of them were having sex every time they got an opportunity. Every time, and everywhere.

They thought they were pretty smart, but they were still young so they had to slip up somewhere. One weekend when Macy was staying over, she came into the kitchen where Jayquan was talking to his father and uncles, Cas and Wise.

Macy had come to tell Lil' Jay to sneak in her bedroom later on, but when she saw the grownups she just got something to drink instead. Before she left the kitchen, she said, "Good night, y'all." After that, she just smiled at Jayquan.

While she was walking away, he stared at her booty sort of appreciatively with a sly grin on his face.

Wise was the only one who caught that. When Jayquan went upstairs, he pulled Casino and Jay's coat. He said, "Yo, somethin' is goin' on between those two. I think Lil' Jay might be smashing that! What y'all think?"

Jay laughed, and shook his head. "*Nah*, man. Macy's a good girl. They just real cool. She's into all that boy shit he's into."

Cas co-signed with Jay. But Wise disagreed. He said, "*Nah*. I'm *tellin'* you. I'll put some money on that. Look how Lil' Jay was lookin' at her butt."

Cas scratched his chin, and Jay shrugged his shoulders.

Wise nodded his head knowingly. He said, "Trust me, somethin' is about to pop off. If it hasn't *already*. Y'all better act like y'all know. How many "good girls" *we* done took down? I hate to say it like that, but it is what it is. The kids are growing up. They're in high school now."

Jay just looked at Wise for a second, and didn't say anything. Cas didn't either. They didn't know what to say. They didn't know what those kids were up too. With children, you never knew what to expect.

CHAPTER TWENTY ONE

Any suspicions Wise had about Lil' Jay and Macy were sort of confirmed when Jayquan called him and said he needed to speak to him and Cas about something. Wise told Cas, and together they went by the house to see what their nephew had on his mind.

Jay and Portia weren't at home when they got there, so Lil' Jay let them in. The three of them played a little pool while they kicked it. To their surprise, Jayquan said he wanted to ask them a few things about sex.

Jayquan was young, but like any other man, he had an ego. He wasn't cool with the fact that Macy always seemed a little more experienced than him when they did it. He needed some pointers, and he didn't feel comfortable talking to his father or Portia about sex. They were always asking him stuff, but he wasn't ready to talk with them just yet.

Jayquan asked his uncles a few questions about how to please a woman. They laughed at him a lot, but they both got a kick out of him coming to them. That was what they were there for. They were both flattered that he chose to talk to them.

It was funny because Cas tried to be the serious one, and tell him the right thing to do when it came to girls. Wise on the other hand tried to teach him from a pimping sort of perspective. He told him just about all the wrong stuff to tell a fifteen year old boy. Wise would never change. He was a natural born comedian.

But it was funny as hell listening to him.

Wise said there were only three things Jayquan had to remember when it came to sex. He said, "Listen here, nephew. There are three little rules to follow. Rule number one is "never trust a big butt and a smile". No matter how bad a chick is, she still can have some type of disease. AIDS, or anything. It's okay to pipe, but just make sure you strap up. You only take the rubber off after you find yourself a good wife, like we all did."

Wise saw that Lil' Jay was really listening, so he continued. "Rule number two is simply "you don't love them hoes, you fuck 'em!" That's pretty self-explanatory." Wise thought about Macy, and changed that part up a little bit. Just in case that advice was for her, he said, "That applies to the hoes, not nice girls."

Next, Wise said, "And always remember rule number three, baby boy!"

He paused, and got real serious. He grabbed Jayquan's shoulders and looked him in the eyes. Wise said, "Rule number three. "Don't let the first pussy you get whip you." Because I'm telling you, pussy is a beautiful thing. When you skeet, you might hear trumpets and horns, and shit. But listen to me, nephew. You gotta whip that pussy!"

Cas and Jayquan started cracking up. Wise was a fool but Cas didn't intervene in his teachings. Though he had been a little graphic and raw, he hadn't told Jayquan anything wrong. It was nothing the boy hadn't heard already anyway. He probably used those same words sometimes. That was how teenagers were.

$ \quad $ \quad $ \quad $

Jay and Portia's knee-baby, Jazz's birthday was two days after Christmas, but they were having her birthday party in mid-January. Portia had been planning it since Halloween, so she already had everything together.

She couldn't believe how fast her babies were growing up.

Jayquan was fifteen, Jazmin was nine now, and Patrice was just about two. They were having a birthday party for her too.

Portia loved all her kids equally, but Jazmin's birthday was particularly sentimental to her. If Portia had carried her full term, Jazmin would've been born in February. But she was born premature, after Portia was raped and shot in her collarbone while she was pregnant with her. Jazz was her miracle baby.

Jazmin didn't know yet, but Jay got her the pony she wanted. Portia was probably more excited about it than she would be. She couldn't wait to see the look on her little girl's face.

That year Jazz wanted her party theme to be the Disney Princesses. Portia was excited about it as well. They had recently introduced the very first African American Disney princess, Princess Tiana. She was featured in the new movie, "The Princess and the Frog". Back in December, Portia, Laila, and Fatima took all the kids to see it when it first came out. They enjoyed it as much as the children did.

When the day came, Jazz was dressed up as Princess Tiana. She had the whole outfit on, including the dress, the gloves, the shoes, and the tiara. You couldn't tell Miss Thing nothing.

Portia went out on a limb and bought the frog costume for Lil' Jay to be the Frog Prince. She just assumed he wouldn't mind wearing it for his little sister at her party, but Jayquan said he refused to "dress up in no tight frog suit lookin' all stupid." Portia begged him, but to no avail. She couldn't even bribe him to do it. He was going through that stage where he thought he was too cool for everything.

Portia was frog-less, so she had to try to hire someone at the last minute. She told Laila and Fatima her dilemma, and they started looking online for a company. They found a couple, but Uncle Wise volunteered before Portia could make the call. Portia laughed, and thanked him over and over. Then she told him to hurry over so he could get in character.

Wise didn't mind being the frog at the party. It gave him an excuse to attend one of the family celebrations. He didn't go to any and everything because he couldn't risk being seen.

Wise drove himself, Fatima, and Falynn over to Jay and Portia's crib. Their little girl was dressed as Cinderella. Halfway there, he had to turn around and go back because Fatima left Jazmin's birthday gift at home by mistake. Wise fussed about it, but he still went back.

He laughed at Fatima while she was walking in the house. She was six months along now, and her belly was getting big.

When she got back in the car, Wise asked her if she'd reactivated the security system. She nodded, and told him to drive.

When they got there, Portia quickly ushered Wise in her office downstairs to change. When he came out, she laughed, and told him what a fine damn frog he made. She said she especially loved his webbed feet.

After they laughed, she grabbed his hand and took him out there to introduce him to the children. They roared in excitement, and were all over him.

Wise did his best to entertain. They had no idea who he was underneath that mask, so he acted like a silly fool. The children loved him. He had a good time too.

Fatima kept laughing about the way Wise's legs looked in that frog suit. She and Portia snapped a million photos, and Jay and Jayquan took turns videoing. It was for the kids, but they would never let Wise live that one down. They would laugh about that incident for a long time.

The party invitations had specified Jazmin's wishes to have all the other little kids dress up as Disney characters too. There were little Snow Whites, Cinderellas, Sleeping Beauties, Tinkerbells, Little Mermaids, there was a Minnie Mouse, and any other Disney princess, fairy, or diva you could name. The only two little boys there were dressed up as Pinocchio and Prince Charming. Jazz's first cousin, Jahseim was Prince Charming.

The birthday cake was a real castle with a little Princess Tiana on top. It was beautiful. Everything was fit for a princess, and Jazz acted like she was real royalty too. She was prancing around, and acting all dainty and ladylike all day. She was nothing like the little tomboy who liked to play fight with boys. Any other day, she would wrestle her big brother and cousin Jahseim fearlessly.

Jay and Cas' man, Eighty, had a daughter around Jazmin's age. So Jay had invited him and his little girl over that day too. His daughter's name was Janessa. She was dressed as Princess Jasmine from Aladdin, and she and Jazz hit it off immediately.

Casino and Jay had recently put Eighty on their payroll. They created a job for him as part of their security team at Street Life. He still worked at BJ's nightspot too. Eighty was a good dude. He was trying to get it right lately, and they wanted to help keep him on the right track.

Portia had also invited her cousin Melanie. She was tired of Mel calling and asking her for help with that porn production company. She had to be honest with her and tell her she changed her mind. She was glad her cousin had showed up because they had to talk. She had to explain to her that she couldn't do it because she had daughters. She couldn't bring herself to get involved in that lifestyle again. She was done.

Portia pulled Mel to the side, and told her she couldn't help her. She let her know she had too many maternal responsibilities to dedicate herself to the project. She apologized for backing out on her, and wished her luck. She told her she would see if she could introduce her to somebody else that could help her.

Mel grinned at Portia, and told her she was getting old. She said she was a real square now, but it was all good. She said she understood how she felt. And truthfully, a part of her envied Portia. She had a husband that loved her and took good care of her, and they had the perfect family. Mel was thirty now, and she sometimes thought about settling down too. But she still had a wild streak she had to get out of her.

Just then, Mel caught the eye of this dude across the room who was talking to Jay. He looked at her for a second, but he didn't show much interest. The brother was looking kind of good to Mel. She knew she was a perfect ten, so she was sure he liked the way she looked too. The fact that he was so nonchalant about it sparked her interest.

She stared at him for a minute. He was basically ignoring her now. Mel decided she wanted to get to know him. She asked Portia who he was, and if he was alone.

Portia looked over to see who Mel was referring to, and she smiled. She told Mel who Eighty was, and then she told her he was too hard for her.

Mel looked at her like she was crazy. She said there was no such thing as a dude too hard for her. She said she loved it hard. She and Portia both laughed, and then she demanded to be introduced.

Portia told Mel she didn't really want her messing with Jay's friends because she didn't want her to get a bad reputation.

Mel acted like she was offended. She said, "Damn, P, I just said I wanna meet him, not fuck him. Give me a little bit of credit."

After she said that, Portia sighed, and agreed. She walked Mel over there and introduced her to Eighty, and then she grabbed Jay's hand and told him she needed his help in the kitchen.

When Portia pulled him by the arm, Jay knew what time it was. He laughed, and told Eighty they would holler in a minute.

Melanie struck up a conversation with Eighty, and they actually hit it off. He treated her like a gentleman, but she could tell he was a thorough type of dude. And there was a mystery to him. She was feeling his persona.

During their brief chat, she learned that he had a daughter there with him at the party, but he said he was no longer with his baby mother. He said that was his only child. She was a twin, but her sister didn't survive during birth.

Mel asked for his number, and keyed it in her cell phone. She called him right there on the spot, just to give him her number too. When he saw her number, he gave her a little smile. Mel flashed her pearly whites and gave him a big one. She liked his swagger, so she was definitely looking forward to hooking up with him.

$ $ $ $

That following Saturday, Portia, Laila, and Fatima had a meeting with the wedding planner to see where they were. They had set a date for Valentine's Day weekend. The wedding was to be held on Saturday, February 13, 2010.

The wedding planner, Teresa, said they were on schedule. She said she just needed their opinion on a few changes she had made. She assured them the changes were for the better. After they discussed her final ideas, Laila said she was feeling a bit overwhelmed because it was coming so fast.

Fatima made a face at her. She said, "Look, Lay, you need to let *us* worry about that. If them Kardashian bitches can pull off Khloe and Lamar Odom's wedding in ten days, then we can damn sure do this. All it takes is money. Money makes the world go 'round, baby."

Portia laughed, and gave Fatima a high five. Then she looked at Laila, and said, "Don't go turning into no Bridezilla, bitch. Just relax, and let us handle it. All you gotta do is show up, and look pretty."

Laila grinned. She said, "I ain't gon' front, all this shit sound good. But it would be just my luck that it'll turn out to be the wedding from hell. And then I'ma wanna kill you bitches for making me do this."

They all laughed together. Next, Fatima asked about her dress. She was starting to show, so hers would definitely need to be let out. All their dresses were designed by Vivienne Westwood. Befittingly, they chose Valentine's Day colors. Laila's wedding gown was winter white, and their bridesmaids' dresses were different shades of red. They had an appointment the following weekend to have their final fittings. The brothers would keep it simple in black custom tailored Tom Ford suits, and red ties.

Laila told them Cas had the flu, so she had to get home to look after him. Her girls sent him lots of well-wishes. Laila said she would tell him what they said. She laughed, and told them her whole house smelled like garlic because he preferred natural remedies instead of taking over-the-counter stuff. Everybody knew Cas was a health fanatic, so they just laughed.

Portia suggested that she take their kids home with her until Cas got over that bug. Laila took her up on that. Their house was huge, but she still didn't want to take any chances on them getting sick. She told Portia to follow her home so she could pick up Macy and Skye, and take them with her.

CHAPTER TWENTY TWO

When Portia got home, Jay was waiting for her. He greeted Macy and Skye, and then he kissed Portia and said he hoped she wasn't tired. He told her they were going out to dinner with two young, promising associates of his.

Portia smiled, and told him to let her take a shower and get ready. She asked him if it was "black tie".

Jay laughed, and said, "Not at all. Wear what you wanna wear."

Portia didn't ask him any more questions. She headed upstairs, somewhat flattered that Jay had asked her along. It wasn't all the time she got to be with him when he handled business.

Portia dressed in a fitted black Gualtier sweater dress, and a pair of high heeled Christian Louboutin ankle boots she had bought in Paris. Underneath her dress, she put on sexy lace stockings, garters, and lacy underwear. She planned to seduce Jay later, somewhere between their after-dinner cocktail, and the time they got home.

She sprayed on Yves Saint Laurent's Parisienne perfume, and then she put on a few brilliant pieces from the latest diamond collection Jay had given her. After that, she threw her mahogany colored mink stroller over her arm and headed downstairs. Jay was already dressed, and watching the ball game. He let out a whistle when he saw her. Portia held up her arms and twirled around for him. He nodded appreciatively.

Jay had on a nice Ralph Lauren Purple Label sweater and

slacks, and wine colored shoes. Portia told her man he looked good in his ensemble. She asked him to do a little spin for her.

Jay made a face. He said, "What I look like, twirling around like I'm some fruity ass model, or somethin'?"

Portia laughed. She knew that was how he would respond. Her baby was so hardcore. She walked over for a hug and kiss. Damn, Jay smelled good. She bought him that cologne herself.

Jay held Portia for a minute and kissed her. Then he pushed her away, and adjusted his hard dick in his pants. He said, "Damn, Kit Kat. Now I got wood. We better chill, P, 'fore we fuck around and be staying home tonight. But I know what you want. Don't worry, I'ma beat that thang up later."

Portia laughed, and rolled her eyes. She said, "Promises, promises."

Jay said, "Hold me to it, sexy." He winked at her, and smacked her on the ass. "Come on, ma. Let's go."

He helped his wife into her fur, and then he slipped into the wool Ferragamo coat he was wearing. Lil' Jay, Macy, and all the little ones were up in the rec section. They said goodnight to them, and Portia told Macy to put Trixie, Skye, and Jazz in the bed soon. Jay told Jayquan not to wait up because they would be getting home sort of late. After that, he and Portia headed out on the town.

After all those years, Jay was still a gentleman. He opened his Bentley passenger door and helped Portia inside. And when they got to the restaurant, he took her hand and helped her get out so the valet could park the car. She took his arm, and together they headed inside.

Portia loved when Jay made her feel like a lady. She was all smiles. She loved her man so much she couldn't stop cheesing.

When they got to their table, they saw that their guests had already arrived. When Portia saw Vino and Five from L.A. sitting there, her smile quickly faded. She was so caught off guard, she almost choked.

Portia didn't know why she was tripping. She knew Jay did business with them, so she should've known she would see Vino again. She was just surprised to see him that night. She quickly got it together before her husband noticed she was acting weird.

Jay hadn't said a word to Portia about it, but he and Cas had decided to fly Five and Vino to NY to talk about Kira's project. He thought it would be a nice surprise for Portia to see them while they were in town, seeing as though they had looked after her and Fatima when they went out to L.A. But from the look on her face, she wasn't really thrilled to see them. Jay wondered what that was about.

Five and Vino stood up to greet them. Jay smiled at his little homies, and welcomed them to his coast. The men gave each other dap, and hugged.

Portia smiled at them too, but she was so nervous she almost peed on herself. The only thing running through her mind was the words *"Oh shit! Why me?"* She said a quick prayer, and tried to keep her cool. She was with her husband so she couldn't blow it. Portia took a deep breath, and kept her composure. Above all, she was a lady.

Every ounce of her regretted the fact that she'd put herself in that type of predicament. She prayed Vino wouldn't blow it up. If Jay knew they had sex in L.A. he would've probably ordered a hit on both of them. No, he would've killed them himself. That was personal.

Jay told Vino and Five that Cas was at home sick, so he wouldn't be joining them. He turned to Portia, and said, "Y'all already met my wife, Portia, when y'all took care of her for me in L.A."

Portia almost turned red when Jay said that. If he only knew how much Vino took care of her. She smiled, and said, "Yup, sure did. Y'all looked out for me *and* my girl, Tima. It's good to see y'all." She extended her hand to each of them for a ladylike handshake.

Vino and Five both said, "Likewise." They were gentlemen. They both smiled at her, and kissed her hand.

Jay was a good sport. He knew his wife was stunning, so he just grinned. Portia smiled politely, and sat down in the chair he pulled out for her. After that, they all had a seat. Jay summoned a waiter, and ordered a bottle of their best bubbly.

Five and Vino asked how Fatima was doing. Portia's face lit up, and she told them her girl was expecting another baby. They told her to congratulate Fatima for them. Five said he had a kid on the way too, so Portia congratulated him on that. So did Jay.

When the waiter brought the champagne over, he popped the cork and filled everyone's glass. Jay held up his glass and proposed a toast to prosperity. After they all clinked their glasses together, he thought about the look on Portia's face when she first saw them. Was it his imagination, or had she looked uncomfortable?

Jay wasn't stupid. He wondered what that look was about. Was she nervous? Did something happen in L.A.? He had this weird type of hunch, but he just blew it off. He wasn't a jealous dude. Besides, his little homies knew better. And Portia would never violate him like that. Right?

Jay just had this weird feeling, but he let it go. They ordered a few appetizers at first. Jay, Five, and Vino engaged in good natured conversation for a while. After the appetizers were served, Jay brought up the reason they were there.

Portia sipped another glass of champagne while they talked about Kira's album. Jay looked over at her, but he didn't say anything. That made her nervous for some reason. She told him she would be right back, and then she excused herself and went to the ladies room.

In the bathroom, Portia quickly got Fatima and Laila on a conference call. When they were both on the line, she said, "Y'all ain't gon' believe this shit. Guess who I'm eating dinner with? Vino, the young guy I screwed in L.A."

They both said, "*What?*"

Portia ran it down for them, and told them how shook she was. Both of her girls gave her a quick word of advice. They said be cool, and don't admit anything. Fatima was especially concerned because she had been with Vino's right hand man, Five. If Portia got blown up, it would be easy to figure out that they had couple fucked.

Portia admitted to her girls that she felt like the scum of the earth. She said she was foul for crossing Jay like that. They were split up at the time, but still. She had slept with a guy he hired to protect her. That was some real whorish shit. How could she stoop so low? She really played herself.

Laila said what was done was done. She told her to sweep that shit under a rug, and get it together. Portia said she was straight now, but there were some things you just had to tell somebody.

Fatima was so silly. She said, "You better go back to the table before everybody think you in there takin' a shit. We been on the phone for a minute, P."

Laila and Portia cracked up. That was on time. Portia needed a laugh. They agreed to talk later, and hung up after that.

Portia looked in the mirror at herself, and took a deep breath. She loved Jay, and she would let nothing ruin her marriage. Absolutely nothing. They had been through too much. She reapplied her lip-gloss, and then she held her head up and walked back to the table to finish dining with her husband and his associates.

When Portia got back, Jay smiled, and told her they had been waiting for her to order. He summoned the waiter, and said, "Ladies first, ma."

After dinner, Jay told his little homies he had his assistant get them on the VIP list at an upscale gentleman's club. He had prepaid for a two-hour session for them with two of the club's best girls, so they could "enjoy" themselves. Five and Vino took him up on that, and then they all parted on a positive note.

It had turned out to be an enjoyable evening after all. Portia was relieved because Jay didn't seem to notice anything. But she still felt guilty for putting her husband in a situation like that. He was treating a dude who had bedded his wife to dinner. Portia was so sorry.

She felt so bad she wanted to make him feel good. So when they got home that night, she was totally submissive. She asked Jay how he wanted to be pleased. She said she was his freaky American Geisha Girl that night, so his wish was her command.

Jay was feeling that. He made his first wish, and of course it was a wet one. So Portia did him like she was trying to apologize. And she enjoyed doing it. She gave her baby head until he came, and then she started again. But she was so tipsy from all that champagne, she dozed off with him in her mouth like his penis was a pacifier.

Jay was enjoying himself, but he looked down at Portia and laughed. She gave new meaning to the words "sleepy head". He slipped Rocky out of her mouth, and got up and went to the bathroom to take a leak.

Jay had never really spied on Portia, or checked her messages since they'd been married. They didn't do that. She got in her moods sometimes, but he wasn't really with it. She was asleep at the time, and the text alert on her phone was vibrating and beeping. He picked up her BlackBerry, and saw that the late night text was from Fatima. The first few words said, *"R u ok? What happened…"*

That was enough to raise his concern. He opened up the text and read the rest. The whole thing read, *"R u ok? What happened in your "situation"? Are we safe? LOL."*

Jay raised an eyebrow. He had this funny feeling. What "situation" was Fatima referring to? Were they "safe" from what? He thought about the way Portia had looked when she first saw Five and Vino. Something was up.

He thought about waking her ass up, and asking her a few questions. He wanted to know what the fuck that was about.

Were they safe from what?

Jay caught himself. He wasn't that type of dude. But he had a feeling Five and Vino had some dirt on Portia and Fatima. He figured they probably knew about them flirting or hanging out with some dudes out there. Portia was probably scared that they were going to tell him.

He put his suspicions on a backburner for the time being. They had a great time that evening. There was no point in him ruining the night with an argument. It was usually Portia who initiated those.

Jay already knew from his own misdeeds and fuck-ups that anything Portia might have done would come to the light. Everything done in the dark always did. To be fair, they weren't really together when she went to L.A. So if she did do a little socializing, he couldn't even trip. Portia was a sexy woman so he knew lots of dudes tried to holler.

$ $ $ $

About five AM, Portia got up to go to the bathroom. She realized she had been out for a while. She smiled at Jay, who was sleeping peacefully beside her. He was so cute. She leaned over and planted a feather light kiss on his ear. He didn't even budge.

After she came out the bathroom, Portia decided to check on the kids. She had fallen asleep without peeking in on them. That was something she never did. That alcohol and guilt trip had her bugging.

She looked in on the little ones first. Jazmin, Trixie, and Skye were all asleep in Jazz's room. Portia went to check on her big babies next. She peeked in Macy's room, and saw that she wasn't in there. For a second, Portia wondered if she had left the house and gone somewhere. She thought about the way Macy's sister, Pebbles, had sneaked out of her house that time and met her demise. Portia got real worried. She hurried down the hall to

Lil' Jay's room to see if Macy was in there.

Jayquan's bedroom door was closed, but she could see the light from his TV under the door. That was her son, so she didn't bother knocking. Portia barged in without even thinking twice.

What Portia saw when she opened that door shocked the shit out of her. Jayquan and Macy were asleep together under the covers, and it looked like they were naked! Macy was laying on Lil' Jay's chest. Portia could not believe it. Wow! It was pretty obvious what those kids had been up to.

She just stood there for a second. She didn't know what to do. If they had sex, it was already done. Portia was a realist. Lil' Jay and Macy were both at that curious age.

Portia was no hypocrite. She was around Macy's age when she'd started having sex, and so was Laila. And Jayquan was a boy. Sex was all they thought about. Portia wasn't really surprised that either of them was doing the do. She was just shocked that they chose each other to do it with. She hoped and prayed those kids had protected themselves.

Should she wake their little fast asses up and ask them? Portia was so unsure how to handle it, she decided to just close the door and walk away. She felt like she was stuck between a rock and a hard place. The situation definitely needed to be addressed, but she wanted to talk to Jay first. She wasn't afraid to tell him.

Now telling Laila was a completely different story. That news could force her into cardiac arrest. Portia went back in her bedroom and woke Jay up.

Jay was displeased that she was disturbing his good sleep, but he got up. When Portia pulled his coat about the kids, the first person he thought about was Wise. He told Portia, "Yo, Wise said something was up between them two."

Portia made a face at him. She said, "So why didn't you say something, Jay?"

Jay just shook his head, and shrugged. "Because it didn't seem like it to me."

Portia felt him on that. She said she hadn't suspected anything either. Macy and Lil' Jay had always been tight, but they acted like cousins. Brother and sister even.

Portia and Jay both sat there for a minute, absorbing the fact that the kids got busy. Damn, right under their noses. They wondered how long this had been going on. Maybe they had been too naïve. Had they trusted them too much? And what if there were repercussions?

CHAPTER TWENTY THREE

Khalil came home from jail in late January. He was so relieved to finally touch ground, he bought himself a bottle to celebrate. But Khalil's biggest problem was that when he partied, he never did so in moderation. He always went hard and indulged. He was a bit of a hog. When he started, he couldn't stop. That was how he got hooked on crack. Every time he took a little hit, he went on a mission. And he drank alcohol the same way.

Khalil had been drinking for two days. Lucky for him, he was downstairs in the basement apartment of his mother's home. While he was pulling his two-day drunk, he had been calling Laila and harassing her. He told her he was going to get her back for what she got her man to do to him.

Laila didn't know what he was talking about. She thought Khalil was referring to the way Cas had forced him to sign the divorce papers. She didn't know about the L-shaped cut he got on his face in prison, so she just kept hanging up the phone on him.

Khalil was in a terrible mood. He was pissed that his life was so shitty. He had it all, and lost it. He was miserable. Misery loved company, so he dialed Laila again. He just wanted to fuck up her mood.

When she answered the phone, he just started going in on her and calling her all kinds of names. He said, "Bitch, you ain't hot shit! You try'na be all Hollywood now, but remember *I* made you, bitch!"

Laila cursed him back out, and slammed the phone down again. He got so mad that she wouldn't hear him out, he shouted out a string of obscenities.

His mother was upstairs humming church songs, and preparing a sweet potato pie for an ailing church sister of hers. Mama Atkins overheard Khalil acting out again. It sounded like he was losing it down there. She wiped her hands on the front of the old, faded "Kiss the Cook" apron she was wearing, and quickly made her way downstairs.

She only had one child in the world. Khalil just came home from prison, and she was sick of him already. She was tired of her grown, thirty five-year-old son living with her. Sometimes she couldn't even get her proper rest, and that was a crying shame.

She opened the basement door, and started down the stairs. "Khalil! What are you making all that noise for? What are you doing down here?"

Khalil was too angry to talk to her. He looked at his mother, and said, "Go back upstairs, and finish doin' what you were doin', Ma."

His mother saw that he was enraged, and got worried. Her first thought was that he was messing with that stuff again. She was short of patience with him. Mama said, "Boy, what's *wrong* with you?"

Khalil still had the phone in his hand. He cursed angrily, "*Fuck!*", and threw it across the room. The phone hit the concrete wall, and broke into pieces.

That phone didn't belong to him, it belonged to his mother. She didn't appreciate him breaking up stuff that he didn't pay for. She got fed up, and said, "You better *quit* tearing up my damn shit! What is *wrong* with you, boy?"

Khalil heard his mother curse, so he knew he'd upset her. She never cursed. He calmed himself down, and told her the reason he was so mad. "Ma, I *hate* Laila! Pardon me, but I *hate* that bitch! She keep on try'na style on me, like she brand new!" He angrily kicked the mini refrigerator in the corner of the kitchen.

Khalil's mother didn't like ruckus, and she wasn't about to accept it from her son. She couldn't believe he was carrying on like that over Laila. They were divorced now. Mama Atkins was tired and impatient, so she broke it down to her son. She gave it to him straight, like the Black mother she was.

"Boy, you up in here with your blood pressure boiling, about to pop a blood vessel in your head over *Laila*? Fool, Laila don't want you. Y'all are divorced, and that girl done moved on. She got a new man, and a new baby now. She just try'na live her life, and take care of her kids. Just leave that girl alone!"

Khalil's response was, "I should kill that fuckin' hoe!" He knew deep down inside that his mother was telling the truth, but his pride wouldn't allow him to just let Laila dis him the way she had. He couldn't let it die. He still loved that fucking bitch.

His mother kept trying to get through to him. That was her job. She said, "Son, listen to me. You signed the papers, remember? And the girl paid you all that money, so that's that! It's over, son. Let it go. *Please*. You're making a fool out of yourself."

Khalil had been acting out ever since he came home. He saw a photo Laila had given his mother of her new baby. He asked him moms whose little girl that was, and she told him she was Laila's. He was shocked beyond words. That was the ultimate betrayal.

Ever since then, he had been calling Laila sporadically to harass and disrespect her. What really pissed him off was the fact that she was so cool about it. He wanted her to react like she gave a damn, but she just kept hanging up. She wouldn't even argue with him. That got him tight.

Khalil nodded at his mother to let her know he was cool. He said, "Sorry to disturb you, Ma. Go back upstairs. I'm good."

She peered at him, and asked, "Are you sure?"

He nodded again.

Mama Atkins said, "Thank you. Good night, son." She started back up the stairs. Just to make sure they wouldn't have to go through that again, she looked back and said, "Laila's engaged, son. She's getting married soon. Like next month."

She looked in her son's eyes to see if he got it. He just nodded, and looked away. She couldn't help but feel sorry for him, but she kept on upstairs.

Mama hadn't meant to hurt Khalil. That was just tough love. That was what mothers did. He was in denial, and needed to be told like it was. He had to get over Laila. The two of them would never be again, and that was it.

Mama knew it was hard for him, but it was a life lesson nonetheless. Hopefully, he would stay strong, and learn what his mistakes were. Heartache was often the best teacher. Khalil wasn't a bad looking man. He would love again, if he gave himself a chance. And then he would know how to treat the woman. Khalil's mom left his basement apartment, and went back upstairs with the impression that she and her son had an understanding.

As Khalil watched his mother walk off, that was the furthest thing from his mind. His thoughts were screaming, *"I should kill that bitch, Laila! Her, that fucking baby, and that nigga Cas. That lowdown, dirty bitch! She thinks she's getting married, but over my dead body!"*

Khalil told his mother good night, and he sat down to think for a minute. He needed a master plan. He had to figure out a way to stop that wedding, and that was all there was to it. He had no intentions on letting Laila marry another man. Fuck that, he couldn't.

$ $ $ $

Portia didn't want Laila to blame it on her negligence, so she still hadn't told her about the "Jayquan and Macy" incident. But she called Laila one day just to see how she was doing, and talk about her wedding.

When Portia called, Laila had just hung up her cell phone on her ranting and raving fool for an ex-husband. The jail time hadn't done that asshole a bit of good. He was still a complete loser. Now he was hounding her about her decision to re-marry. He had some nerve. That was none of his fucking business.

Laila greeted Portia, and filled her in on the biggest loser's latest tired antics. She said she was thinking about changing her number because his threats were starting to really creep her out. She said she wasn't going to tell Cas what he said because she was afraid he would kill Khalil's dumb ass.

Portia couldn't stand Khalil either, especially after he'd tried to ruin her and Laila's friendship by revealing that foul secret about him getting her pregnant. Thank God they got pass that. She told Laila to change her number if she had to.

Before they hung up, Portia casually threw in a comment about Macy. And then she asked Laila if and when she planned to take her to the doctor to get on some type of birth control.

Laila said she didn't see a point because Macy wasn't thinking about sex yet. She figured her daughter would just tell her when she was ready. Especially since she was such a cool and down to earth mom. She said Macy didn't even have a boyfriend yet.

Portia told her that she thought it would be a good idea to talk to her about birth control, but she didn't say why. She simply said that they both knew Macy was at that sexually curious stage, so they should just take precaution. She left it at that.

Laila thought about it, and wondered if she was being a little narrow-minded. She had to agree with Portia. She was around Macy's age when she had given her virginity to Khalil.

Laila wasn't a naïve mother. Especially considering what had happened to her baby daughter, Pebbles. Pebbles was brutally raped and murdered. Laila preferred to know what was going on with her children, so she asked Macy questions about sex a lot.

She just prayed she was getting honest answers from her.

Laila said, "You know what, you right, P. I gotta take her to the GYN."

Portia said, "Good, that's what's up."

Laila noticed Portia almost sounded relieved when she said that. She asked her if something was up. She knew Portia like a book. She wasn't fooling her. There was something she was holding back.

Laila tried to pull it out of her, but she was unsuccessful. She decided to just take heed to what Portia had told her. She had to have another sex talk with Macy. She wanted her daughter to know she could confide in her.

$ $ $ $

Portia hadn't said anything to the kids since she caught them in Jayquan's room, looking like they just had sex. But what she did do was make sure they weren't together alone anymore. Portia knew she needed to address that incident, even if it embarrassed them. They were a little too bold with their affair. They had some nerve laying up in her house like they were grown. No matter what they did, they were going to show respect.

Portia was kind of glad they slipped because if she hadn't caught them in the bed, she would've never known. She decided to approach Macy first. Macy was a young lady, and she was like her niece. If she was grown enough to lay up in her house and have sex, then she better be grown up enough to talk about it.

Portia waited until she came over to stay the weekend again. She intentionally didn't make any plans to leave the house. She was going to keep an eye on their little hot asses.

That Saturday, Portia took Macy to the salon with her. After they got their hair done, they went out for lunch. While they were eating, Portia brought it up. She was blunt with her, and asked her if she was having sex yet.

Macy blushed at first, and she was just quiet. She told Portia she was afraid to say because she didn't want her to tell her mother. Portia told her she could speak freely to her. After that, Macy put down her fork and grinned. She admitted to Portia that she was having sex, and with a boy she really cared about.

Portia played dumb. She asked who he was, and where he was from. Macy said she couldn't tell her just yet, but she swore they were practicing safe sex. Portia asked her when she planned on telling Laila. Macy shrugged, but she promised she would tell her soon.

Portia wondered if she was really referring to Jayquan. She asked how many boys she had sex with. Macy made a face, and said only one. She said they just did it their first time over the Christmas holiday.

Portia asked her if her mother ever asked if she was sexually active. Macy said Laila did, and admitted that she lied to her. She said Laila just asked her again the other day, but she didn't think her mom was ready to accept that yet. Portia told her that her mother was really cool, and she was the first person who should've known.

They ordered desert, and Portia continued schooling her niece. She told her she was too close to graduating from high school to get pregnant and blow it. She said it was okay to like boys, and even have sex sometimes, as long as she was responsible and careful, and kept her priorities straight. She begged her to never let boys distract her from her goals.

Portia thought about telling Macy she knew exactly who she was having sex with. She changed her mind and decided to let Macy tell her when she was ready. Instead, she told her to stay focused on going to college, and becoming a successful young Black woman. She told her that whoever the boy was, carrying herself like that would only gain his respect, and make him want her more.

$ $ $ $

Meanwhile, Jay was at home having "the talk" with Jayquan. After they shot a few hoops, Jay started asking questions. Lil' Jay was a little more honest than Macy was. He admitted to his father that he'd had sex with Macy. He said he was her first, and it happened during Christmas break. He said they had done it lots of times since then.

Jay asked him if Macy was his first too, and if he had strapped up. Lil' Jay said yes to both questions. Then he paused, and admitted that Macy let him "just put the head in one time without a rubber".

Jay appreciated his son's honesty, but he told him what was real. He told him he was too young to be a father. And he let him know that a lot of other stuff came along with having unprotected sex too. Jayquan said he knew all that, but Macy was a good girl. He grinned, and said he was her first, and only. He told Jay that was his.

Jay asked him if he cared about her. Jayquan didn't hesitate to say yes. Jay asked him if they were a couple now, or something. Jayquan said he wasn't really sure. He said they were more like best friends, but she was definitely special to him.

CHAPTER TWENTY FOUR

The next day, Ysatis was drunk again, and up to her usual antics. She spent day in and day out trying to do the same thing. She was still campaigning hard to win Jay. Lately she was sad all the time because she just wanted them to be together, and it seemed like he didn't. She couldn't take it anymore. But every time she spoke to him he kept on telling her to just wait.

She had started drinking again because she couldn't get in touch with him. Over the last two days she had called Jay well over a hundred times, and she left about twenty voice messages. She would've left even more messages but his phone started saying his voice mailbox was full. She had also texted him about a hundred times. He hadn't responded to anything yet.

Reality had started to sink in. Now Ysatis felt like he had just been stringing her along. Again, but that was the last fucking time. Jay shouldn't have lied to her. He promised that he would be with her.

Ysatis was pretty scorned. She got fed up with him ignoring her, so she sent him another text threatening to go to the police about her brother's murder.

Jay was with his main man, Cas, when he got the text. They had just finished handling some company business. That week they had been so busy they had barely even slept. That was part of the reason he had been ignoring Ysatis' annoying ass for the last two days. She kept calling him begging, crying, and sounding all needy, but he had bigger shit to worry about. She wasn't talking or texting about shit.

But her last text was different. When Jay read that particular text, he paid attention. She had threatened to go to the police again, so he got pretty angry. Now she wanted to start that shit again. A quiet rage started building up inside of him. The bitch wanted a reaction from him, so he decided to give her one. He was tired of tiptoeing around her ass, and having to lie about shit. The way he felt now, he didn't give a fuck what the hell she did. He really fucking despised Ysatis. She irked the shit out of him.

After their last meeting, Jay and Cas had just said that they were going home to rest up. Jay let his right-hand know they had to make a detour. He showed him the text, and let him know he had to pay his stupid ass baby mama another visit.

When Cas saw the text, he just shook his head. She was at it again. He told Jay it was a good thing they were still in the City. He understood why he felt the need to go by there. That Ysatis chick had become a real nuisance. She took "baby mama drama" to a whole new level.

Jay hit the Brooklyn Bridge, and headed over to that bitch's apartment. He had something to tell her, and he had to do it in person. He purposely didn't call first, so she wouldn't be expecting him.

When they got there, Ysatis was surprised when she answered the door. Jay and Cas walked right inside. The first thing they noticed was the baby hollering and screaming.

Cas just stood to the side, and out of Jay's business. All he did was have a look around to make sure there was no one else there. He wasn't being nosy, but it was always safety first. She may have had some dude over there, or something.

Cas wasn't trying to be the enforcer, or anything. He just didn't like surprises. It would be just their luck that some dude would pop out of the shadows blazing at them. Ysatis had set up her own brother, so he wouldn't put anything past her. Cas didn't trust anybody. Especially a scorned woman.

There was nobody else there but the baby. The poor kid was screaming his lungs out. He was in the bedroom, so Cas peeked at him. The little fellow's face was red. Cas hated to see a child mistreated. He could tell that baby had been laying there for a while. The good in him prevailed, so he picked the baby up and tried to quiet him down.

Cas immediately smelled the reason he was crying. He had pooped, and needed to be changed. Cas wanted to go spit on Ysatis for that. What kind of mother was she? He had smelled alcohol when they came in, and saw her little bottle of Grey Goose on the table. She should be ashamed of herself. Damn, poor Jay had a real bird for a baby mama.

Cas laid the baby back down for a second, and took off his jacket. Then he looked around for the diapers and baby wipes. He knew how to change a diaper. He was a father, and he had been involved hands-on with both of his children when they were born. His heart wouldn't allow him to see a baby suffer like that.

He found the diapers and wipes, and cleaned the kid up. While changing him, he discovered that his little bottom was severely chafed. It was red and inflamed, and letting him lay in feces didn't help. Cas tried to be as gentle as he could, but the baby hollered something awful while he was cleaning him.

He looked for some diaper ointment but he didn't see any anywhere. He doubted she had even purchased any. That girl must've been retarded or something. She didn't seem to know anything about taking care of a baby. Cas thought about telling Jay to get his kid out of there. That bitch was clearly unfit.

He had no choice but to just sprinkle lots of baby powder on the little dude's chafe skin before he closed the diaper. He knew the little fellow needed more than that, but he hoped that would at least help.

Meanwhile, Jay was out front telling Ysatis what it really was. He was tired and grumpy, so he didn't waste time with small talk.

He got to the point, and told her she was really agitating him with her little threats, and shit.

Ysatis had done some heavy drinking that day, so she was pretty bold. When he asked her what her problem was, she said she was tired of being lied to. She said she loved him, and wanted to be with him.

Jay couldn't believe how pitiful she was acting. He asked her what happened to her. She looked like a drunken, defeated shadow of her former bright eyed, determined self. He told her she wasn't doing anything with her life but stressing him. She was a college graduate, for God's sake. So what if she had a kid. There were single mothers all over the world. And those women were handling their business.

She stared crying, and said, "What *happened* to me? *You* did this to me. *You* made me like this, Jay! Why you keep doin' this to me? Why? We could be so happy together!"

Jay said, "You don't need no nigga to make you happy, Ysatis. And if you do, then at least find somebody who wants to!"

Ysatis couldn't believe he said that. She knew it! He had been lying to her all along. She looked at Jay through teary eyes, and promised him she was going to hurt him back. She told him that if she couldn't be happy, he wouldn't be happy either.

Jay had tried to be patient because he realized the girl was missing a few screws. But after she said that, he kind of lost it. He grabbed that snotty nosed bitch by the neck, and told her he wouldn't tolerate being threatened by some dumb ass broad.

Ysatis had the nerve to turn it up even more. She got in his face and yelled, "I don't give a fuck *what* you say. If you ain't telling me when we're leaving, then don't say shit to me! And if you keep on lying to me, I'll go to the fuckin' police on you, nigga!"

Jay looked at her like she had lost her mind. He slammed that bitch up against the wall, and sneered, "Bitch, are you *crazy*? You can go to anybody you want! Fuck you *and* the police! That's right I been lying to yo' stupid ass. I'm never leaving my wife for you! I wouldn't even have a dirty ass, ready to snitch at the drop of a dime, broad like you! You *know* all I did was try to help you when that shit went down. And now you wanna run your mouth? Do what you want, you triflin' ass bitch!"

Jay let her go, and then she started hollering and screaming. She yelled, "Nigga, don't put your fucking hands on me! I'm telling you, don't fucking play with me. You *know* you killed my brother! I will get you put away for the rest of your *life*, mothafucka!"

Cas had managed to quiet down the baby, so he came back out front and overheard the last of their conversation. That bitch was yelling like she was crazy, so he knew it was time to go.

Jay was at a lost of words after Ysatis said that. He really had to restrain himself. A large part of him was ready to just do away with that bitch. If she had been anyone else, she would've been dead already.

Cas wanted to tell Ysatis what a hole she was digging for herself. He saw how upset Jay was. He knew Jay, and the only thing stopping him from killing that girl was the fact that she had that baby. Cas was a witness that Jay had tried hard to be fair with Ysatis. He had given her a lot of passes. He'd even tried lying to her so he wouldn't have to hurt her.

Cas could smell disaster brewing. Jay got pissed and stormed off, but he knew the perils of turning your back on a scorned woman. She would probably do something drastic and irrational. Cas didn't want that bitch to go running to the police that night, so he tried to talk to Ysatis to calm her down.

He told her to name a price, and urged her to take the money and chill. But she wasn't trying to hear him. She said she didn't give a fuck about money. She said Jay was doomed, and told Cas he was going to go down with him because he had helped kill her brother too. She obviously wasn't thinking, because she was running off at the mouth to a stone cold killer.

That girl was too bold. She really started going in. She told Cas she would no longer be made a fool of. She said it was now or never that she and Jay were going to be together. Then she had the audacity to give Jay a timeframe. She said he'd better get his shit together before Valentine's Day, or she would give V-Day a whole new meaning. She told Cas he'd better go talk some sense into his "codefendant". Then she went in her pocket and pulled out a business card. She flashed him what she said was the number of her police detective friend.

That's when she really shot herself in the foot. After that, Cas wanted to kill her right on the spot. But that would be too messy. And the baby was there. He just smiled at her, and promised her he would talk to Jay. After that, he suggested she pay closer attention to her baby. He told her she should really get something for that diaper rash, and then he said goodnight.

After Cas left her apartment, Ysatis slammed the door closed behind him.

On his way downstairs, Casino was saddened by the reality that set in. He had to kill her. She was completely unreasonable. The threats she had made could very well be idle, but he wasn't willing to take a chance. Shorty had a big ass mouth, and that's what had sealed her fate. She said Jay was doomed, but she was the one marked.

Downstairs, Cas saw that Jay was already in the car. He just got in, and didn't bother to speak on the fact that that would be Ysatis' last threat. Cas wasn't a talker. He knew what had to be done, so that was that. That bitch was out of control. They had too much at stake to let her hotheaded ass snitch on them about some old shit.

Cas wasn't going down behind no bitch, so it was settled. She had to go, and it was him who had to send her. Jay was too wrapped up in it to entertain the thought, so he would do that work. Jay was his main man, and he wasn't going to allow that jaded bitch to destroy him.

$ $ $ $

That evening at home, Cas was still pondering about how he would rectify the situation. He knew what had to be done but he didn't quite have a plan. He thought about calling Jay, and getting him to call Ysatis up and invite her out on a romantic date. He could tell her he wanted to take her sailing on his private boat, or something.

But the more Cas thought about it, he really didn't want to involve Jay. The bitch was a snake, but she was still the mother of his seed. No matter how the kid was conceived.

Late that night, Laila gave Cas some unexpected loving. He thought she was asleep when he got in, but she fooled him that night. When he laid in the bed, she turned over and seduced him. She acted like she wanted to take charge that night, so he let her do her.

Cas was laying there getting some toe-curling head, when he happened to look over at the closet door. Laila's purse was hanging on the doorknob. He stared at her alligator Birken bag, and got an idea. It was like a light bulb came on in his head. But he was currently more interested in the dark chocolate on him, so he put it on a backburner until they were done.

They went at it for about an hour. And they went hard. Afterwards, Laila laid on his chest while they talked about their wedding. It was coming up in just weeks, and they both said they were looking forward to it.

After Laila fell asleep, Cas got up out the bed and went to his study to make a phone call. He used *67 to block his number, and he called Ysatis. He and Jay had been best friends for the last thirty years, so he could impersonate Jay well enough to fool his own mother over the telephone.

Ysatis answered, and he pretended he was Jay sneaking on the phone and calling her while his wife was asleep. He told her he was so sorry about what had happened earlier. He said he had to see her. He told her he really cared about her, and wanted to be with her. He said he just had to tie up all the loose ends on their "evacuation plan".

Then "Jay" told her the plan. He said he would send a car for her that Friday, which was in exactly two days. He told her he wanted to take her shopping, and then they were going on vacation.

Ysatis literally cheered when he said that. And when he said he would hire a sitter to keep the baby while they were away, so she could get some "me time", she cheered again. She was pretty excited.

Still talking low like he was hiding in the bathroom, "Jay" promised to call her soon. She told him she loved him, and blew him a kiss before he hung up the phone.

Cas had worried that his plan wouldn't work. He thought she would probably be too smart to fall for something so obvious. But Ysatis was so naïve, it went right over her head. She leapt at the opportunity to get away with him. She really thought her and Jay had a future, even after all that slick shit she had said earlier. He couldn't believe she was really that dumb.

$ $ $ $

Cas had a couple of days to perfect his plan but he needed assistance pulling it off. He needed two people he knew he could trust, one of which was a female. Kira was the perfect candidate because she was Jay's sister. He knew she had his best interest at heart. Cas called her and told her he had a proposition for her.

They met up in person, and discussed what he had in mind. Kira agreed for two reasons. For one, Jay was her brother. And two, she sort of felt like she owed Cas one. She had set Laila's house on fire when his baby was inside. And then he turned around and helped pay for her lawyer when she got charged for it. He was mad, but he had been so cool about the situation it was unbelievable. No matter what had happened between them, Casino was a good dude.

Kira had the easiest role in Cas' plan. He simply wanted her to befriend Ysatis, and take her shopping for the all-expense paid vacation he was sending them on. He said he just wanted her to make Ysatis feel like a part of the family.

That seemed easy enough, so Kira told him he could count on her. She just reminded him that she was filming her reality show, and working on her album, so she couldn't be away too long. Kira didn't bother to mention that she had a little thing for one of her producers, Vino, so she wanted to hurry back and see him.

Next, Cas needed to get with Wise. He called him and told him he needed to holler at him about something. He scooped him up from home that evening, and they rode off for a minute. Along the way, he ran his plan down to Wise.

It wasn't hard to convince Wise because he knew how that bitch was wilding, and running her mouth. In his opinion, loose lips sank ships. It wouldn't be the first time he had done work with Cas. That was his man. They had done a lot of shit together. The only difference this time was that the job involved a female. Wise had never killed a woman before. But then again, he never had to.

After he thought about it, he didn't even care. A rat was a rat, no matter what its anatomy was. When a mothafucka was threatening everything you had, the decision wasn't gender specific. Wise nodded to let Cas know he was in. He was bored anyway. He could use some action in his life.

Neither of the men told their women what they were really up to, but that night Cas and Wise told them they had to go away. Laila was a surprised that Cas gave her such short notice, but she didn't say anything. If he said it was necessary, then it was necessary.

Fatima reacted differently. She was pretty upset that Wise

was going away, so she outright complained. That baby she was carrying made her extra emotional. She started crying, and begged him not to leave her alone.

Wise knew it was the pregnancy. They went through the same thing when she was pregnant with Falynn. He laughed to himself, and promised her he would back in two days. He held Fatima and caressed her until she stopped crying.

CHAPTER TWENTY FIVE

Friday morning, "Jay" called Ysatis and told her they were going on a couples' retreat. He told her the limo would be there to pick her up at around noon. The sitter he had hired got to her apartment around ten, and she spent the rest of the time packing.

When the limo arrived to pick her up, Kira was inside. She introduced herself brightly, and hugged Ysatis. She told her it was great to meet her new sister in-law.

Ysatis knew exactly who Kira was. She was a little star struck so she just stared at her for a minute. She was a huge fan. She knew the lyrics to all her songs. Ysatis was thrilled. Even more so after she told her what a grand time they were going to have on vacation. Kira said they had to get fly for their trip, and then she directed the driver to Fifth Avenue.

They went shopping in stores Ysatis had never been in, and bought clothing by fashion designers she couldn't even pronounce. When they finished splurging, they stopped at a ritzy salon Kira attended regularly. They got their hair and make-up done there.

By the time they were done, Ysatis was convinced she had the coolest sister-in-law in the universe. She told Kira she was her new BFF. Kira grinned, and told her that was sweet. She said she was flattered to be her "best friend forever", but she reminded her that Jay was financing everything because he cared so much about her.

Ysatis blushed. She felt like a real live princess. She totally loved her new life. When she and Kira were done getting pampered, they headed for their five o'clock flight.

Cas was sending them on the company plane, so they would be flying in style. Before their flight took off, "Jay" called Kira to make sure they were okay. After they spoke briefly, he asked to speak to Ysatis. His goal was to make sure she got on that plane.

When she got on the phone, he told her he couldn't wait to see her. He said he had some prior business he had to handle, so he would catch a later flight, and meet her there as soon as he was done. He told her not to hesitate to tell Kira what she wanted because the sky was the limit. Ysatis was cheesing when she hung up the phone.

When she and Kira landed in Miami, there was a hired car waiting to take them straight to their destination. "Jay" had a friend who owned a vacation home there, and that's where they were staying.

When they got there, they discovered the vacation home was more like an estate. And the property had an exquisite Greek theme. The huge, white columned house sat on acres of picturesque lawn, adorned with beautiful foliage. To Ysatis, it looked like one of those houses on MTV Cribs.

In front of the house there was a small lake with a fountain in the middle of it. On top of the fountain was a stone statue of a nude Greek goddess. In the back of the house there was a pool and an outdoor spa, and there was even a small golf course off to the left.

To their delight, there was a live-in housekeeper on the grounds. She kept the house up, and was there to serve them. Her name was Magdalena, and she actually lived in a separate, smaller house behind the big one. Her husband, Pablo, lived there too. He was the landscaper, and he took care of fixing things.

Magdalena had been informed by her boss, Manuel, to expect

guests. She welcomed Kira and Ysatis warmly, and showed them around. She wrote down her telephone extension so they could reach her if they needed anything, and left them alone to get settled in.

The three-story columned house had four huge bedrooms that each had their own private bathroom. Kira picked the biggest and best room. Staying there was like staying at a five-star resort, with all amenities included. She and Ysatis spent their first evening getting massages from the on-call masseuse, and getting their drink on. Their "men" were due to arrive the following day.

The next day they slept until about eleven AM. Ysatis was used to having to get up early with her baby, so she really liked that part. After they showered, they started their day with a late breakfast, and then they headed for a nearby spa. They sipped on white wine, and got the whole works. They got facials, exfoliating sugar body scrubs, manni/peddis, and hot stone massages.

Ysatis was enjoying her time with Kira. She'd never had the pleasure of being around an actual diva, so she was elated. Kira was a celebrity, and the way she carried herself intrigued her. She snapped her fingers to get things done, and dished out orders like it was second nature. Ysatis was thrilled to be in her presence. She started trying to emulate her. In fact, she had sort of developed a little crush on her.

Ysatis was a lot like a stray puppy. She fell in love with anyone who showed her some affection. She never had anybody, so if someone took care of her, she was theirs forever.

Kira knew Ysatis admired her because she kept telling her how beautiful she was, and how she wanted to be like her. On more than one occasion she caught her staring at her breasts. But she never commented.

When they got back to the house, they decided to go down to the pool for a while. They put on the swimsuits they'd purchased when they went shopping in New York. After Kira changed into hers, Ysatis practically undressed her with her eyeballs. She told her she had a great body, and said she wished she was shaped like her. Her eyes lingered on her hips when she said that.

Kira felt a little uncomfortable, so she tied a wrap around herself. They headed downstairs, and had a couple of cocktails. Afterwards, they got in the water for a little while. Kira could swim like a fish, so she tried to give Ysatis lessons. It was useless, but it was pretty funny. They had a good time. About six o'clock, they decided to head back upstairs to change.

Kira was feeling nice from her cocktails. Ysatis drank twice as much, so she was tipsy as hell. She was stumbling along the way, and she kept on giggling. On the way upstairs, she made a comment about Kira's ass. She said she liked the way it was shaped, and the fact that it was all one color. Kira had to laugh at that one because she knew her ass was just as black as the next chick's.

When they got inside, she looked over at the time. "Jay" would be there soon. She decided to shower off the chlorine from the pool, and re-moisturize. She went up to her room and grabbed some clean undies, and a pair of Juicy sweats. Kira headed for her bathroom. She took her pocketbook with her, in case that bitch felt like going through her stuff.

Kira closed her door, but she didn't lock it. Ysatis decided to come in when she was in the shower. She actually had the nerve to come in the bathroom. That alcohol had made her ass too bold. She told Kira she just wanted to watch her take a shower.

Kira snapped on her, and told her to get out. Ysatis apologized, and said she just thought she was so cool. She said everything she did was cool, and then she went back out of the room.

After she left, Kira finished her shower and thought about it for a minute. Ysatis had creeped her out a little. Homegirl was acting like a mental case. No wonder Cas felt like they had to get her out of Jay's hair. She was a fucking stalker. Being obsessed with Jay was one thing, but she was acting obsessive towards her too. What part of the game was that? That bitch was really crazy.

Kira dried between her legs, and accidentally bumped her clit with her towel. She felt a little jolt, but all it did was remind her how lackluster her sex life was. Damn, she was horny. She had been all business since she came home. Not for nothing, but she had other needs too. Every now and then she would masturbate, just to get off. But she really needed a dude to put it on her. She thought about Vino, and smiled. She made up her mind to let him know she was feeling him. He was a sexy, chocolate mothafucka.

Kira was feeling nice from the drinks she had, and her freshly showered skin was tingling. She felt like a woman. She wished she could pleasure herself right then. But that bitch Ysatis was there, so she didn't have any privacy.

Kira got an idea, and dismissed it immediately. Thinking of something like that made her feel ashamed. But the thought crept back into her subconscious, despite her efforts to suppress it. Since that groupie bitch was sweating her so much, she should make her eat her out. Ysatis kept leering at her ass and tities anyway. She acted liked she wanted to.

Kira was no lesbian, but she hadn't got wore out since she'd been home. She had never done anything gay, not even while she was in jail. She was just horny as hell that day. She couldn't masturbate, so she just wanted to get her pussy eaten.

The only reason she chose Ysatis was because she knew she could get her to do anything. The bitch was there, so she might as well make use of her. And Kira knew she wouldn't be around long, so there was no way she would ever be able to tell anyone.

Kira didn't bother to put on her sweats. They were there alone, so she went down to the kitchen in just her bra and panties. She got a bottle of champagne from the fridge and poured herself a glass. Then she clicked on the stereo, and kicked back on the sofa.

Ysatis ran behind Kira like a puppy, and sat on the arm of the sofa. She poured herself a glass of champagne as well. She drank it fast, and poured another.

She kept on staring at her, so Kira finished her glass of champagne, and tested her. She said, "Ysatis, how far would you be willing to go to prove to me that you're really my BFF?"

Ysatis said, "Are you kidding? I would do anything for you, girl. For real!"

Kira said, "*Anything?*"

Ysatis grinned, and nodded.

Kira was feeling so naughty she decided to exercise her power. Ysatis was a nobody, so she put it to her rather blunt. "I want you to lick my pussy."

At first, Ysatis looked kind of surprised. But it only took about three seconds for her to make up her mind. She said, "Okay, I will. You want me to do it now?"

Kira said, "Duh! I just want you to make me cum."

Ysatis got up and walked in front of Kira. She got down on her knees, and stared at her crotch for a second. Kira stood up, and put it right in her face. Ysatis tugged at her thong anxiously.

Kira could see that homegirl was ready, so she stepped out of her panties. Before she could say a word, Ysatis' face was in her pussy. Kira had to admit, so far it felt good. She just needed to get comfortable and relax. She sat back down and spread her legs.

Ysatis gently pulled her vaginal lips apart, and looked at her feminine flower like she was mesmerized. She nuzzled it with her nose and sniffed it, and then she kissed it a few times. Kira coaxed her softly, and she started licking and sucking her clit.

Kira moaned, and held the back of her head. She asked her if she liked how her pussy tasted. Ysatis' mouth was too full to speak, so she nodded and gave her a thumbs up. She kept eating her out like she couldn't get enough. She was determined to please Kira, and she was loving it.

Kira didn't know if it was her first time or not, but the girl could eat some pussy. Damn, she had her shaking and shit.

Ysatis spread her legs wider and stuck her tongue deep inside her. Kira leaned back and grinded on her face, smearing her juices all over her in the process.

Ysatis zoomed back in on her clit, and that pushed Kira over the top. She wrapped her fists in her hair and fucked her face hard. She commanded her not to stop. She was panting and breathing like she was having an asthma attack. "Ooh yeah, that's it! Bitch, don't stop!" A few seconds later, she came all over her face.

That experience was different for Ysatis. She had never got down like that before, but she really enjoyed herself. She was fascinated with the sweet stickiness of Kira's essence. And while she was eating her, it felt like she was in control.

Ysatis couldn't get enough. She wanted to make Kira cum again. She stared at her hungrily, and then she spread her lips wide open and went headfirst. She devoured that pussy like it was her favorite gourmet dish. This time she stuck her fingers in and out too. She licked the honey off them every few plunges. It was delightful. She took her time and savored it.

After a while, Kira was damn near screaming. That shit felt too good. She couldn't take it anymore. Ysatis had drained her. Kira kept telling her to stop but she wouldn't obey. She damn near had to beat that bitch off her pussy.

After she recovered from the powerful cum-quake she'd just experienced, Kira went and got cleaned up. When she came out the bathroom, she told Ysatis to keep their little tryst between the two of them. Then she laughed to herself, and told her she had earned the right to be her "Best Friend Forever."

Ysatis almost jumped up and down. She was thrilled to hear that. Kira was her BFF! She smiled from ear to ear, knowing that forever was a long time. The poor thing had no idea how little time she had left.

Kira looked at Ysatis grinning, and she felt kind of sorry for her for a minute. It was mad foul to have set her up like that.

She had pretended to be her friend, used the girl for oral sex, and everything. That was some grimy shit.

But Ysatis wanted to do what she did. Kira didn't hold a gun to her head. And her fate wasn't up to her anyway. Kira remembered the fact that the bitch had threatened to destroy her brother. And after Jay had tried to help her ungrateful ass. When Kira thought about it like that, she had it coming. Ysatis brought it on herself.

$ $ $ $

About two hours later, Cas rang the doorbell. He and Kira hugged, careful to stay in character as a couple. Kira couldn't front, it was nice to hug Cas like that again. But she knew their thing was of the past.

Cas greeted Ysatis, and smiled at her. She took that as a sign of warmth, and smiled back. If she had been more informed about Killa' Cas, she would've known his smile wasn't always friendly.

She asked him where Jay was. Cas told her he'd stopped off to get her a gift. He assured her he'd be there soon. After that, Cas ran down their dinner plans. He told Ysatis that "Jay" wanted to spend the evening alone with her, so they wouldn't be dining together.

Ysatis beamed. There was no doubt in her mind that Jay was really feeling her. He had rolled out the red carpet for her. He wanted to be with her pretty bad because she was getting the star treatment before he even appeared. She felt like a queen.

Ysatis was excited about her current situation. She had it made. She was going to be Jay's main squeeze, and also be able to enjoy playtime with his sister here and there. She imagined her and her new BFF up in all the industry hotspots, both dressed to kill. That was a lifestyle she had only dreamed of.

Ysatis told Cas and Kira goodnight, and she went to her room. She hurried because she was anxious to get ready for her man before he got there. That night she wanted to skip all the eating and stuff. Fuck that, she wanted to be Jay's dinner.

About forty five minutes later, she awaited Jay clad in sheer, sexy, white lingerie. Kira had knocked on her door and hand-delivered an expensive bottle of celebration champagne for them. She told her Jay would let himself in, so she should just get comfortable.

Ysatis took her advice. She lit a few candles, and turned off the lights. She poured herself a glass of Dom Perignon Rose, and sat back sexily posed on the bed. She sipped on her bubbly while she waited.

Unbeknownst to Ysatis, the champagne was spiked with powerful sleeping pills. Cas had gotten his hands on a bottle of Ambien, and those were the good ones. Ysatis poured herself another glass, but she never got a chance to drink it because she dozed off.

Shortly after, "Jay" entered the bedroom. The first thing he noticed was all the candles burning, and then he saw Ysatis asleep on the bed. Wise chuckled to himself. She was knocked out. Things couldn't have gotten easier for him.

He looked at the outline of her breasts in the flimsy lingerie she was wearing, and a natural reaction occurred. His dick got hard. The devil told Wise to take advantage of the situation. Now he wanted to fuck her. She was laying there half naked, waiting to get smashed by "Jay" anyway. Wise told himself he was in character, so he had to play the role. When the lights were off, a dick was a dick. Especially to a drunk, doped up bitch.

He blew out the candle on the nightstand. Wise cursed under his breath because he didn't have a condom. He wasn't going up in it raw. Fuck that, he didn't want it that bad.

Now he wanted to wake her up so she could give him some head. But then again, he didn't want to leave his DNA in her mouth. Wise laughed to himself when he remembered how they planned to dispose of her remains. He could smear cum all over that bitch if he wanted to because they would never find her. He just had to make it quick. He shook Ysatis awake.

When Ysatis woke up she was a little groggy. She noticed it was sort of dark in there now. She smiled when she saw that Jay had shown up. And his hands were all over her. He must've been pretty happy to see her. He massaged her nipples for a minute, and then he ran his hands through her hair romantically. After that, he sort of started pushing her head down towards his lap.

Ysatis smiled to herself. She figured she had made him feel so good when she sucked his dick before, he wanted another taste. Anxious to please him, she kneeled down in the dark and swallowed his immenseness.

He held the back of her head, and forced himself further and further down her throat. She choked a couple times but she didn't complain. She was determined to show Jay she could take anything he threw at her. If he liked it rough, she would just be tough and take it. He was leaving his wife for her, so she had to.

Wise was power stroking the shit out of that bitch's throat. He grinded his back teeth, and showed no mercy. After seven more deep strokes, he clenched his ass cheeks and exploded. His dick was so far down her throat, he probably busted on her esophagus.

There was too much cum to swallow, so Ysatis gagged. She wanted to spit some of it out, but "Jay" wouldn't let her. He held her head real tight so she couldn't move. He said, "Nah, bitch. Swallow it all."

She gulped, and did as she was told. She noted that he had called her out of her name. But she couldn't lie, it turned her on. If that was what he was into, she wanted to be his little slut.

Wise laughed to himself. Temptation was a bitch. He knew he was wrong, but he was still a dude. Now that he got his shit off, it was back to business. That cum thirsty, loose lipped bitch was a potential threat, so she had to go.

Wise wanted it to be clean. All the gory stuff wasn't necessary. She was just a girl. He actually hated that he had to kill her, but there was no way they could allow her to talk to the police about that shit they did to her brother. There was just too much at stake to let some scorned broad's bitterness destroy everything. Jay wasn't going to ever give her what she wanted, so the bitch was like a walking time bomb. If she exploded, there would be one hell of a mess. She had to go.

Wise prayed silently, and asked God to forgive him. He didn't want to miss, so he reached over and turned on the lamp on the nightstand.

When he turned on the light, Ysatis was completely surprised. That wasn't even Jay! She covered her mouth in shock. Wow, she had just swallowed some fucking stranger's cum! She couldn't believe it. She demanded that he identify himself. She said, "Oh my *God*, who *are* you? Where the hell is *Jay*? I thought you were *him*!"

That shit was so funny, Wise laughed out loud. He said, "Yeah, I can see that. You really like that guy, huh? I'm not Jay, but I'm a close friend of his. Just think of me as a representative."

Ysatis was mortified. She looked at Wise like she saw a ghost. All of a sudden, she recognized him. She said "Oh my God, *you're*... Oh shit, *you're Wise*! The *rapper*! I thought you were dead!"

Wise laughed. Damn, she knew who he was. Even with the new beard. He shook his head. "You right, ma. That's me. I ain't dead... But *you are!*"

Before she could respond, he grabbed the bed pillow closest to him and smashed it over her face. He applied a lot of pressure, in effort to cut off all her oxygen.

Ysatis realized he wanted her dead, but she wouldn't go out without a fight. She tried to get him up off her. She started kicking, scratching, and screaming. Her cries were muffled by the pillow, but she fought for her life with everything she had.

Wise hadn't anticipated Ysatis being so feisty. The bitch was pretty quick. She kneed him in the nuts, and made a run for the bathroom.

Pain exploded in Wise's scrotum. He yelled, "Oh shit!" He watched her heading for the bathroom, and couldn't believe she got away. He ignored the throbbing in his nuts, and jumped up and chased her ass. He managed to stick his black Nike ACG boot in the bathroom doorway right before she slammed the door.

Ysatis was frightened to death. She pushed the door as hard as she could and tried to close it, but her strength was no match for his. Wise busted right in with his shoulder. *Boom!*

The impact knocked Ysatis backwards. When she fell to the floor, she hit her head on the corner of the sink. That head injury dazed her for a minute.

Wise stepped inside the bathroom and stood over her. He bent down and picked that bitch up by her neck. She started wilding again, and trying to claw his face. That made him so mad, he pulled the gun from the back of his waist and shoved it under her chin.

Ysatis froze, and started begging for her life. She told him she would do anything for him.

Wise just tuned out her pleas. He had the gun in his right hand, and he kept his left hand wrapped tightly around her neck. He started to just shoot her in the face, but a part of him thought that was a little too harsh. He decided to kill her with his bare hands.

He laid his gun down on the sink, and tightened the death grip he had on her throat. He squeezed harder and harder, until her eyes bulged out of her head. Ysatis frantically tried to pry his knuckles off her neck. She gasped for air, and desperate tears rolled down her face. But it was useless. Wise was unmoved by her crying. He was determined to finish her, so he only choked her harder.

Ysatis began to feel faint. And it was getting darker in there. Wow, she was dying. She couldn't fight it anymore. Her last thought was about her son. He would be alone in the world now. She hoped he would be okay.

She stopped struggling and squirming, so Wise knew she was gone. He looked down at her face. She had died with her eyes wide open. That shit looked crazy. He just stared at her for a minute. Being that close to death was bone chilling, even when you were the killer.

He closed her eyelids, and then he washed his hands. The next thing he did was call Cas' cell phone to let him know it was taken care of. Now it was time for phase two. They had to dispose of her body.

$ $ $ $

Cas was seeing Kira off when he got the call from Wise. She was flying out that night because she had a studio session the following afternoon. She said she wanted to get back, and get ready. Cas thanked Kira for her assistance. She smiled, and said it was nothing. He hugged her, and told her to have a safe flight.

Next, Cas headed straight upstairs to the bedroom Wise was in. When he got there, Wise showed him Ysatis' body slumped on the bathroom floor. Cas stood there with his hands in his pockets, and looked at her for a minute. Quite naturally, he wasn't thrilled about what they had done. He wished that damn girl would have never started all that drama.

Cas picked up the telephone on the nightstand, and dialed extension 432. A man with a thick Hispanic accent answered on the third ring. Cas told him there was a "mess" in the house he needed assistance with. In broken English, the man told Cas he would be right there.

Pablo got up and put on his boots. He told his wife he would be back to bed soon, and headed towards the big house. Inside, he went all the way upstairs and called out to them to find out where the "mess" was.

Pablo was a middle-aged, illegal Cuban immigrant who had been employed by Manuel ever since he came to the United States nine years ago. He worked in exchange for room and board, and also a stipend big enough to care for his family back home. Four years ago, his wife Magdalena had joined him, and Manuel gave her a job too. He was a good man, so Pablo didn't mind cleaning up a mess for him every now and then. There was usually a bonus associated with it anyhow.

Pablo had undoubtedly witnessed worse "messes" than the cleanup Cas and Wise had for him. He just wanted to get it over with so he could get back to bed.

Cas heard Pablo calling him, so he opened the bedroom door to let him know where they were. While he waited for Pablo, he recalled a conversation he and his friend Manuel had a few years ago. Manuel had boasted of the many alligators surrounding his Florida vacation property. He had jokingly told the tale of the way his traitor for a brother-in-law was eaten by them. His face had lit up when he described the gory details. He was quite fond of his deadly pets.

Cas had called his old friend two days ago, and asked if he still had that property. Manuel was in Colombia at the time, but he was a hospitable guy. He had been happy to give Cas access to his vacation home for the time he needed. And he had assured him that he had a man onsite to assist him with "anything" he needed.

Pablo came inside the room. When he saw the dead girl on the bathroom floor, he didn't even bat an eye. He had seen far more atrocious crime scenes. He pulled a black, contractor-sized trash bag from his back pocket, and opened it up. Together, Cas and Wise put Ysatis' corpse inside. Pablo tied the bag, and then he told them to follow him. He dragged the body down the steps.

Downstairs, they put her in a big wheel barrel, and Pablo carted her out the house. Ysatis was only about 130 pounds, so it was no big deal. They all exited through the back of the house. It was dark outside, but Pablo knew the grounds so well he could've led them while he was blindfolded.

Pablo knew from experience that it would be better if the body wasn't whole. He told them they had to "process her first", and he led them to the utility shed where he kept his power tools. There were a lot of contraptions in there, including the grinding machine that was used to turn logs and big tree branches into sawdust.

They put Ysatis inside the machine, and then Pablo attached a heavy-duty trash bag to the other end. After that, he turned on the power switch. There was this awful sound when her body passed through the blades. It was almost sickening. Then they could hear micro-bits of her just shooting out and splattering into the bag attached.

When Wise first saw the machine, he was under the impression that they were about to be sprayed with tiny pieces of flesh and bones. He was glad to see that wasn't the case. When the bag was full, Pablo unattached it. He opened it up for them to see, and laughed at the faces they both made. He tied the bag, and they wheeled it over to a canal on the edge of the property.

It was a pretty long walk. They kept going and going, until they were out of safe territory. Pablo ignored the warning signs that were posted. They passed another one, and another one. The next one clearly said "**DANGER! Alligators! Do Not Proceed Beyond This Point!**" They just kept going.

Wise nudged Cas. He wondered if that nigga Pablo was trying to feed them to the gators too. Cas just shrugged at him. He didn't want to ask any questions because he believed they were too close to alligators to be making any noise. They had to be as quiet as possible.

When they finally stopped, they were right at the mouth of a huge alligator pit. Pablo quickly slit the bag with a box cutter he had in his pocket, and dumped it right there. The bag of remains rolled a couple of times, and then landed right by the water.

Cas had done a little research, so he knew alligators naturally feed at night. He had a pamphlet from the Florida Fish and Wildlife Conservation Commission. A passage in it said,

"Never feed gators, or swim or wade in waters where large alligators are known to occur. Normally, alligators avoid humans, but alligators that have been fed by humans will move toward humans, and can become aggressive. Alligators that have been fed by humans are dangerous and should be reported immediately."

Cas was no different from Wise. He was kind of ready to go back too.

It was dark out there, but they could see because there was a full moon out. Pablo quietly pointed at what appeared to be a log in the water. They all just stood there, and didn't make a sound. About a minute later, the log began to move.

Wise started backing up. He was pretty nervous. Casino's heart was pounding too. They weren't from those parts, so they weren't used to fraternizing with alligators.

All of a sudden, the log sprang out of the water. They didn't see what happened after that because all three of them ran for their lives. Wise, Cas, and Pablo. They were all trying to get the hell up out of there.

While they were running away, Wise slipped and fell. That nigga screamed just like a bitch, so Cas and Pablo turned around to see about him. When they looked at him, he was down on one knee struggling to get up. The look on that dude's face put them in stitches. He looked like he was straight terrified. You'd have sworn the alligator was right on his ass.

That shit was so funny, Cas and Pablo doubled over in laughter. When Wise realized he wasn't in danger anymore, he didn't mind them laughing. He was a good sport. He looked behind him one more time, and then he joined them.

The three men shared a good laugh. Wise was lucky that time. He got a pass because none of them was crazy enough to go up against no alligator.

When they finally got back to the house, they shook Pablo's hand, and thanked him for his assistance. Cas knew he had helped them on the strength of Manuel, but he still wanted to show his appreciation. He made a metal note to do something nice for him.

Cas told him he had to trouble him one more time. He needed to know where they could burn a few things. Pablo told him they could use the incinerator he used to burn trash. Cas said that would be perfect.

He and Wise gathered all Ysatis' belongings, including the luggage she came with. They filtered out the new stuff she and Kira had shopped for, and gave it to Pablo for his daughter. The rest they carted straight to the incinerator. After they tossed everything inside, Pablo assured them it would be burned to fine ashes.

Cas and Wise decided to stay over, and leave in the morning. It had been a pretty long night. Pablo must've been tired too because he kept on yawning. He bid them both a goodnight, and disappeared.

The following morning, Cas and Wise got up early. They played a little golf, and then they had a hearty breakfast that was prepared by Pablo's wife, Magdalena. She was a good cook, and she served them with a smile. They tipped her very nicely for that too. A thousand dollars, to be exact. She smiled, and thanked them like seven times.

When they were done eating, Cas and Wise took a walk over by the alligator pit. They just wanted to make sure all of the remains were gone. When they got there, it looked like everything was gone. They didn't even see the plastic bag anymore. Lucky for them, they didn't see any alligators either. There was no trace of Ysatis left, so their mission was accomplished.

The gators were probably resting at that time of day, but they didn't take any chances. Casino and Wise got the hell out of dodge. When they got back to the house, they gathered their stuff and brought it downstairs. It was time for them to go. They were just waiting for their hired car to arrive.

Pablo was there to see them off. He was a pretty alright dude. When their car showed up, he walked them outside. The three men all shook hands, and said goodbye.

Before Cas got in the car, he handed Pablo an envelope with ten gees inside. Pablo didn't open it up in front of him. He just shook his hand firmly again, and thanked him.

On the way home, Cas and Wise's minds were at ease. They weren't proud of what they had done, but they were glad it was over. That was one less thing their team had to worry about. The problem was taken care of, and Jay didn't even have a clue yet. They were all going down to Miami for the Super Bowl, so they would probably wait until then to tell him.

CHAPTER TWENTY SIX

Kira was back in New Jersey at her house. It felt good to be home. Spending over a year in that jail cell made her really appreciate the space and luxury her home offered. Cas' money bought that house, and then he gave it to her in the divorce settlement. Now Kira was grateful. It was prime real estate, so she had no intentions on relocating any time soon.

It was too much space for just her and her son, but Kira loved kids, so one day she planned on filling up those other bedrooms with children. She just had shit to do first. Lately, she had been thinking about adopting too. When she settled down a little more, she wanted to help as many children as she could. She could see herself with a whole rainbow tribe in the future.

Speaking of children, she had flown to New York from Miami and picked up Ysatis' baby like Cas had instructed her to do. She had paid the sitter, and then she gathered some of his belongings, and locked up the apartment. Kira took the little fellow home with her. She couldn't front, her brother's son was handsome. He resembled Jay quite a bit.

Kira felt bad that he would never see his mother again, but what was done was done. And it was necessary. She knew the baby would be okay because he was a Mitchell, and they were good people. The type of dude Jay was, he would make sure his son was taken care of.

Her little nephew was a cutie pie. She had enjoyed playing

with him but she was ready to pass him off. As far as she was concerned, she had helped out enough. She even bought the A&D Ointment Cas told her to pick up, and rubbed it on the baby's chafe bottom. He was good. She fed him, and he was smiling.

Now it came down to her dropping him off with either Jay, or her mother. But Kira knew their mom would ask a lot of questions. And furthermore, she didn't know if her mother even knew about Jay's new kid yet.

She decided to call Jay. That was his child. She knew that might cause some issues between him and his wife, but that was his problem. She called her brother and told him she needed to see him pronto.

Jay was at home when Kira called. He sensed the urgency in her voice so he hurried over her house, hoping his little sister hadn't done something stupid again. When he got there, he was pretty surprised when she handed him his kid. He looked at Kira for an explanation.

Before Jay could ask her any questions, Kira just told him to speak to Cas about it. She told him she had kept the baby overnight, but she couldn't baby-sit anymore because she had to get ready to go to the studio.

Jay knew about her studio session with Five and Vino, so he didn't argue with her. He just had to decide what to do with that baby. After Kira told him to speak to Cas about it, he didn't even bother to ask how she got the baby, or where his mother was. He knew Ysatis was gone, and she wasn't coming back.

$ $ $ $

Portia was downstairs cleaning up the kitchen. She had just finished washing the breakfast dishes when she heard Jay come back in the house. She dried her hands, and headed out there to greet him. He had left the house in a hurry, so she wanted to make sure everything was okay.

To Portia's surprise, he wasn't alone. He was holding a baby in a carrier.

Portia screwed up her face, and shook her head. Jay was hard on his self. She guessed she had handled that shit too well. Did he think he could start bringing his mistakes home now? Around her children? Hell no!

Portia was ready to set that nigga straight. She said, "Jay, what the hell do you think you're doing? What is that baby doing here?"

Portia was tight. Jay knew she would be. He just told her the truth without saying too much. "No disrespect, P. I'm sorry, but there's no one else to look after him right now."

Portia crossed her arms, and looked at him like he was crazy. "And where is his mother?"

Jay sort of looked away. He said, "She left."

Portia said, "Oh yeah, and when is that bitch coming back?"

Jay paused, and then he said, "She's not."

There was a brief silence after that. He knew Portia was thinking about what he said. She stared at him for a second, but he was glad she left it alone.

Portia didn't ask any questions. She was his wife, so she would ride with him no matter what. Truthfully, she didn't even want to know any details. Jay looked like he was stressed. She knew him well enough to know that whatever happened had taken a toll on him. That couldn't have been easy.

Portia thought about all the times she had secretly hoped Ysatis would just die out of their lives, and she felt bad. Maybe it was guilt.

Jay broke the silence first. He cleared his throat, and said, "He shouldn't be here long. Okay? I just gotta get in touch with my sister, Laurie. Hopefully, she can help me out. I'll call her now."

Portia walked over and looked at the baby whose mother she had wished dead a thousand times. Her heart went out to the little fellow. She couldn't front, he was handsome. He had Jay's eyes. He looked like Jay just as much as Jayquan and Patrice did. Jazmin looked just like Portia, but Jayquan and the baby were Jay's spitting image.

Ysatis had no family, so if Jay didn't step up, the child would wind up in the foster care system. Portia wasn't that kind of woman. She wouldn't deprive Jay of the right to be in his child's life.

Just then, the baby started crying. He was going to need somebody to look after him. Portia knew he needed to be nurtured. He probably missed his mother already.

Portia said a quick prayer for strength. The decision she was about to make, she knew she was going to need it. With the help of God, she overlooked all the malice in her heart about the baby's conception. That very second, Portia accepted Jaylin into their family. She had a feeling that was what her mother would've done, God bless her soul. Portia took the screaming baby out of Jay's arms.

Jay looked surprised. Whatever Portia did made the baby stop crying. It must've been a woman's touch. It was another one of those moments when Jay was moved to thank God for his wife. She brought that out of him a lot. Portia was golden. What a woman.

$ $ $ $

The story Jay and Portia gave their kids about the new baby in the house was simple. They said he was adopted. Jayquan was the only one who wasn't going for it. He said it was a little suspicious that they had suddenly adopted a baby that they had never once mentioned getting before.

Jay didn't want him sore at him, so he sat him down for a man to man talk. He told him the truth, which was he had made the mistake of getting another woman pregnant. He told him he regretted it more than anything in his life, but he had to face up to his responsibilities.

Jayquan asked him why he would take a chance like that, knowing how sad it would make Portia. He asked him how he could be so irresponsible. Then he asked where the baby's mother was, and why he couldn't live with her.

Jay had to lie to him with a straight face. He said that she ran off, and left the baby with him. He said she had signed her parental rights away, and wasn't coming back. He told Lil' Jay he was sorry to spring a new kid brother on him so unexpectedly, but he promised him the baby wouldn't affect their relationship. Jay reminded him that he was his firstborn, and said he would always be special to him because of that.

Jayquan didn't miss a beat. He used the situation as a means to manipulate his father. He shook his head like he was in despair, and said, "I don't know, Pop. This is heavy. This gon' take some time to get over. You know what would probably help? We should probably go looking at some cars this weekend, man."

Jay shook his head. He didn't believe his son was trying to bribe him at a time like that. That little dude was fiending for a whip, and he wanted it by any means necessary. Jayquan must've figured he had him by the balls.

Jay knew he could drive pretty well. Lil' Jay had been steering a car since he was three. Back then, Jay used to put him in his lap and let him "drive". He grinned, and promised his son a car in the near future. He wanted to wait until he was at least sixteen, but he might just go ahead and make that happen for him. But Lil' Jay would only be able to look at the car for a few months. He would have to wait until he got his license to actually drive it. As long as he understood that, Jay wasn't against it. He knew he would be spoiling his son, but he needed Jayquan's forgiveness about that baby thing. To Jay, a car was a small price to pay for that.

Over the next few days, they all tried to get adjusted to having another baby in the house. Portia had to give Jay credit. He was definitely trying not to inconvenience her. He had hired a nanny to do basically everything for the little fellow. The first few days, Portia had limited contact with the baby.

Portia knew she had to get pass whatever issues she had with that child. She had forgiven Jay and opened their home to that baby, so she had to accept him. But it was hard because Jay made him with another woman. Even though she knew Ysatis was out of the picture, it was still difficult.

It was actually her kids who unknowingly broke the tension. Jazmin and Trixie loved their "adopted" baby brother. Trixie was going on two years old, so she thought she was a big girl now. She tried to pick Jaylin up just like Jazz did. Even Jayquan played with him a little bit.

While Portia was watching the kids play with the baby, she started to fall in love with the little rascal too. He was so precious, bless his little heart. She couldn't help but hold him and play with him.

Jaylin acted like he loved Portia too. He would smile and start jumping every time he saw her coming. He was so cute. He had two little bottom teeth growing in.

As the week went by, Portia started feeling guilty. Little Jaylin was down the hall in one of the guest rooms with some stranger who was being paid to care for him. He was one of Jay's children, for God's sake. It just didn't seem fair. What was she, the wicked step-mother?

The second week the baby was there, Portia fired the live-in nanny. She paid her for the rest of the week, and then she told Jay she would just get a part-time sitter to come in when she needed help. She started doing a lot more for the baby, and treating him like he was hers. He was a part of their family now, so in a sense he was hers.

It was a totally different situation, but Portia hadn't birthed Jayquan into the world either. But she had still raised him, and she loved him like he was her own. She would do the same thing with the new baby.

She had talked it over with her girls, Fatima and Laila, and they both commended her. Laila said she was an angel, and was truly going to be blessed. Fatima agreed. She said she knew that couldn't have been easy. She told Portia she was a hell of a woman, and said Jay's ass better know what he had. Laila said amen to that.

CHAPTER TWENTY SEVEN

Laila had made an appointment to take Macy to the GYN to talk about birth control. When the day finally came, the doctor visit ended in sheer surprise. The one time Macy sort of slipped up came back to haunt her. She just let Jayquan put the head in for a minute one day. He must've had super sperm because she was five weeks pregnant.

Laila was utterly shocked, to say the least. It felt like her heart actually stopped. She couldn't believe her daughter was pregnant. She hadn't even noticed Macy had missed a period. Hell, she didn't even know she was having sex.

Laila just started crying. That news really hurt. Not her Macy. She was a good girl. She had never given her any problems. Never. Laila had just known she was going to make her proud. But what about college now? Laila was heartbroken.

Macy was just as shocked. She really had no idea. But she realized how much her life was about to change, so she was frightened. She was having a baby. Wow. She was only sixteen years old. She watched the silent tears roll down her mother's face, and felt horrible. She guessed she had really let her down.

Macy didn't know what to say, so she just apologized. "Mommy, I'm sorry."

Laila didn't even respond. She didn't want to lose it up in that place, so they left the doctor's office, and headed home. On the way, the silence in the car was heavy.

Mid-route, Laila asked her daughter if she was okay. Macy nodded, and asked her if she was.

Laila reached over and squeezed her baby's hand. She said, "Macy, let's keep this between us. We don't have to tell anybody, okay?"

Macy smiled weakly, and said, "Thanks, Ma, but how long do you think we could hide a baby?"

Laila raised an eyebrow. She wondered where that chick was going with that. Her ass wasn't having no baby. Laila kept cool for the time being. She had questions, so she grilled Macy instead.

"So how long you been having sex? And with *who*? Damn, Mace, I thought you would've told me. I thought we were close. Didn't we agree that you would come to me when you were ready? Girl, tell me who the hell got you pregnant?"

After a few seconds of silence, Macy said, "If I tell you, you might laugh."

Laila made a face, and snorted. "I doubt that! Why would I laugh?"

Macy sighed. "Because he's younger than me."

Laila got impatient. "Girl, what is the little bastard's name? What is he, some boy from school? Where is he from?"

Macy shrugged. "He don't stay too far from us. Ma, I might as well go on and tell you... It's Jayquan."

Laila's eyes popped. If Macy wasn't her daughter, that *would've* been funny. Laila said, "*What*? Are you *lying* to me?"

"*No*, I'm not lying. It's him."

"Jayquan is like a *brother* to you, girl. How long y'all been having sex?"

Macy said, "Ma, but we're not *blood* relatives. I *care* about him. He cares about *me too*. And we ain't been having sex that long. Just since the day after Christmas."

Laila didn't even know what to say. That little mothafucka Jayquan done got her baby pregnant. Boys always had to be so

273

damn fast. She wondered if Portia knew her son was screwing her daughter in her damn house. She felt like cutting his little horny ass balls off.

Macy must've read her mind. She said, "And please don't be mad at Jayquan. It wasn't even his idea. *I* initiated sexual intercourse with *him*, okay Ma."

Laila looked at her sideways. Her little ass was too grown. But she was right, she couldn't blame Jayquan. Hell, Macy was older than him.

Laila was blunt with her knocked up teen. She said, "Well, if you're so *smart*, and so *in control*, how could you be dumb enough to get pregnant the minute you start having sex? Did you plan this?"

Macy said, "*No*." After that, she just dropped her head.

Laila didn't mean to be harsh, but she was mad as hell. The girl looked so pitiful, she toned it down. "Look, baby. People make mistakes every day. Don't worry, we'll take care of this. The sooner, the better. Okay?"

Macy took a deep breath. She was afraid of her mother's reaction, but she stood for her beliefs. She said, "I'm keeping it, Ma."

Laila was driving, but she looked at her like she lost her mind. She said, "You ain't ready to have no baby. Girl, you wouldn't know shit if you fell in it. I'm your mother. *I* know what's best for you. *You* don't know shit! You are not about to let no pissy tail ass boy mess up your life!"

Macy started crying hysterically. She never got that emotional before. She yelled at her mother for the first time in her life. "See, that's where you wrong! This ain't even *about* Jayquan! This is *my* baby! It's *my* decision!"

Laila couldn't disagree, but she told her not to raise her voice at her. She got an idea, so she took a detour. She headed for Jay and Portia's place instead of going home.

When her mother turned down the down the long, winding

driveway to Jayquan's house, Macy said, "Ma, please don't embarrass me."

She had the nerve. Laila didn't even respond. She just parked the car, and hopped out. Skye was asleep in her car seat in the back. Laila picked her baby up, and told Macy to come on. She rang the bell, and waited for someone to come to the door.

Jay answered the door. He was on his way out in a minute. He actually thought she was Cas because he was expecting him. Jay smiled at Laila and Macy, and greeted them pleasantly.

Neither one of them was smiling, so he knew something was up. The baby was reaching for Jay, so he took her out of Laila's arms, and invited them in. Skye looked up at him and sleepily said, "Hi, Uncle Jay. Where's Cwixie?"

Jay smiled, and gave her a kiss. She talked so cute. He said "Trixie is sleeping. She's taking a nap like you were." Skye said, "Okay", and laid her head on his shoulder.

Jay looked over at Laila. She looked uptight. He had a feeling this had something to do with Jayquan's recent admission that he and Macy were having sex. She must've found out.

Jay said, "What up, sis? What's wrong?"

Laila just shook her head. She crossed her arms, and said. "Jay, we got a serious problem. I just found out that our kids been having sex. And my daughter is pregnant by your son."

Jay had planned to act like he was surprised, but that shit shocked him for real. No wonder Macy looked like she'd been crying. He said, "What?! Oh shit!"

Laila nodded. "Yes. I can't believe it either. Where is Jayquan? And Portia? We need to talk."

Jay was still stunned. He nodded, and told her Lil' Jay hadn't got home from school yet. He was due in any minute. He told them to have a seat while he got Portia from the kitchen.

Laila sat down, and Macy stood up by the door. A few seconds later, they heard Portia scream, "Jay, you better stop fuckin' playing! Macy is *what*? By *who*? *Oh my God*!"

Portia rushed out of the kitchen to Laila. When they looked at each other, they both just started crying. Macy started crying again too. Jay just stood there wishing he wasn't home at the time. Women were so emotional. He didn't know what to do.

Laila stammered, "Portia, m-my daughter is p-p-*pregnant!* By y'all son! And she wants to keep the baby. I brought her over here for y'all to help me talk some sense into her. What in the world are they gon' do with a *baby* at their ages?"

Macy tearfully sobbed, "Auntie, she try'na make me kill my baby! And I just can't. If I do that, I'ma go to hell! I can't do that! My sister got an abortion. What if that's why that happened to her?"

Everybody just looked at her when she said that. Wow.

Macy's nose was running, but she didn't care. She looked at all of them, and said, "I'm sorry for saying that. I'm not being mean, but I really feel like that could be true. God bless Pebbles' soul. Nobody loved my sister more than me! But maybe she would still be here if she wouldn't have killed that baby."

She looked at Laila. "Ma, I'm sorry, but you made Pebbles do that. She was real young, so I understood your logic. But I'm *sixteen*. I can make my *own* decisions!"

Laila was so hurt she couldn't even speak. Her daughter had voiced something she had struggled with for years. She had often wondered if that abortion she forced Pebbles to have had something to do with her dying so young. But it was too painful to say it out loud.

Portia told Macy to calm down. She didn't want the situation to get anymore out of control. They just had to talk about it.

Just then, Jazmin and Jayquan came strolling in. Lil' Jay had unknowingly walked right into a hot frying pan. All eyes were on him.

The first thing he noticed was that Macy was crying. And then her mother looked at him like she wanted to kill him. Oh shit, something was up. He wanted to turn around and leave, but he knew he had no wins. Especially with his parents standing right there. Jayquan turned off his iPod, and took out his earphones.

Laila said, "Well, hello. Just the person I wanted to see the most." She got up and walked over there where he was standing.

Portia and Jay looked at each other. They thought Laila was about to jump on Jayquan. Portia knew Laila wasn't thinking straight, so she got ready to intervene.

Instead of slapping their boy, Laila patted him on the back sarcastically. She said, "*Congratulations*, Jayquan. You better pull up them pants, boy. 'Cause guess what? You 'bout to be a father, baby!"

Jayquan looked like Laila just slapped the shit out of him. He said, "*What?*" He looked over at Macy, expecting her to disagree with what her mother said. But she didn't. Jayquan's heart fell in his ass. Wow.

Laila pointed at him, and shook her head. She said, "Thank you! I wanted *her* to see your reaction. You ain't ready to be no father. Tell her, Jayquan! *Please* tell her. 'Cause ya' little *girlfriend* talkin' about she wants to keep it."

Jayquan took off his fitted Yankees cap, and scratched his head. He looked over at Jay and Portia, but they just shrugged. They let him know he was on his own that time. He had to man up.

To everyone's surprise, Lil' Jay did. He said, "Look, no disrespect to none of y'all, but it's whatever *Macy* wanna do. It's *our* kid, so if she wanna have it…" He paused, and shrugged. "Then we'll have it."

Macy looked up when he said that. She looked like he had given her a ray of hope. She had been afraid of his reaction. She stopped crying, grateful for the support. She really loved Jayquan. Even more so now.

Laila said, "Oh *really*? That's what you think? Well, you are wrong. What the hell y'all think this is? This is real life! This ain't the movie "Juno"! What y'all think, you have a baby, and then just sing, and play folk songs on a fucking guitar? This ain't television! Macy is *my* child, so it's *my* decision. And *I* decided that neither one of y'all little asses is ready to bring no child into this world. So we gon' take care of this ASAP! I hope we're all clear on this. Now Macy, let's *go*."

Laila took Skye out of Jay's arms. She put her down so her butt could walk, and then she looked at Portia. She said, "Portia, our babies are not even two years old yet. How tacky is it that they could actually be *aunties* before they turn three. That's some real *project* shit."

Laila turned to Jay next. She said, "Bro, I don't know 'bout y'all, but *I* ain't ready to be no damn grandparent. I love y'all, and I will speak to y'all later."

She and her daughters headed for the door. Macy looked back at them with fresh tears running down her face. Her and Jayquan locked eyes for a minute. You could tell he wished there was something he could do.

Portia felt the same way, and Jay did too. But Laila was right, that was her child. Jay made a mental note to speak to Cas about it. He had to get him to talk to Laila before she did something irrational.

$ \qquad $ \qquad $ \qquad $

Before bedtime that night, Laila peeked in on her daughter. Macy hadn't come out of her room since they'd been home. Not to eat, or anything. When Laila walked in there, she wouldn't talk to her. Laila just told her she loved her, and asked her to trust that she knew best.

Macy spoke then. She said, "No disrespect, Ma. But I'm an American, and I have the constitutional right to choose. I'm afraid to get an abortion. If I do, God is gonna punish me. That's *murder*, Ma. I choose life. This is a life I have inside of me. I'm the one who's gon' have to answer to God for that, not you."

Laila wasn't heartless. That made her want to cry, but she said,

"Baby, God will forgive you for your sins, if you ask him. Now we gon' go ahead and take care of this thing while it's still early. We're going tomorrow morning, and that's final. You'll thank me for this one day. Trust me, baby."

Macy looked real glum. She said, "I doubt I'll ever thank you for forcing me to kill my child. Good night, Ma." She turned over on her bed.

Laila guessed that meant she was dismissed. She walked out the room without another word.

Laila waited up for Cas that night. She had spoken to him on the telephone earlier, so she knew he already knew. But she needed to speak to him face to face. She had to see his response. And their wedding was coming up in a matter of days. Was he still in? How did she know he wanted to marry a would-be grandmother?

Most importantly, Laila needed Cas' advice. That was her man, and she valued his opinion. Cas was usually right about stuff.

When he finally got home, the first thing he did was give her a hug. Laila smiled for the first time that day. She always felt better when he was around. When he asked her if she was okay, she nodded and told him she was all cried out.

She fixed Cas something to eat, and ran him a bath. After he got comfortable in the hot tub, Laila sat on the side and washed his back. She casually asked him his take on the situation.

Cas said he firmly believed in a woman's right to choose. But then he said he truly didn't believe a baby was the worse thing in the world. He loved kids, so he especially didn't have a problem with Macy keeping her baby. He told Laila the girl was already pregnant, so maybe it was meant to be. He said they could certainly afford to have the baby, so why not give it a chance.

Cas even went so far as to say he would hire a nanny to help out, so the baby wouldn't be a burden on her while Macy went to school. Laila smiled at him, touched that he had even thought that far ahead. Macy's father acted like he didn't give a hoot about her, so it meant a lot that he cared so much.

Next, Cas reminded her that Macy's baby daddy was from a good family. He said it wasn't like she was pregnant by some no-good ass deadbeat. Jayquan was young, but Jay and Portia would definitely do their part.

Laila knew that was absolutely true. Jay had been so kind to her in the past. He had welcomed her and her children into his home. As far as Laila was concerned, that dude was platinum.

And Portia had a heart of gold. She had just taken in a baby that Jay made on her in an affair with a younger woman. She said she planned to raise that baby like it was her own. So Laila knew she would surely spoil Jayquan's child.

She kissed Cas on the cheek, and told him she would definitely think about it. Then she asked him to put her to bed. Cas grinned, and told her he would be happy to assist her with that.

He stood up out of the water and reached for a towel. Being wet defined his chiseled muscles even more. Laila's eyes rested on his tattooed chest, and then traveled south. Cas was well endowed, and he looked sexy as hell with all that water dripping off him. Laila licked her lips, and gave him "the look".

Cas knew what it was. He encouraged her with his eyes. She smiled seductively, and leaned over and kissed his hardening manhood. Cas nodded appreciatively, and stroked her hair.

Laila loved the way Cas always made everything seem so simple. She needed that in her life. He always took control and made everything alright. He had made her feel a lot better that night, so she wanted to make him feel good too. She ran her tongue along the length of his shaft, and proceeded to please him right there in the hot tub.

Laila would do just about anything for Cas. She really loved that man. He had stood by her side through thick and thin. Even when she was in a coma, and then paralyzed. He loved her unconditionally, and always made her feel beautiful. That was exactly why she was marrying him.

$ \qquad $ \qquad $ \qquad $

Macy had always been an obedient child. She had never once openly defied her mother. The thought had never crossed her mind. But this situation was different. Laila wouldn't see things her way. She wanted her to abort her child.

Macy was convinced there was a miracle growing inside of her, so she wasn't even trying to hear that. As she packed an overnight bag, she thought about the hypocrisy of Laila's logic. How dare she raise her to be God-fearing, and then force her to commit sin? Macy felt like abortion was murder, so that night when Laila went to sleep, she hopped in her red Mercedes and fled.

Macy couldn't go to her aunts, Portia or Fatima's house because she knew they would tell her mother she was there. She used the GPS system on her car to get directions, and drove herself all the way to her Nana's house Brooklyn.

Macy didn't call first because she had the feeling her grandmother would've called Laila. She just parked outside, and walked up to the house. She knew her father stayed downstairs in the basement, so she prayed he didn't come to the door. She rang the bell, and waited. She got no response, so she rang it again.

A minute later, the outside light came on. Macy knew her grandmother was looking out the window to see who it was. She didn't want to scare her, so as quietly as she could, she said, "It's me, Nana. It's Macy".

Mama Atkins opened the door immediately. She just knew something was wrong. She quickly let her granddaughter inside, and hugged her. Then she asked her what in the world she was doing out that time of night.

Macy's first question was, "Nana, who's here with you?"

Mama Atkins told her she was home alone. She knew Macy

was referring to her father, so she waved her hand and told her there was no telling where he was.

Macy was glad. She had some issues with that dude, so she didn't want to see him. Especially at the time. She asked her grandmother if they could go sit down. She told her she had to talk to her about something. Before she could ask, Macy was honest and told her that her mother didn't know where she was.

When they were seated in the kitchen, Macy sipped the hot cocoa her Nana fixed her, and tried to think of a way to make her plight sound better. She finally decided to just level with Mama Atkins. She was sitting there being so patient with her.

Macy didn't want to put her through the suspense, so she said, "Nana, I kind of messed up. Umm, I'm sort of pregnant. My mother wants me to get rid of it, 'cause she thinks I won't be able to go to college anymore. But I'm not gettin' no abortion. I wanna keep my baby. And I'ma *still* go to college."

Mama Atkins said, "I see. And just how "sort of pregnant" are you?"

Macy said, "I'm only like five weeks."

Her grandmother was just quiet for a minute. She wasn't ecstatic about the news, but it certainly could've been worse. Thank God the child was alive and well. Teenagers got pregnant every single day. It wasn't the end of the world. Finally, she said, "Well, I guess you gots to grow up now, little girl."

Macy smiled. Her grandmother always called her "little girl" as a term of endearment. She was surprised she took the news so well. She'd half-expected her to yell, or lecture her, but she was pretty cool. Macy was grateful for that. She appreciated her understanding.

Mama Atkins and Macy sat up talking for a while. Macy left out a few details, but she filled her grandma in on how things had come to be. She told her all about Jayquan, and the fact that they had recently started having sex.

Mama Atkins didn't judge her granddaughter. She had been

young once. She even had a sense of humor. When she found out Jayquan was younger than Macy, she joked that he was barely old enough to know where to put it. She asked her if she had left the light on and showed him.

Macy just laughed, happy to have found a place where she wasn't the bad girl. What she need was unconditional love at the time. She figured her mother of all people would've known that.

$ \qquad $ \qquad $ \qquad $

The following morning, Laila noticed Macy wasn't up yet. When she went in her bedroom to wake her up, she saw that she was gone. Her bed looked like it hadn't even been slept in! Laila got real scared. The first thing she did was call Portia to see if she had gone over there.

Portia said she hadn't seen her. When she got off the phone with Laila, she was worried too. She kept on calling Macy's cell phone, but she wasn't picking up.

Laila tried calling Fatima too. She said she hadn't seen or heard from Macy either. Laila just kept praying, and called her cell phone again and again. The situation reminded her of the way she couldn't find Pebbles that time. She was sick to her stomach. She prayed to God that Macy would return to her safe.

Laila knew her daughter left because she didn't want to get rid of her baby. Now she wondered if she should've handled things differently. She hadn't meant to push the child away. Laila figured Macy was upset with her, and didn't want to answer her phone. She decided to text her, and tell her to come home so they could talk.

While Laila was typing the text in her Sidekick, her phone rang. The caller ID said "Mama Atkins". Laila figured she was just calling to check on Macy. She loved her granddaughter, and did that quite often.

Mama Atkins had always been there for Laila to confide in. She was quite an understanding woman, and she always had a kind word of advice. She was so concerned about her granddaughter, she called to check on her three or four times a week. So Laila didn't see the point in keeping things a secret.

She told Mama Atkins the truth about her grandchild being pregnant, and running away. To Laila's surprise, she didn't get upset. She wasn't judgmental, and she didn't make any snide comments about Laila's parenting skills. She simply said, "Well, God knows better than we do. Macy just got to grow up now."

Laila told her she was worried sick. She admitted she'd tried to coerce her to abort, and said she felt bad about it now. She said she should've been more supportive and understanding.

Mama Atkins told Laila to calm down, and let her know Macy was in Brooklyn with her. She said Laila just needed to pray about the situation, and put her trust in God. She said when she did that, everything would be fine.

Laila was relieved to hear that her daughter was safe. She asked Mama Atkins to accompany Macy home because she didn't want her driving on the main highways during heavy traffic hours. She told her she would send her back home in a hired car whenever she was ready.

After Laila found out Macy was safe, she called Portia and Fatima to let them know where she was. They were both relieved to hear the good news.

Laila said, "Boy, the devil is a liar. That mothafucka really got it in for me. Y'all think this is a sign to postpone the wedding?"

In unison, Portia and Fatima responded, "No!" There was no need for that. Macy was okay, and Laila and Cas were in love.

Laila's best friends told her to keep an open mind, and not jump the gun about Macy's pregnancy. They said if she kept the baby, they would raise it together. They assured her that she wasn't alone. They were a family.

Laila thanked her girls for the talk. They had always been the core of her support system. They all agreed to talk later.

Mama Atkins and Macy got to the house about two hours later. The first thing Laila did was hug her daughter, and tell her she was sorry. Cas was right there too. He hugged Macy, and kissed her on the forehead. He asked, "You okay, lil' mama?"

Macy smiled, and nodded. She proudly introduced him to her grandmother. Cas greeted her respectfully, and shook her hand.

Mama Atkins got a great first impression of the man Laila was marrying. He truly seemed like a genuine person. And she could tell he cared about her granddaughter. And Macy spoke highly of him too.

Mama Atkins was just glad that Macy was living in a stable environment. That was all that mattered. Especially while she was pregnant. Sadly, Khalil had taken that away from the child when he got hooked on that stuff. She was glad Laila had settled down with a man so decent. And their house was beautiful.

Laila sat Macy down, and they talked. She told her that the child she was carrying was hers, and she had no right to make that decision for her. She hugged Macy again, and told her she had her blessing. She said she would support her, but she warned her that motherhood wasn't easy.

Macy said, "Ma, I know that from all I've seen *you* go through. I'm the daughter of the strongest lady in the world. I have your genes, so I'll be fine."

They locked eyes for a second after she said that, and Laila thought about what she said. What a compliment. She loved her daughter. Macy had always been real mature. And she was good at taking care of babies too. When Laila was paralyzed from her accident, and going through a crisis right after she first had Skye, Macy had helped Portia take care of two newborns. So Laila had to give her daughter the benefit of a doubt.

Macy said, "Don't worry, Ma. I'm still gonna graduate from high school, and I'ma still go to college. I'm even still going to my junior prom. And I'ma be gettin' down too! Big belly, and all. Watch." She danced a little two step and did a dip.

Laila just laughed at her silly daughter. She really felt like they would be okay now. She made a mental note to call Portia and Fatima. She had to tell them they were keeping the baby.

$ $ $ $

Portia and Jay were across town discussing Macy's pregnancy too. It was still hard to believe. Especially since Jayquan was only fifteen. They couldn't even picture him being a father. Macy was so young too.

They had spoken to Jayquan, and he seemed pretty cool. He said he felt like they would be okay, considering all the mommies the baby would have. He pointed out the fact that by the time the baby came, Macy would be seventeen, and in her last year of high school. And he would be sixteen.

There was one thing they all agreed on. They wouldn't be the first young parents in the world, and they certainly wouldn't be the last. It would just be one more baby they would have to get used to. Portia joked that they were "gonna have a damn daycare in the house after a while." She laughed, and said she was thinking about hiring another nanny.

Jay laughed too. All of a sudden, he started feeling pretty good. He figured he was blessed to live to see his son have a kid. He knew a lot of dudes who never lived to see their children be born, let alone their grandkids. He grinned at Portia, and said, "Oh well, P. It is what it is."

Portia smiled back at him. She said, "Okay, daddy. Sorry, I mean *granddaddy*."

Jay smacked her on the ass, and said, "A'ight now, *grandma*. 'Wit your sexy, juicy, fat ass." He winked at her, and laughed. They hugged, and shared a little kiss.

Portia had to laugh when she thought about it. She and her girls all had new babies in their lives. She had to call them later, and point out how ironic that was. Portia had taken in Jay's outside child, Fatima was expecting a son in a few months, and Laila's daughter was pregnant. They'd soon have a whole new set of little ones to bring up. They'd all be mamas again in some fashion, and none of them had planned it. Life was just funny like that sometimes.

Portia reminded Jay that it was just days before Super Bowl weekend. Him, Cas, and Wise already had tickets, so they had plans to head down to Miami. Jayquan was going too. Everybody was cool now, so it looked like their trip was still on.

Chapter Twenty Eight

Mama Atkins prayed on it for a few days, and her spirit told her to inform her son that his daughter was pregnant. Now she didn't believe he wasn't going to help take care of it, or anything. Khalil didn't even do anything to help out with Macy. She just felt he had the right to know.

Khalil was pretty angry when he found out Macy was pregnant. He blamed it all on Laila. His mother told him he had no grounds, and pointed out that his absence in his daughter's life may have been a contributing factor as well. She told him there was no time for pointing fingers.

Khalil was selfish, and just ignored all that. He really had a one-track mind. He was still convinced that it was all Laila's fault. That was just easier to believe. He believed it so much, he called her cell phone to tell her.

When she answered her phone, he went off. After a string of insults, he said the most painful things he could throw at her. His last words in the barrage of verbal assault were the worse. He shouted, "She's pregnant because you raised her to be a whore like you! Dick suckin' and fuckin' is all you know, so that's all you could teach her!"

How dare he? Laila wished she could've jumped through that phone. She had tried to be a woman, and have an adult conversation in case he was concerned about his child, but he was an ignorant ass Black fool. She had planned not to stoop to his level, but she had to respond to those last words that disrespectful asshole said.

She said, "And if Macy had stayed with you, mothafucka', then what would she have turned out to be? A damn *crackhead*? Sure, Khalil. *You* were a *great* role model for our kids."

Khalil couldn't say anything at first. Her words had cut him deep. It got real ugly after that. He venomously spat, "Yeah, you had the kids with you, but you couldn't take care of 'em. You got one killed, and the other one pregnant. *Great job*, Laila. Great fuckin' job! You should've brought them over here to my mother! 'Cause you *obviously* ain't know what the *fuck* you were doin'!"

Laila was so shocked that he said that, she was just quiet for a minute. She knew that weak ass, recovering crackhead mothafucka wasn't trying to belittle her parenting skills. She had held their family down and kept a roof over their heads, while he sold all the shit in the house, and smoked up their savings.

She went off on that nigga. "You *son of a bitch*, don't you *ever* talk to me like that again. Maybe if your triflin' ass would have been more of a *man*, shit would've turned out differently. When you hit rock bottom, I did the best that I could for my girls. That's why I left, 'cause I wasn't gon' let you bring me down to your level. I left yo' ass to give my children a better life. What ever happened after that was in God's hands."

She paused for a second. "And as far as Macy and the baby she's carrying, *we* gon' be fine. We don't need you for *shit*. Now you go to *hell*, bastard."

Khalil couldn't even respond. Laila won that round. He hadn't expected it to go that way. She cut him long and deep that time. He was really hurt. And the fact that he knew she was right made it worse. He should've been more of a man.

The last thing Laila said to him was, "Now if you'll excuse me, I have a *wedding* to get ready for. I'm marrying a *real* man this time!" After that she hung up on his ass. *Click!*

Khalil sat there dumbfounded, staring at the phone. He felt so low tears came to his eyes. His pride was shot. He felt like killing that bitch. He wanted to kill Laila and that nigga Cas. He didn't have anything left to lose, so he might as well.

Laila was a dumb bitch. She had been so wrapped up in planning some stupid wedding, she fucked around and let his daughter get pregnant. Khalil couldn't believe she had the nerve to throw that fucking wedding in his face. That spiteful bitch had already sent his mother an invitation. So now he knew exactly where that whore was getting married.

He needed a fucking drink. Khalil grabbed his liquor bottle off the table and turned it up to his lips. He guzzled damn near half of the bottle of E&J Dark in one swig, and then slammed it on the table. He felt like he needed more. He hadn't smoked any crack since he came home, but he couldn't think of a better excuse. He was so low, he needed to get high. He had been clean for a while, but he was seconds away from going to buy himself a hit.

Khalil thought about his mother again. She acted like she was planning to attend Laila's little funky wedding. And he had seen the new, pretty dress she'd bought hanging up in her room. He got so angry about that, he went upstairs and told his mother off. He let her know he thought that was fucked up that she had taken Laila's side in everything that went down. He accused Mama Atkins of conspiring against him.

She reminded her foolish son that Laila was the mother of her granddaughters. She told him they had to maintain a relationship. She said it was his fault he had been weak and got hooked on drugs, and he couldn't fault Laila for moving on.

She asked Khalil a question that left him ultimately dumbfounded. She said, "Be honest, son. What have *you* done to prevent this? You're just as much responsible as Laila is, if you wanna get technical. It takes two to parent, and you stepped off."

He shouted, "Ma, *she* left *me*! Remember!"

His mama didn't back down. She said, "*Why*, son? Why? Because you got on that stuff! You messed up, so I don't blame her. And you ain't did a damn thing for Macy since. So boy, hush that fuss up in here!"

She shut him right up. The truth hurt. Khalil just had to eat that because it came from his mother. He had no defense anyway.

Laila thought she was hot shit, throwing her little wedding up in his face. He was seriously contemplating crashing that shit. He should just show up, and mess up her big day. He wanted to piss on that bitch's parade bad as hell. He ought to kill both of them mothafuckas. Right before they said "I do". That liquor Khalil had guzzled had him thinking he was Superman. He felt like he could do anything.

$ \quad $ \quad $ \quad $

Miraculously, after a few days passed, Laila's life seemed to return to normal again. She had accepted the new baby her daughter was having, and moved on. So did all the other parties involved. That baby was going to affect everyone in their family's life in some way or another, but everyone seemed to be at peace with it.

Macy said if she had a girl, she was going to name her after her sister, Pebbles. Pebbles' real name was "Khalia". Although Laila had named Pebbles after Khalil, she didn't have a problem with that.

Macy was knocked up, but she was still a good girl. She was a huge help to Laila. She knew how nervous she was with the wedding coming up, so she had really been holding her down. Macy watched her baby sister, Skye, and she cleaned up the house a lot too.

Laila couldn't believe how fast time was moving. It seemed like the big day was approaching at the speed of light. It was

Wednesday, and she and Cas were getting married that Saturday. There was only one more wedding rehearsal to go.

$ \qquad $ \qquad $ \qquad $ \qquad $

Mama Atkins had RSVP'd the wedding invitation Laila had sent her weeks before. So when the day finally came, she was ready to go. She was looking forward to seeing how beautiful Laila looked in her wedding dress. And Macy was one of the bridesmaids, so she was sure she'd look pretty too.

As far as Mama Atkins was concerned, Laila would always be family. She was her daughter-in-law, and her granddaughter's mother. Right before she got dressed for the wedding, she phoned a friend of hers to get the right route. She wasn't that familiar with that part of New Jersey.

Khalil was downstairs drinking. He'd been going hard on the booze, but he overheard his mother on the telephone getting directions from someone. She was going to that fucking wedding. He couldn't believe his own mother would stab him in the back like that. The woman who had brought him into the world. That was a real slap in the face.

While his mother was getting ready, Khalil tried to conjure up a good plan. It all came together in his head, so he quickly changed into some decent clothes. After he was dressed up, he retrieved the new gun he had copped from a neighbor from the top of his closet. He made sure the gun was on safety, and tucked it in the side of his waist. It was a cold February day, so he grabbed an overcoat and a hat. He picked up his liquor bottle, and then he quietly exited the house.

When Khalil got outside, he looked around. The coast was clear, so he nonchalantly used the spare key to open the trunk of his mother's car. She drove a big ass Chrysler LHS, so the trunk was huge. Khalil looked around again, and he got inside. Now he was going to the wedding too. But it wasn't on no happy go lucky shit.

$ $ $ $

It was Valentine's weekend, and Laila's big day finally came. She was pretty nervous. She was more excited than afraid, but she had a bad case of pre-wedding jitters. Laila was in the back doing a last minute mirror check, and Portia and Fatima were right there by her side. Fatima was pregnant and emotional, so she kept crying and telling her how happy she was for her.

Laila kept fidgeting in the mirror, but her girls kept on telling her she looked beautiful. They said the only way she could mess things up was if she tripped over her dress and busted her ass while she was walking down the aisle. Laila laughed, but she told them that was easier said than done.

Laila had done a lot of thinking the past few days. She had taken a serious look at her life. When she took inventory, her journey always seemed uphill. But in all actuality she couldn't complain. God was so good to have placed people in her life who she could count on. People who had been crutches for her, and made her journey easier.

One of those people was Jay. Laila thought of the countless times he had been kind to her, and to her children as well. Every single time she was down and out, he offered a helping hand. He didn't even turn on her when she had a fistfight in his house with his little sister, Kira. Jay was good peoples. That dude had a big heart. She thought about the time he gave her that huge painting of Pebbles as an angel in heaven. That was so thoughtful of him.

Laila had a lot of love for that guy. She considered Jay her real brother-in-law. And he was sort of like her big brother too. So at their final wedding rehearsal the day before, she had decided to ask him to walk her down the aisle. He looked surprised by her request, but he said he was flattered. Then he grinned, and said he'd be honored.

The road had been rough, but it felt like everything was going to be okay. Laila was happy. At one point in her life, she believed the notion of that was impossible. She had a word with God, and thanked him for making her whole again. She was whole physically, mentally, and spiritually. Around that time a year ago, she couldn't even walk. But now she had her health and strength back, and she had true love. What were the odds?

Laila looked at her girls, and grinned. Portia and Tima looked so pretty. She was blessed to have them as friends. It was her wedding day, but she told them how beautiful they looked too.

They both looked happy to see her smile. Portia grabbed Laila and Fatima's hands, and suggested they say a quick prayer. They all closed their eyes and bowed their heads, and she led. Each time one of them got married, they had the same ritual.

When they were done praying, the girls all said "amen", and thanked God. Laila squeezed her best girlfriends' hands excitedly. She was so happy her eyes were shining. It was about to be official! Cas and her were about to tie the knot. She would become his "old ball and chain" in just minutes, and the thought was exhilarating.

$ $ $ $

Around almost around the same time, Cas with his boys. Moments ago, he had a word with God too. He thanked Him for His patience, and asked for forgiveness for all the wrong he had ever done. Especially for the latest "extermination" he was responsible for. Believe it or not, he really felt bad about having to get rid of Ysatis. It was necessary, but he knew it wasn't right.

Cas knew how it went. He might have to pay for that one day. And it would probably serve him right because he had gotten away with a lot of shit. He wasn't proud of the bad he had done, but he asked God to allow him the chance to do some more good.

He knew he wasn't still there just because he was smart. Or

because he was invincible. Cas gave God all the credit. He knew he was blessed, so he made a deal with God that day.

It was his wedding day, and he wanted to turn over a new leaf. He promised God that, in exchange for His continued mercy, he would walk a straight line. Cas just wanted to focus on being successful, and being a good husband and father. Family was everything to him, so nothing else really mattered. He smiled at the thought of the sunshine in his life finally becoming his wife. He only had a few more minutes of being single left.

Jay was Cas' best man, so he was suited up nicely. Wise was dressed up too, but for obvious reasons he wasn't in the wedding party. He couldn't really participate in any of the festivities, but he came out on the low to show support. He just had to stay in the cut.

Wise was a jokester, so he really wanted to see the look on Cas' face when he said "I do". But the great time the three of them had the night before made up for him missing that. Wise had wanted to create a makeshift bachelor party for Cas, so they had gone to a strip club and partied until the wee hours of the morning. As usual, Wise acted up a little more than Cas and Jay. But they had a good time too.

Cas' two best friends in the world told him he looked quite dapper that day. He thanked them, and said "ditto". After that, they both slapped Cas on the back, and asked if he was ready to go get hitched. Wise and Jay laughed, and joked that the fun he had the night before would be his last.

$ $ $ $

Minutes later, Laila walked down the aisle holding Jay's arm. She had to admit she was totally pleased. The red and white floral arrangements were lovely, and the wedding turnout was amazing. The place was packed. Laila kept up with Jay's long strides, and looked over at the live orchestra to her left. There were about twenty five instrumentalists, and they were playing an old classic, "Always and Forever". Everything was beautiful.

Everything she had prayed for had come to pass. She looked great in her dress, her makeup was flawless, and she got to walk down the aisle in couture high heels. Instead of Jimmy Choos, the wedding shoes she chose were some very stylish 3 ½ inch heels from Fillapa Scott's "Fifi" collection.

Jazmin and Falynn were the flower girls. They walked ahead of them in their pretty white dresses, sprinkling red rose petals on the fancy aisle runners. Cas' son, Jahseim, was the ring bearer. Kira had opted not to attend, but she didn't stop him from participating in the wedding. He had on a little tailored suit just like the men had on. So did Jayquan, who was one of Cas' groomsmen. Macy was a bridesmaid, so she had on a lovely red dress similar to Portia and Fatima's.

Laila stared down the aisle at her wedding party. Everyone looked absolutely great. And there was her groom. Cas looked real handsome in his fine tailored blacksuit. He was gazing at her like she was beautiful.

Laila had protested against a big wedding, but Portia and Fatima had compiled a guest list that kept on growing. It was so long, they had to narrow it down to a hundred people. Each person was allowed to bring one guest.

Maybe if Laila had gone with her original plans to have a small wedding, someone would've noticed Khalil in the vicinity. But in a sea of close to two hundred faces, he went virtually unnoticed. Especially in the hat he donned. He was there the whole time, and no one had any idea.

Khalil's mother didn't know he had hitched a ride in her trunk. He had waited until long after she parked the car to get out. And luckily, he wasn't seen by anyone. He had himself another drink in the parking lot, and went inside the ceremony. He sat close to the back and blended in, but he was seething.

Khalil was sick when he saw Laila marry Cas. When they

said "I do" to each other, he had to restrain himself. Before they kissed, the preacher asked if anyone objected to the two of them getting married. He almost stood up. He had a gun, and that was the perfect time to run up there and kill them. But there were so many people there, he lost his nerve. He told himself he would do it when the time was right.

Khalil knew he had no business there, but he stuck around for the reception. He had already thought of what he would say if someone approached him. He would just pretend he had come out to wish Laila well in her new life. To back up the lie that he was no longer bitter, he had even grinned and posed for one of the pictures the professional team of photographers was snapping.

It really killed him to admit it, but Laila's second wedding upstaged their wedding severely. They had shit like indoor fountains, and ice sculptures. That nigga Cas had clearly spared no expenses. All the fancy shit they had in there, he knew it cost a grip.

They had a seating area that was sectioned off. It was decorated real fancy, and all the tables in there had place cards on them. There were people in charge of the seating, and there was a red carpet leading up to the entrance. You could peek inside, but your name had to be on a table to get in. That side was obviously for the wedding party, and all the important and elite mothafuckas there.

Khalil couldn't front, some of the people there looked like they had some bread. He thought back to when he and Laila were happy, and had opened up a sporting goods store. Back then, he was determined to have something. The level those high roller mothafuckas up in there were on was the level he was trying to get to back then. Khalil knew he would never get to go in that red carpet VIP section now, so he wanted to take a piss and shit on that damn carpet.

In another room, there was a huge buffet set up for the

"common folk". Khalil had been going hard at drinking the past couple of days, so he hadn't had a full meal in a hot minute. He helped himself to about three plates. He sampled just about everything, except the caviar. He wasn't fucking with no fish eggs. The thought alone nauseated him. But he had to admit the rest of the food was proper.

After Khalil got his belly full, he took advantage of the open bar. He quickly threw back about four shots of the good stuff. He was so greedy because it was free. The whole time he drank, he got up his nerve more and more. He thought about the L-shaped cut Cas had ordered on his face, and his thirst for vengeance accelerated. He had lost his nerve and let those mothafuckas get married, but there would be no honeymoon.

CHAPTER TWENTY NINE

At their wedding reception, Laila and Cas were seated at the main table with the rest of their wedding party. They had jumped the broom about two hours ago, so now they were newlyweds. Laila was officially the "Mrs." now, and she was loving it.

Laila had made a beautiful bride, but after the wedding she had changed into another bad ass dress. That was her reception ensemble. In that dress she was showing a little more skin, but it was still elegant. And her shoes were so bad they were ferocious.

Laila really looked the part of a happy wife. She was all over her new husband. Especially when they had their first dance. They danced to "Forever My Lady" by Jodeci. Now she sat on Cas' lap feeding him. And girlfriend was smiling so much she was showing all thirty two teeth. She was literally glowing. Cas looked happy too.

The champagne was plentiful, so most of them were pretty tipsy by now. After dinner, Jay stood up and proposed a toast to their future together. Cas and Laila raised their glasses, and then they crossed their arms and sipped from each other's champagne flutes.

Khalil stood outside the door looking in. Their happiness was nauseating. He was infuriated by it. Especially when he saw his mother sitting at the main table with them. She was seated on the end next to Macy, and she even joined in on the toast. Mama Atkins was smiling, and looked happy too.

That shit had Khalil tight as hell. All the women in his life were over there with that nigga. His mother, his daughter, and his wife. That mothafucka Cas took everything from him.

And that bitch Laila looked like she was so gone over that nigga. Khalil was fucked up off all those drinks, but the image of her gazing lovingly at another man and spoon feeding him was sobering. Enraged, he bit his lip so hard he tasted blood. He decided that was it. There was nobody at the entrance at the time, so he walked right up in there.

He went up to the table, and stood right in front of those mothafuckas. He banged on the table to get everyone's attention, and took off his hat. Just about everybody's jaw dropped in surprise, including his mother's. Khalil had to admit, he enjoyed having the stage.

All eyes were on him, but nobody looked scared. They were just looking at him like he was crazy. He was eager to change that. He couldn't wait to see the looks on those mothafuckas' faces when he pulled out that gun. Then their asses would start ducking, and shit.

Khalil sneered at Cas, and thought about the times he had laughed at him, and beat his ass. This was the revenge he had dreamed about. He wanted to kill him so bad his dick was hard. He smirked, and said, "Congratulations! I brought a gift." He pulled out his weapon.

Macy saw her father brandishing a gun, and was terrified. She screamed, "No! Daddy, please! No!"

Khalil ignored his daughter's pleas, and didn't think twice. He cocked the gun, and pulled the trigger three times. He had wished many nights that Laila, and all his pain and misery would just die, so he tried to kill that bitch too!

When Khalil fired on them, Cas reacted as quickly as he could. His first instinct was to shield Laila from harm, so he threw himself over her and dived on the floor. In the process, one of the bullets struck him in the chest.

That was one of the very rare times Casino was unarmed. He couldn't believe that nigga caught him with his pants down like that. It was his wedding day, so he hadn't anticipated any gun play. He guessed he had really slept that time. Damn, he was hit. He said a quick prayer, and managed to duck the third bullet Khalil fired at him.

The sound of those gunshots caused total chaos. Everybody that was sitting at the main table jumped down on the floor, except for Macy and Mama Atkins. The rest of the reception attendees scattered every which way searching for cover. People were screaming frantically, and running for their lives.

Cas was a well loved dude, and there were lots of homies from the hood on the premises. Dudes who toted hammers everyday, and killed at will. They were all suited up that day for the occasion, but there was nothing sweet. So that third shot was the last one Khalil got off.

He had committed suicide the minute he fired his weapon. But he was so caught up in his rendition of revenge, he didn't realize yet. He was focused on trying to kill Cas and Laila, so he didn't see the dudes rushing at him on his left and right. BJ and Eighty got there first. They football tackled Khalil to the ground so hard he didn't know what hit him. He tried to shoot at them, but they wrestled the gun from him.

Handy Andy grabbed the gun, ready to empty it on Khalil, but there were no more slugs left. The nigga only had three bullets! When Andy realized the gun was empy, he screwed up his face. He would've preferred to kill him quick, but instead he used the hammer to beat that mothafucka in the face.

Pain exploded in Khalil's left eye. He laid there on the floor looking up at the angry mob surrounding him, and he realized he made a big mistake. It looked like Cas' boys were going to kill him. He was outnumbered ten to one, so he knew he was done. Somebody kicked him in his head real hard, and then those niggas started beating him like a runaway slave. He was kicked and stomped, and pummeled with fists. Those hard bottom shoes them dudes had on really hurt.

The minute those men jumped on Khalil, Macy ran over there and tried to help him. He was dead wrong about what he did, but he was still her father. She loved Cas, and she was praying he was okay, but she didn't want them to kill her father. She would understand if he had to go to jail for the rest of his life, but she didn't want him to die. She kept trying to pull those men off him, and she kept on screaming, "Get off my father! Oh my God! Daddy! Get off my father!"

Mama Atkins felt the same way Macy did. She would rather her son be dealt with by the police then endure the brutal street justice he was being served by that gang of angry men. She tried to help him with everything she could, but her attempts were in vain. All she could do was pray for her only child. At that point, prayer was the only protection she could offer him.

Khalil felt his ribs cracking, and he even spit out three teeth. By now, he was actually coughing up blood. The pain was just excruciating. All he could do was ball up in the fetal position, and try to cover his face. He could no longer see, and he couldn't hear out of one of his ears. It wasn't long before he lost consciousness. He was hanging on by a thin strand.

Macy tried desperately to stop the mob from kicking and stomping her father. However, her sixteen-year-old girl strength was no match for a group of angry, bloodthirsty, grown men. Somebody shoved her out of the way, and knocked her to the floor.

When Mama Atkins saw her granddaughter fall, she quickly helped her to her feet. Macy was pregnant, so she hoped the baby was okay. That was a sure sign for them to get out of the way. Mama Atkins just kept on praying. She had to put her son in God's hands.

Khalil was out, but another blow to his head awakened him. He realized that he was still being berated, beaten, stomped, and kicked. Amidst the blows, he wondered if it was all even worth it. He guessed he'd proved his point. He shot that nigga Cas. He wasn't sure, but he may have even taken his life. But it looked like he gave up his life in exchange.

Khalil couldn't hold on any longer. He was in a lot of pain, and he was weak and tired. He wished someone had just shot him. He would've suffered a lot less. He had told Laila she would get married over his dead body, and it looked like that had come to pass.

His eyes rolled back in his head. The last vision floating through his mind was his daughter. He saw when she and his mother tried to help him. Macy looked pretty in her red dress. He wished he'd been more of a dad to her. He couldn't remember the last time he told her he loved her.

Khalil prayed that God would take his soul. Someone stomped on his head again, and blood came out of his ears. He took his last breath. The angry men just kept on stomping and kicking him.

Macy was crying so hard she almost had a seizure. She watched in disbelief, and wondered how that could happen. She would never forget the horror of seeing her father killed right before her. She and Mama Atkins both just stood there powerless, and cried their hearts out. How was it possible that such a joyous occasion like a wedding could've ended so heinously?

$ $ $ $

Meanwhile, Laila and the rest of the fam were on the opposite side of the table from Khalil. They were all praying to God, and seeing about Cas. Mama Atkins wasn't the only mother in tears. Cas' mom, Ms. B, was crying and praying too. And so was Mama Mitchell. It was quite a sad occasion.

Cas was hit, but he was conscious and holding on. The paramedics had been called, and were on their way. Jay was right by his main man's side. He was scared for Cas, but he held up a strong front. He kept telling him he was going to be fine if he just stayed calm.

Laila was unsuccessful at trying not to cry, but she stayed right by Cas' other side the whole time. Everything had just happened so suddenly. She felt like she was living in a bad dream. The situation was that unbelievable. She kept thinking about the fact that she hadn't told Cas about Khalil's threats.

She couldn't believe that lunatic had showed up at her wedding reception with a gun. That mothafucka was really crazy. She wished she had taken his threats more serious. If Cas hadn't knocked her out of the way, he could've shot her too. Laila was in shock, but the warm blood seeping from Cas' wound through her dress was a reality check.

It was a good thing that Portia and Fatima had rounded up all the little ones, and hoarded them off to safety. They didn't need to see Cas laying there bleeding like that. The poor kids had already seen too much that day.

Laila said another quick prayer that her husband would be okay. She was a registered nurse by trade, so she pulled it together as best she could. There was a chance that she could help Cas. There was no way he could die on her, so she got her head together so she could take a look at his wound. She needed to get his shirt and jacket off first. Laila told Jay she needed help getting Cas' clothes off.

Jay knew Laila was a nurse, so he knew where she was going. She didn't have to tell him twice. He got Cas out of that jacket, and ripped his shirt open so she could see the wound. Jay's hands were shaking the whole time. He was worried sick. Damn, he was seated right next to Cas when the shooting occurred. He couldn't believe Khalil caught them off guard like that.

Laila's hands were shaking too. There was so much blood she was almost afraid to look.

Cas saw how scared his wife was, so he squeezed her hand and told her not to worry. He told her he was okay. But he couldn't front, he was scared himself. He damn sure didn't want to die. His happy days had just begun.

Casino thought about the irony of the situation, and he almost laughed. He couldn't believe that pussy ass nigga Khalil had really put a hole in him. After all the passes he gave that lame. Damn, he should've just killed him.

Cas was a man. He wasn't about to cry about it. That was how life went. You got it just how you gave it. He had shot quite a few people before. So if he had to take a bullet, then he just had to take one.

Cas looked up at Laila's tearstained face. She was beautiful, with the most doll-like features. While she was checking him out, she kept looking in his eyes and asking him how he felt. He insisted that he felt pretty okay, considering.

Laila looked real hopeful when he said that. She said the bullet appeared to have struck him high in the chest, just below his shoulder. She told him she believed he was going to be fine.

Cas sure hoped so. He just nodded, and said another silent prayer. He thought about the way he'd recently had Ysatis killed. Boy, karma was a bitch. That was probably why he got shot.

In a way, Cas felt sorry for Khalil. He knew there was no way that nigga would get away with violating like that. He would literally have to shoot his way out of there. Cas had so many peoples there, he didn't believe the dude had enough bullets. He knew his mans would ride for him.

Cas tried to sit up, but Jay kept telling him to just lay there. He said if he moved, he would risk making the bullet travel.

Jay told Laila to make sure he didn't move, and he got out the way so Cas' mother could see about him. Jay told Ms. B. not to worry, and squeezed her hand, and then he took a walk over there to see how dudes had handled that nigga Khalil. He found out that dude was finished, and went back to Cas with the report.

Cas just shook his head. He wasn't really happy about that.

He really hated that all that shit had happened while Macy was there. But taking Khalil down was necessary for their safety. Their families were there, and all those wedding guests.

Laila heard Jay say Khalil was dead. She was deeply saddened by the thought. Damn, why couldn't he have just moved on? Deep down inside, she felt like it was her fault. Laila had to go see about Macy. The poor child's father had been killed. She had to be upset.

The paramedics finally arrived, and so did the police. A lot of the dudes there were on the other side of the law, so they dispersed before the pigs got there. Especially after they participated in bludgeoning and beating Khalil to a bloody pulp.

Cas must've read Laila's mind. He told her to stick around to make sure Macy and Mama Atkins were okay. He said she could come down to the hospital after that. Laila kissed him, and told him she loved him.

Cas just looked at her for a second, just in case he never saw her again. He told his wife he loved her too, and told her to kiss the kids for him. He squeezed her hand and promised he would see her in a little while. After that, the paramedics stuck an oxygen mask on his face, and put him in the back of the ambulance truck. Jay and Ms. B. jumped in there with them.

Laila stood there for a second watching them roll off. She had tears in her eyes. It just wasn't fair. She and Cas were supposed to be rolling out on their honeymoon, but instead they were rolling her husband out on a stretcher. She took a deep breath, and put her faith in God. God hadn't put her through a test she couldn't handle yet, so she prayed he would be okay.

Laila looked down at herself. She imagined she looked a sight with all that blood on her dress. As she walked over there where her daughter was, a few people asked her if she was alright. Laila just nodded.

She found her daughter standing over there with Jayquan. He had his arms wrapped around her, and she was crying on his shoulder. You could tell he really cared about Macy.

Laila hugged both of them, and then she asked Macy if she was okay. Macy wiped her eyes and nodded, and then she asked Laila the same about herself, and Cas. So did Jayquan. Laila told them she was okay, and said she hoped Cas was too.

They asked her why she wasn't going to the hospital with him. Laila told them she had to make sure Macy was alright before she left. Jayquan looked at her sincerely, and assured her that he would look after Macy, and make sure she got home.

Macy looked comforted by his words. Laila could definitely see their bond. Those two were really close.

Macy said, "Ma, I'm good. I'ma stay here with Nana, to make sure she's okay. You go on ahead."

Laila kissed her baby on the forehead, and then she squeezed Lil' Jay's hand and thanked him. He told her it was nothing.

Macy looked a lot better now. She managed a little smile, and said, "Ma, your dress is ruined. You look like the girl in the bloody prom dress, Carrie, from that scary movie."

Laila looked down at herself, and smiled weakly. She shook her head sadly, and shrugged. She didn't even care.

The police had taped off the area where Khalil's body was. Someone had taken the liberty of covering him with a white tablecloth. Laila walked over by his corpse. While standing there, she was moved to say a prayer for his soul. They had shared a lot of years. Some were good, and some were bad. It was hard to believe he was gone.

Damn, Khalil had brought it on himself. He had no business there in the first place. His erratic, suicidal behavior had gotten him no where. The grave he had dug for himself was the one he'd be buried in. Laila just hoped he would rest there in peace.

The police were walking around trying to get statements from witnesses, but there weren't many people still around. When they approached Laila, she told them she was still in shock so she couldn't talk about it yet. She said she had to get to the hospital to see about her husband.

The detectives gave her business cards, and asked her to call them. They said from what they understood, she had ties to both men involved in the shootings. They asked her to confirm that Khalil was her ex-husband. Laila didn't deny that, but she told them they would have to talk later. She knew she would have to deal with them, but not at the moment. She had to go.

There was one thing she had to do first. She had to find Mama Atkins, and let her know how sorry she was. She spotted her talking to a police officer. Laila waited until she was done, and then she went over and hugged her, and offered her condolences.

Mama Atkins had witnessed her son pull out a gun, and open fire on Laila and her new husband with her own two eyes. She knew it wasn't her fault. She asked how Cas was doing. Laila said he looked okay when the ambulance took him off, but she wasn't sure about his condition since.

Mama's eyes were full of tears. Laila really felt horrible for her. She knew how it felt to lose a child, but she couldn't even imagine seeing them get killed. She told Mama Atkins that Cas had said tell her he was very sorry. She tried to smile, and told Laila to thank him for her. She said her son had made a foolish mistake, that he had paid for with his life.

Laila started crying again. Khalil was an idiot. She couldn't believe he was dead. She squeezed Mama Atkins' hand, and promised her they would bury him together. She assured her that they would put him away nicely.

Mama Atkins smiled weakly at the notion. It wasn't going to be easy planning her son's final arrangements, so she told Laila she would appreciate her assistance. That was very generous of her, considering the circumstances. Laila was a decent woman. No matter what had happened, they would always be family. Mama Atkins hugged her tight, and then she told her to get down to the hospital to see about her husband.

Laila thanked her. That's exactly what she planned to do, as soon as she located her girls, Portia and Fatima. She needed them to drive her. All she could think about was Cas. She prayed he was still okay.

Laila looked around for her girls, and told herself that she and Cas were still going on their honeymoon, as soon as he was better. She pictured them frolicking on the beach in Rio, and prayed God wouldn't take away her happy ending. They had been through a lot that day, but she had a lot of faith. She had witnessed God's power too many times to doubt Him. She knew He would bring them through.

Just then, Portia ran over and grabbed her by the elbow. She told Laila to hurry because Wise and Fatima were waiting outside in the car. They were all going to the hospital to see about Cas. Laila grabbed her hand, and the friends hurried out to the car.

If you love these characters, stay tuned…

Coming Soon from Synergy Publications...

"A Dollar Outta Fifteen Cent"
Volume 2

"Another Day...Another Dollar"
A series of novellas

By Caroline McGill

Spring, 2011

**Turn the pages to check out more heat
from Synergy Publications!**

In Stores Spring, 2010

ANYTHING 4 PROFIT

By Justin "Amen" Floyd

"Think you really know about the dirty south? Think all street novels are the same? Think again!"

Read this excerpt from "ANYTHING 4 PROFIT", the hottest new urban novel in the game…

THE INTRODUCTION

BOOM! BOOM! BOOM! The hail of shots fired from the .44 caliber cannon pierced the silence of the dark, hot, humid summer night. The flash from the muzzle of the gun briefly illuminated the horrific scene that was taking place. A body dropped to the ground, and two figures dressed in all black from head to toe fled the scene as fast as their legs would carry them. Left behind on the asphalt was a lifeless being lying face down in a pool of blood. His white on white Nike Air Force Ones were now the color of crimson, and his new Coogi jeans were now filled with the stench of his own piss and shit. His face was so badly disfigured from the gun wounds, that if not for his teeth, his body would have remained unidentified. Needless to say, at his funeral the casket would remain closed.

This is the story of three friends from the bottom. Born into poverty, pain, and despair, and tired of being pawns in the white man's chess game, they all made a vow amongst themselves to get rich…by any mothafuckin' means possible. Murder; robbery; extortion; kidnapping; fraud - ANYTHING FOR PROFIT. And any opposition to their goals was met with violence so savage that only those who were also raised in the gutter could possibly understand or relate to. Either you rolled with them, or you got rolled the fuck over. Real simple. No mercy, no remorse.

Again, this is the story of three friends. Their hate, their fears, their dreams, and their thoughts. But most importantly, their struggle to rise above the squalid socio-economic conditions they were born into.

GREENVILLE, SC A.K.A. "THE VILLE"

August, 2006

A woman's voice came blaring from a cheap television that was bolted down to a cheap nightstand: *"Tonight on the Fox 10 0'clock news… Police have found an unidentified body in the Kennedy Park section of Greenville. The body has suffered numerous gun wounds to the face and chest area. Authorities believe that this murder was the result of a drug transaction gone wrong. If you have any information pertaining to this crime please call 1-800-crimestoppers, or the Greenville county sheriff's office. More details to follow…"*

"A yo', Ant, did you see that nigga's face when I pulled the pistol on his ass?", asked Mike. He and Ant sat in a cheap motel room, reliving the murderous events that they'd committed only hours earlier.

"Man, that nigga's eyes got bigger than a deer's caught in the headlights of an 18 wheeler", laughed Ant D.

"But do you think he shit on his self befo' or after I peeled his shit back", asked Mike jokingly.

"Probably befo', dog. Er'body know Tremone was more pussy than three dikes in a bed together. I'm surprised that old Sideshow Bob, Homey the Clown ass nigga was even out here try'na hustle, dog."

"You ain't even bullshittin'. That was the quickest 30 G's I ever made in my fuckin' life, my nigga."

"Damn right," Ant D said.

"Man, look here. Over the past few months we done licked mothafuckas for bout 250 grand..."

"At least" said Ant D.

"That's my whole point though, my nigga. We just blowin' that shit, homey. We ain't doin' shit wit' it. We gotta slow down and start try'na figure out how we gon' wash all this paper without 'dem boys getting on our ass. I ain't try'na go in and do no time, and you know they like flies on shit once them alphabet boys figure they got a case."

"I'm already on it," said Ant D. "You remember my uncle Bug, right?"

"Yeah", chuckled Mike. "I remember that ugly ass mothafucka. Man, they gave that nigga the right name too. Dude look like a fuckin' bug for real", said Mike, laughing. "Big, black, ugly mothafucka! I know he be paying for pussy, 'cause thats 'bout the only way he gon' get his dick wet...except fo' when he wash. And shiiiiiit, the way that nigga be smelling, I ain't even sure he do that." Mike started cracking up.

"Yeah, yeah, yeah. But all bullshit aside though, peep game, Mike. He was telling me 'bout this building that's on sale in the burg for 'bout 400 G's. He said it used to be a storage facility but that shit shut down. All we gotta do is buy it, fix it up, and open up our own shit. You always talkin' 'bout having your own strip club and shit, right? Well this the spot, my nigga. We can put our paper through the cleaners, and at the same time have the baddest bitches in the south workin' at our club", said Ant D animatedly. "Nigga, we'll be the youngest, flyest niggas in the Upstate with our own spot. Doin' it!" He rubbed his hands together excitedly.

"That sound like a plan", Mike stated. "But as of right now, we only got 'bout 100 to play with. We gon' need at least a good 900 to a mil to make that shit pop like it's 'posed to. So you know what that means."

"Mo' money, mo' murder," they said in unison.

"Ant D, go head and stop bullshittin', and roll one up, dog", Mike said. He passed Ant D a clear plastic baggy with big buds of that purple in it.

"Yeah, I better roll this shit, 'cause I swear yo' non rollin' ass will have the whole blunt fallin' apart." Ant D took a bud out, broke it down, and rolled a blunt that looked like it was about 9 months pregnant. He grabbed a lighter off the dresser. He lit the blunt, and took a pull, savoring the way the smoke filled his lungs.

"Take two and pass, nigga. You know what it is", said Mike. Ant D passed the blunt to Mike, already feeling a little buzz from the potent, exotic weed they were smoking.

The Camelot, the motel where they had rented a room to count their blood money in, was nothing but a hole in the wall where the hoes came to get fucked, and heads came to get high. Where dope boys came to trap, and jack boys came to lick.

So when they heard a woman outside screaming for the police, they both looked at each other thinking the same thing. It was time to get the fuck outta dodge!

"Let's get light, Ant D. Ain't no point in try'na explain to the police what we doin' in here with 60 stacks of cash money."

"Shiiiiiiiiiiiiit, I was thinking the same thang, my nigga."

They both grabbed what few belongings they had, and hurried outside to Mike's money green box Chevy Caprice. It was sitting high on 26 inch Giovanni rims wrapped in low profile Pirelli tires. Mike started the car up, and put that old shit from Tip's album Urban Legend on blast.

"Ride wit' me nigga, let me show you where we kick it at/ where hustlers get them chickens at, and T.I.P. be chillin' at..."

As Mike was pulling out of the parking lot he looked in the rearview mirror, only to see the blue lights of a Greenville County police car flashing behind them, signaling for him to pull over.

Without even so much as a second thought, Mike slammed

his foot down on the accelerator. The Pirelli tires screamed and left a trail of burnt rubber on the asphalt. Ant D, who was in the passenger seat bobbing his head to the beat, was forcefully thrown back into his seat as the Chevy propelled down the road. The chase was on!

He said, "*What the fuck…*" Before Ant D could finish his statement, Mike ran a series of red lights and swerved onto a side road. The dark blue police cruiser followed close behind, sirens blaring.

"Man, these pussy mothafuckas is on our ass!!" yelled Mike. He gripped the steering wheel and sped through the night, attempting to shake the county car that was behind them.

"Gotdamn! Boy, I swear to *God* I ain't tryna see that county tonight, nigga! My mama cookin' ribs for dinner tonight *too*", Ant said irately. He glanced in the rearview mirror.

Mike chuckled, and said, "Nigga, I got this here…" While laughing, he temporarily took his eyes off the road.

His hands fiercely gripping the dashboard, Ant yelled, "*Oh shit*!!! Watch out!"

Mike turned his attention back to the road, and swerved to the right just in time to avoid a head on collision with an oncoming car in the other lane.

He said, "Damn, that was close! Nigga, it sounded like you was 'bout to shit on yourself though." He was fucking with Ant. Truthfully, nervous beads of sweat had started to run down his *own* forehead after such a close brush with death.

Ant said, "Nigga, fuck you. Just drive this mothafucka!"

By now they had reached speeds in excess of 70 mph. And on those small unpaved back roads, one wrong move could be fatal. "Gotdamn, this mothafucka is still on our ass!" Mike said, as he continued to swerve recklessly in and out of lanes. He was hoping that the cop would lose heart and give up on the chase. But no such luck.

"Mike, look here. Just get us to that lil' cut over there by

Lakeside Park, and we'll jump out and split-up on his monkey ass. Then meet up at Neesy's house over there in Rockvale. As good as we know them woods over there, ain't no way that cracker gon' be able to catch us."

"Yeah, but that mean I gotta leave my Chevy behind", said Mike, with a hint of regret in his voice. He steered the car onto the wrong side of the street, hoping to scare the pig off. But once again, no such luck.

He continued, "Which means they still gonna know it was me and you, 'cause this shit registered in my name. Plus our prints is all over this bitch."

"Look here nigga, you try'na be sittin' up in the mothafuckin' county tonight, in one of them pissy ass, packed ass holding cells, with a bunch of drunks and crack heads all night, waiting to see a judge to make bail?! I know I ain't!"

Mike had to think fast. His Chevy was his baby, but an O.G. named Big Rick had schooled him a long time ago that once you embraced the streets, you could never become attached to anything that you couldn't walk away from in 30 seconds, or less. His exact words were, "...Because young blood, sometimes 30 seconds can be all the time you got between death, a life sentence, or living to see another day."

With that thought in mind, Mike swerved recklessly onto the road that would take them in the direction of the park. He was driving so fast and wild that he nearly wrecked and flipped the car over more than once. Yet Greenville County's "finest" still refused to stop the chase.

"Ok nigga, we almost there! As soon as we get to the cut, you already know what it is", said Mike frantically.

"Fa' sho'. We hop our asses out, toss the guns, split up, and hit the woods 'til we lose this clown. Then we meet up at Neesy's house."

Suddenly Mike made a hard right onto a dirt road, and killed his lights. The road was illuminated only by the dim glimmer of the moon. The Chevy almost spun out of control, and a cloud of dust went up into the air. That road led into some woods that were part of Lakeside Park. At the end of the road was a small opening that led into the woods. On the other side of the woods there was a hood called Rockvale. That was where one of Ant's numerous girlfriends, Neesy, stayed in a house with her sister.

As Mike approached the woods he attempted to pump the brakes. But the dirt road made it difficult for him to keep control of the car, let alone slow down. As the forest raced towards them, he slammed his foot down on the brake. The car skidded forward until it collided with a tree at the beginning of the path. The impact was bad, but not bad enough to prevent Mike and Ant from jumping out and running into the woods like two runaway slaves!

The officer who had initiated the high speed chase brought his car to an abrupt stop. He jumped out and ran into the woods with his gun drawn, and flashlight out. "Greenville County Sheriff's Department!! Stop!" He might as well have been talking to one of the trees because Ant D and Mike was ghost.

Within seconds, there were several Greenville County police cars at the scene with their spotlights on, and their blue lights flashing. The K-9 unit was dispatched, and there was also a police helicopter circling overhead like a vulture waiting to swoop down and pick off its prey. But it was all for nothing.

Ant D and Mike had escaped the long arm of the law...At least for the moment.

ANYTHING 4 PROFIT

Spring, 2010

Get yours today!

Summer, 2010

Guns & Roses

Street Stories of Sex, Sin, and Survival

IN STORES NOW!

Sex as a Weapon
A Caroline McGill Exclusive

Preview excerpts at **www.SynergyPublications.com**

Fall, 2010

Sex as a Weapon 2

The highly anticipated sequel to the most controversial novel in the game

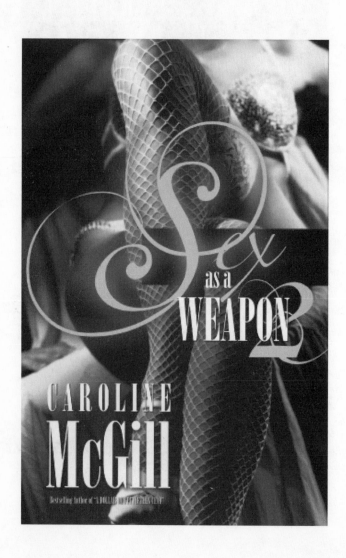

IN STORES NOW!

Sex as a Weapon

By Caroline McGill

A Dollar Outta Fifteen Cent
An Urban Love Story of Sex, Money, and Murder

By Caroline McGill

A Dollar Outta Fifteen Cent II:
Money Talks…Bullsh*t Walks

By Caroline McGill

A Dollar Outta Fifteen Cent III:
Mo' Money…Mo' Problems

By Caroline McGill

A Dollar Outta Fifteen Cent IV:
Money Makes the World Go 'Round

By Caroline McGill

Contact and Ordering Information

www.SynergyPublications.com

Synergy Publications
P.O. Box 210-987
Brooklyn, NY 11221

Phone: (718) 930-8818

Fax: (718) 453-6760

Email the author at CarolineMcGill160@msn.com

www.MySpace.com/CarolineMcGill

www.Facebook.com/CarolineMcGill

www.Twitter.com/CAROLINE_MCGILL

Order Form
Synergy Publications
P.O. Box 210-987   Brooklyn, NY 11221
www.SynergyPublications.com

_____ A Dollar Outta Fifteen Cent	$14.95
_____ A Dollar Outta Fifteen Cent II: Money Talks…Bullsh*t Walks	$14.95
_____ A Dollar Outta Fifteen Cent III: Mo' Money…Mo' Problems	$14.95
_____ A Dollar Outta Fifteen Cent IV: Money Makes the World Go 'Round	$14.95
_____ Sex As a Weapon: The Grudge	$14.95
_____ Sex As a Weapon 2	$14.95
_____ Guns & Roses (Vol. 1) *Street Stories of Sex, Sin, and Survival*	$14.95
_____ ANYTHING 4 PROFIT	$14.95
Shipping and Handling (plus $1 for each additional book)	$ 4.00
TOTAL (for one book) _____ TOTAL NUMBER OF BOOKS ORDERED	$18.95

Name (please print) :_____
              First   Last

Reg. # (Applies if Incarcerated): _____

Address: _____

_____

City: _____ State: _____ Zip Code: _____

Email: _____

*25% Discount for Orders Being Shipped Directly to Prisons
Prison Discount: ($11.21+ $4.00 s & h = **$15.21**)
**Special Discounts for Book Clubs with 4 or more members
***Discount for Bulk Orders - please call for info (718) 930-8818
WE ACCEPT MONEY ORDERS ONLY for all mail orders
Credit Cards can be used for orders made online
Allow 2 -3 weeks for delivery
Purchase online at **www.SynergyPublications.com**